MISERY
HATES
COMPANY

MISERY
HATES
COMPANY

A NOVEL

Elizabeth Hobbs

CROOKED
LANE

NEW YORK

Copyright © 2025 by Elizabeth Hobbs

All rights reserved.

Published in the United States by Crooked Lane Books, an imprint of The Quick Brown Fox & Company LLC.

Crooked Lane Books and its logo are trademarks of The Quick Brown Fox & Company LLC.

Library of Congress Catalog-in-Publication data available upon request.

ISBN (hardcover): 978-1-63910-973-9
ISBN (ebook): 978-1-63910-974-6

Cover design by Marisa Ware

Printed in the United States.

www.crookedlanebooks.com

Crooked Lane Books
34 West 27th St., 10th Floor
New York, NY 10001

First Edition: November 2024

10 9 8 7 6 5 4 3 2 1

For Holly Ingraham, editor and enthusiast, for early encouragement, for loving Marigold as much as I do, and for keeping me from the worst of my Gothic excesses, but mostly for the singularly brilliant idea to make Marigold an archaeologist.

I'm embarrassed I didn't think of it first.

PROLOGUE

The first thing Marigold Manners noticed was the scarecrow's hat, battered and torn but still somehow familiar, tilted at a rakish angle as if the wearer had some style or panache—but panache was what gave one style, if you asked Marigold.

But no one asked.

Because Marigold was alone, staring in dawning horror at the hat, which was set at that angle not because of panache or style or any such thing. The hat was set at that angle because the neck it was attached to—the neck that should have been stuffed with straw—was unnaturally bent.

Because it wasn't straw.

Because the person under the hat was dead. Quite dead.

Marigold opened her mouth but couldn't scream. She was too astonished to find that someone else seemed to have been murdered instead of her.

Chapter 1

Boston, Massachusetts
April 1894

> *Go West, young man, go West. There is health in the country, and room*
> *away from our crowds of idlers and imbeciles.*
>
> —Horace Greeley

Death lay heavy upon Marigold Manners's mind the late winter morning that set her on the path to the scarecrow—death but not yet murder.

That gray morning, Marigold gripped the seat of the cheap, chilly hansom cab trudging through Boston's cold, cobbled streets, closed her eyes, and wept. Quietly. Intensely. Briefly.

One didn't want to give way to emotion or make too much of oneself. Nor ruin one's looks. Not now, when she needed to preserve every advantage she might have. Because the gold that had given its name to the age had tarnished into tinsel. Her gilded youth had come to an abrupt, inconvenient end.

Today she would count the family lawyers amongst the crowds of Horace Greeley's idlers and imbeciles, for they did not give her such sage advice as Mr. Greeley—and even his advice was sadly lacking. Why did no one ever say, "Go West, young *woman*"?

Why were the modern, forward-thinking Miss Marigold Mannerses of the world not given such expansive advice? Why did the attorneys harp and carp like moralizing old puritans, insisting she retreat and retrench instead of boldly going toward the future?

Why was everyone not so superbly, rationally modern as she?

Marigold dried her eyes, paid the driver from her dwindling purse, and stepped over the late-season slush on Fenway's Park Drive quite determined to forge her own path forward—to do what she was meant to do and let the world learn to catch up. Behind her were the hours she had spent within the austere offices of Ropes, Grey and Loring, Esquires. Before her stood a tall, handsomely appointed townhouse, the door flung wide in welcome.

It was a wonderful thing to have rich friends.

"How was the reading, darling?" Her confidante and dear friend, Isabella Dana, kissed her cheek and swept her into the townhouse's opulent, cocooning warmth.

"Dreadful," Marigold admitted. "Nearly as dreadful as the funeral." She unpinned her black velvet hat with the chicly netted mourning veil—there was no excuse for looking dreadfully unfashionable, no matter the dreadful occasion—to better let herself be cocooned. "In fact, I've quite resolved never to have one of my own—neither a funeral nor a will to be read out."

"But you'll have to have a will now that you're an heiress," Isabella soothed as she steered Marigold toward the elegant sitting room. "You have my congratulations along with my condolences. I've poured sherry."

"That, dear Isabella—Oh, thank you! You have no idea how welcome this is." Marigold took the proffered glass gratefully. "That is the most dreadful news of all—not that losing my darling parents to the influenza has been anything but the most awful wrench." Her only comfort was in the knowledge that they had died within hours of each other—neither would have wanted to live on alone. "But I am told I am not, in fact, an heiress. It seems my sweet mater and pater squandered it all."

"What, all?" Isabella clutched the back of a velvet armchair to steady herself. "Harry and Esmé lost all the Manners money?"

"Lost is not quite the right verb." The shock had already passed for Marigold. All she had left was the damning truth. "But yes, all." She took a fortifying sip of the sherry and let the rich wine restore what was left of her equanimity. "Not that I'm surprised—my parents always were spendthrifts, the poor dears."

She had been a child when she first understood what the leaking mansions and hasty departures from hotels really meant—her beloved parents were absolute fools with money. Still, she had admired their verve, if not their unsound personal fiscal practices.

"I know your dear father liked to gamble, but Marigold, darling, to spend it *all*?" Isabella put her hand to her stylishly rounded bosom as if to hold back the enormity of the loss. "The Manners family is so distinguished, so very industrious—how could several hundred years' worth of New England thrift be gone?"

"Indeed," Marigold agreed on a sigh. "One would think it a Herculean task to run through so much money in just one lifetime, but they managed it quite spectacularly."

"Good Lord." Isabella was still aghast. "I know you were estranged from them, as they didn't approve of your devotion to your education—"

"Heavens, no." Marigold had peacefully separated herself from her parents' hurly-burly lifestyle by the age-old convenience of boarding school, and then—horrors of all horrors—enrolling in Wellesley women's college. She was a modern, academic New Woman in all ways, with a strong, well-regulated mind residing in an equally strong, well-regulated body. *My darling changeling*, her sweet mother had laughed—for how could such beautiful profligates as her parents have produced such a serious-minded child? "By their account, marriage is the only way a young lady of good breeding should secure both her future and her family fortune. But now there is no fortune left to secure."

Isabella was still too flummoxed to appreciate Marigold's attempt at humor. "The Beacon Hill townhouse?" Isabella seemed to be going through a sort of inventory in her head, searching for potentially hidden assets. "The summer place on the Cape?"

"Gone, sold on the sly for debts last year, the lawyers tell me." Marigold tried to maintain both her good humor and her good sense, but the truth was, it was quite an off-putting experience to find oneself a pauper.

"My darling girl!" Isabella gasped in companionable disbelief. "Not that you ever cared about the money—but to have none! I can't imagine the shock." She hastened to refill Marigold's glass.

"Thank you. Though the lawyers did manage to secure me a small annuity of one hundred dollars per annum, I know very well that I can't live the life I'd chosen on such a pittance in this day and age."

"Oh, no," Isabella agreed on a solicitous gasp. "Not and maintain any reasonable kind of style."

"Exactly," Marigold confirmed. "Nor afford to even finish my degree in classical studies—apparently my college tuition has not been paid for quite some time. Which also means I must cancel my plans for the archaeological field season on Kefalonia this summer." Everything she had worked so hard to accomplish was now out of reach. "You see why it's all so dreadful." Marigold allowed herself some small measure of bitterness at the unfairness of fate. "This is supposed to be the Progressive Era, but my life does not seem to be progressing at all. The august attorneys of Ropes, Grey and Loring have advised me that if I wish to remain a lady of good repute, I must fall back on finding some family relations to take me in."

"Relations?" Isabella uttered the word in the same tone one might normally reserve for *rodents* or *reptiles*. "Oh no, you must stay here with me instead. I adore your company, we get along famously, and there's plenty of room." She waved her hand at the gracefully spacious surroundings. "Just the thing for a well-positioned widow like myself to take on a protégée."

Marigold's pride had already prepared her for just such a generous offer. "You are a dear, Isabella, but I think we both know I'm far too independent to be anyone's protégée, let alone yours. I don't know enough about fashion—apart from being fashionably dressed—to be of any help in your atelier."

"Nonsense—you're a walking advertisement for the utter perfection of my creations. The House of Dana is daily visited by young ladies vying to look as smart and effortlessly elegant as the inimitable Miss Marigold Manners."

"Thank you, but I am hardly unique. And what happens now that I can no longer afford to look so smart?"

"Darling! What kind of friend would I be if I charged you to wear my clothes?"

"What kind of friend would I be if I let you give me clothes for free?"

"The well-dressed kind," Isabella rejoined with some exasperation.

"You know it won't do," Marigold countered. "It's bound to get out that I'm a pauper, and then where will I be—pitied!" Marigold shuddered at the thought and took another deep, meditative sip of her sherry. "And despite all this, I'm still quite set on becoming a fashionably iconoclastic, classical archaeologist. I am in the process of convincing myself the harsh realities of poverty will be instructive in the art of living in archaeological encampments."

Marigold had spent the winter in detailed planning, imagining her summer on the Greek island of Kefalonia, digging at the classical period site at Leivathos—the evening breeze off the Ionian Sea would waft across her journal, which would be filled with drawings of artifacts and site plans . . .

"Life is never as one imagines, darling," Isabella objected. "Real poverty is bound to be exceedingly tedious and messy, and you know how you feel about messes, Marigold. You're always tidying up and improving things."

This, Marigold acknowledged with a sigh, was the result of a childhood spent in uncertain wandering. Her parents had been first-class nomads, always in search of somewhere suitably chic to shore up. Always leaving a messy string of unpaid bills and disgruntled shopkeepers behind. All that traipsing about had left Marigold with an excellent vocabulary, a strong sense of self-reliance, and an abiding wish for structure and stability. The Viennese physicians might write of unmet needs and wish fulfillment, but Marigold thought her penchant for creating order out of chaos extraordinarily rational—and altogether the perfect mind-set for an archaeologist.

"Well, you need absolutely no improving," she told Isabella. "You're already perfection."

"Thank you, darling," Isabella cooed. "Then why not just stay here as my friend and companion and improve someone else? I can think of several young gentlemen—and quite a few older ones, too, for you know how profitable such an alliance can be for a young lady of your age and sophistication. You're perhaps not a superb beauty, but you have something more—you have panache."

It was a lovely compliment coming from Isabella, who was one of the languid beauties of the age and had both looks and panache. She had consequently married young and profitably to a wealthy bon vivant some forty years her senior, who had had the good manners to die in time to leave Isabella an attractively rich, stylish young widow.

"I should like the advantages of widowhood without having the inconvenience of marriage," Marigold admitted on a sigh. "My plan has always been to become a leading academic archaeologist. But now even my expensive education will do me no good. Without the backing of my college, I can't afford to go to Greece on my own. And without either extensive field experience or a finished degree, I can't teach."

"You'll have to do something to remain independent," Isabella warned. "If you won't marry, do you think you might try your hand at some"—she searched for a tactful word—"lesser job? A typist, perhaps? At least you'd have pin money."

"What a dismal prospect. Not that I'm afraid of work, but I had hoped to be working at something more . . . *important*." Marigold was a progressive woman of a progressive age, but to what purpose? "Mr. Ropes, the lawyer, insisted letters be sent to each and every one of my remaining relatives, so I shall have to deal with that as well, for I can't imagine any of them will come up to scratch."

Isabella nodded. "Quite right to have standards. And speaking of standards—I thought we'd have a quiet dinner here then go out for some dancing."

"Dancing? Not even a week after my parents' funeral?" It was finally Marigold's turn to be shocked. "Dear Isabella—"

"A celebration of life, just as they would want, for life goes on, and in your particular situation, life *must* go on." Isabella pursed her lips. "And certainly, when everyone finds out the state they've left you in, no one will begrudge you a little dancing before you're forced to face the wolves at the door."

"Let us hope Mr. Ropes and his firm will deal with any wayward wolves."

"Well, I have a very different sort of wolf in mind for your evening." Isabella set aside her glass. "The sporty set are hosting a little soiree down at the boathouse on the Charles. And you are quite sporty—the collegiate champion at golf and rowing for Wellesley?"

"*Was* sporty, for that's all in the past, now that I must leave college. One doesn't want to make too much of oneself—especially now."

"No indeed. But the right sort of people will be there."

What Isabella invariably meant by the "right sort" were Harvard men.

"You know my views, Isabella. I'm *modern*—I have no plans whatsoever to marry." Most colleges and universities insisted their female academics remain strictly single. "No plan, no inclination, and now no money—for what man in his right mind would want a pauper? And you know I could never countenance a man who was not in his right mind."

"I commend your forward thinking, darling, but even a pauper—especially a pauper—doesn't want to put herself too far beyond the pale. I don't think you'll like the social wilderness," Isabella warned.

"Perhaps I should consider the real wilderness," Marigold mused. "Perhaps I ought to take Mr. Horace Greeley's advice in the newspaper and go west instead of going to Greece. That's what that savage old man, Mr. Clemens, did to make himself into Mark Twain."

"Savage?"

"The man evinced outright disdain for the works of Jane Austen," Marigold replied. "What else is such a man but a savage?"

"There won't be any savages at the boathouse this evening," Isabella assured her. "Cab is sure to be there."

Marigold's breath bottled up in her throat, but she carried on as if nothing had happened—as if every fiber of her being hadn't been instantly doused in secret delight. "Cab who?"

"You know very well Cab Cox."

Jonathan Cabot Cox was just the sort of fellow Marigold might have expected to encounter at a Charles River boathouse. Scion of one of Boston's oldest families, Cab had grown up basking in the sunny rays of wealth and privilege, excelling at any number of expensive sports and attending the requisite exclusive boarding school before enrolling in college at Harvard, where he had joined the right clubs and rowed crew before processing onward to Harvard Law. All as if it were preordained by a right-thinking, puritan God.

She had met him at various regattas and picnics over the years, but Marigold had never actively pursued anything more than friendship—she had too much pride to allow herself to admire a man everyone else idolized.

He was simply too handsome, with the sort of strong, blade-sharp jaw one would expect to find on a fellow who rowed stroke and captained the varsity eight. And there was something too casual about the sweep of sandy hair that often fell just so across his broad forehead. Something too flawless about his conservatively tailored clothes.

He was, simply put, too tidy, too strong, and too self-assured to be an interesting subject for any improvement. Or affection.

So naturally, he could not have attracted her more.

CHAPTER 2

To lose one parent may be regarded as a misfortune;
to lose both looks like carelessness.

—Oscar Wilde

Cab Cox was also the sort of fellow who had never had to wait for
anything—opportunity was always well-mannered enough to come
calling at his immaculately polished front door.

Which was why Marigold was determined to never be amongst those
hammering on his proverbial knocker. She resolutely avoided him—he was
stationed like a lighthouse in a tailcoat, guarding the entrance to the bar—
and instead slipped into the boathouse in Isabella's flamboyant wake, a sleek
catboat in the tow of a far more eye-catching yacht.

Yet, even with such rectitude, Marigold was instantly mobbed. The
ghastly rumor had already been put about that her parents had left her desti-
tute, and everyone seemed to want to get a good last glance at the inimitable
Marigold Manners. She pasted on her fashionable, crocodile smile—all
bright teeth and cynical eyes—and put up her chin, steeling herself against
that curious, demeaning pleasure people seemed to take in the misfortunes
of others.

But she needn't have worried—this sliver of Boston society seemed singularly devoid of anything too much like pity. Perhaps it had been bred out
of them. Condolences were murmured as an afterthought while her hand
was solicited as a dance partner.

"Bad luck, that, old thing. Care for a spin?"

"Terrible news, but you do look divine."

"I say, Marigold, mourning becomes you."

And so she danced, handed off from one sporty, turkey-trotting gentleman to another, until a firm voice asserted itself. "You look run off your feet by those mashers." Cab Cox managed to find the soft skin on the inside of her glove-clad elbow to lead her outside under the awning-covered porch.

"Cab. What a surprise," she lied as he led her toward a wicker armchair. "It's been an age. What have you been doing with yourself?" she queried, all careless, surface civility.

"What's expected of me, naturally." His smile was so subtly derisive, she might have imagined it.

The truth was, she *had* assumed he would quite naturally do what was expected—gladly take over his father's law firm, marry a beautiful, well-bred debutante from an equally well-bred family, settle into the family estate on the south shore, and raise a nonvulgar number of beautifully towheaded children, who would eventually follow in their parents' expensively shod footsteps.

Everything she herself wished to avoid.

"I'd ask what you've been doing with yourself," he continued, "but the gossips are full of it—my condolences on the loss of your parents. It's never easy, is it, no matter how estranged you were."

Marigold felt her smile slip at the earnest, almost angry sympathy in his tone. She might have expected consideration—Cab was raised to be a gentleman—but not such fellow feeling. "Cab, how did you know? But I forgot that your father passed away recently. My condolences to you too."

"Thank you." He signaled a waiter to bring them a bottle of champagne. "Let's drink to the graceful art of surviving."

She impulsively reached for his hand. "That sentiment is too much like truth to be easy banter. I had no idea."

"That's the trick of it, isn't it?" he allowed. "The never letting on."

"Cab. I'm so sorry."

"As am I." He gave her hand a sympathetic squeeze, but he withdrew quickly enough to deflect any further foray into emotions better left unsaid by pouring the champagne into two wide-mouthed crystal coupes. "To better days."

"Better days," Marigold murmured before she let the cool bubbles dazzle her tongue. "Ooh. That tastes divine." Another luxury she would have to give up. But not just yet. Tonight, the champagne was exactly what she needed—forgetfulness in a glass.

"Here's to dear old Boston." She raised her coupe. "Home of the bean and the cod—"

"Where the Lowells speak only to Cabots, and the Cabots speak only to God," Cab finished with a dry laugh. "Such is our world."

"I wish it weren't our world, so strict and narrow. So narrow-minded." She poured another. "I want my world to be . . . larger somehow. More expansive."

Cab's laugh held just enough scorn to please her. "Don't we all."

"No!" she disagreed, before she waved her glass at the rest of the party. "They're all quite content to be 'cold roast' Bostonians, resting comfortably upon generations of good breeding and bushels of old money. None of them want it to be any different."

"But you do." He leaned forward as if he might say something more before he seemed to change his mind. "Then a different New England toast." He held up his glass. "To a willing foe and sea room," he toasted.

"Yes!" Such astonishing fellow feeling. She covered her awkwardly reawakened attraction with another toast. "And to luck," she added, "which I'm going to need as much as sea room."

"Ah, yes—I had forgotten your plans for Kefalonia."

Trust Cab to get the details right. Even if they were now wrong. "Not this summer, I'm afraid," was all she allowed before she stilled her bitter tongue with champagne.

"I say." Cab grew serious, his frown marring the perfection of his broad brow. "Is it true, then? Isabella's been putting it about that you're going to have to throw yourself on the mercy of relatives."

Marigold's cheeks heated. "I'll have to speak to Isabella—it isn't like her to be so indiscreet." She tried to muster what she could of her usual panache. "I'll think of something."

"Of course you will—you're the accomplished, incomparable Miss Manners. I should expect nothing less."

His pronouncement prompted a giddy mixture of pleasure and gratitude. While she had always believed in herself, she had never dreamed anyone else might share her outsized confidence—it had seemed too much to ask of her parents and certainly far too much to ask of a man as perfect as Cab Cox.

"Cab, you needn't try to be so transparently kind—it smacks of pity."

"Nothing to pity, Marigold. Plenty to admire. But you don't like being admired."

"Nonsense," she countered. "Everyone likes to be admired, and I am no different."

"But you want to be admired for being an accomplished academic and a rational New Woman."

"Just so." An accomplished, thirsty New Woman, who couldn't think of what to say to such an astonishingly understanding man until after she had finished her drink. "Don't you think the world would run a great deal smoother," she mused as she refilled her glass, "if one could pick one's family in a rational manner?"

"Naturally," he agreed. "Isn't that what a marriage is—choosing one's intimate family?"

"And that is what is wrong with marriage," she said airily, because she was the incomparable Miss Manners and a New Woman even if she were a wee bit tipsy. "It's all the fashion to allow the heart to make that choice instead of the head."

"And we must be thoroughly logical," he agreed. "But is it true, what Isabella said? That you require assistance from sympathetic relatives?"

Marigold took another ruminative sip before she sputtered to a stop. "Oh heavens, Cab! I hope you don't think that because the Coxes and Manners are distantly connected through some long-dead, grim Pilgrim ancestor, I was angling for you to take me in!"

"And why not?" Cab leaned forward as if he wanted to make sure she could hear him—or make sure that no one else heard. "Mother adores you—as anybody with an ounce of sense would. She would love nothing more than to have you with her at the house in Cohasset."

The mention of mothers put a damper on whatever strange hopes might have stirred within Marigold at the first part of his declaration. "Thank you, you're very kind to offer, but no." She made sure her voice was calm but firm. "While the Oaks is lovely and your mother an absolute lamb, I'd have absolutely nothing to do. Nothing to think. Nothing to feel."

Nothing to *accomplish*.

"You must understand how it is—I need a change from—" She shrugged and waved her champagne coupe at the whole of Boston twinkling in the gaslit night across the Charles. "From all this."

All this being everything she had lost—her past as well as her future.

"I suppose I do understand." Cab took a deep breath and sat back. "Feel that way often enough myself."

"Do you really?" Had she misjudged him? It really was unfortunate that he was so handsome, for he was otherwise a sensible, unobjectionable, right-thinking young man. And he did dance divinely. "Take a turn with me, will you, Cab, for old times' sake?"

"Love to."

She took the hand he offered, and they glided into a lively two-step that was just the thing to banish her incipient blues. But when the orchestra changed tempo and added another note to the rhythm, Marigold found herself being twirled into the slower three count of a waltz.

And urged subtly closer to his chest.

Cab danced as well as he did everything—with unhesitating skill—and it was everything Marigold could do not to let the champagne go to her head and say stupid, sentimental things. Not to let her head rest upon his broad, exquisitely tailored lapels and give in to the impulse of the moment.

But she was, as he had just reminded her, the accomplished, incomparable Miss Manners, and it wouldn't do to rest her head against anyone's chest, even one so nice as Cab's. Because if she let herself rely on him once, what was to keep her from relying upon him again and again, falling back into the clubby, closed society to which she'd been born? Setting aside all her ambitions and accomplishments for suffocating social ease?

No. No matter how relying on Cab would solve most of her more pressing problems—especially her more pressing bills—she could hardly set up housekeeping with the unforgivably handsome man. Even with the presence of his doting mama as a chaperone, the matchmaking mothers of Mayflower-obsessed society would tar and feather what remained of her good name in great Bostonian style—with cold, calculated innuendo.

No. "I want something different."

"Be careful what you wish for, Marigold." Cab's voice rumbled down to her. "It's a strange, illogical world out there."

"Well, it's strange and illogical here as well," she said before her cheek seemed to rest of its own accord against the sleek lapel of his tailcoat. "And I can't stand the idea of leaving my fate in someone else's hands."

"So you'll take it in your own? I don't believe in predestiny any more than you do—we make our own fate by our choices. But—"

"But you're a man," she objected. "And just by dint of your sex, you get so, so many more choices. It just isn't fair."

"No," he finally answered. "That isn't fair. But such—"

Marigold sighed and finished for him. "—is our world."

But not hers for much longer.

CHAPTER 3

The letters from relatives began to arrive in droves—so many that Marigold began to suspect Messrs. Ropes, Grey and Loring had invented relations to query.

Marigold eyed the pile with something more than distaste.

"The sooner you get it over with, darling, the sooner you can put all this nonsense about leaving from your mind," Isabella advised.

"On the contrary, I've decided that all I need is a room where I can write a comprehensive collection of translations of the Greek myths and fables—that old bowdlerizer Mr. Bulfinch's attempts to do so fall far short of academic standards. It shouldn't be too hard to find such a situation," Marigold predicted before steeling herself to read the letters, one by one, to Isabella. And one by one, reject them.

"Too dreary," was Isabella's opinion of Uncle Wooburn's aches and woes in Wellfleet.

"Far too folksy," Marigold objected to Aunt Parthenia and Uncle Orman and their too-numerous-to-name offspring on their sad farm in Swampscott. "I fear I couldn't bring myself to share a room. Even as a pauper, one has one's standards."

"Quite right," Isabella agreed as Marigold put Swampscott in the *no* pile.

"What have we here?" Marigold picked up a particularly battered specimen. "From Great Misery Island?"

"Great Misery? How positively Gothic." Isabella turned up her nose. "I've never heard of such a place. And one can barely read the writing, so ill is the penmanship. You know how you feel about penmanship, darling."

While Marigold acknowledged that her feelings on the subject of penmanship were quite strict, she was also curious. "Do you have an atlas?" She slit open the letter. "Why, it is from a person who claims to be my mother's cousin, Sophronia Sedgwick Hatchet—my mother was a Sedgwick, you see. But just listen to this: *Be you Esmie Warren Sedgwick and Henry Minot Manners's daughter at long last? I've been expecting your letter these twenty years past.*

"Imagine that," Marigold wondered. "I'm only twenty-one years old—she should hardly have expected me to write before the age of at least four or five. I will admit to being a precocious child, but that does seem to be pushing the boat out a bit far from the shore."

"Very strange—and not in a good way," Isabella warned.

"*You will know by now that my man once did your mother, Esmie Manners as was, a great and godless wrong.* She keeps spelling my mother's name wrong," Marigold observed, before she continued. "*I am obliged to invite you to come to us and if you will, I will do my level best to make it right in the eyes of the law and in the eyes of God, though time has compounded the grievousness of the sin.*"

"Grievous sin?" Isabella asked in astonishment. "Whatever could it be?"

"I have absolutely no idea," Marigold admitted. "I've never heard of either this person or this place, nor this 'wrong' before. But I must know now!"

She read on. "*But if you do come to take up your rights, girl, be warned—we are a queer lot out here away from the world on our Great Misery, best left to ourselves and our own odd, peculiar ways. The decision be yours. On your shoulders alone will this wearisome burden rest, for I can carry it no longer.*"

"How appalling," cried Isabella. "Not to mention dangerous."

"Nonsense. She is my mother's flesh and blood, and she says I have rights. She is a Sedgwick born and bred, despite all this queer great-misery nonsense, which I fancy is just a ruse to put me off claiming my due."

"I don't care what she is," Isabella objected. "I don't like it at all. You had much rather stay here and be comfortable and safe with me."

"Isabella," Marigold warned in a tone that indicated she was not going to be drawn in by the trap of comfort. She turned the envelope over—and was disappointed. "It's postmarked Salem." That was just up the coast of

Massachusetts—hardly the wilderness. "Why, this island is right on the North Shore, opposite Pride's Crossing." Marigold mentioned the fashionable, old-money enclave to discourage any further dramatics from Isabella. "You can hardly object to me visiting a private island estate off the North Shore with the likes of the Searses and Spaldings and Fricks as neighbors."

"The Fricks are New Yorkers," Isabella sniffed.

"They hail from Pittsburgh, actually."

"That's worse."

This deficit Marigold would not acknowledge. "You're always saying that sea air is reputed to be a great benefit to health."

"Your health is just fine."

"Then there is no danger." Marigold had to smile at the ease of proving her point. "What harm could come of a summer visit to such a place amongst such a set of people?" Mansions of all sizes and styles gilded the coast from Marblehead to Manchester. "And think of how such a setting will be just the thing to recover myself by"—she borrowed her next argument from the poet Mr. Whitman—"experiencing *the untrammel'd play of primitive Nature* along the coast."

"Hearken *primitive*, darling, denotes a lack of plumbing."

"I'm quite sure that in this modern day and age, indoor plumbing will be found along the North Shore. It will be the perfect setting for me to write my Greek mythology." Marigold could already imagine herself in the estate's cool, cocooning library. "And I am vastly curious of all this talk of their queer and peculiar ways and righting wrongs done to my mother— who never hurt a fly but herself."

"Is there nothing I can say to stop you?" Isabella asked. "What would Cab say?"

Whether Marigold was surprised by the mention of his name or the involuntary pang that accompanied the mention of said name, she refused to decide.

"I see that blush you are trying to hide." Isabella was happy to prove a point of her own. "I noticed he took a very particular interest in you at the boathouse the other night."

"He is a very distant cousin, and your dire accounts had put the wind up him that I might be angling for an invitation to live at the Oaks with his mother," Marigold scolded. "It is a wonder you didn't frighten the poor man to run away to sea."

"He didn't look frightened from where I sat. He looked, if I may say so, like he was extraordinarily taken with you."

"Nonsense—he's merely a gentleman, so you may not say so." Marigold tried to dismiss any thought of Cab, or *being taken*, from her mind. "And I *must* go—how else am I to reclaim what is rightfully mine? I have enough money to get me that far. And if it isn't Kefalonia, it is at least an island where I can work on my mythology until I figure out a way to resume my academic career. It will be a grand little adventure—see if it isn't."

Marigold felt all the pleasure of decisiveness. "I have nothing else to do now but write them back, repack my trunks I had ready for Kefalonia, and consult the train schedules."

Isabella sighed unhappily. "Then I suppose it falls to me to make sure you have something suitable to pack. Whatever does one wear on a Great Misery Island?"

Marigold laughed, relieved to have it settled between them at last. "The same as for my fieldwork, I should think. Something practical. And waterproof."

"Good twill it is."

"Just so. Thank you, dear Isabella."

Isabella shook her head. "Don't thank me yet."

★ ★ ★

Marigold had sworn to be ruled only by the archaeological principles of logic and practical necessity. And the two trunks and four cases of luggage were absolute necessities. Not to mention the boxed crates carrying her books and bicycle—if she was to maintain any independence at all in the hinterland, she would need her steel-made safety bicycle.

Clad in one of Isabella's brilliantly tailored traveling suits of practical, charcoal herringbone tweed—discreetly trimmed with black velvet in deference to her mourning—Marigold felt herself almost equal to the day of departure. Almost.

Because now that the time had come to make the leap from the platform to the train, Marigold was uncharacteristically hesitant. Her normal decisiveness had vanished, leaving her palms damp inside her gloves.

Isabella mistook her unease for vanity. "You look a treat, darling." She patted Marigold's arm in comfort and consolation. "Though I wish you weren't going."

"But I am, so we'll say no more." Indeed, if she said any more, Marigold might think better of independence and primitive adventure, and that would never do.

"You might say no more," Isabella groused, "but I'll regret not speaking up if you think you can't come straight back home at any time."

"Thank you, my dearest friend." Marigold clasped Isabella's hand in gratitude. "That means the world to me. As does your purchase of my parlor car ticket."

Isabella could not resign herself to Marigold's newly budget-conscious state. "We can't have you crossing the countryside in a third-class rail car— that would never do. And neither will my weeping like a maiden aunt upon the platform." Isabella shook her head briskly to ward away her tears. "Promise you'll write. Or better yet, wire me, and I'll send anything you might need."

"I'm only going twenty-five miles north, Isabella, not across the ocean. But thank you, and I promise, I will." But before Marigold could climb the steps to the plush parlor car, a deep baritone voice called her name.

"Marigold!" Cab Cox came striding down the platform as if she had conjured him from her overworked imagination, perfection in a dark wool overcoat and smart houndstooth lounge suit, bearing an equally perfect bouquet of hothouse flowers. "I hoped I wouldn't arrive too late."

"Cab." That she had not allowed herself to expect him was no defense against the flutter in her veins. "What's all this?" she asked to cover the sudden irrational heat in her cheeks.

"I thought you deserved to be seen off in style." He pressed a paper-wrapped bouquet of blushing blossoms into her arms and a kiss to her cheek.

She fumbled the flowers—peonies, her favorites—as her heart made a rather riotous, entirely unauthorized cartwheel inside her chest.

"I hope you've come to stop her," Isabella put in.

An unreasonable, unrestrained hope burst into Marigold's brain before she could stop it.

"Wouldn't dream of it," Cab returned. "Just what a modern gal like our Marigold needs to do—what we all need to do—go out and meet our fates."

"Oh, Cab." Marigold could only overcome her bout of unseemly sentiment with a laugh. It was almost too much—and far too late—for such extraordinary understanding. "Thank you."

"Bon voyage, Marigold." He gripped her hand and looked serious, and for one moment that irrational hope rekindled in her chest. "I hope you know—"

"All aboard!" the conductor called.

"Well then. I'm off." There was no time for anything more private.

Cab gave her one of his blinding smiles and handed up the last of her bags as Marigold climbed aboard. "All the best!" he called.

She blew him a first and last kiss. "You are a lamb."

"Remember that," he called over the clamorous hiss and clank of the train. "Always."

Always? He said *always* as she was leaving?

Marigold knuckled the hot splash of tears out of her eyes and covered her awkwardness with another laugh. "I'll write!" she promised over the grinding roar of the engine straining to life. "As often as I might."

"Remember," Isabella cried as she waved, "you can always come home!"

And for just one moment Marigold truly wished she had a real home to come "home" to.

But then she forced herself to be logically unsentimental and face the uncertainty ahead with a cheerful, confident attitude. She was the independent, incomparable Miss Manners—she had best act like it.

CHAPTER 4

All you need in this life is ignorance and confidence, and then success is sure.
—Mark Twain

The peonies had wilted by the time the train steamed to her destination.

"Pride's Station!" the conductor bawled. "All out for Pride's Crossing."

Marigold rose, but found the aisle blocked.

"Well, how do you do, missy!" A bearded, middle-aged man poked the brim of his bowler hat upward in greeting. "Don't you look pretty as a pick-chah," he drawled in his countrified, New England way. "Look just like one of those Gibson Girls come to life."

Marigold felt the uneasy mixture of wariness and mistrust that was so unfortunately well-known to women traveling alone. She knew she was meant to be flattered—Mr. Gibson's drawings of the female archetype of the age were all the rage—but when the fellow's hairy smile slid into a leer, unease became umbrage. Nothing brought out the intrusive familiarity and condescending littleness in men of all ages like an independent, unaccompanied young woman.

"Lonely country for such a delicate-lookin' little lady," was his next gambit. He might as well have twirled his over-oiled mustache as a substitute for announcing his intentions.

Though Marigold might appear delicate to him, at the moment she had the finer feelings of a catamount. She was a modern New Woman and would not be frightened into politeness. "Let me pass, sir. I have no wish for your, or any other, company."

"Hey, now." His toothy grin was all condescending smarm. "That any way to treat a fellow who's just trying to be friendly?"

Marigold gave the fellow her crocodile smile. "No," she agreed pleasantly. "This is." And with that, she all but harpooned him with the business end of her stylish but steel-shanked umbrella.

"Hey, now!" he yelped as he jackrabbited out of her reach. "If you ain't just the harpiest thing." But he rubbed his abused, well-padded posterior from a distance of proper respect.

"Quite so," she agreed with the same cold-blooded smile. "And I should like nothing more than to demonstrate my harpiest prowess." Her coursework in physical education at Wellesley had been comprehensive, including a vast deal of self-defense. "If you do not clear the way immediately, I will feel free to do you a more deliberate harm."

The fellow obligingly fled the car.

Marigold allowed herself a moment of triumph. But only a moment. Because the station platform was empty of any person who might be taken for a greeting relative, though she had wired her expected time of arrival. The efficient parlor car porter had expertly managed the transfer of her stack of trunks to the platform, but the step down to the rustic stick-and-shingle-style station was where all such luxuries ended—the velvet couches, plush banquettes, and silver flatware of the parlor car gave way to the bare wooden benches of the lone station wagon for hire idling in the lane.

Still, Marigold was made of sterner stuff than to wilt at the prospect of minor physical discomfort—indeed, she had long looked forward to the physical as well as mental challenges of archaeological fieldwork. She fancied she would have met with similar conditions transporting her baggage to the Greek islands, although the temperature in New England was a vast deal rawer than what she imagined Kefalonia would have offered.

"My good man," she called to the gray-haired driver, "I desire a wagon to the pier for Great Misery Island." Since her cousin had not met her at the station, surely she would be awaiting Marigold at the pier, where a sleek, awning-covered motor launch would no doubt ferry them out.

"Great Mis'ry?" The spindly man's bristly chin slowly telescoped into his neck, like a turtle withdrawing into its shell in consternation. "Cain't get there from here."

"*I* am going there from here." Marigold's rejoinder was firm. "You have only to tell me how."

"No pier is what I mean to say, miss." He touched his hat in a belated gesture of respect. "Tho I s'pose I could get you as far as the beach."

That would have to suffice. "Thank you. And a porter to assist with my baggage?"

"There's a dolly 'round the side," was all he offered.

"Naturally." Marigold fetched said dolly—a squeaky hand truck with wobbly wooden wheels that looked in imminent danger of splintering—and managed by a great deal of athletic exertion to load her various smaller cases into the well of the station wagon, glad of her decision to wear her healthful, elasticized sporting corset. "I shall require your assistance, sir, with these heavier trunks."

"By jeezum." The driver let out a low whistle. "Cain't fit all that, miss. Reckon we might take them trunks, seeing as you're strong enough, but them big crates'll need to go on another wagon."

Her books and her bicycle! But this was merely a setback and not insurmountable. "And how does one arrange for a second vehicle?" She cast a glance at the empty lane.

The miscreant raked his fingers through his whiskers. "Reckon I could come back and fetch them along. For another full fare."

"Naturally." It was *damnably* remarkable how often the sight of a calm, confident, independent woman brought out the littleness in any man, even one who resembled a turtle.

Marigold controlled both her ire and her tongue. "Miss Marigold Manners, Hatchet Farm, Great Misery Island. Payment in cash upon delivery. I leave it"—she gave him both her bluster-proof smile and her calling card—"in your capable hands. Thank you."

He gaped at her as if she had eaten her wide-brimmed hat. Speaking of which—the weather along the coast was turning rawer by the minute. Rain looked imminent.

Marigold opened her carpeted handbag and shook out the long, heavy duster Isabella had tailored to her requirements, along with a veil for her hat and a pair of protective safety goggles she had packed to shelter her complexion.

There was no excuse for looking unfashionable or being unprepared, no matter the raw occasion. Or the raw audience. "If that don't beat all," the driver drawled.

"I hope it does." Marigold was not a collegiate athletic champion and a New Woman for nothing. She scaled the rudimentary step up to the well of the cart with ease and settled onto a precarious perch atop her luggage as serenely if it were a padded deck chair on a luxury liner and not an overloaded station wagon.

Yet the moment the vehicle was bawled into motion, serenity was thrown to the wind—it was everything she could do to hang on as the horse tore down the narrow, rutted lanes at a rattletrap pace.

She loosened her hold on the seat rail only long enough to button the collar of her heavy duster against the cutting cold of the April wind off the Atlantic as the wagon wound its shuddering way toward the water. Salem Sound appeared at the end of the lane, gray, tumbling, and foaming as it rushed against the shore, breathtakingly beautiful in a relentless, almost overwhelming sort of way.

"Is that the island?" she asked of the small, manicured landmass just offshore.

"Naah, miss," the driver tossed over his shoulder. "That's Chubb. Mis'ry's larger, farther out." He cast her a long look as he reined the cart to a halt. "Beg pardon, miss, but what in gumption do you want with Great Mis'ry?"

"I'm visiting my relations, the Hatchet family, there."

He gawked at her. "On purpose?"

Marigold was taken aback but refused to give in to the feeling of creeping unease. "Naturally."

"By jeezum." He scratched his grizzled chin. "If that don't beat all. Cain't for the life of me think of why any decent lady would want to do that."

"Whyever not?"

"Things ain't right with them folk," he swore. "You mark my words, miss, afore it's too late—them Hatchets out to Great Mis'ry just ain't right."

Marigold was having none of his gloomy, Gothic predictions. "Nonsense," she said as firmly as possible while attempting to descend from her rickety seat. "The Hatchets are my family, and I'll brook none of that talk about them, if you please."

"Cain't say as I didn't warn you," the bewhiskered driver muttered, tossing his beard at a derelict dory drawn up some distance away on the otherwise empty beach. "There's for Great Mis'ry, I reckon, if you're dead set on going. Cain't think why else old Cleon'd be here—besides the obvious."

The obvious was not apparent to Marigold. "Am I to understand that boat to be my transport to the island?" The vision of the fashionable motor launch sank from her imagination as the specter of the primitive rose.

"Ayuh," the fellow confirmed in his New England way. "If old Cleon ain't all womble croft—halfway to Concord," he clarified.

"I see," she said, though she did not, in fact, understand his garbled reference. Of this Cleon she saw no sign. But the chill afternoon was rapidly fading into chillier twilight, so Marigold turned her collar against the relentlessly raw April wind and wrestled her baggage into a pile where she could keep an eye on it before she approached the dory—which appeared empty but for a heap of stained, stinking fishing nets.

Marigold had half climbed in to bail out the briny bilge water collected in the bottom when the ragged heap of net she had kicked aside roared to life.

"Lawd, help me from being murdered!" the heap cried.

Marigold managed to keep both her footing and her composure only by the slimmest of margins—and by grabbing hold of the thin gunwale. "Control yourself, sir," she advised in her sternest tones, while attempting to impose the exact some control over her wildly beating heart. "You are not in the least being murdered."

The man to whom she spoke was a specimen so straight out of Mark Twain's imagination—all wide, pale eyes and ruddy, windburnt face, with uneven tufts of white hair sticking straight out of his head at all angles—that he could only be termed a *codger*. Between the ogler on the train, the turtle of a driver, and now this addled old coot, Marigold felt as if she had somehow fallen into one of Mr. Twain's novels as revenge for calling the author a savage.

When the old fellow subsided into a heap on the cross bench, Marigold drew a calmer breath. "Kindly explain yourself, sir."

The dung heap of a man looked up at her with rheumy gray eyes. "I be Cleon."

"Naturally." She tried to smile in an encouraging way and soften her voice, the way one did when soothing a stray dog. "From Great Misery Island?"

"Ayuh." He squinted up at her. "Be you Esmie's girl?"

She corrected his pronunciation of her mother's name. "Esmé Sedgwick Manners was my mother, yes." Marigold unwound the enveloping veil from her hat and removed her goggles so he might better see her. "I am her daughter, Marigold Manners. How do you do."

"That's a-right, then." He nodded in apparent relief. "I'm to get poor Esmie's girl."

"Then you've got her." Now that introductions had been sorted, it was time to return to practicalities. "I would appreciate some help with my baggage. The larger trunk is far too heavy for me to lift alone."

"I don't know 'bout no baggages." Cleon rolled his way over the side of the dory and staggered to his feet. "I'm only to get poor Esmie's girl."

"Esmé's girl comes with luggage, which you see arrayed behind you," Marigold explained with some exasperation. "I should like the trunks arranged carefully, to take care not to lose them overboard." The farther she traveled, the more she was coming to realize that some of the things in her possession were now quite irreplaceable.

"Lawd, where we gonna put 'em?" he wondered aloud.

While Marigold could not expect the efficient expertise of the parlor car porters from such an addlepated codger, she had strict opinions about incompetence. "In this capacious dory," she instructed with precision and far more patience—or confidence—than she felt. "I'll show you exactly how I should like them stowed."

But in the process of loading, it became apparent that the old man's state of befuddlement was at least in part due to a recent overindulgence in intoxicating spirits—he reeked equally of fish scales and strong rye whiskey. *Halfway to Concord* explained.

"I'll row, if you please." Marigold climbed aboard the dory and rewrapped her veil to protect her complexion against the incessant wind before she squared the oars. "You may push us off."

Cleon complied with a gusty amount of huffing, puffing, and groaning, but once the vessel was finally afloat, he sloshed aboard and slumped himself into a rumple in the stern. "Don't look much like poor li'l Esmie. Bigger n' darker," he opined.

Marigold was a brunette where her mother had been blonde, athletically built where her mother had been delicately boned. "How did you know my mother?"

"Seen a picture Miz Sophronia—my cousin Hatchet's missus—keeps of her. Our Daisy's the spit of her."

Marigold tacked that information onto its proper leaf on her sprawling family tree—Cleon was from the opposite branch of her cousin Sophronia's family and no actual relation of Marigold's. "And Daisy is your daughter?"

"Oh, nay. Miz Sophronia's."

"Ah, then I suppose Daisy is my"—Marigold did the requisite assorting of generations in her head—"second cousin."

Cleon agreed. "Must be on account they look so like."

Marigold attempted to sort Cleon's ambiguities out. "My mother and Cousin Sophronia, or her daughter Daisy?"

"Oh, you'll see," Cleon said with a shiver. "You'll surely see. Bad blood atwixt 'em," he averred. "Nothing but bad blood atween the whole bed-amned lot."

CHAPTER 5

The emerging woman . . . will be strong-minded, strong-hearted, strong-souled, and strong-bodied . . . strength and beauty must go together.

—Louisa May Alcott

Marigold would not countenance the notion of bad bloodlines—people made their own choices, regardless of their family's blood. "Yes, well," she said in her crispest tone to dispel the ridiculous feeling of foreboding. "I am quite sure I will."

What she also saw as she attempted to put her back to the oars, was that, despite being an experienced oarswoman, she was making little progress.

"Tide's running in," Cleon remarked unhelpfully. "Shoulda waited on the ebb. Be a long pull out to Mis'ry."

Marigold stiffened her determination along with her spine and braced her feet hard against the thwart. The light was rapidly fading, and over her shoulder, the dark hulk of the island seemed to be dissolving into the sea. "How far is it exactly?"

"A good long pull," he repeated imprecisely.

But to the west, the sunset painted the shore in deepening amethyst, turning the water as Homerically wine dark as she might have wished. She wouldn't have an archaeological summer field season on Kefalonia, but she would still work on the translations of the early Greek myths and fables she had planned for her honors paper. She would find a way to progress even if she wasn't at college.

A flash of contrasting color—a wine-dark mulberry red, like the velvet dinner dress she had packed because, well, because she had packed everything in her possession—swirled past like the flotsam of a shipwreck. And then it was gone, leaving Marigold staring at the water, wondering if she had only imagined it.

No—there it was again, just below the gray surface of the water, truly wine dark and not just the product of her ancient-Greek-literature-influenced imagination! "I think there's a woman—there!"

Cleon spared the barest glance over the side but did nothing more.

Marigold was not used to being ignored. "There is something—or someone—in the water," she insisted, shipping the oars. "There!" She pointed over the side.

It was real and not some overwrought, literary vision. An apron, perhaps?

Marigold leaned over the gunwale toward the water. "Do you not see it? Pass me that rope or net or whatever—"

She reached out blindly, trying to keep sight of the flash of color through the dark waves, only to be met with a shock of pain ricocheting up her arm from Cleon ineptly trying to pass her the spruce spar instead.

"Cleon! Careful!" she cried, forcefully enough to make him cower away. Marigold snatched the offending oar from his hand and snapped it back into its proper place in the rowlock. "What on earth do you think you're doing?" Only the fact that she was strong and athletic had prevented her from being struck senseless. "You might have knocked me overboard!"

Cleon slumped back into the stern. "Pardon, Esmie's girl," he said by way of apology. "Din't mean nothing by it."

"It was extremely careless. Not to mention ill-timed." Because whatever it was she had seen—and she *had* seen something—was gone in the cresting waves. "We've lost whatever it was now."

"Din't see nothing myself, Esmie's girl," Cleon finally offered. "Nobody oughta be in that water this time o' year. Too cold and too fast."

"Naturally," Marigold agreed more reasonably than he deserved. "That's precisely why I wanted to help." But there was no one to help now. Marigold finally resumed rowing but kept a careful, if stern, eye upon the addlepated idiot.

Who remained cryptic. "Takes some getting used to for some peoples, Esmie's girl," Cleon mumbled into his soiled beard, as if she were the one making mad suppositions. "The lonely ocean."

Marigold felt herself bristle like a cat with its fur rubbed the wrong way. She was not "some peoples." She was a rational creature of sense and logic and integrity, and she knew what she had seen—the color and shape were impressed upon her brain.

She had seen *something*.

Marigold took her frustration out in the rhythmic physical exertion of the long pull, straining somewhat at the oars in the rougher water mid-sound, but by the time she finally piloted the dory into a small, rock-bound inlet on Great Misery Island, her forearms ached and her hands were cramped and sore, with blisters beneath her gloves.

Nothing but years of rigorous self-discipline and an unqualified belief in herself kept her from showing any sort of consternation—or any symptom of her present injuries—when the chilly inlet proved as empty of any greeting relation as the station had been. Or from showing any sign of alarm when Cleon simply abandoned the dory and wobbled away into the gathering night.

"What about the boat?" Marigold called as she struggled to pull the heavily laden vessel up the sand, past the high-tide mark, where it wouldn't float away. "And my luggage?"

"S'pose you oughta take what you'll need for your comfort," Cleon advised over his shoulder. "Reckon someone'll have to come back with the mules for the rest."

As loath as Marigold was to abandon her luggage a second time, she was even less eager to be left behind in the eerie wilderness of her cousin's estate. She quickly snatched up two of her nearest valises and raced after Cleon, down a rough track leading into the darkened woods.

The night seemed to close in around her, and the sounds of the woodland—the beats of unseen wings and the scuttering of creatures behind the tumbled-stone walls—set her surprisingly susceptible heart to racing.

And that would never do. Marigold took both her imagination and her baggage firmly in hand to keep from letting the clammy discomfort shifting between her shoulder blades unsettle her.

On they plodded—well, Cleon plodded, while she trudged along under the weight of her bags—following the rutted trail that meandered like a deer path across the arcadian island.

It was nearly full dark when the woods at last gave way to a clearing where a single flickering lantern gave scant illumination to a number of structures—a larger, darkly shingled edifice, several shacks, coops, or sheds, and a weathered, tumbledown barn—all perched along the granite-strewn edge of the sea, hulking in black silhouette like crows over a carcass.

Marigold shook her head to dispel such a dire, illogical image—real life was not like the imaginings of a Gothic novel. But she couldn't help asking, "Is it much farther to the main house?"

"This be the house." Cleon pointed to the dilapidated shingled building. "Cursed it is." He spat out the side of his mouth as if he could rid himself of some evil. "And us'n all with it."

Unease cloyed across Marigold's skin like a cobweb, insubstantial but still keenly felt. If before she had imagined herself in one of Mark Twain's stories, now she felt as if she had chanced into one of Edgar Allan Poe's—she would certainly be leery of any cellars or casks of amontillado.

But it took only a moment before she reasoned that Cleon's mutterings were likely the second of two painfully obvious attempts to scare her out of her rights. The Hatchets were likely proving themselves reluctant to part with whatever inheritance she might be owed—however unlikely the chances of such a shoddy place providing any inheritance might be.

And if Hatchet Farm wasn't the private estate she had imagined, it still harbored the potential to become one—the real estate had value even if the farmstead had fallen into disarray.

Up close, the house was a moldering, Gothic-looking pile, clad in warped clapboards topped with blackened, cedar-shake shingles. It might have once been an imposing edifice, but the present appearance of the place was quite persistently dismal—all skewed angles and shuttered gables without a glint of light or warmth. The shiplap framing the entry was cracked and canted as if the place had withstood successive years of Nor'easters with nothing more than salt and spite.

Presently, the chapped front door creaked open and a wizened woman held a flickering oil lantern high. "Be that Esmie's girl?"

The old woman was dressed in clothes nearly a century old, with worn patches at the wrists and elbows, and her shoulders were draped in at least two layers of shawls. Gray and black-streaked hair wreathed her pale, lined face.

The word *crone* rose unbidden on the tip of Marigold's tongue, and nothing but the strictest application of her best manners prevented her from speaking the term aloud. "Good evening, ma'am." Marigold nodded graciously to the housekeeper, who was most likely Mrs. Cleon. "I am Miss Manners, of Boston, to see my cousin, Mrs. Sophronia Hatchet."

"By Gawd," the woman muttered. "Look at you."

"Evening then, Miz Sophronia." Cleon slouched his hat at the frizzled creature. "Found 'er up the beach, just like you said I ought," he confirmed, as if Marigold were a stray cat he'd happened upon. "Rowed us here, she did, poor Esmie's girl. Took the oars, straight off—t'were like she knew the way." He rolled his eyes to the pitch-dark sky. "Powerful eerie it were."

"Nonsense." Marigold might have been shocked to find this crone was her mother's cousin, but she would give no sway to old Cleon's ridiculously ominous talk. "It was simple enough navigation to point the bow at the island," she suggested more reasonably than she felt, clenching her fists around the handles of her luggage in defiance of her blisters. "I rowed crew at Wellesley College, you see."

But she took the next moment to remove her hat and veil and recover some of her aplomb before she stepped closer into the circle of lamplight. "Good evening, Cousin Sophronia. I'm your cousin Esmé's daughter, Marigold Manners."

"My Gawd above," the old woman whispered as she held her lantern higher and reached out a shaking, talon-like hand toward Marigold's cheek. "Of course she called you Marigold."

Marigold felt just the whisper of cold caress against her skin before she flinched away in revulsion. Which wasn't at all like her—normally, she had complete control over both her emotions and actions. "Yes, ma'am, she did."

"You're the spit of him, you are," Sophronia muttered, "with Black Harry's coloring."

"Black Harry? Do you mean my father?" While Harry Manners might not have been the most sterling of characters—gamblers rarely were—Marigold had never heard him referred to in such damning tones.

"Black hair, black eyes, dark as the devil, wicked as sin." Cousin Sophronia continued to mutter under her breath as if she were talking to herself and not her new-met niece. "Sinner he was—you could see it from the day he set his eyes on . . ." Her voice faded to a whisper. "Only a matter of time before doom devoured them both."

While Marigold might have been estranged from her parents for her own differences of opinion about education and their erratic style of living, she would not stand by while a comparative stranger tarred their good names so blackly.

"I should like it known that my parents were not devoured but passed away from the influenza epidemic that has swept up the globe. It was the highly transmissible disease, coupled with a lack of care"—they had fallen ill from the grippe in a hotel suite far from home—"and nutrition"—their condition had been exacerbated by their decided preference for dry gin cocktails over foodstuffs—"and not any defect of their souls, which were, as should be, entirely their own business and nobody else's."

And while she was on the topic—"I hope to find that you take the usual sanitary precautions here, against such agents of disease as influenza?" Marigold looked at the rust-rimmed pump some distance across the littered dooryard and resigned herself to only rudimentary plumbing. But even with plumbing, the scope for sanative improvement was vast. "I have some experience in implementing a scrupulous system of hygiene." Her Wellesley College coursework in the sciences had been as practical and extensive as her physical education.

Cousin Sophronia looked at her as if any idea of sciences were quite beyond her. "Best take you up before the night falls upon us like sin," she intoned with a narrow-eyed look at the sky.

Another involuntary shiver crept up Marigold's spine to the back of her neck. "We left my luggage back at the beach—"

"Hired girl'll get those." Cousin Sophronia gestured across the yard, where a young Black woman reluctantly stepped into the light. "Leave t'others here. You're not to lift a hand for Hatchets."

"Thank you." Marigold was relieved to set down her bags.

"Best come along then, Esmie's girl"—the woman beckoned her into the unlit house—"before the night creatures get the scent of you on the wind."

With such a dire warning—wolves at the door took on an entirely new meaning—Marigold did not need to be asked twice, though good manners dictated she wait for her cousin to precede her through the uneven entrance and wait in the drafty dark of the hall while the woman laboriously shut the creaking door behind her.

"What about the others?" Marigold thought there might have been other people besides the hired girl in the dooryard, but it had been too dark to make out their features.

"They're on their own, each to find their own way. That's how it is at Hatchet Farm." The heavy wrought-iron latch fell with an ominous clack. "Each to fend for themselves."

The interior of the house was fitted with the same chipped shiplap as the exterior. The peeling posts holding up the stairway and doorjambs seemed to be listing like drunken sailors. Marigold peered up the steep, narrow staircase into the inky, cobwebbed rafters of the place, looking for some sign of warmth or comfort. Or gaslight.

There was none.

Isabella's warning against the primitive came swiftly to mind, but it was far too late to heed her words now.

"You're here at last." Cousin Sophronia picked up a tarnished oil lamp that couldn't hope to dispel the gloom of the dim interior. "Just as I always saw. Just as I knew you should be. Welcome, poor girl, home to Great Misery."

CHAPTER 6

My courage always rises with every attempt to intimidate me.
—Jane Austen

Marigold shook off the frisson of fear that laddered up her spine. Fear meant she was relinquishing logic, the very bedrock of her carefully educated persona. She would not give in to the clutches of illogic. She refused its tawdry invitation.

In the fitful, eerily marbled light cast by the oil lamp, Marigold could see that her mother's cousin must have once been a handsome woman—there were traces of the Sedgwick family nose and delicate bone structure—but years of hardscrabble living had taken their toll. The woman resembled nothing so much as a cracked walnut shell, worn and wrinkled on the outside, jagged and hollow beneath.

Marigold would take care not to get scratched.

Presently, they came out of the creaking hallway into a large, ill-lit kitchen, redolent with the pungent, greasy smells of kerosene and bacon fat. The room had once been the old-fashioned keeping room typical of New England farmhouses, with a long-board table with chairs and benches in the center and a cavernous fireplace that now housed a hulking cast-iron stove.

"You've come all aback for supper," Sophronia advised her.

"I am sorry for that," Marigold said, trying to understand her cousin's peculiar vernacular, though the dirty dishes littered across the table gave no clue as to what sort of foodstuffs she was too late to be offered. "Would it be possible to get a plate of bread and butter in my room? Or perhaps some hot tea and milk? It has been a rather long day."

"Same length as all the others," Sophronia countered.

"Milk and butter!" A scornful murmur came from the dim shadows at the end of the room. "Did you bring us a dairymaid in the dory?"

Marigold felt the hairs prickle at the back of her neck, but she would begin as she meant to go on—logically and confidently.

"I'm sorry"—she addressed the shadows—"but I don't take your meaning."

"Pa's not going to like this."

"Mind yourself," was Sophronia's advice, but whether she was speaking to her niece or to the sneering shadow, Marigold could not yet tell. "Come and meet your cousin first I take her up," Sophronia ordered the shadow. "My sons, Wilbert and Seviah. This is your cousin Esmie Manners' girl."

Two tall forms detached themselves from the gloom and lurched forward. One was a handsome young man, roughly about her own age, with dark hair, tanned skin, and piercing golden eyes in a superbly well-fashioned face. The other was clearly his brother, perhaps older and still handsome, though his eyes were less piercing and his bone structure held a heavier share of ruddy flesh. They were attired in rough workingmen's canvas vests and pants over soiled shirtsleeves, and their dark expressions, as they stared at her, were idly hostile.

But Marigold had dealt with opposition from men of all sorts and ages all her life and could give as good as she got. "Marigold Manners. How do you do?" She stepped up and shucked her glove to extend her hand despite her blisters. "I am pleased to meet you."

"Come to take the place from us, have ye?" the older son growled.

Marigold was shocked by the suggestion. "No indeed," she stated baldly. "I'm only here for a visit." She would abide the filthy place only long enough for Sophronia to tell her what "godless wrong" had been done to Esmé.

"Come to live with us, she has, as is her right," their mother contradicted. "She's naught but a poor orphan now, with no money and no home, as needful of our charity as we are of her forgiveness."

The insult of pity was somehow sharper than it had been in Boston, coming from this arguably more pitiable creature. "I do have *some* money," Marigold assured her with cool, Bostonian hauteur, "which I hope will be put to my room and board as long as I'm here. You needn't fear I won't pay my fair share."

"We'll not take so much as a penny," Sophronia swore.

"Won't take her money?" muttered the younger son, before he spat on the floor. "Don't know as I'd take her forgiveness either, though there's other things I might like to take."

"There'll be no liberties, Seviah Hatchet, unless you'll want to burn in hell."

"Perhaps I will. Perhaps it would be worth the heat." The handsome young man laughed and made a show of flicking a wooden match to make it light. The sulfur flame winked deviously before he snuffed it out between his blunt fingers.

The suggestion was as crude as his behavior was rude. Marigold suddenly understood the urge to wash someone's mouth out with soap.

"Leave off." The other brother—Wilbert—shoved Seviah toward the door. "You heard her, no liberties. Likely no forgiveness either."

"I am sure I'd be happy to forgive," Marigold interjected, determined to be progressive in her judgment. "Only I've no idea what I'm to give forgiveness for."

They did not laugh at her attempt at humor. They did not so much as smile. They simply stared at her until they'd looked their loathsome fill, then shuffled off, back—judging by the dirt on their hands and the mud under their nails—to whatever stinking hole they must have crawled their way out of.

Which left her with her mother's cousin for answers.

Marigold took the moment to strip off her other glove and remove her outer garments, though she was mindful of the letter in her coat pocket. "I must say, Cousin Sophronia, I was quite surprised by your letter and your reference to a great wrong done to my mother, as that's the first I heard of it."

"She never told you?" For the strangest moment, her cousin gawped at her, as befuddled and slack witted as old Cleon. And then she seemed to come back to her narrow-eyed self. "Then I've said what I've said and I'll say no more." Sophronia waved a hand over her lips, as if that settled the matter. "Me and mine'll know what they're to do, and that's my first and last word on the matter."

She looked so foreboding and forbidding, Marigold was temporarily silenced. "But what am I to do?"

Sophronia shook her head before she turned away. "Ask me no more this night, for the hour grows old and I am weary of this talk." She took up the lamp again. "Come along."

Marigold set herself to follow her cousin through the inky gloom, but the house was acting strange underfoot—like a ship on the storm-tossed sea, rising and falling on the tide, shifting and wavering with the wind. Or more reasonably, shimmying side to side, like the train.

Marigold put a hand against the wall to steady herself.

"You drunk, Esmie's girl? Perhaps you're your father's daughter?" Sophronia narrowed her eyes.

Marigold bristled anew. Her father might not have been the most sterling of characters, but he was not a drunkard. Nor, certainly, was she, even if she did rather want a fortifying sip of Isabella's best amontillado sherry—there were no dank cellars at Isabella's house.

"Not a'tall, ma'am, I assure you." Marigold worked to keep her tone even. "I expect my condition is merely travel fatigue—a product of the continuous motion of the train carriages in concert with the exertion of rowing the dory. The phenomenon often happens after one takes a sea voyage." From Sophronia's dour, uncomprehending look, Marigold was sure her cousin had never traveled. "And please do call me Marigold—or Cousin Marigold will do, if you're feeling particularly formal."

Sophronia did not take the gentle invitation. "They'll be no alcoholic spirits in this house, Esmie's girl," the woman answered without emotion. "Your room's along here, separate from the others." She led her shuffling way down a meandering wing that seemed to turn left and right at random, as if the builder had been drunk when he pegged the house together out of the scattered bones of a shipwreck.

At the end of the hall was a door, next to which was a table with a dinner tray—complete with empty, scraped plates.

"Looks like someone enjoyed their supper," Marigold observed, not without a touch of envy. She'd certainly take "cold roast" now.

"Pay that no mind. It's no business of yourn," Sophronia warned. "Your room's here." She indicated a narrow, slatted attic door, which, when opened, revealed an even narrower set of attic stairs. "Up here."

Marigold followed with some trepidation, fearing a cold, dusty garret. But while the room did smell strongly of seaside damp, some small effort had been made at homeyness—the river-rock fireplace had a thin fire already laid, and a tattered gingham coverlet was spread across the tarnished brass bedstead. And there, on a weathered wooden stool next to the bedstead, was a chipped jam jar with a small posy—a golden-orange marigold with a few sprigs of wild rosemary. "How thoughtful."

It wasn't the height of style or fashion, but it would certainly do for the rudiments of shelter. Of course, Marigold had sensibly packed her own sheets in her valise. Even without bread or butter, she could clearly survive the night. "Thank you, Cousin Sophronia."

The older woman shook her head and knelt to light the fire. "I knew you'd have to come. I saw it in the flames with my own ruined eyes. The curse will work its way. So don't thank me yet, Esmie's girl. Don't thank me yet."

Marigold felt she was being purposefully frightened. But to what end?

Even though her skin chilled, she returned her cousin's warning with her calm crocodile smile. "Of course not, Cousin. There's plenty of time for us to set things right."

Sophronia's dark eyes narrowed with some strange combination of malice and sorrow. "Oh, no. There's a well of wrong runs so deep, you'll never drain it dry. You'll drown in it first."

CHAPTER 7

One need not be a chamber to be haunted. One need not be a house.
—Emily Dickinson

Left alone with her misgivings—along with that eerie reminder of the woman she was sure she had seen drowned on the tide—Marigold took the sensible precaution of angling a chair under the doorknob to allay any misapprehensions about drownings and attics and wells and wolves, and especially sullen, match-wielding cousins, and retreated to the rickety bed.

She had made it all the way from Boston on nothing more than optimism and determination, but in the chill confines of her garret, she could not avoid the conclusion that it had all been a terrible mistake. That if she had been less stubborn or less proud, she might this very moment be tucked up in one of Isabella's fine feather beds with a generous stem of well-aged sherry.

But such sentiments were the normal product of exhaustion and overexcitement at having finally arrived at a place that looked nothing like the North Shore estate of her imaginings. She would feel more of her optimistically practical self in the morning.

Yet by the middle of the cold night, the courage of Marigold's convictions was quavering under the blankets. The ramshackle house creaked and groaned like an old woman, and its high, dark rafters seemed to hold specters that moaned and moved in the moon shade overhead.

Almost as if it were putting on a show.

Naturally—if she were frightened away, she would never find the wrong done her mother, nor receive her due. Marigold was determined to ignore the eerie sounds, even if it meant burying her head between the musty pillows to shut out the noise. She soothed her thoughts by creating practical lists of improvements she would make on the morrow—laundering and sun-bleaching musty pillows was first on that list.

Yet despite her best sensible intentions, only when the first thin, red rays of daylight peeked over the top of the windowsill, banishing the shadows, did her true sense of practical logic return. But just as she was finally drifting off into an exhausted sleep, a row erupted under her window.

"For the love o' galoshes, would you let me have a say?" a man's voice growled. "I bought them hogs with my own actual, saved up to make something better outa this wretched place."

"My money, you mean." Another man's voice, hoarser and somehow nastier than the first.

"My own dang money," the first countered. "Worked for fair and square, tho' wrestled from your miserly clutch."

"Why, you ungrateful, unholy succubus," the other rasped. "Watch yer foul mouth, or so help me I'll—"

Whatever other invective followed was lost to Marigold's ears as she clambered out of bed and crossed to the window, where a broken pane left the tattered curtains slapping against the jamb like a loose tent flap to let the full cry of the argument in.

Red sky at morning, sailor take warning the old adage might have been, but Marigold was too annoyed to take heed. She shoved up the rickety, sticking sash of the broken window and poked her head into the raw morning to find Cousin Wilbert facing a gaunt, grizzled older man in an old-fashioned fisherman's woolen smock.

"As ye sow, so shall ye reap!" the old devil quoted.

"Well, you ain't sowed nothing but discord in years," Wilbert returned.

"Shut your clamshell," the older one roared. "Or I'll shut it for you."

"If you don't mind," Marigold broke in. "Would you please take your argument elsewhere? Some of us are trying to sleep."

The older man turned a face as rough and raw as a prizefighter's fist toward her. "Some of uz are trying to work, you hu—"

"—houseguest," she finished for him before he could say anything unkind. "Then I suggest you argue wherever that work might be,"

Marigold advised reasonably, "instead of filling the dooryard with your unseemly row."

She shut the window to discourage them from any further argument or abuse, but as she was now fully awake, she turned her mind to her surroundings.

Last evening, she had been hesitant to believe the evidence before her own eyes. As impoverished and down-at-heel as her cousin's and her family's appearances might be, Marigold had learned never to make assumptions about a New Englander's solvency—there was a miserly, keeping-back tendency among them, a grim Puritan distaste for finery or showiness in any form, that might have kept them from profligate spending.

But in the clear light of day, her chamber was very nearly derelict—the corners were enmeshed in cobwebs, the curtains faded and filthy, the rugs thin and threadbare. And a peculiar New England sort of smell, of must and mildew mixed with salt, signified that the room had been left vacant and stale for too long.

There was much, much work to be done. And Marigold, with her penchant for orderliness, was just the one to do it. She could spend the day until she convinced Sophronia to trust her by being trustworthy and useful. And she would start on her scheme of hygienic improvement just as soon as she was bathed and dressed for the rigors of the work.

Yet a search of the cupboards revealed nothing that could be taken for a water closet, and the basin on the washstand was filled with dust. The only thing that passed for personal relief was a chipped old-fashioned china chamber pot Marigold's grandmother Manners would have called a *bourdaloue*.

But Marigold was a resourceful New Woman who would overcome such obstacles by availing herself of the pot before completing her ablutions with a practical application of astringent, scented toilette water from her bags. She dressed as warmly but as smartly as possible—given the fact that there was also no mirror—in a thick sportswomen's sweater, wool walking skirts, and boots. Her version of athletically rational dress was certainly more suited to a fashionable summer estate than a barren farmstead, but such attire was sturdy enough for whatever difficulties or travel the day might hold.

One might adapt one's standards but never let them down.

Cleon alone was present in the kitchen, sprawled facedown upon the long, slatted table with his mouth gaping wide, as if he had been frightened into an apoplexy midscream. So still was he that for a terrifying moment, Marigold feared the worst.

"Cleon?" she whispered, almost to herself. "Are you dead?"

"Dead and gone," he croaked as he bolted awake. "Gone to the fallow fields and unmended walls. Out."

"All of the family? Cousin Sophronia and her daughter Daisy have gone out as well?" How progressive that the women of the family might be accorded equal status on the farm. Not that she had seen any evidence of actual farming.

"Miz Sophronia?" Cleon looked at her as if she were daft. "Reading her cards and embers, she'll likely be. Talking to the departed spirits."

"Perhaps she can speak to my parents and find where all the money went." Marigold also wondered where all the food had gone. "Is there any breakfast left? Tea or coffee? A piece of toast?"

"It's each to their own here, but I can make mush for you, Esmie's girl."

The thought of "mush" was unappetizing in the extreme. "It's Marigold or Cousin Marigold, I suppose, since we are vaguely related. Or even Miss Marigold, if you're still quite determined to be feudal."

"Ayuh," he answered, though she had little idea if he had understood her. "Or I can fry you up a special egg, Miss Esmie's Girl." He held up just such an object from the depths of his copious—and copiously filthy—pockets. "Got just one left."

A glance at the dirty pans littering the top of the cast-iron range made up her mind. "That is very kind of you, but you needn't wait upon me—I'm perfectly capable of boiling an egg for myself." Once she had scrubbed the grime from every inch of the place. "But this morning I should just like some tea and toast, if possible. I've brought some—tea, that is." She produced the canister of gunpowder tea she had packed for just such a contingency. "And if you'll just show me where I might find a kettle to boil the water and a toaster?"

"The toaster?" The old man gaped at her. "What be a toaster?"

Surely he was joking. "An implement to make toast—a little metal rack to put in the range to toast the bread?"

Not a flicker of recognition.

"Do you know what toast is?"

"Ayuh." He nodded eagerly. "Bread all burnt round the edges."

"Naturally." The description was sufficient, if entirely unappealing. "How do you make toast, Cleon?"

"I got me a fork." He fished an ancient, iron prong from a hook beside the chimneypiece and held it out to her like a trophy.

"Naturally." The place was fulsome with quaint eeriness. Marigold began a mental list of Items Necessary for Civilized Living alongside Items to Be Cleaned. First on that list, a toasting rack. "How about hot boiling water for tea?"

"There were some Adam's ale heated for the oats, but it's gone cold as an old whore now."

Marigold's attention to that particularly revolting, if colorful, metaphor was diverted by a sound very much like the eerie moans she had heard in the night. In the light of day, it was easier to reason that the noise was only the wind, or the waves crashing rhythmically against the rocks cresting the shoreline, because Cleon took no notice of it.

And having no real idea what he was talking about—what on earth was Adam's ale?—Marigold tried another tack. "Perhaps if you could show me the larder, I could find the bread and butter and a kettle, perhaps, for the water?"

Cleon shook his head. "Only herself has keys to the foodstuffs."

The idea of a locked larder seemed like something straight from an antiquated Victorian Gothic. "How positively Dickensian. And where might Cousin Sophronia be found this time of day?"

"Her? Dunno. Could be anywheres, I s'pose. After I gets the eggs from the hens and she counts 'em, Miz Sophronia leaves me be to my fishing, and I leave her be to her own business."

"And what does her business entail—"

There it was again, only louder—an eerie moan that worked its way up Marigold's spine like a chill wind.

"I beg your pardon, Cleon, but did you hear that?" she asked without any real hope of an answer—it would only be fitting if the old man were as deaf as he was befuddled.

"Ayuh. That's the curse and no mistake. The watery souls calling back. The house herself moans and groans, holding herself onto this piece o' rock like a naked whore cleaves—"

"Cleon!" Marigold did not care that her voice had become sharp. "Don't be vulgar. I collect you are of a superstitious nature, but there really is no call for such language." She changed the subject. "If my cousin Soph-ronia is not to be disturbed, where can I find the hired girl? I didn't catch her name?"

"Lucy Dove, from across the sound, is the skivvy. Her mam used to cook here, time was, but she don't now. Got a boardinghouse up the shore, she does." He lowered his voice to an overly dramatic whisper. "Does a few things like for *herself.*"

Marigold did not understand him. "She does for her daughter? Or Sophronia?"

Cleon's answer was as enigmatic as it was confusing. "Couldn't say."

"And Mr. Dove? Does he work here as well?" There had been a great many plates and bowls on the table last night—in fact, most of them were still dirty—but Marigold was trying to understand just how many souls inhabited Hatchet Farm.

"Mr. Dove, as was, passed on some years ago. That's when his widow, Bessie Dove, started taking in work—washing and cooking and the like—long afore Lucy come to skivvy."

"And Lucy does the washing and the cooking now?"

"Oh, no. That's my job now, Miss Girl."

Which explained the state of the kitchen, which was as filthy and dilap-idated as the old man. "And Lucy?" Marigold refused to use Cleon's rather offensive, old-fashioned term, *skivvy*. "What work is she hired to do?"

"Couldn't say, Miss Girl, excepting she does for *herself.*" Again the old man lowered his voice to a whisper, as if whatever the hired girl had been hired to do was meant to be a mystery.

How curious. "And where might I find her?"

"Couldn't say."

"Naturally." Marigold had to smile at the absurdity of it all. The Hatch-ets were in sore need of a good cleaning out, both practically and rationally.

A good cleanout had never hurt anybody. See if it wasn't so.

CHAPTER 8

If you have knowledge, let others light their candles in it.
—Margaret Fuller

"I shall be gathering some necessary things," Marigold concluded, mentally going over the store of hygienic and cleaning items in her trunks. She had hidden the stash of carbolics from Isabella, but she knew her friend would approve of such precautions now. "And then I shall need you to help me set to work, Cleon."

"Ayuh, Miss Girl," he agreed docilely, as if it were his penance, but then he brightened. "But there's Miz Sophronia now!"

Marigold turned in time to register the impression of an eye staring at her from behind the crack of the door before her cousin disappeared, as if she were afraid to be seen. "Cousin Sophronia?" Marigold called. "I thought I might assist you—"

Her cousin halted on the threshold. "You? How could *you* help me?"

Marigold's determination wavered a little in the face of such dour pessimism. "I am not afraid of hard work, cousin. I have extensive experience—"

"Experience is pain," Sophronia muttered. "Life is naught but suffering and sorrow. Drawn in like moths to the flame, women are, helpless. All of us doomed."

Although Marigold was taken aback by such an unaccountable segue, she was not afraid to disagree. "There is a great deal to be said for one's choice, Cousin," she returned matter-of-factly. "I am a woman, and I, for one, am not helpless. I don't feel the least bit mothlike or doomed."

Sophronia's eyes widened, as if she could not conceive of such a thing. Then her gaze narrowed on Marigold. "Mayhap," the woman considered in her measured, New England way, "there is something in you—some old magic come through the curse."

"Rational thought needs no magical assistance." Marigold could not help but correct such backward thinking.

Yet Sophronia plodded across the dusty, rutted dooryard, unswayed.

In the light of the overcast day, the farmyard—or whatever the collection of semidilapidated buildings that included the once-proud house, bowed barn, canting chicken coop, and various shanties and sheds was called—was even more bleak and down-at-heel than it had appeared last night. Litter of all sorts, large and small, was strewn about the place. Broken-down blades of equipment lay rusting where they had been abandoned. A few skinny chickens pecked through the dust and detritus. The appearance of the whole was persistently, dismally dirty.

And then Marigold heard it again—the eerie moan.

"I beg your pardon, Cousin," Marigold called after Sophronia. "But was that . . . the house moaning?" She fell back on Cleon's ridiculous explanation in the hopes that it might make sense to the odd woman.

"The house?" Sophronia stared at Marigold. "Have you lost your wits, Esmie's girl? Or are you drunk again?"

Marigold bristled anew. "I am most decidedly not drunk now, nor was I last night, as I have taken naught—and been offered naught—since I arrived." She curbed her tart tongue to add, "Cleon was the one who said the house was haunted. I myself think there must be some logical explanation for the noise."

"Ayuh," Sophronia agreed with a weary nod. "Because it's not the house giving out those sinful moans but the barn." And off she plodded, kicking up dusty straw as she went.

Marigold followed, mostly because now that she listened closely, the quality of the moaning was taking on an altogether different sound—entirely less eerie and more far more throaty. And decidedly more carnal.

"Seviah," Sophronia called upward to the hayloft. "Get down from there. Do you want to break your mother's heart?"

"Why not?" came the laughing answer from above. "Might as well get that in, too, while I'm breaking other things."

Sophronia looked pained. "Damn your handsome eyes. Get out of there and get to work."

Though what work she was referring to remained undiscovered, her son's knowing smirk appeared at the hay door of the loft above, where he stood, buttoning the few buttons that remained on his worn pants. "Just finished up here anyways," Seviah said. "Unless my little cousin, Miss Delicate City Manners, wants to have a go?"

"No, thank you," Marigold managed as politely as she might while containing her shiver of scientific revulsion at the very thought of copulation with one's cousin.

Seviah began to descend the ladder, but with him came a heeled half boot—a women's boot—that fell onto the muddy ground.

Sophronia sighed as if the weight of the world were dragging her down. "Get back to the parsonage, Minnie." She shook her weary head. "Preacher's child from Pride's Crossing, as wicked and wild as the wind. Get home before you come to grief!"

Seviah swung himself down to the ground and tossed the boot back up without a word of care to this still-unseen Minnie. "Showing our little cousin around, are you, Ma?" He tucked in his soiled shirttail. "So, she knows what she'll be taking from us?"

His aggressively snide tone prompted Marigold to defend herself again. "I'm not taking anything that doesn't belong to me."

He swaggered closer, crowding her back, attempting to intimidate her with his height. "And just what does belong to you?"

"I don't know," Marigold was forced to concede. She looked to Sophronia for some indication of what her "rights" might be, but Sophronia, with her mission to interrupt her son's coitus done, had disappeared. "Well, no matter what might belong to me, I am quite sure I want nothing that is rightfully yours."

"And we're to take the word of a citified, pert lady with her nose all turned up at the very stench of us earthy, hardworking men?"

"You don't appear very hardworking at the moment," Marigold observed.

"Oh, I'll bet I'm hard enough for the likes of you." He lowered his voice to a suggestive growl. "Hard enough to put you on your back and give you what you want."

Marigold might have answered him with a *hard* slap, at the very least—but she saw that what the wolfish young man wanted more than anything else was an argument, and so she set herself to thwart him. "If you're done with your louche attempt at being a Lothario, could you kindly tell me where I might find the hired girl?"

He immediately retreated. "Why do you want to know? No business of mine. I'm sure I don't know." Seviah hitched up his pants one last time before he swaggered away across the farmyard, singing a popular Tin Pan Alley tune: "*Boys and girls together, we would sing and waltz, while Tony played the organ on the sidewalks of New York.*"

What a strangely urban song to hear in the middle of a ruined New England farmstead.

But then somewhere farther away, another voice took up the song—a mellow alto, meshing with Seviah's rich tenor in perfect, easy harmony before it trailed off.

Marigold followed the sound around the back of the barn and down a slight slope to a shed, where the hired girl was opening the steep bulkhead door to a root cellar.

"Hello?" Marigold called as she neared. "Miss Dove? Might I have a moment?"

In the light of day, Lucy Dove proved to be a tall, handsome, young Black woman with warm skin and a cooler nature. Servant she might be, but her appearance was everything the Hatchets' was not—her clothes were as clean and neat and fashionable as anything on Beacon Hill's Cambridge Street, from her sharply pressed shirtwaist collar and apron to her well-polished half boots. Her hair was just as neatly dressed, wrapped in a soft blue calico scarf that matched the hue of her spotless skirts. "Is there something particular you want, miss?"

"I'm Mrs. Hatchet's cousin, Marigold Manners." Marigold felt some introduction was in order. "Thank you for your help with my bags last night."

"You're welcome, I guess. Anything else you want?"

"I understand you're the hired girl, and I wanted to see about hiring you myself."

"I've already seen to your trunks. You'll find them outside the breezeway door."

Marigold shaded her eyes to look across to the sun-bleached dooryard. "I thank you. Cleon made no mention." She turned back to see Lucy's wry smile. "But what I wanted to propose was a rigorous course of cleaning and disinfection in the house—"

"I don't set foot in the house," Lucy interrupted. She crossed her arms over her chest as if delivering an ultimatum. "Not a toe inside."

It confounded Marigold's sense of logic that a girl who had been hired to work in a place would not actually enter that place. "May I ask why?"

The girl took a long, considering look from the top of Marigold's soft chignon to the bottom of her now-dusty cycling boots. "No."

How forthright. Not to mention curious. Clearly, more than just Sophronia had secrets they wanted to keep. But Marigold had not come all the way across Salem Sound to let sleeping dogs lie to her face. No indeed. She had come to find the truth about a wrong, even if no one at Hatchet Farm wanted to tell her.

"I suppose I'll see if I can spend my money elsewhere." Marigold turned to survey the yard, as if that elsewhere might magically appear.

Lucy laughed. "I thought you were supposed to be a poor orphan?"

"My parents are deceased, yes, though I am of age and so not technically an orphan. And I do have a small, private income."

Lucy accepted that information with a nod. "Then let me tell you I'm not hired for the house," she explained, "but for the old lady, Mrs. Alva Coffin Hatchet, Mr. Ellery's mother."

This was a name Marigold felt she might remember. Her mother had once or twice mentioned an Alva Coffin—Esmé had always referred to her as *a terror*. But many things in life had terrified darling Esmé—like the prospect of getting a job.

"And does she live here?" Marigold eyed the mossy, shingled roof of the shed.

"Oh, no!" Lucy's laugh rolled down the rise. "She's got herself all set up in a big room in the house that she likes so much she never leaves it, not in all the years I've been here. This back house is all mine. I've got it all fixed up the way I like. All private. With a good lock."

After barring her own door with a chair last night, Marigold was all appreciation for the protection of a good lock, if not the need for it. "However private, it is a very poor lot to live in a fish shack."

"Don't let them hear you calling it that. This back house Mr. Ellery's father built himself first thing when he settled out here on Great Misery. I keep it just so. Take a look." Lucy gestured down the cellar stairs.

"Thank you, there's no need," Marigold responded, for her readings of Mr. Poe's work had taught her that it was entirely nonsensical, not to mention dangerous, to follow a person one didn't know into an unlit root cellar on a rather decrepit New England farmstead.

And she could see from where she stood that the walls were stacked with storage bins and canning, along with a burlap-wrapped ham that hung from the rafters on a wicked iron hook that looked as if it had been there since the original construction of the edifice. Which made it a historical shack, but a shack nonetheless.

"If you're employed by Mrs. Alva Hatchet, who never leaves her room, why do you not live in the house with her?" Judging by the many dark, vacant windows staring down from the roofline like sightless eyes, there appeared to be a vast number of empty rooms under the warped eaves.

"Oh, no." Lucy's mouth curved into a smile that would have been lovely had it contained a smaller share of derision. "Too close for some people's comfort." Her glance skittered casually away, but Marigold fancied there was a definite glance toward the path Seviah Hatchet had so recently trod.

Marigold took a second look at the half boots Lucy wore, but her long skirts obscured Marigold's view.

Such an interesting and varied lot of secrets the folks on Great Misery seemed determined to keep. And perhaps Marigold might let them—it was no business of hers if Lucy wanted to dally with Seviah Hatchet in the hayloft. The only business Marigold was interested in was the "great and godless wrong" that had been perpetrated against her sweet mother.

The rest of their secrets, these difficult, fornicating Hatchets might gladly keep.

CHAPTER 9

There is a healthful hardiness about real dignity that never dreads contact and communion with others, however humble.

—Washington Irving

Lucy was proving far more openly curious than Marigold. "What do you want out here, anyway?"

"As I said, assistance in cleaning the house—"

"No. Why have you come out here to Great Misery? Someone like you?" Lucy eyed her up and down. "Pride's Crossing's full of your sort of people, all stylish and knowing."

"I daresay." Marigold was nothing if not self-aware. "But I might ask you the same. Cleon said your mother keeps a boardinghouse on the North Shore. Surely such a place is better that this small sh . . . house?" she corrected.

"I told you, I've fixed it up just as I like, like my momma did when she lived here. Got a good stove—a clean stove. Clean dishes. Everything just so. And everything's mine. All I have to do is cook for Mrs. Hatchet and bring it over to the big house. Three squares, as they say. And I'm good at it."

That explained the tray outside the door last night. "Can you do that for me? For pay, for the duration of my visit?" The hope of cleanly prepared food delivered to her room made Marigold more than willing to part with more of her meager funds.

"Maybe." The girl shrugged. "I'd have to ask."

"Naturally." Great Aunt Alva seemed to wield a great deal of influence for an old woman who never left her room. "Why might she not be agreeable?"

"No reason, any reason," Lucy laughed.

"If she is so changeable, why do you work here?"

"I got my reasons," she demurred. "The work's pretty easy. And it's got its advantages." The smile hooking up the corner of the girl's mouth intimated just what those advantages might be.

"Seviah is a handsome young man," Marigold admitted. If one liked that type of Lothario. Presumably Lucy did, which made Marigold more determined to educate the girl into having higher standards for herself. "But handsome is as handsome does."

"Now, don't go getting the wrong idea." Lucy shook her head, but then she smiled ruefully. "Haven't you ever got the idea you could make something of a man?"

"No." Marigold had never had such a feeling. She had only ever wanted to keep a man from thinking *he* could make something—something different or nonarchaeological—of *her*. "I say, make something of yourself first. Do what you're meant to do, and the world will learn to catch up."

"I'd rather nobody catch me up, thank you very much."

Marigold decided she liked Lucy's wry humor. "Then it is incumbent upon me to ask if you are employing the right precautions?" Lucy might *say* she had the wrong idea about Seviah, but Marigold had eyes. And ears— those moans had been particularly melodic.

"No, thank you." Lucy laughed. "I've no want to be filling my house up with by-blows."

"An admirably independent stance." The young woman was clearly sensible and rational—one could become a New Woman no matter one's education or economic status. And as a New Woman herself, Marigold knew it was her duty to help other women find the path of logical fulfillment. "We all deserve a life of our own choosing, with the opportunity to make our own choices."

"Do we now?" A one-sided smile split Lucy's wide mouth. "You sound just like my old schoolteacher in Salem, Miss Tibault. I have met a vast many white ladies like you, all improving. Usually, they're from some church. Are you Methodistical?"

"I am a-theistical, though my people were Unitarians—or contrarians, as my father liked to joke, which is a very New England thing to be." But Marigold knew her faults as well as her strengths. "I daresay it is the hallmark of my personality, this penchant for improving things." And she also knew when she was wrong. "I can see now that you, like my dear friend Isabella, need no improving from me. In fact, I fancy it is quite the other way round—I should be taking lessons from you in how to get along with these Hatchets."

"Getting along may be a stretch." Lucy laughed again. "Surviving, now—I might know a thing or two."

"Then I shall follow your lead," Marigold vowed. "And get a good lock on my door."

"That's better thinking." Lucy nodded approvingly. "Though I suppose you've come to the right place if you like to improve things." She surveyed the littered farmyard up the rise. "Like a bag of rusty nails, this place is."

"Yes," Marigold agreed with a sigh of her own as she added another item to her list—hauling away scrap metal. "I notice that stoved-in washing mangle there. I'll start with seeing if I can repair that"—even if she did not have her bicycle maintenance kit, there were bound to be tools somewhere on a working farm—"and then move on to the washing, if that would suit?"

"Told you I don't go into the house. If you've work I can do outside, then I reckon I can help you."

"And for payment in cash," Marigold clarified, determined to improve Lucy's lot. Now that Cousin Sophronia had refused the hundred dollars per annum for room and board, Marigold felt free to dispense her money elsewhere.

Lucy's indifference changed to pragmatic enthusiasm. "Then it surely does suit."

"Excellent. Whenever you're ready—all in good time and no need to rush."

"No rush?" Lucy's laugh was a rollicking, musical thing. "That just means you haven't needed to use the outhouse yet."

Now that the unfortunate outbuilding had been pointed out to her, Marigold held her nose and made use of the facility. And promptly added a load of lime and sanitary paper to her list.

And then she manhandled—or rather woman-handled, because she used levers and a wheelbarrow to do the lifting instead of brute strength—the abandoned washing mangle out of the rutted dirt and across the yard to the sunny area outside the kitchen door, where a small shed roof made a convenient alcove for the washing.

But repair was more easily imagined than done. Though Marigold had long cultivated a mechanically utilitarian bent—practical reality dictated that an archaeologist acquire competence with a tool set—the rust proved extensive and resistant to everything but repeated oiling and sanding. It took hours of discommoding toil, two broken fingernails, and one aggravating tear of her tweed skirts before Marigold was able to reassemble the refurbished parts into a workable whole.

"You look like you walked across a banana peel," Lucy laughed, but she proved herself an equally hardy soul and turned the crank over every last scrap of dirty linen Marigold could find in the ramshackle house, although her search didn't get far past the few public rooms—most of the house's narrow, warped doors were locked. And while it bothered her to think of the potentially soiled antimacassars lurking behind closed doors, Marigold took great satisfaction in the work she could do.

When they had the clean linen pegged out on a line, drying in the stiff wind off the Atlantic, Marigold turned her mind to her next project—the kitchen. For what good would clean linen do in a dirty house?

She worked around the ominous-looking pot of glutinous fish stew resident upon the stove, but nothing else—dishes, pots, pans, stove, floors, tables, walls—escaped a thorough scalding. Once the room had been scrubbed and scoured, Lucy was set to polishing up the old copper pots and pans to a hygienic shine on the steps of the breezeway while Marigold went after the more delicate assorted tableware on the cobwebbed kitchen hutch.

More than once she felt a strange chill across her arms or up her neck, though she could find no cause. Watchfulness settled upon her, but she did not slacken her efforts, and by the afternoon she had unearthed and cleaned a dust-coated tea service and put it to good use in quieting her growling stomach.

"Polishing up the silver to steal away, are you?" Seviah slouched into the room, all narrowed eyes and sharp accusation.

"I hadn't thought of that." Marigold gave him a laughing smile, as if he amused instead of irritated her. But if Lucy, who was clearly a sensible young woman, saw something of worth in the young man, Marigold had only to find it. "I thought to institute the taking of afternoon tea. Would you care for a cup?" She held a china teacup out to him.

He squinted in suspicion. "Where you'd get that?"

Marigold indicated the ancient-looking hutch behind him, now full of clean crockery. "A good cleaning makes everything cheerful and new, don't you think?"

"That what you're doing, then—attitudinizing us up with your cheerful city ways and wiles so you can slip us some poison?"

His blunt query shocked her. There was something aggressive and challenging in his stance, and although Marigold knew perfectly well that her mere presence was somehow a challenge, she was canny enough not to provoke the young man. "Hadn't thought of that either. Just trying to earn my keep the best way I know. I can't reasonably claim any wiles, but I will say I'm very good at tidying things up."

"You're very tidy yourself," he observed, not without a slight leer. "All buttoned up and not a hair out of place." He leaned over the table, one long, well-muscled arm on either side of her, caging her with the open fall of his shirt and his musky scent, intimidating her with the lit match that just seemed to appear out of nowhere under his right palm. "Wonder what it would take to muss you up?"

"Oh, a bicycle ride," she said breezily, and purposefully poured out enough tea to douse the match, quite determined to give as good as she got. "I am an accomplished and enthusiastic wheelwoman. I often go so fast I muss my hair quite considerably. It's better than sex. Do you know how to ride a bicycle, Seviah?"

"No." He was taken aback—either by the frankness of her query or the unexpectedness of her action. He stepped away from the table, tossing the spent match to the floor. "But I seen 'em. Or pictures of them."

Marigold allowed herself to sigh—not least for the dirty match marring her clean floor. "That's a pity. I do so love to bicycle. I quite like the speed and daring of it all. I had to leave my machine behind at the Pride's Crossing station, and I am anxious for it to arrive."

He seemed not to know what to do with that information, so Marigold pressed her momentary advantage. "What do you like to do, Seviah? Besides girls in the hayloft, I mean." There was more than one person who might benefit from information about the precautionary arts. "The sex is all well and good, and a healthy expression, I suppose, if you're being responsible and taking the necessary precautions with your inamoratas."

"In-an-mor . . ." The young man turned a gratifying shade of deep crimson red. "Now listen here—"

"I did listen." Marigold continued amiably. "And I saw, just as you intended me to. I must say, you did an admirable job of vexing your mother with your sexual liaisons—which I assume is the real gratification you derive from the encounters."

He tossed up his shoulder in a strangely aggressive shrug. "Maybe I just like to fu—"

"What's all this?"

Seviah lapsed into silence when his brother Wilbert bulled his way into the kitchen like an errant calf, dragging a tall, lethal-looking scythe behind.

Such a penchant for intimidation these young men seemed to have.

"It's tea, if you should care for some." Marigold held the cup she had proffered to Seviah out to Wilbert instead.

"That's mine!" Seviah snatched it away.

"Naturally." Marigold refused to be either annoyed or alarmed by such behavior. At the moment, she was more determined to simply set an example. "Let me pour you a fresh cup, Cousin Wilbert, while you put your scythe out back, please, where it won't be a hazard or muddy the floor, thank you so much."

She smiled sweetly to mitigate the order, but Wilbert proved as stubborn and belligerent as his younger brother and promptly laid the sharp scythe across the table in front of her, as if throwing down a metaphorical gauntlet. "Making the place over the way you'd like it, I suppose?"

"Cleaning up the place to do my share of work, yes," she agreed calmly, moving the lethal implement to lean against the wall. "How do you take your tea?"

"Never taken it," Wilbert confessed a trifle mulishly. "Never had money to waste on such fripperies."

"Then I am glad I can treat you to it." Marigold gave him a sunny, cheerful smile. "We'll try it with just a dash of sugar." A small sugarloaf was also part of the limited stores she had brought with her from Boston. Just in case. "See how you like it."

"Is it poisoned?"

"Heavens no." Their bluntness was rapidly losing the power to shock, but what a mistrustful lot they all seemed to be. "I'm drinking it too!"

"As if that means anything." But Wilbert took the tea and retreated to a nearby corner, while Marigold took the conversation in hand.

"I overheard your . . . discussion"—she chose her words carefully—"with your father this morning? I take it you've purchased some hogs?"

Wilbert blew on the tea and look a tentative sip. "Just a Hampshire sow and a boar to start, but they cost me a passel of actual."

"They were expensive, do you mean?"

"Yup." He slurped up a deeper, more curious drink of the tea. "Took months of saving up what I could, a little here and there, from selling extra eggs on the main." And then his face fell as he realized what he had confessed.

Marigold allayed his alarm. "How very economical. Well done."

"Don't cost nothing much to keep, them hogs. They feed up on acorns in the woods, and Cleon saves up the slops from dinner—though the devil knows the dinner is slops beginning to end."

"Is it?" Marigold was reminded by the pang in her middle that she had not taken supper with the family. "And Cleon does the cooking? He seems to be something of a jack-of-all-trades."

"More like the dog's body, doing chores nobody else wants to do. Don't get me wrong, miss—I'm fond of the old man. Fond as can be. But . . . he's not like other people—not right in the head. Ma calls him *gawney*." He shook his head ruefully. "Then again, our family ain't like other people neither. We're a cursed, unhappy lot."

"Mmm." Marigold encouraged his confidences with some of her own. "Cleon mentioned that—the feeling-cursed part—as did your mother, in her first letter to me. She also mentioned a great wrong her husband—your father—had done my mother, though I have no knowledge of what that was. Do you?"

"Nope." But this mention of the bone of contention within the family seemed to remind Wilbert of his suspicions of her, as he put down his teacup. "I'm obliged to you for the hot drink, miss. But I've work needs doing."

"Then don't let me keep you from it. But speaking of work—do you mind if I keep on tidying things up here?" Cleaning was a good first step, but there might be other things she could do to improve their lot and earn their trust.

Wilbert shrugged. "Don't suppose I mind, if nobody else does. Be a nice change from all the dirt."

"Excellent. And if you should like your clothes laundered as well, you have only to leave them in the basket I've placed next to the kitchen door." She pointed to the receptacle.

"Fancy that," he said, taking up his scythe.

"Yes," Marigold answered with a smile. "Very fancy indeed."

Marigold saw him off with a friendly wave as Cleon crept in the kitchen door.

"Lawd," he croaked. "What happened here?"

"Cleaning," she said succinctly. "Everything has been put away where it belongs, not left to molder on the table." She wanted to set an example of how a hygienic kitchen ought to be kept.

But Cleon paid no attention to the table or cupboard, rushing instead to the narrow shelf of the chimneypiece around the stove. "Where's my little sugar pot?" he demanded.

"That rusty old jar? I didn't realize it was sugar. It looked so old and contaminated, yellow with dirt and rust flakes, that I threw it out." At the old man's distressed look, she hastily added, "But I've provided sugar from my own stock. There, you see." She gestured to the tea set she had filled from her sugarloaf.

He peered into the silver bowl at the unevenly crushed grains. "Is it poison?"

It was one thing to be asked twice, but a third time gave an entirely different impression of the Hatchets' fears—what on earth made them so suspicious of her? "No, Cleon." She dipped her pinkie in the bowl and put the sugar onto her tongue. "You see. Nothing but pure, sweet sugar."

He shook his wispy head. "I can't like it, Miss Girl. I gotta account for the foodstuffs."

"And here is your account." She held the sugar bowl out to him. "A full jar of sugar. I also thought to find some other condiments and spices, like salt and pepper and herbs—"

"Ain't got none o' that, Miss Girl." Cleon was so flummoxed he harrumphed himself out the kitchen door, while Marigold stayed put in the quiet kitchen to contemplate both what she had learned of her relatives and what she had yet to learn.

Because the thing about tidying up and organizing things was that it wasn't really about the dust on the shelves or the soiled linen—it was about discovering why people were so unhappy they didn't notice the dust or the soiled linen or the lack of spices. Improving a place really meant finding out how to help people make themselves happy.

One thing alone was abundantly clear—no one at Hatchet Farm was happy.

CHAPTER 10

It is better to be beautiful than to be good.
But it is better to be good than to be ugly.
—Oscar Wilde

While Marigold might not count herself among the unhappy, she was still among the impatiently curious. And hungry.

So as soon as she saw Lucy at the door carrying a tray laden with savory cheese and sausages for Alva Hatchet's afternoon meal, Marigold stepped up. "I'll take that in," she volunteered.

"Not in," Lucy warned. "Just knock and leave it on the little table next to the door. Understand? And don't think you can sneak a bite."

"Naturally." Despite protests from her empty stomach, Marigold left the delicious-looking meal intact and even added a fresh cup of tea before she took the heavy tray to the end of the hallway. "Great-Aunt Alva? It's Marigold Manners, Esmé's daughter. I've brought you your tray."

No answer came from behind the door, though Marigold was sure she could hear some furtive movement—and certainly there was a shadow under the door. "It's Marigold, Esmé's girl." She crouched down so the old lady might see her if she were peeping through the keyhole. "I'd like to speak to you."

"What do you think you're doing?"

Marigold whirled to face her inquisitor and found herself looking up at the most beautifully belligerent young woman she had ever beheld.

"I said, what are you doing?"

"I'm leaving your grandmother her tray." Marigold could only state the obvious.

"Did you poison it?"

Somehow the accusation was easier to take the fourth time—Marigold had become inured by its repetition. "No, it is not poisoned. You must be Daisy. I've been hoping to meet you. Especially because our family seems to have a penchant for floral names—I'm Marigold." The darker, shorter counterpart to this slim, wildflower daisy.

Marigold made sure to smile in what she hoped was a kindly manner, because her brain was too distracted to be entirely sure. Cleon had said—she realized now—that Daisy resembled Marigold's mother. And though the girl was tall—far taller than either Esmé or Marigold, and nearly as tall as her brother, Seviah—she had all the delicate Sedgwick bone structure and porcelain skin that had made Esmé one of the breathless beauties of her age.

But this beauty had none of Esmé's air of innocence—she regarded Marigold with narrowed eyes, all leery, cynical suspicion. "I know who you are. Ma's always gawping on about you."

"Is she?" How odd, when Sophronia seemed to have so very little interest in speaking with Marigold directly. "No matter. I am glad to finally make your acquaintance."

"Well, the feeling ain't mutual." The girl tossed back an untidy braid of long blonde hair.

Her costume, for lack of a better word, was a hodgepodge of patched garments that appeared to have been handed down equally from her brothers and her mother. She wore a long leather skirt with a tattered hem, topped by an overlarge blanket-wool wrap that looked as if it might once have been under a saddle. Practical if not rational dress.

And still she was so beautiful she took Marigold's breath away.

"I'm sorry," Marigold said, judging that the direct approach was best. "I'd like for us to be friends."

"I don't give a bleached barnacle what you'd like. You're just like them—all for what you can get. And I hate you for it. I hate you, do you hear?"

"I do." As surely had everyone else in the house, especially Great-Aunt Alva. Marigold heard the door latch behind fall—the tray had disappeared into the old lady's room without another sound.

But this old bird in hand would stay in hand, so Marigold set out for the bush, determined to follow Daisy, if for no other reason than to gaze at her mother's face again. Despite the late-afternoon hour, Marigold followed her out of the house, across a dry weedy area that might once have been a kitchen garden, and down a twisting path through the woods.

She just managed to keep the girl in sight on the ankle-twisting trail along the eastern shore before she finally caught up to her cousin at the northernmost point of the island, where the underlying granite had thrust up to form a small bluff.

Daisy stood at the edge, looking out across the dark, gray water with a sort of reverent longing at the sunshine on the other side.

"What an extraordinarily lovely view," Marigold said as she came by her side.

A wicked little pistol appeared in Daisy's hand so fast Marigold stumbled back with her hands up in instinctive, horrified plea. Such an almighty affinity for weapons, these Hatchets had!

"You're awfully dang soft-footed for a city girl," Daisy accused.

"I'm sorry." Marigold wanted to refuse to be frightened—again—but it was ferociously hard. "Please put that away. I mean no harm." She forced herself to look at Daisy, not the flashing barrel of the pistol, and made her voice as level and as friendly as possible whilst experiencing the vulgar, heart-pounding terror of being held at gunpoint. "And I'm not really from the city. Where I made my home most recently is very much the countryside."

And in that frantic moment, Marigold felt a desperate sort of longing for the beautifully landscaped, rolling hills and scenic walks that made up her college's bucolic but highly civilized campus. To be there in the cradle of learning, sheltered in its verdant park instead of quickly composing a plea for one's life on a primitive island . . . "I'm sorry," she repeated.

Sorry for leaving Boston. Sorry for coming to this godforsaken place. Sorry for thinking she knew better that her friends. For the first time in Marigold's life, she felt the sort of regret she had fancied other, less logical, less determined people felt when facing the consequences of terrible decisions.

Yet Marigold had not survived her tumultuous, nomadic childhood and eight years of boarding schools with clever, rich, cruelly overprivileged girls to be so easily cowed. She used the only weapon left in her arsenal of logic— honesty. "I'm here to help, if you'll let me."

"Huh." Daisy's response was little more than a huff of disbelief. "How could you help me?" But she put the pistol away into whatever sleeve or pocket it had so swiftly appeared from. "You never should have come here. You'll end up drowned like the rest of them."

That glimpse of red fabric floating on the tide filled Marigold's mind. "The rest of them?" Her curiosity—and outrage—instantly overcame her regret. "And who are *they* to be so callously disposed of?"

The indifferent beauty tossed up a shrug. "Them girls."

Girls wearing red skirts, floating just below the surface?

Marigold looked with sharper eyes at the stretch of Salem Sound coursing between the island and the mainland and was gladder than ever that her physical education had included water sports—she was quite determined to be hard to drown.

And harder to misunderstand.

"Then I'll withdraw my offer of help and leave you to your callous view." Marigold had seen more than enough. "It is as extraordinarily beautiful as are you yourself, though more's the pity."

"I don't want your pity. Or your help." But the tall girl's voice and expression held less force, and perhaps at least a little more . . . shame?

What else was she ashamed of?

Marigold followed her gaze across the sound. "Whose house is that over there, anyway?" The imposing redbrick edifice crowning the rock ledge on the opposite shore was everything Hatchet Farm was not—structurally, and presumably financially, sound. "Somebody you know—or would like to know?"

Daisy spared her a sideways glance. "You're awfully danged clever."

Marigold decided to work her way around the resentment in her cousin's tone. "Goodness, they must be very rich to own such a place. But it is beautiful." She switched her own focus from the vista to her cousin. "Like you. I meant what I said, but you're clever too—you pulled that gun on me quite cleverly."

Cleverly being a euphemism for any number of other words. *Appalling,* Isabella had rightly suggested. *Not to mention dangerous.*

But Marigold wasn't trading ironic asides with Isabella in the comfort of her Boston sitting room now. She needed to sharpen her wits if she was going to do anything more than merely survive her short stay on Great Misery Island. Or find out if girls had actually been drowned. "Are you any good with it?"

Daisy didn't bat a blonde eyelash. "I could shoot your eye out."

"Please don't. But I'd like to be able to do that." Marigold made sure her voice was admiring, even as she wondered why Daisy had needed to acquire such expertise.

"Fancy you wanting anything of mine." Daisy's scoff was very nearly a sneer. "But that's what you're here for, ain't it, to take away everything that's ours?"

"No," Marigold assured her with the same sincerity she had assured the girl's brothers. "I give you my word that I am only here for a visit. I do not want, and pledge never to take away, any part of Hatchet Farm." Not unless it was hers or her mother's by right—but she could not imagine how that would be. "My ambition is to be an archaeologist, not a farmer."

"Don't know what that is. And don't know you well enough to take your word." For all her ethereal looks, Daisy was as eminently practical as Marigold—which, of course, earned Marigold's respect.

"You are quite right—we don't know each other at all. What would you like to know about me?"

"Why're you here?" Daisy asked the same question Lucy had. "Fancy Boston girl like you out here in all this everlasting loneliness and wind? I'll never believe you came out here just to boil our laundry."

"Because your mother wrote me to say I needed to come right a great wrong done to my mother. Do you know what that wrong was?"

"No," Daisy answered with a return to her native cynicism. "And even if I did know, I don't know as I would tell you."

"Naturally." These Hatchets all had secrets they were determined to keep. But with every minute that passed, Marigold was becoming equally determined to unravel them all.

See if she wasn't.

CHAPTER 11

Let everywoman, who has once begun to think, examine herself.
—Margaret Fuller

Daisy eyed her askance. "You're awfully fancy looking for someone who's a poor orphan."

"Yes, I suppose I am." Marigold decided Daisy's bluntness spoke of a pleasing lack of artifice. And she also heard the faint echo of envy in her cousin's voice. "Which goes to show you that style should never come at the sacrifice of cleanliness. I'd be happy to launder your clothing with my own, which I will admit I own only because I am fortunate enough to have a friend who was very generous in giving my wardrobe to me."

"I wish I had a friend to give me pretty clothes."

"Then I will be happy to introduce you to my friend Isabella Dana, the couturier. She would adore dressing you in the latest fashions." Marigold judged that rational dress might not exactly appeal to Daisy in her current state. "You're absolutely stunning—beautiful and with the perfect, willowy figure for the styles of the day."

The girl's suspicion softened into heartbreaking disbelief. "Do you really think so?" Daisy blushed a revelatory shade of pink while looking wistfully at Marigold's smart sportswomen's tweeds. "If only I had clothes like that, Taddy wouldn't think I was so no-account—"

Marigold's idling curiosity took its cue. "And who is Taddy?"

Daisy tossed up one shoulder with the same defensive shrug both her brothers employed. "Just a fellow."

"Just a fellow you admire?"

"Mayhap," the lovelorn girl admitted on a sigh before she returned to her more cynical posture. "But don't go repeating that to anyone at home, you hear?"

"Naturally." Another secret to add to the tally. "I give you my word." Marigold let a long moment of companionable silence pass before she asked. "Is he very handsome, your Taddy?"

"The handsomest you ever did see!" Daisy answered quickly. "And cleverest and kindest and sweetest. And he just has the bluest eyes."

"Just as a young man ought to, if he can." Marigold could imagine the sort of callow youth who might attract Daisy's interest. But even as she tried to picture what this boy might look like, Marigold's mind's eye conjured up a different set of clear, piercing blue eyes.

How strange that she should think of Cab Cox at such a time. But she strove to put that clever, handsome man from her mind and recalled herself to her purpose. "And does this Taddy know how you feel about him?"

Up went Daisy's shoulder in that characteristically dismissive shrug. "I reckon he does."

"And does he feel that way about you?"

Her shoulders slumped. "I reckon he might. 'Cept . . ."

"Except . . . ?" Marigold prompted. "Why can't you mention this Taddy fellow's name at home?"

"Because Taddy told me we need to keep it a secret. Swear you won't tell, because Pa'd forbid it, too, on account of—" She shook her head and shut her eyes and stamped her feet all at the same time.

"Because?" Marigold asked, already out of charity with both Daisy's beau and her father. Any young man who wanted a girl to keep his wooing her a secret was up to no good. And any father who forbid his daughter from exercising her right to self-determination was no father at all.

"Because Pa says it's for him to decide and he's already promised me."

"Promised you? In marriage? To whom?"

"He won't say exactly and neither will Granny—just that he intends to give me to a God-fearing sort of man. But they don't let anyone from the main come on the island and they forbid us all from going off, so it's just so awful."

"Do they mean for this God-fearing man to come here, then?" Marigold grew increasingly concerned for Daisy as she sorted through the possibilities. "Someone to help with the farm?"

"I don't know." Daisy kicked a rock into the sea in frustration. "Pa's always tormenting Will by saying he won't leave him the farm when he's gone, nor Sev. But who in their right mind wants this fearful old place?"

Perhaps someone who understood the value of coastal real estate.

"I hate it here," Daisy went on. "It's dirty and mean and makes me feel small and worn, and all hand-me-down and tarnished up!"

Marigold grimaced at the knowledge that she had thought the same of the poor girl.

But she had the power to change that. She could help Daisy—she could get her suitable clothes and help her find a job. Practical considerations before the theoretical—but the theory was righteously strong.

"An arranged, forced marriage will never do. You must tell your father—politely, but firmly." Marigold strove to make the complicated situation as straightforward as possible. "Simply refuse, and that will be an end to it."

Daisy gaped at Marigold, completely dumbfounded. "I couldn't."

"Of course you can," Marigold insisted. "This is the year eighteen hundred and ninety-four and not the Middle Ages—no one can force you to marry against your will. There are laws, even in such an isolated place as this. You are legally entitled to follow your own heart's inclination. We owe our parents—and our suitors—civility and respect, but nothing more." Marigold's opinion on the matter was firm. "No matter what your father says, you do not owe him your very self, even if he expects it. He has no *right* to expect it! The law is very clear."

Daisy's eyes were as wide as the sound. "You mean I really could marry someone else?"

"Certainly." Marigold was all calm assurance—with caveats. "Just how old are you?"

"I'll be twenty come August."

"Then you are legally of age in Massachusetts." Marigold felt she was on solid ground after her recent education on legal adulthood from the prim graybeards at Ropes, Grey and Loring. "Your father can't legally stop you from marrying whomever you like." Though Marigold would certainly have to look into who this Taddy might be before she counseled anything so restrictive as marriage, she could at least admit to the financial benefits of the institution—for others, not herself. "Does your beau have an income?"

"Like a job? Oh, yes. He's a journeyman, he said—which is good, ain't it? But I don't really care about that. All I care about is that he's tall and strong and just . . . just the swooniest." The poor girl let out a lovelorn sigh. "When I'm with him, I just feel so free and happy. Oh, you should see him—he swims like a dream. That's how we met—he swam over from the main the first time. As a challenge to himself, he said."

"I'll bet he did." He would have to swim like a dream to get across Salem Sound without being drowned *like them girls*.

But Daisy was a girl who needed saving, too—if Marigold could win her over. Surely then her cousin would be more forthcoming with any number of the secrets of Great Misery Island. "I can help you. I can help you with this beau of yours."

"Oh, I don't know." Daisy made another strangled sound of frustration and despair. "His family is some pumpkins, and I'm . . . well, I'm a Hatchet, and the Hatchets are donkey dust—no-accounts. At least that's what they say about us on the main."

Though Marigold had never heard the country terms *some pumpkins* and *donkey dust*, she understood them clearly enough in relation to *no-account*. And she heard the hurt in Daisy's voice.

"Might as well be the moon," Daisy continued. "And I hate all the sneaking around, cuz Granny and Pa don't like us leaving Great Misery. Especially now, after things got all sideways with the banks. But I oughtn't tell you that."

"It's quite all right." Marigold nodded in understanding. The recent banking panics had brought misfortune to many, including Marigold's parents—although Harry and Esmé Manners had been well down the road to ruin before that. "My family has had their own troubles with the banks too."

"And that's why you're here?"

"That's why I'm here. For a visit," she amended. Which was why she needed to focus her energies and skills upon Daisy's predicament. "And I am more than happy to invite you to come away with me when this visit is over." Surely she could find such a beautiful specimen some gainful employment with Isabella? With some small education, Marigold might be able turn the girl into Isabella's ideal protégée.

"I don't know." Daisy's native skepticism returned. "The truth of it all is—". She hesitated, perhaps not yet sure if she could totally trust Marigold. "The truth is, I fear Taddy's just too fine for me."

"Impossible—you're a very beautiful girl, Daisy," Marigold assured her. "Perhaps you don't know that, because you haven't been out much in the world, but you're as beautiful as any Boston debutante. In fact, you quite remind me of someone I knew who was renowned as a society beauty." The family resemblance was, as Cleon had said, uncanny.

"But I'm not schooled and learned or refined like a Boston lady—like you."

"Thank you for the compliment." Marigold was happy to be gracious and set a good example for the girl. "But I am also happy to share my knowledge. Would you like to gain some learning and refinement?"

"Would I?" Daisy sighed. "Though Taddy says he doesn't give an empty oyster shell for city airs and graces, I know his folks do."

Marigold's solution was as practical as it was aspirational. "Then I propose that I help you gain refinement to make you absolutely irresistible to your darling Taddy—or anybody you might fancy."

"Will you? Can you? Really?"

"I give you my word," Marigold swore. She would educate Daisy for her own sake, independent of any idea of marriage—a New Woman who could decide what was best for herself. "But I warn you, it will not be easy."

Daisy didn't hesitate. "I don't care. There ain't nothing in not trying."

Despite the offense against proper grammar, the sentiment was so like Marigold's own feelings, she had to smile. She put out her hand to shake. "Excellent. You won't regret this, Daisy. We'll get started right away, with reading."

"I'm pretty good at reading." Daisy was enthusiastic. "Ma taught me longer than either Will or Sev."

It was instructive to find that not all of Marigold's Hatchet relatives might be literate—the scope for improvement was proving more vast than she had imagined. So vast, Marigold was momentarily overwhelmed by pity—she had always valued her own education and had known it as an infinitely valuable gift to herself.

And now was a chance to pass that gift on. "We'll start with Jane Austen for wit, confidence, and conduct. And we'll also go over your wardrobe, to survey your clothes." Isabella would know just what to do to fledge such a fashion novice. "But first, in exchange for my knowledge, I should like yours—I should like you to teach me how to handle a gun."

Daisy's surprise was equal only to her enthusiasm. "Well, come on!" She laughed as she raised her weapon and aimed it at a piece of driftwood. "Where's Pa now, when we could use him for target practice?"

CHAPTER 12

Experience is simply the name we give our mistakes.
—Oscar Wilde

The long day's rigorous work led to a better night's exhausted sleep on fresh sheets and a fresher outlook on the following morning. Marigold felt boldly industrious as well as hungry, but she still could not bear the thought of eating anything prepared by the unwashed Cleon, so she turned her attention shoreward.

"Cleon?" Marigold called loudly in the morning ritual she decided to dub Waking the Dead.

"Gone," he barked as he bolted awake at the kitchen table. "I got to go fishing."

"Naturally," Marigold soothed. "How often might the mule cart be available?"

Cleon pulled a baffled face. "Cousin Ellery'll have to give the say-so. But I reckon he might be persuaded anytime the mules ain't being used to plow."

"And how often are they used to plow?" Marigold had yet to see any signs of cultivation on the island.

"Must be years, now that I think on it. Time was, used to harvest what hay there was on the field above North Cove come summertime." Cleon heaved out a sigh. "But now this rock is as bare and barren as a witch's teat, and just as cursed. The seeds fall to the ground like the sulfurous drops from Satan's d—"

"Yes, thank you, Cleon, I take your point." While Marigold could only agree with the present state of affairs, she wasn't about to accept it.

She found Lucy drawing water at the pump. "That reminds me—I need to get some soap out here." Practical considerations before the theoretical. Marigold took over the chore of pumping for her. "Are you free to accompany me to the mainland? I should like your help in navigation."

Lucy tipped her turban-clad head to the west. "It's that way."

"Yes, but once there, I will need help. I'm planning on taking all of this"— Marigold gestured to the junk strewn about the yard—"to an ironmonger."

"You mean like a blacksmith?" Lucy straightened up with a laugh. "Oh, I want to see this."

Marigold was happy to give her an exhibition of competence. "And also, I should like to meet your mother."

Lucy's ebullience faded. "What for?"

Marigold's interest in the absent Mrs. Dove was both mercenary and epicurean—she was perilously hungry. "I like making new friends." Especially friends who knew how to cook. "But mostly I'd like your company. As I said, I should like to follow your lead."

If Marigold had another reason to avoid crossing Salem Sound by herself, she kept it to herself. She couldn't forget Daisy's reference to drowned girls, nor rid her brain of that flash of dark mulberry red against the icy blue of the water. Lucy seemed the sort of person who would not fumble about with oars at such a moment.

Still, Lucy hesitated. "Then my first piece of advice would be that Mr. Ellery isn't going like you taking his mules and cart without his say-so."

"You are doubtless correct, Lucy," Marigold agreed. "But I learned long ago that it is far more expedient to ask for forgiveness than it is for permission."

"Is that what you meant by 'Do what you're meant to do, and the world will learn to catch up'? I'll be praying Mr. Ellery don't catch you up."

"What we need to catch is the tide." Marigold didn't fancy another row against the current. "You let me worry about Ellery Hatchet—"

"Oh, I surely will."

Lucy's laugh followed Marigold into the barn, where putting the mules into harness was easier said than done—the harness was as complicated as it was dilapidated, the cart heavy and the mules mulish. And the assorted pieces of rusted iron, tin, patinated copper, and steel were a heavier chore to load than she had anticipated. It took Marigold the better part of two hours to emerge, as exhausted and bedraggled as if she had been wrung out through the washing mangle.

"I tell you what." Lucy laughed when Marigold finally led the loaded wagon into the yard. "You might look all delicate and city raised, but you aren't scared of real work, are you?"

"No, I am not." As a New Woman and future archaeologist, Marigold relished the sort of vigorous physical exertion that women of her mother's and grandmother's upbringing had disdained as unladylike.

"Pride's Crossing isn't Boston," Lucy was saying, "but I'd still recommend you wear a hat if you're wanting to look respectable-like."

"I want to look more than respectable." One had one's standards, even on a mule cart. Marigold took her cue from Lucy's ensemble of a practical but spotless pressed-wool coat and fashionable felt hat. "I'll be right back."

Five minutes, an astringent wash in rose-scented toilette water, and a fresh shirtwaist, tie, and well-tailored wool jacket later, Marigold pinned her boater hat on at a jaunty angle that brought out the best of her otherwise delicate jawline. As she'd said, she wanted to look more than respectable—she wanted to look memorable.

But it was Lucy who appeared more than memorable—in the interim, she had strapped a leather belt over her coat with a long leather sheath housing an equally long knife. "Just in case," she said in answer to Marigold's unspoken, but clearly articulated, question.

"In case of what?"

"Trouble." Lucy shrugged the same way the Hatchets did—as if trouble were both inevitable and not worth mentioning all at the same time. "I don't take anything or anyone"—she drew the wicked blade out of its sheath and let it glint in the sunlight—"at face value. Not even you, Miss Girl. That's an even better lead you ought to follow."

Such an array of lethal weapons these Misery Islanders were wont to brandish. At least none of them was an actual hatchet—although Marigold's odd relatives might surprise her yet. "So noted. I pledge you'll get no grief from me."

"I wasn't expecting any." Lucy gave her a slow smile. "Not anymore."

"Perhaps not, but I am." Marigold decided to be frank. "I am quite sure I saw woman—or actually her skirts—floating on the tide the first evening I rowed over."

"That so?" Lucy's expression narrowed. "What happened?"

"To her? I don't know." Marigold felt all the frustration of that moment. "Cleon claimed not to have seen her, but I know what I saw." She was used to being believed. "I am not given to flights of fancy."

"I don't imagine you are," Lucy rejoined. "But you're going to have to manage a flight of some sort to unload this all into the boat and then take the mules back to the barn without getting the wind up Mr. Ellery."

"Naturally," Marigold said, though she had not yet conceived of the best possible course of action—the one that would keep her from Ellery Hatchet's notice.

Lucy was excellent, reassuring company through the dark loom of the wood and provided a welcome surprise when she steered Marigold toward the far side of the cove, behind some large rocks, where a small slipway was hidden at the edge of the woodland with a pristine, perfectly balanced sailing skiff.

"This one's mine for when I need to come and go, which Mr. Ellery doesn't like the Hatchets to do," Lucy explained. "Keeps me independent."

"Like my bicycle," Marigold answered. "Which I miss dearly." Had it been a mistake to trust her machine to the indifferent care of the driver? Perhaps the Hatchets were considered of such low account that the man felt he could get away with it?

Marigold would disabuse him of that idea at her first opportunity.

She and Lucy set to loading the skiff with alacrity, as Marigold was more than anxious to be off the island. Once done loading, she quickly set the cart back down the bumpy track to the farmyard in a state of awareness that was too close to alarm for her liking. She let the mules have their heads—they went at a steady clip at the prospect of returning to their barn—and concentrated her own energies on convincing herself that there was no logical reason for her strange dread. She was doing her Hatchet relatives a favor, and who could object to that?

Much to her relief, the barnyard was still empty when she reached it, and she had far less trouble unhitching the animals than she had had harnessing them up—it seemed no time at all before she could start back up the path at a brisk pace that was only just short of a run.

She eagerly marked her way by various landmarks she was beginning to identify—the great arching elm tree, the small stand of birches, the great, protruding glacial rock—but no sooner had she rounded that very rock than she came upon Ellery Hatchet.

At least she assumed he was Cousin Sophronia's husband, Ellery, as he was the same gaunt, blade-faced man who had argued with Wilbert yesterday morning. He had the sharp, cagey look of a rat terrier—all grit and antagonism as he stabbed his shovel into the ground at the base of a nearby boulder.

Marigold's only comfort was that he started just as violently at the sight of her as she had at him. "What are you looking at?" he growled.

"Good morning, Cousin Ellery." Marigold began as she meant to go on—with a confidence she did not entirely feel. "I am Marigold Manners, your wife Sophronia's cousin."

"I know who you are," he groused. "And you're no cousin of mine." He shifted to hold the shovel with both hands, as if he might swing it at her. "What are you doing here? Spying on me?"

"Not at all," she answered instinctively, while what she might command of her logical mind was already telling her to make for the densest part of the undergrowth if he so much as moved another step closer. "I was merely going for a walk, this being the clearest path to follow from the house."

"Well then?" He glared at her from under his wiry white eyebrows. "What are you waiting for? Get on with yourself."

"I will," she agreed, while trying to calculate to the inch how close was too close to the clearly irate man, who still gripped the shovel as if he would use it as a weapon.

At least it wasn't a hatchet.

Marigold edged by on the verge of the path, never turning her back to him, until he finally returned his attention to his strange hole in the middle of the woods. But whatever he wanted to plant there was no business of hers.

She took the rest of the trail at a run, not easing her pace until she was finally within sight of Lucy, who waited calmly with her feet crossed as she leaned against the skiff.

"Look at you!" Lucy teased at Marigold's blousy appearance. "You look like you got one foot on that banana peel and the other on your grave!"

"I ran into Ellery Hatchet."

"Say no more." Lucy gestured for Marigold to join her in launching the boat immediately. "Let's get going before he catches us both up—they say the devil's got long arms, and I don't want to test that out!"

CHAPTER 13

Mediocrity knows nothing higher than itself, but talent instantly recognizes genius.

—Arthur Conan Doyle

They made speedy progress across the sound with Lucy's perfectly balanced skiff pushing them along on the bluff easterly. Lucy added to the atmosphere of escape by singing spirituals as they sailed along. She had a lovely voice, and her calm company helped keep Marigold from dwelling on the possibility of mulberry-clad bodies floating just beneath the waves—though she did look.

Lucy piloted them past the private beaches of mostly empty summer estates until they reached a small reed-ringed cove, where she made fast at a small pier.

"My momma's place is back along the marsh." She pointed down the boardwalk they were to take. "Doc Oliphant's place." Lucy gestured to a well-maintained two-story house with a picturesque porch across the water. "If you ever need doctoring."

"I am in excellent health, thank you, but that is a good thing to know—if he is a well-trained, well-read medical doctor and not a patent medicine-dispensing quack? What has your experience with the man been?"

"No experience at all." Lucy's smile gave way to careful blankness. "Doc Oliphant is just for you white folks."

"Even in such a rural place?" Marigold was shocked. She knew doctors in Boston might have exclusive practices, taking only well-to-do patients, but she had never imagined that a doctor might refuse patients based solely on their race. "I apologize for my ignorance, Lucy, though I do deplore that you should have no doctor to see you. What if you became ill?" She thought of the perilous number of casual threats she had endured in only two days with the Hatchets, and especially how they had all feared poisoning. "What if something went wrong?"

"We got doctors and learned people of our own, you know, though maybe not so many out here as in other places, like Boston. But my momma used to nurse, back in the day, back in the war. She still makes her own medicinal notions and tonics, so she does for what might ail me, though nothing does."

The list of Mrs. Dove's virtues increased.

Lucy pointed out other landmarks as she led the way down the boardwalk. "Gloucester branch of the railroad cuts this part of town off from the rest, which is how my momma could afford it." She gestured in the opposite direction to orient Marigold. "The smithy's at the other end of the cove, up against the old quarry at Snake Hill. We'll send a message to him when we get to Momma's."

"And to purchase some supplies for cleaning, along with materials for a garden?"

"What garden?"

"The herb garden I am planning to start to improve the culinary situation." While Marigold had never before kept her own garden, she had excelled at botany in college—indeed, she had excelled in every discipline to which she had applied herself.

"Unless you can cook," Lucy opined, "you're not improving anything."

"I cannot." While Marigold's peripatetic lifestyle might have kept her from learning to cook, she had the advantage of having eaten food that had not been stewed to a pulp—Isabella's chef was an effervescent delight of sauce-making wonderment. Which meant that though Marigold might not have skills, she had standards. And she was hungry. "What about you? Why do you not cook for the whole of the household but just for Great-Aunt Alva?" Marigold tried to keep the hopeful expectation from her voice.

Lucy regarded her with a sidelong glance. "You can ask that of my momma."

"I will."

Bessie Dove's house was a respectable, two-story boardinghouse from whence the tantalizing aroma of spiced ham wafted to tempt Marigold's starved taste buds. "Cleon said your mother used to cook at Hatchet Farm before? Before what exactly?"

"Afore she had a set-to with Mr. Ellery on account of him saying her soul was as black as her skin because she was demanding her back wages that he owed her."

Marigold already thought her cousin's husband a frightening person as well as a dreadful father—this report only confirmed her less-than-flattering opinion of the man. And given her parents, Marigold had strict feelings about unpaid debts. "Was it a large sum?"

"Enough to buy this boardinghouse."

"Excellent." Marigold very much approved of women owning their own property. "So now Cleon does the cooking?"

"What passes for it. One reason I'm glad to have my own place to cook and store foods and preserves from my momma. And there she is!" Lucy waved as they passed through the picket gate into the neatly swept backyard. "Hey, Momma."

Bessie Dove proved to be a small woman with ebony skin, steel-gray hair, and a butter-soft smile, who met them on the wraparound porch with her arms outstretched to her daughter. "Come here, baby girl, and let me give you some love. I been worried about you."

"Me? You know I can take care of myself."

Mrs. Dove enveloped her daughter in a hug that ought to have creased her starched, lace-edged apron but somehow didn't. It was clear where Lucy had gotten her sartorial sense—her mother's clothing was every bit as immaculate and well put together as her daughter's.

Mrs. Dove shook her head and lowered her voice, but Marigold heard her tell Lucy, "They found another girl. Washed up just down-sound at the Point."

The word *another* blared in Marigold's brain like a siren.

"Dead?" Lucy asked with a speaking glance toward Marigold. "Who was it?"

"Minnie Mallory, the reverend's daughter. You remember her?"

Marigold had three conflicting thoughts simultaneously. First, vindication—she *knew* she had seen someone in the water two days ago. And second, alarm—how many local preachers' daughters might be named

Minnie, the very name she had heard Sophronia call the unseen girl in the hayloft with Seviah yesterday morning? And third, terror—how often did girls get drowned that the local populace, including Marigold's Hatchet relatives, talked about their deaths so casually?

"I remember her," Lucy said. "Hard to forget a girl like Minnie. What are they saying?"

Mrs. Dove spared a wary glance at Marigold before she answered. "That she drowned by mistake or mischance. But that's what they always say when they seem to be finding dead girls down-sound."

You'll end up drowned like the rest of them.

Marigold felt her skin go cold and clammy in the chill spring wind.

"Did Minnie have a bun in her oven?" Lucy's question was blunt.

"They didn't say," Bessie Dove said, though her skeptical expression rejected that answer. "What they did say is she got herself disappointed in love and fell in—likely because she's the reverend's daughter." Mrs. Dove shook her head. "Like there couldn't be no one else to account for her being in the water," she said, almost too low for Marigold to hear.

Almost. "Does that mean you think there is someone to blame?" Marigold queried.

Mrs. Dove pressed her lips between her teeth, as if she were deciding how much she might say. Or if she'd already said too much.

Marigold was torn between her affront that such an obviously white-washed tale was being put about—it seemed an outrageous injustice to the deceased young woman—and her newfound understanding that not everyone was as able or prepared as she to tackle such sanctimonious nonsense.

"It's all right, Momma," Lucy put in. "You can't shock her—she's modern. And I reckon she might have actually seen Minnie's body in the water when she rowed over to Great Misery two nights ago."

"If that's so, maybe you ought to introduce me to this sharp-eyed lady you brought with you today."

"She's Miss Sophronia's kin from Boston," Lucy offered.

"I am Marigold Manners, Mrs. Dove." Marigold had to recall herself to her own manners, when all her brain wanted to do was ruminate on dead girls and their possible relationship to her Hatchet relatives. "Honored to make your acquaintance, ma'am."

Mrs. Dove took her hand. "Call me Bessie, and you're welcome here. That make you Miss Esmie's girl?" she asked as she led Marigold into her clean, comfortable kitchen, where a well-polished cast-iron stove radiated soothing heat and mouthwatering aromas.

"Yes, Esmé Sedgwick Manners was my mother, ma'am. She recently passed away."

"I'm sorry to hear that, child." Bessie covered Marigold's hand consolingly. "Bless her soul."

Marigold realized with a pang that none of her Hatchet relatives had offered any word of condolence at the loss of her parents. Until that moment, she hadn't realized how much she would have welcomed it. "Thank you very much, ma'am. You are very kind. Did you know my mother?"

"No, child," Bessie disappointed her. "I never had that pleasure. But she sounded like a real sweet lady, and I seen her picture that Miz Sophronia kept."

This was the second reference to a photograph—Cleon had mentioned it as well. Marigold made a mental note to seek it out. After she had some answers about this poor young woman in the water—who, she now realized, could not have been the Minnie making the most of her time in the hayloft with Seviah yesterday morning if she had been drowned two days ago. "You were saying you thought there might be someone else to blame in Miss Mallory's death?"

Bessie took another moment before she said, "Let me just say this about that—ain't no girl ever got a bun up her oven by herself. But that's got nothing to do with us. Now, what brings you home?" she asked Lucy. "You ailing? I got a new cranberry tonic I brewed up—"

"Not me." Lucy looked to Marigold. "She's got a load of junk metal out from Hatchet Farm she wants to sell to a smith."

Bessie nodded approvingly. "Let me send for Samuel. He'll deal with you fair."

"Thank you, ma'am," Marigold answered. "I appreciate your help."

Something in Marigold's behavior—perhaps the way her nostrils flared to take in the scent of the cooking or the way her eyes kept sliding back toward the oven—gave her away to Mrs. Dove. "You had anything fit to eat out there yet, honey?"

"No, ma'am." Even Marigold could hear the rather desperate hope in her voice.

"She already asked me to cook for her, Momma—for pay," Lucy added. "But you should see what she's done to that old kitchen. She might look like a flannel-mouthed piece of calico, all delicate and fancy, but she scrubbed that place to a shine. Almost like you said it used to be," she reported.

"Bet it still don't taste like it used to," Bessie laughed as she heaped a plate high with ham, baked beans, and soda biscuits.

Only the strictest application of self-discipline and good manners kept Marigold from falling to it like a stray cat. "Thank you, ma'am. You have no idea—" Marigold's words would have to wait until she could spoon beans, sweet with molasses and whiskey, onto her tongue.

"Oh, I got a pretty good idea." Bessie was still laughing.

"This is absolutely delicious, ma'am," Marigold began. "And as you say, far superior to the mush and fish stew being ladled up by Cleon."

"That poor old man." Bessie shook her head. "My advice to you would be not to eat a thing out of that kitchen."

"I feel very much that way myself," Marigold agreed between bites. "Is there any way I can persuade you to come back—"

"Oh, no." Bessie held up her hand. "Save your breath. I won't step foot on that island again. I tell Lucy only to go to the door of the house and no further. To keep herself to herself. You can't wallow with pigs and not but get dirty," was Bessie's blunt opinion.

"But, as Lucy said, I've already made great strides in banishing the dirt. Together—"

"You made considerable progress on that kitchen," Lucy agreed. "But there is nothing you're ever going to be able to do about *them*."

"Is it their air of decaying eeriness," Marigold asked with all seriousness, "or something more specific?" Something Bessie, with her long experience of the duplicitous Hatchets, might know that the others didn't.

Lucy broke into guffaws. "*Decaying eeriness*. Oh, I gotta remember that."

Bessie laughed along with her daughter. "You got a way with words, child."

"Thank you, ma'am." Marigold tried not to let the compliment sway her attention. "I do mean to be an academic author someday and publish tales of ancient civilizations, but at the moment, what I wish I had was a way with food. Or could convince someone who knew her way around a stove—"

"No, child. No." Bessie's tone was firm but kind. "Even if I wanted to—which I don't—Ellery Hatchet won't have food made by a Black hand in his house."

"But—" Marigold's powers of logic and reasoning were being stretched thin in the face of Hatchet's bigotry. "Lucy makes the food for his mother, and that's in his house."

"I make it in *my* house that no one else is allowed in," Lucy corrected.

"But—"

"I ain't saying it makes sense," Bessie countered, "just what is. Lucy will cook for you." She nodded at her daughter to confirm their understanding, and Marigold was struck by the fact that it was Bessie who gave Lucy permission—not Alva or Ellery Hatchet. How instructive.

"Now, you get that good food in you." Bessie brought her a cup of blessedly scalding coffee. "And never mind things that can't be changed."

"Everything can be changed," Marigold insisted, "if only one wants to change and puts in the effort required. And that is what I'm prepared to do."

"But what about *them*? You mark my words, child." Bessie was emphatic. "Them Hatchets ain't prepared to do nothing but make trouble for themselves. Years and years of it. Nothing but everlasting trouble."

Chapter 14

Few things are harder to put up with than the annoyance of a good example.

—Mark Twain

"Now, let me send for Samuel."

Bessie and Lucy left Marigold to herself long enough for her to fill both her stomach and her curiosity. The tidy, gingham-curtained kitchen looked to be a meeting place of sorts—pamphlets for the Salem Colored Convention were neatly stacked on the table. Outside the window was a lush garden in which morning glories grew alongside scarlet runner beans, and honeysuckle rambled over the whitewashed fence to spill over the carefully swept dirt paths.

Practical considerations before the theoretical. "You have a beautiful garden, ma'am," Marigold complimented when Bessie returned. "I'm hoping to start an herb garden out on Great Misery Island and wondered if you might have some herb plants or vegetable seeds I might purchase from you?"

"I got some chives divided out just this week all ready. I might could see what else I've got to hand." Bessie crossed her arms over her chest in much the same skeptical way her daughter had yesterday. "But what grows down here in this patch along the marsh might not take to growing out on that bald, dry rock."

"I take your meaning, ma'am. It is curious how dry and barren it is when the coast here is so arable. But I have an idea to set out raised beds with well-rotted chicken manure—they seem to have plenty of that at Hatchet Farm."

"I reckon you do," Bessie agreed. "You sure are a determined little thing."

"She's like that," Lucy confirmed with a laugh. "She's already done more in two days than those Hatchets have done in two years."

"I thank you for the compliment, Lucy." Indeed, it was a lovely thing to be admired by people worth admiring. "But I have more to do yet—I'd like to visit a mercantile store and then a wire office?"

"There's Mercer's Mercantile up the commercials street, next to Crestfield's Druggist and a few doors down from the telegraph office."

"Thank you. And thank you for the ham. I don't think I've ever had better."

"I got a smokehouse back out behind the garden—my property goes all the way back to the edge of the cove. Most folks round here, even the butchers, get their hams from me," Bessie said with some pride. "Now, listen, Pride's Crossing is a right enough place," she advised Marigold, "but like a lot of places out in the country, they don't exactly take to strangers."

"And am I so strange?" Marigold asked with an attempt at humor.

"Strange enough," Bessie laughed. "You're an eyeful, for sure, but most especially because you're a Hatchet."

"Technically, I am only related to Mrs. Sophronia Hatchet's side of the family, but I take your point. But what is it about the Hatchets that the residents of Pride's Crossing might object to?" Marigold probed with a nonchalance she didn't feel. "Was there some scandal or infamous incident that I should know of?" Like something that qualified as a great and godless wrong?

Bessie pursed her lips shut and wiped her hands with her apron as if she could wash the Hatchets from her experience. "Let's just say that the Hatchets don't go out of their way to make themselves peaceable and friendly. And the town feels the same."

Marigold had to admit her own introduction to her cousins had been neither peaceable nor friendly—what with the curses and lit matches and scythes and guns and shovels, not to mention the lack of hygienically prepared food. Yet there was so much scope for positive, forward-thinking change.

"But I reckon folks on the North Shore are going to be mighty interested in a pretty new Boston lady in town, Hatchet or not," Bessie was saying. "My advice is to be careful of what you let on—you don't want folks to judge you wrongly just because you're kin to Hatchets. They'll treat you respectful-like if you keep respectful. That's my experience."

Marigold nodded at Mrs. Dove's undoubtedly well-meaning advice. Her own experience of the world was that curiosity very often combined with fear and suspicion.

But here was her opportunity to allay fear and set aside suspicion, especially for Daisy and her young beau's sake. Who could be a better representative of the face the Hatchets ought to be presenting to the world than she herself?

"Here's Samuel now." Bessie called through the screened front door as an oxcart drove into view, "Come on in here and meet Miss Manners. She's come to sell a load of scrap she's got in the skiff down at our dock."

Samuel was a large Black man with arms as bronzed and well muscled as any Rodin sculpture. "Don't get many ladies come trading for themselves," he said as he climbed onto the porch.

"Perhaps they have not learned the pleasure of driving a hard bargain," Marigold answered, offering her hand. "Bessie gave me her word that you were a man who would bargain fairly."

"Oh, surely." The smith's smile was as reassuring as his calloused hands were gentle. "I'll head out to take a look, but if it ain't too rusted, I believe I'm prepared to go to twenty-two cents a pound for a friend of my momma's. But don't you go telling that tale around the town."

"No indeed." Marigold noted the easy affection between mother and son. She also noted that the smith looked at least ten years older than Lucy and bore little familial resemblance to her.

"That's a special price," he explained, "cause my momma likes you. And you know how mommas are." He laughed. "I make it a point not to disappoint her."

"Naturally," Marigold agreed with some chagrin. She had done her best not to let her own mother down, but sweet Esmé's disappointment in her forthright, forward-thinking daughter had seemed inevitable.

"A man would do a lot for his momma." Samuel snuck a piece of ham into his mouth. "Mmm. Especially one who can smoke and cook like that."

"Indeed." So would a woman who had just eaten her only edible meal in days.

"You new to town?" the smith asked.

"New to the area," Marigold clarified. "I'm staying on Misery Island with my relatives, the Hatchets. I sailed across with your sister, Lucy, this morning."

"What do you know?" Some of the warmth faded from the man's smile. "Isn't that something." But he shook his head ruefully, much like his mother had. "I know it ain't none of my business, but you seem like such a nice lady. You be careful of them out there on Great Misery, you hear? Those people out there just ain't right."

Marigold no longer brushed off the warning. She had rationalized and dismissed the Hatchets' strange variety of threats, but she had to admit she had been truly frightened of Ellery Hatchet on the path that morning. And this whole business of Minnie Mallory didn't sit right. "Indeed, I will."

Perhaps she ought to rethink her residence on the island? If only there were some other way to find the information she sought about Ellery Hatchet's mistreatment of her mother. "Does Pride's Crossing have a public library?"

"Up Hale Street," Bessie answered. "Once you get over the railroad tracks, just follow the main street back up to the north. You can't miss it."

"Excellent." Marigold's own curiosity to see the town—and let the town see her—urged her to take her time finding the ivied stone library building in the center of the small municipal and commercial district. And as a New Woman, she never minded the physical exertion of a good walk.

Marigold dusted her skirts off before she entered and stepped up to the circulation desk, where a young woman was also attired in a smart shirt-waist and tie. "Good morning. I should like to apply for a library card. I'm new in the area and very happy to find such an excellent facility here."

"Certainly." The young woman adjusted her pince-nez spectacles and produced an index card for Marigold to fill out. "Welcome to Pride's Crossing."

"Thank you. I'd like to check out a copy of *Pride and Prejudice*, funnily enough." Her own copy was still in her crate of books, which, like her bicycle, had yet to be delivered—but Daisy's education could not wait until she tracked the cart driver down. "And I wondered if you have an archive of local newspapers from the last twenty to thirty years or so?"

"Of course, miss." The librarian was a model of both rational dress and rational competence. "If you'll step into the reading room, I can bring you the relevant issues of the *Pride's Evening Times* and the *Manchester Cricket*, although that will only go back to '88. But I'll also bring the bound copies of the *Salem Register* and the *Gloucester Daily Times*."

Marigold felt the giddy attraction of meeting an equal—an educated woman who knew her business. "Most excellent. You are a godsend, Miss . . . ?"

"Morgan. Amelia Morgan. Mount Holyoke College, South Hadley."

Marigold put out her hand to shake with genuine pleasure. "Marigold Manners, Wellesley College, Wellesley."

"Oh, how lovely!" The young woman's handshake was a boon to Marigold's hope to make like-minded friends. "So very pleased to make your acquaintance, Miss Manners. Let me show you the stacks where you'll find your Austen—who is my personal favorite, I must say." She flushed with her own pleasure. "The reading room is that way. If you'll make yourself comfortable, I should have the archived newspapers to you momentarily."

Marigold was buoyed by her friendliness—her plan to make a good impression was already working wonderfully. "Thank you. I wonder if I also might trouble you with the latest edition of the local newspaper? I understand the body of a young woman was recently found down the sound?"

Miss Morgan blanched. "Yes, such a tragedy. You should find today's issue of the *Evening Times*, as well as the *Salem Register*, in the reading room."

Marigold retrieved the copy of dear Miss Austen from the stacks before she found a table with a pleasant aspect out the window toward the leafy street and began scanning the local newspapers for information regarding Minnie Mallory.

The story was tucked away at the bottom of page four. Miss Wilhelmenia Ann Mallory had been the daughter of the Reverend Angus Mallory, the pastor of the First Parish Church, and was presumed to have drowned at the tender age of nineteen by mischance in the frigid spring-melt waters of Salem Sound.

Marigold could not suppress the shiver that ran across her skin. There was no mention of exactly when the young woman's body had been pulled from the water, nor of what she had been wearing, but Marigold was convinced that the glimpse of red skirt she had seen that first evening in the dory must indeed have been poor Minnie.

But if Minnie had been dead in the water, then who was in the hayloft with Seviah?

"Here you are, Miss Manners." Amelia Morgan appeared at the table with a stack of bound newsprint. "Let me know if there is anything else I might find for you."

"As a matter of fact—is there a modern police force in the town?" Marigold wondered if she ought to make some report of seeing the young woman's body, though to do so might raise more questions than it answered.

Miss Morgan frowned and lowered her voice. "I wouldn't exactly call them modern or forward-thinking, but there is a small police office housed in the town hall. Officer Parker is occasionally there during the daytime."

"Thank you." Then the answer was no—the last thing Marigold wanted to experience was being "little-missyed" by a part-time, rural officer. The best course was undoubtedly to find the answers to her own questions first, before she consulted any authorities. Accordingly, she turned her attention to the newspapers, searching the close-printed pages for any mention of a member of the Hatchet family, or of her mother's name. Or of other drowned girls.

Excepting a short obituary of one Captain Elijah Hatchet of Great Misery Island passing away at home back in the year 1844—which she guessed was shortly after Ellery Hatchet must have been born—there was no mention of any scandal or trouble that might be construed as a great and godless wrong. Or of other drowned girls.

How frustrating.

But the day was growing long and there were still her purchases to make, her scrap metal to be paid for, and Salem Sound to recross.

She returned the materials to the desk. "Thank you very much, Miss Morgan. It was a pleasure to meet you, and I hope I'll see you again on my next visit."

"Yes, indeed." The young woman's enthusiasm was a cautious, hopeful thing. "I look forward to that. We don't get many new faces in town. I keep rooms at Mrs. West's, up on Grove Street, and sing in the choir at St. John's Episcopal down the street—we're always looking for new voices."

"Thank you, but I live too far from town to attend services." Marigold kept her own religious beliefs—or lack thereof—to herself for the time being. "I'm staying at Hatchet Farm on Great Misery Island—" She reached for her calling card.

"Great Misery?" Miss Morgan's tone was aghast. "But you said Wellesley College?"

As if being an educated, rational creature automatically precluded any association with her relatives. Marigold's misgivings returned, despite her determination to be positive. "I did. I am here for a short visit. Mrs. Sophronia Hatchet is my second cousin."

Miss Morgan's reply was tactful. "I can't say as I've had the pleasure of meeting Mrs. Hatchet."

Marigold's smile was purposeful—she had to think of Daisy. "I'll have to try to get her into town more often, as I'm sure she'd enjoy such a well-stocked and tended library. And my young cousins as well."

"Yes, I'm sure." Amelia Morgan's expression conveyed the opposite of her words as she handed Marigold her library card.

Marigold stuck to her principle of setting a good example. "Thank you again, Miss Morgan." She put her new library card safely into her pocket. "It shall be my dearest possession. Until next time."

"I hope there is a next time," Marigold heard Amelia Morgan murmur as she headed for the door. "Heaven help you out there on Great Misery."

CHAPTER 15

Nobody minds having what is too good for them.
—Jane Austen

Marigold headed for the mercantile with more determination than ever to create a positive view of her less-than-socially-acceptable relatives. But from the moment she stepped under the merchant's clanging bell, she was met with narrow-eyed suspicion and a silence so sharp it was pointed—directly at Marigold.

"Well." The floor clerk smirked behind his mustache, and Marigold's ire rose when she recognized the dratted woolly ogler from the train. "What do you know. Wondered if you'd turn up."

Wasn't it damnable how often the sight of an independent, unaccompanied young woman brought out the condescending littleness in a man? No matter. Marigold never minded a challenge.

"Good afternoon," she said brightly. "I require thirty feet of one-inch-diameter, nineteen-gauge Norwich wire fencing, rolled, if you please, into a bale."

"Aren't you mighty particular? Where you been hiding yourself?"

She adjusted her approach to such ill-bred curiosity—she softened her voice. "If you do not have Norwich wire fencing of that specification, what do you have?"

"Chicken wire, I s'pose you mean?" the clerk said, as if it were something of a privilege for him to share such information. "I can cut you thirty feet in length, but it'll cost you a pretty penny."

As Marigold had silver in her pocket and a congenital dislike of unsolicited information from men who were invariably less well-informed than she, she asked again. "What is the diameter and gauge of the wire fencing you *do* have?"

The answer was of such indifference to the clerk, he couldn't bring himself to exert the energy required to shrug. "Do you want it or not?"

"If it is less than two inches in diameter, I should like it very much"—and here she let the full reptilian chilliness of her crocodile smile glint at him—"baled, along with a Yale cylinder brass padlock and hasp, an eight-pound sack of carbolic powder, two large cakes of lye soap, a twenty-five pound sack of lime, and a carton of Gayetty's medicated paper for the water closet."

"And a partridge in a pear tree," the man sneered. "That's an awful lot of privy paper for such a small a—"

"Also"—she overrode his doubtlessly crude innuendo—"I require eight yards of that very pretty blue-and-green calico cotton, one pane of clear window glass cut to eight inches by ten inches, wrapped, as well as a tin of putty, to be delivered forthwith to Mrs. Bessie Dove's boardinghouse on Cove Street."

"Dove's?" he scoffed. "Where'd you say you were from?"

"I did not say," Marigold rejoined, never letting her icy smile falter. "But the place from whence I hail is renowned for minding its own business. None of which is your business, which, I should think, is more properly the selling of goods requested to paying customers."

"Which," the clerk echoed in a tone just shy of mimicry, "brings *me* to asking if you're a *paying* customer and not wanting to be extended a line of credit."

Marigold reached into her pocket and withdrew a silver dollar. "Payment in cash, my good sir." She made her tone everything condescending. "If it's not too much trouble? Or too high to count."

He was buffeted back enough to satisfy Marigold's feelings, though he took his own good time in pulling the requested items off the shelves and measuring out the fabric, glass, and wire.

"Anything else, Your Majesty?"

This time Marigold let herself laugh. "Indeed, yes. A toasting rack, if you have one. And if not, would it be possible to order one?"

"Special orders come three cents extra."

"Naturally." She laid her calling card upon the table like a poker player revealing a winning hand. "Order for Miss Marigold Manners, resident at Hatchet Farm, Great Misery Island. I expect I'll be back within the week to receive it. How much do I owe?"

The fellow closed his gaping mouth in startlement before he totted up the total on a notepad and thrust it toward her without any further discourse or innuendo.

Marigold paid the sum in exact change from the coin in her purse. "There you are—minus ten cents to correct your small error of addition. I'm very much obliged. I'll expect the goods to be delivered to Mrs. Dove's promptly. I have the tide to catch." She hoped her smile was dazzling in its icy coolness.

"Good gravy." The man swore. "Ain't you just something? Old man Hatchet's like to make a meal out of you, if he don't murder you first."

"Don't be ridiculous. Or rude." Marigold wished she had thought to arm herself against impertinence with her umbrella; as it was, her wit would have to do. "Sarcasm is no substitute for customer service, my good sir. Good day."

She sailed out under the bell like a nimble yacht cutting across the bow of a workaday Gloucester fishing schooner just for the pleasure of the feat and charted her course for the wire office, where she sent a telegram to Isabella asking for advice about Daisy, before she returned to the Doves', where she drank a glass of much-needed lemonade, collected her money from Samuel, and loaded her provisions into Lucy's skiff.

But the moment the boat cleared the dock, Marigold's righteousness and native positivity lost ground to the misgivings the townspeople's repeated warnings against the Hatchets had planted in her head.

Was tidying the place up and liming the outhouse enough to make her cousins trust her with the truth about whatever had passed between her mother and Ellery Hatchet? Were the advantages she might be able to give Daisy—and Wilbert and Seviah and maybe even Lucy as well—worth the risk of returning to a place where she was so clearly unwelcome? Where *them girls* might have drowned?

She was more than thankful that she had Lucy, imperturbable and singing a soft ballad as she sailed the skiff, or Marigold might have given way to the strange, dreadful frustration that clouded her normally sunny outlook. If Lucy had no qualms about returning to Great Misery, then neither would she.

And she was cheered by the sight of Wilbert standing on the dark shore of North Cove waiting in welcome—until they drew close enough to the sheltered beach to see that his countenance was as stormy as a nor'easter.

"You sure made yourself to home with our things," he accused. "Where's all the . . ." He gestured in frustration back toward the woods and, presumably, at the now-empty farmyard. "All them things we was storing out in the dooryard?"

"Leaving metal to rust and ruin is not storage, Cousin Wilbert. And what could not be repaired, like the mangle—and how do you like having your clothes laundered regularly? It looks well on you—matches your eyes. But as I was saying, what could not be repaired at beneficial cost, I sold for scrap metal. Here is your profit." She handed the dumbfounded man his money. "And you'll see I made sure to be paid in silver coin, not paper money."

He looked at her with a charming combination of awe and suspicion, with the greater portion given over to awe. "This is more'n I can take in a two-month."

"Then I am glad I went to the trouble." She patted his arm in genuine pleasure before she returned to practical matters. "Thank you for your company and assistance, Lucy. Do you need any help with your things?"

"No, thank you." Lucy hefted her covered basket and left Marigold with a now-silent Wilbert.

"I expect you could make a favorable report to your father that you asked me to undertake the errand, Cousin." Marigold tried another approach. "I'm sure he'll be pleased at the profit."

"Yeah, I reckon I might could." He stared at the coins, weighing them in his hand before stowing the money carefully in his pocket and taking up the parcels from the mercantile. "Do you think maybe we could keep just how much you got for the junk atwixt us, you and me? Least till I can figure what to do with it?"

"Certainly," she swore, for she knew the value of loyalty to a skittish ally. "I give you my word. But may I ask why?"

Wilbert made sure to check the seemingly empty path before he gave her his quiet answer. "Pa's got some strange ideas. Him and Granny both."

"About the island? Or about money?" A miserly, holding-back disposition would go a long way to explaining the decaying state of the place.

"About everything," he admitted. "Pa's no farmer, though he's tried to farm this salt patch for nigh onto fifty years. But it still looks like a bag o' nails, don't it?"

"Less so now." Which made her all the more glad she had made the effort and even gladder that she had trusted Wilbert with the resultant funds. "He objects to your efforts to change or improve the farm, like with the pigs?"

"That's it." He nodded, grateful for her understanding. "Pa'll pitch a goldang fit if'n I get more pigs—swine he calls them. Says that's what they're called in the Bible and they're pagan and unclean."

"Leviticus, chapter eleven, as I recall."

"Is that the Bible?" He scratched at his stubbled chin. "Pa's always preaching verses at us, but they don't make much sense to me." He looked at her with something that might be respect. "You sure do know a lot of book things."

"I am happy to put that book knowledge to use for you."

"Your book knowledge tell you what to do with this pile of rock and salt grass?"

"Actually, I once read some stories set in Scotland." She remembered one glorious semester devoted entirely to the British Romantics. "And it seems to me their western islands, which are climactically temperate like Great Misery, are foraged very successfully by sheep."

"Sheep?" He chewed the word around in his mouth as if he were testing the taste of it. "The old man'll be sure to look blue at 'em on account they have cloven hooves too."

"Whatever the anatomy of their hooves, I should think you'd need more information on cost-benefit ratios and recommended number of animals per acre before you could make an educated decision."

He let out a low whistle of admiration. "But I ain't educated, nor likely to get so."

"Well, perhaps not in a regular school, but what about the Grangers?" She mentioned an agricultural group she had heard of as being particularly progressive—especially in their views of women and suffrage. If Daisy and Lucy could become New Women, why couldn't Wilbert be brought to an understanding of higher principles as well?

"There's a Grange Hall in Pride's Crossing—Pa rents the hall for his preaching now and again, when he can sneak off island without Granny being none the wiser—but I don't belong. And Granny won't spare any money for dues."

"Now you have some money of your own," she reminded him. "Perhaps that might be your first use of the funds—to join to acquire knowledge in advance of acquiring stock?"

Wilbert still wasn't convinced. "Don't know how folks round here would take to sheep."

While her natural instinct was to let the logical facts dictate the course of action, "folks'" opinions be damned, Marigold certainly wouldn't want to encourage anything that would make Wilbert's position in the community any more tenuous. "Why don't I do some research at the library in town and see what information I can find about sheep farming along the Atlantic coast before you make any decision?"

"You'd do that for me?" The first real smile Marigold had seen on her cousin's face lit him like a bonfire at a clambake. "Thank you, Cousin Marigold."

She patted his arm in companionable agreement. "I'm glad I could help."

"Why don't you take supper with us this evening? It's likely to just be fish chowder and bacon—Cleon can't seem to catch nothing but alewives—but . . ." Words failed him for a moment, before he swiped the hat from his head and said, "I'd like it if you'd take supper with us."

Marigold was torn between the thought of another helping of the ham Bessie Dove had sent out with Lucy and the prospect of what would surely be a miserable meal from Cleon. And there was Bessie's warning—*not to eat a thing out of that kitchen*—to be considered as well.

But some things were more important than food—like family and loyalty and someone else's happiness. "I'd be honored to do so."

CHAPTER 16

Go to Heaven for the climate, Hell for the company.
—Mark Twain

Marigold dressed as carefully as if she were attending a dinner party at Isabella's—after all, one might alter one's standards but never let them down. She chose her dark mulberry velvet dinner gown—with a daytime bodice faced with black ribbon, in deference to her mourning—which was more suited to the Back Bay than Great Misery, but its wonderfully wide gigot sleeves added to her breadth and gave her confidence.

And it gave her the opportunity to see if anyone remarked upon the color—so close to what Minnie had been wearing in the water.

But the gown was such a change from the practical tweed sportswear she had been wearing that Wilbert made an involuntary sound of surprise and admiration when she appeared at the kitchen door. "Golly."

His brother was less subtle, as well as less admiring. "Well, lah-ti-dah," he sneered. "Think you're at Delmonico's?"

While Marigold was surprised to hear the name of a famous, fashionable New York eatery from a cousin who had lived all his life on a rock nearly two miles into the Atlantic, she tucked that piece of information away until she might make better use of it and greeted him politely. "Good evening, Seviah. Perhaps you'd like to make use of the warm water and soap in the basin next to the stove to wash the dirt from your hands before we sit down." She rewarded Wilbert with a smile. "I see you've already done so."

"Used the soap and towel out at the pump," he reported. "Reckoned it was you as put it out there."

"Trying to be helpful," was all the credit she allowed herself as she waited politely for her cousin Sophronia to sit. But Marigold soon found she needn't have stood on ceremony, as dinner appeared to be an informal, uncoordinated affair, with many of the family not even sitting to the table. But the reason for them keeping to themselves was apparent the moment Ellery Hatchet elbowed his way to the table.

"You're still here, then," was his greeting. "Here to take the food from the mouths of hardworking men with your sinful ways."

Marigold would not let his incivility lead her astray. She had standards. "I am indeed here, as you see. Good evening, Cousin Ellery."

"Nothing good in it," he growled before he sat himself at the head of the pine plank table and glowered like a man determined to be displeased with her and unpleasant to all who surrounded him. "You're no kin of mine."

But his unpleasantness seemed to create some fellow feeling in his eldest son, who said, "Why don't you sit here, Cousin Marigold, near me," and held out a chair for her at the other end of the table.

Marigold rewarded him with a grateful smile as Cleon began dishing out the chowder from a cast-iron pot on the stove.

"Why, that's my wedding china," Sophronia exclaimed as she reached for a porcelain bowl that Marigold recognized from the kitchen hutch. "That's not for common use."

"'Tis for Miss Girl." Cleon pulled the dish away from Sophronia's grasp.

But Sophronia met the odd fellow's stubbornness with something that looked, from Marigold's vantage point, to be rather extraordinary determination of her own—Sophronia was so vexed that she swiped at the bowl, knocking it from Cleon's hands, as if she would rather let the precious porcelain dish smash upon the floor, splattering chowder and shattering china, than let Marigold use it.

But whatever spite Marigold might have imagined vanished from Sophronia's face in an instant. "How fearful clumsy of me. Let me get her another. Here, take mine." Sophronia pushed a plainer, earthenware bowl of beans and bacon into Marigold's hands. "Can't have you not fed."

Whatever Marigold might have thought to say was drowned out by Ellery Hatchet's voice. "The wages of sinful covetousness is the same as for all sin," he declared, before clearing his throat in an obvious, over-loud way. "Pay heed, you damn sinners."

Heads flinched downward and away as Hatchet glared at them before he began his prayer. "May any man, or woman, ungrateful for this meal, feel the everlasting fires of hell burning away his soul for all eternity and ever-more," he growled. "May the food turn to ashes in your sinful mouths and the fires of damnation burn the tongues from your skulls." He waited a long moment, as if waiting for some further divine inspiration—or retribution—before he seemed satisfied enough to mutter, "Amen."

The men fell to the meal, hunkering over their bowls, guarding them like prisoners fearing starvation, although Seviah stood to one side, against the wall, to eat. Sophronia, Marigold noticed, quickly and silently mopped up the broken dish and retreated into the inglenook around the stove, as did Daisy, leaving Marigold the only woman at the table. Great-Aunt Alva, she recalled, preferred to take her dinners in her room.

That's how it is at Hatchet Farm. Each to fend for themselves.

The food itself was passable—a bite proved it to be beans hot enough to fill and bland enough not to alarm—but the thought of having her taste buds so denigrated for the foreseeable future had Marigold determined to follow Bessie Dove's instructions to eat nothing from this kitchen in the future.

But it seemed others were taking note of the improvements she had already accomplished. "What's gone on in here?" Ellery looked around with suspicion.

"Cleaning," Wilbert said, before he swiftly changed the topic. "I'm pleased that the gilt is well in season. I expect her to farrow come summer."

"You'll sell her off before then," Ellery bade him. "Swine is the spawn of the devil."

"No sense in selling afore there's a good litter of piglets," Wilbert countered reasonably.

"I'll have no swine on Great Misery."

"And why not? You'll have bacon in yer chowder and fatback in your beans. Nothing but false pride not to keep pigs when we can—"

"False pride?" The old man scraped his chair back. "You sniveling sin-ner. Your pride is a monstrous, hell-bound thing." He pounded his fist on the table. "Hell-bound, I say. You should be caught in the devil's maw and crushed into a bloodless pulp."

"The hell if I will." Wilbert was red in the face.

"Blasphemous!" the elder Hatchet roared. "I should have drowned you in the ocean the day you were born, you miserable—"

Marigold had heard enough. She was on her feet before she knew what she was doing but the assembly gaped at her as if she were the one threatening to murder defenseless babies. Or drown people.

"If you'll excuse me, I'm sure I'm not needed, as I have no idea what on earth a gilt is, and I shall be happy not to know. Thank you, Cousin Sophronia and Cleon, for a lovely dinner. Cousin Wilbert." She smiled, as unconcerned as Joan of Arc at her stake, ignoring the hunger gripping her stomach as she handed Cleon her bowl. "Good evening to you all."

She went only as far as the room at the far end of the hallway, where the fork, knife, and empty plate all indicated Great-Aunt Alva had been given a supper of neither chowder stewed into glue nor bland beans. Marigold's taste buds all but salivated in envy.

"Aunt Alva?" Marigold rapped at the door in another bid to introduce herself.

But the old lady either didn't hear or didn't care—the door remained closed.

Back down the hall, dinner was already coming to a swift close—chairs were scraped back and empty bowls clattered. Marigold returned with Great-Aunt Alva's empty tray to assist Cleon in clearing the remaining dishes from the table.

"No, you leave them be." Sophronia stayed Marigold's hand as she took the tray. "You're not to lift a hand toiling for Hatchets."

"If you insist," Marigold agreed, happy to concede after a long day of just such toil.

"Tho' the cupboard looks right nice," Sophronia said with a quiet nod at the hutch. "Can't remember when it's looked so good."

"I am happy to be of use, though I am very sorry that your dish was broken."

"No matter." Sophronia shook her head, already retreating down a dark corridor from any further conversation.

Marigold was left to join Wilbert in the quiet chimney nook, where he had subsided with a pipe. "I reckon you'll be taking your supper on a tray in your room like Granny from now on," he ventured.

"Perhaps I will." The prospect seemed infinitely preferable to sharing a table with Ellery Hatchet.

Wilbert shrugged in that characteristically careless Hatchet way that seemed to be a ward against hurt. "Suit yerself. Though it sure is pretty to see you togged up so nice in your dress. Don't get to see much prettiness at Hatchet Farm."

"Well, we'll have to see what can be done about that. But I thank you for the compliment. You are a lamb." And speaking of making an effort—"I wasn't sure whom to ask, but I wondered if I might avail myself of some of your chicken manure for making a vegetable garden?"

"Vegetables? What you want with them?"

Marigold decided to bypass the clearly unpopular idea of vegetables in favor of the promise of savoriness. "I plan on growing some herbs—that was those plants in the pots I brought back from town." No need to reveal from whom the plants had come until she better understood the strange, antago-nistic, but somehow close relationship between the Doves and the Hatchets. "I can guarantee the herbs will make everything, from bread to stews, taste better."

"Don't know as I'd know the difference."

Marigold was determined to be positive. "Then it won't hurt to try."

"You are a sunshiny thing, ain't you?"

She felt herself smile. "I'm rather used to being called persistent. And hardheaded."

"With the hard heads around here, I reckon that's a good thing."

"Yes," she agreed. "Things do seem to be hard in more ways than one."

Wilbert shrugged. "Just the way it's always been. Never known no dif-ferent. But I hope you won't let the old man scare you away if you can stom-ach it."

"The food or the hellfire?"

She was happy to have made him laugh. "Both." His smile went a little wistful.

"Wilbert." She made sure to lower her voice. "Now that you have some money, what's to stop you going off and finding a place at a better farm? Wouldn't you be happier not having to argue over gilts and piglets?"

The idea seemed to rattle him. "Oh, no. I could never. Granny won't stand for family to leave the island. She means to keep us all here to comfort her, same as Pa."

Great-Aunt Alva certainly cast a long shadow—though not in person. "I haven't had the pleasure of meeting your grandmother yet."

"Don't know as you will." Wilbert's expression was rueful. "Granny don't ever leave her room. Sees only Pa or Cleon, when it pleases her, or when she needs aught. And the rest of us but once or twice a year, when she wants an account of us blood kin. But I reckon she keeps tabs on us all the same, she does."

"Really?" It seemed a bit farfetched that the malevolent presence that loomed so large over the Hatchets was an octogenarian recluse. "I doubt she cares I'm even here."

"Oh, she cares," Wilbert assured her. "Likes to keep her hand in everything that goes on on the island. She sees the books—the stock book, though it's just the two mules and the two swine and the hens, and the egg book and the larder list—every day. Cleon takes them in to her every morning with her breakfast. Wants to know where every penny has gone, she does."

"Except the eggs and pennies you withheld to buy the hogs?"

Wilbert evinced a sheepish blush. "You're danged smart to remember that, Cousin."

"I am also smart enough to know when something is said to me in confidence, so I will tell you in plain language, I will keep your secret, Wilbert. I give you my word. You may rely upon me not to tell a soul—about the egg money or about the money from the scrap metal."

"Ain't never scared up more'n a dollar at a time," he admitted. "Don't know what to do with it all."

"You may rest assured that I will help you, Cousin, any way that I can. You have only to ask."

"Can't ask you to clear out the place, though, can I?" he joked halfheartedly.

"And why not?" Marigold joked back. "I am rather persistent, and once I set my mind to a thing, I always get my way. See if I don't."

But as determined and sunshiny as she was, Marigold couldn't get one particular dark cloud, or one particular person, from her mind—Minnie Mallory.

She tracked her cousin Seviah down to the dark end of the breezeway where he slouched against the open windowsill, quietly smoking a hand-rolled cigarette. "Come to cozy me up the way you have with Daisy and Wilbert?"

"Not in the least." She returned his sarcasm measure for measure. "I've come to antagonize you, as that seems like a relaxing after-dinner exercise. Might I ask how well you were acquainted with Minnie Mallory?"

His answer was a short laugh as he blew out a stream of smoke. "What's it to you? Jealous?"

"I only ask"—Marigold tempered her vulgar curiosity—"because hers was the name your mother mentioned yesterday morning while you were up in the hayloft with"—she checked to make sure no one else was listening but lowered her voice anyway—"somebody I doubt very much was Minnie."

His expression grew guarded. "Well, ain't you the nosy parker."

"Curious," she corrected, "especially about how well you knew Minnie."

His frown devolved into a smirk. "Bragging about me in town, was she?"

"Did she have something to brag about?"

He tossed up his shoulder in that Hatchet Shrug—all-too-casual, suspect dismissal. Clearly hiding something. "I may have walked out with her a time or two."

"Walked out?" Marigold decided that with Seviah, the direct approach worked best. "Is that your rural euphemism for having sexual relations?"

"Sexual relations." He pursed up his mouth to mimic her. "Aren't you the hot tottie."

While he was clearly no Galahad. "I make no moral judgment about your involvement with Minnie, but a sexually promiscuous young man is a danger to more than himself. Did you use any precautions?"

"Look, I don't know who you think you are to ask, Miss City Manners"—he lowered his voice to a perturbed growl—"but what a man does with his *inamoratas* is no damn business of yours."

Well, someone picked up new vocabulary quickly. "It will be your business if someone in town knows she was your inamorata. Or if you got her pregnant. Because she's dead."

He jumped off the railing as if scalded. "What?"

The moment she saw the very real horror and disbelief on his face, Marigold regretted being so blunt. "I'm sorry, but I found out in Pride's Crossing today. I understand they pulled her body out of the water day before yesterday." The day she was alleged to have been in the hayloft.

Seviah sat back heavily on the sill as if the strength in his legs had given out. "Holy hell."

Marigold watched him carefully. "I read the notice of her death in the newspaper after hearing it from Mrs. Dove, and I put one and one together with your mother's mention of the name . . ."

"No matter what you put together from Minnie and me," he swore, "you won't come up with three." He scrubbed his hand through his hair and lowered his voice even further. "I ain't so stupid or no-account as some folks like to think, Miss Nosy Manners. I got plans for getting myself off this cursed rock, same as Minnie wanted to get out of that damned one-horse town. She didn't want to get herself tied down, no mor'n me or anyone."

"Then why did you not correct your mother the other morning?" Marigold probed. "And since Minnie wasn't with you, who was?"

"Minnie weren't no mor'n a diversion to keep folks from—" He shook his head as if reconsidering what to say. "I mean, she were no more than a passing fancy, just like I were no more'n a passing fancy to her." He looked down at himself and gestured to his appearance. "More like a not-so-fancy, I suppose. But I keep myself to myself," Seviah vowed, "or I'll never be able to escape this curst place."

His vehemence seemed genuine. "Now, don't tell me a modern man like you believes in curses? Don't you want to stay and help your brother make something of the place?"

"Take a hell of a lot more than a flock of sheep to make a go of this place," Seviah sneered.

So Seviah had been listening. What else had he been doing that he oughtn't? "What would you do if it were yours?" she challenged.

"Sell it," he said without another thought. "Sell it or burn it to the ground. Because who would buy it?" He inhaled and blew out a thin stream of smoke that hung in the air like a ghost. "This broken-down old place, where nothing gets better and nothing ever changes except the girls who turn up dead? If that isn't cursed, I don't know what the hell is."

CHAPTER 17

Nature provides exceptions to every rule.
—Margaret Fuller

Marigold was quite determined not to become one of the girls who turned up dead. To leave as soon as she could—once she had learned what she needed to know about her mother. In the meantime, she would stay watchful and careful so she could not be taken unawares.

Hence, she installed her padlock before she set to work on her next project—an herb garden laid out with all the precision of an archaeological site, mapped out with the same stout twine, line levels, and plumb bobs she had packed for the Leivathos dig on Kefalonia—another place in ruins on a Greek, rather than a Massachusetts, island. But using her brass theodolite and surveying skills allayed some of her frustration at needing to remain at her present site.

"Rise and shine, Cleon." Marigold rattled her measuring chain against the cast-iron stove to waken the old man. "Rise and . . . well, shine as best you can under the circumstances. I have a job for you this morning."

While she would have preferred the help of any of her cousins, they had already scattered, each to their own way, to fend for themselves. *That's just how it is at Hatchet Farm.*

"Gone!" He bolted up from his habitual slumber on the kitchen table. "I gots work here." He rose and made as if to clear the table, which had already been cleared—by her.

"I have taken care of the dishes." The offending bowls were already soaking in a steaming caldron. "We'll come back later to scrub them when it's easier."

"I gotta clam today, to add to the chowder."

"The tide is still high, so your clams can wait to go into your never-ending pot." The chowder seemed to always be on a low boil. But something else in the kitchen was giving off an astringent smell, which didn't come from the hot stove but from the narrow hallway where Sophronia had disappeared last night. "What's back there?"

"Couldn't rightly say," Cleon answered. "That be Miz Sophronia's room, and ain't no one else allowed in."

Perhaps Sophronia was brewing up her own moonshine liquor that she didn't share with the rest of the house—maybe that would account for her air of placid disassociation.

But Marigold's knock on the door went unanswered—and she wouldn't allow herself to put her ear to the portal in front of the old man. "Come along, Cleon." She led the way to the chicken coop and its rotting pile of manure. "I'll get a shovel while you get the wheelbarrow."

"What fer?"

"For the garden, in which I will be planting fresh vegetables like green runner beans and peas, and carrots and beets," she explained. "Think of how savory your stews will be, Cleon, with good root vegetables and squashes. You'll have a bounty come midsummer."

"Ain't nothing ever growed on this rock," he fretted. "Barren, it is. Cursed, some say—"

"But not me. I don't believe in curses, Cleon. And neither should you."

"But I seen it with my own eyes," the old man swore. "The earth is as bare and barren as a witch's teat. The rain never comes. The seeds fall to the ground like the sulfurous drops from Satan's d—"

"Yes, thank you, Cleon," Marigold broke in. "I recall that delightful litany from our first meeting. And although I have never seen the devil's big brassy door knocker"—she tossed the astonished old fellow a playful wink—"I can see this chicken manure with my own eyes and certainly smell it with my own nose, which makes it far more real than any curse. The manure, mixed with some fallen leaf mulch from the woods, as well as some grit and seaweed from the shore, will help make fertile raised beds, which we are going to box up from windfallen logs that we are also going to gather from the woods."

"That's a powerful load of work."

"Yes, it is," she acknowledged. "For which you shall be paid hand-somely." Though it occurred to her that she did not know a farm laborer's rate of pay. "What does your cousin Ellery pay you?"

"Don't pay me." Cleon hung his head. "Don't deserve nothing, he says."

"What do you mean, nothing?" Granted, the old fellow didn't do much, but work he did—and work no one else seemed prepared to do. "Everyone deserves to be paid a fair wage, Cleon."

"Not me." He shook his head like a dog. "On account'a I'll only go and waste it on demon liquor. Best not pay me anything but vittles."

"Ah." Marigold recalled Cleon's bout of barrel fever. "While I understand the moral dilemma of not encouraging alcoholic drink, it is highly unethical, not to mention entirely illegal, not to provide recompense for labor."

Cleon shook his head as if he could clear it. "Don't know as what re-com-pen is. But I knows times is hard. And I'm a sinner who don't deserve no cash money to waste on liquor."

"Your sins are your own business, but I shall pay you for your work—perhaps in a jar on the mantelpiece in the kitchen? You can ask Wilbert to help you keep track of it, if you are afraid of wasting it on liquor."

His befuddlement seemed to clear—slightly. "Well, all right then, Miss Girl."

"It will be all right," she assured him. "Because I will make it right."

It was a long day of toil, filling the squeaky wheelbarrow full of manure and hauling it across the yard, taking the mule cart into the woods to load it full of dirt and leaf mulch, returning to Hatchet Farm to unload, and then heading to North Cove for sand and seaweed to layer onto the three patches Marigold had set out with twine.

She kept one eye on the weather, because the gray wind off the water held a raw cold. But the rain never fell, although a different sort of chill did come over her now and again. At one point Marigold thought she might have seen a shadow disappear behind a tree, but having the old man as a working companion kept her far too busy redirecting his missteps and mis-deeds to pursue it.

"Cleon, be careful! You've nearly knocked me into this burrow." Although on second look, it was not an animal's burrow but simply a large hole dug into the ground—the backfill was heaped nearby. Which reminded her of the eldest Hatchet's bizarre appearance with the spade yesterday morning. "I suppose Ellery Hatchet dug this hole?"

"Couldn't say," was Cleon's wary response.

"Naturally." But there were holes all about the woodland, scattered here and there. The illogic of both the holes themselves and Cleon's refusal to give any real answer to any question, along with a continuing sense of creeping unease, was enough to put Marigold on edge. It didn't help that Cleon was fey and skittish, muttering imprecations under his breath and mumbling that he hoped she knew what she was doing.

She did not. And the longer she went on, the less sure she got.

Because there it was again—that uneasy feeling, like a chill across the back of her neck. As if . . .

She whirled around, sure she could catch sight of—

Nothing. There was only old Cleon stepping into her way. "Don't know as why yer going to such trouble," he grumbled, "when the gulls and crows'll just peck up all the seeds first."

"The crows are not going to peck up the seeds, firstly, because I already have the plants in pots on my windowsill"—thanks to Bessie—"and secondly, because we're going to erect a scarecrow."

"I never!" Cleon all but threw his arms over his head, as if he were warding off a spell.

"Cleon, if you must insist upon being gawney and folktale-ish, you should know that scarecrows are meant to ward *off* bad luck." Marigold settled in for a practical explanation. "As well as to scare away the crows."

"No, no. Eerie they be," he insisted, shaking and scratching his head like a dog with a flea in its ear. "Cousin Ellery won't stand for any o' this—he'll say a scarecrow be a graven idol."

"Nonsense." Marigold was determined to put such foolishness from Cleon's head. And to keep the Hatchets from insinuating their way into her own—there was altogether too much eerie decay at Hatchet Farm as it was without adding any more. "The scarecrow is nothing more than a tool to protect the garden. A tool best employed by surprise—so we shall be moving the scarecrow's post and crosstree about the garden regularly, as well as changing the clothes." She had already started gathering garments too worn to be repaired from the washing. "All I require from you is a hat."

"A hat?"

"Yes, Cleon, a hat." No hats had come in the laundry. "Something old and especially tattered." Not that any of the clothing worn by the inhabitants of Hatchet Farm could be called anything but tattered on a good day. "Surely there is an old, broken-down straw hat cast about in some forgotten corner somewhere in that maze of a house?"

"Dunno," the old man quavered. "Usually feed anything straw to the mules."

Marigold kept herself from sighing only by the strictest discipline. "Just keep your eye open for a hat, will you? Or, if you could show whatever hats you might find to me before any feeding to the mules, I'd be obliged."

Cleon took that as his chance to scurry off in immediate search, so instead of instructing him on the repair of the chicken coop—she hadn't argued for that Norwich wire fencing for her own health—Marigold spent some small time with her penciled plan, better judging the layout of the beds with the fall of sunlight and thinking with fondness of her botany courses in college. And all of her courses. Imagining that she was standing in front of the ruins of Leivathos, judging the layout of her excavation grid squares, instead of languishing on a barren pile of rocks two miles off the Massachusetts shore.

But wishing her life was different would not solve her—or the Hatchets'—present dilemmas. She would stick to practical solutions, such as where it might be best to put root vegetables like carrots, parsnips, radishes, and beets, as they would require more mulch while still tender—

This time, the sudden chill was like the shock of a cold hand touching her face. Marigold instinctively whirled away. "Who's there?"

A swirl of dust behind the breezeway door evolved into the long fall of a gray wool skirt. "Cousin Sophronia?"

The woman reluctantly showed herself, the dark hem of her cloak and skirts damp with dew, as if she'd been about the woods or tide pools. "You've gone right out straight," she said in her strange, old-fashioned New England style of talking. "Looks like you scraped up half the foreshore."

"Enough for good, gritted soil," Marigold agreed, determined to foster some conversation between them, "to grow herbs of use in cookery."

"Which?" Sophronia's eyes grew eerily dark and overlarge. "Tell them to me."

Marigold tried not to let her cousin's stare unnerve her. "Chives will go here," she began.

"Usefulness," Sophronia muttered with an approving nod. "Why are you crying?"

"I'm not," Marigold assured her, though she surreptitiously put up a hand to check that her face was indeed not wet with tears. "Are you quite to rights, Cousin?"

"Hang them to dry on the rafters to repel evil spirits, chives." Sophronia motioned toward the kitchen with her dirt-gnarled hands. "Need an awful heap for this house."

"Certainly," Marigold answered. "Anything to help. I will also put in thyme, thereabouts,"—she pointed to the end of the bed—"which will be savory with eggs, since you seem to have a fairly steady supply of those."

"Courage." Sophronia's gaze became unfocused, as if she could see something other than plants growing from the soil.

"I don't think I'll need courage, Cousin Sophronia," Marigold soothed. "Just more mulch, for the sage and parsley, which will go there."

"Ward away misfortune." Sophronia muttered the words, as if she were invoking some strange incantation.

A more reasonable thought occurred. "Are you by any chance talking about the language of flowers?" Marigold asked. "The symbolic meanings of plants?"

"Ayuh," Sophronia confirmed. "Everything has meaning," she said a trifle vehemently. "Everything speaks to us, if only we will listen."

"That's a lovely thought." Marigold saw her opening. "I, for one, should very much like to listen and learn," she assured her cousin. "Especially as to what wrong was done to my mother and what I am to do about it?"

Sophronia instantly backed away. "It is too soon."

"How could it be too soon, Cousin?" Marigold reasoned. "When I've come all this way, by your invitation, to find out? How much longer am I expected to wait?"

"I've said what I've said and I'll say no more." Sophronia retreated toward the house, as if she would end the conversation.

Marigold was having none of it. "Then why did you write me about my rights and bring me all the way out here if you mean not to tell me?" she demanded. "Do you mean to be so intentionally perverse? Or cruel?"

"Poor girl. You've strength in you, I'll give you that." Sophronia looked at her with a sort of fearful pity before she cast another glance over the garden. "But you'll need rosemary. And rue."

"And what are they—rosemary and rue—meant to say to me that you will not?"

"Rosemary is for remembrance." Sophronia's voice lowered to a whisper. "And rue is—" She sighed so heavily that Marigold half expected her to collapse from the weight of her cares. "Rue is regret." Her eyes finally met Marigold's. "And virginity."

"Well then." Marigold was a modern New Woman, and it was time her cousin understood that. "That wouldn't be for me."

"Oh, no." Sophronia nodded, unperturbed. "Not everything is for you."

"Well, I seem to be the only one listening." Marigold drew herself up to her full middling height. "But if you will not teach me what I am meant to learn, I will find some other way. The past, dear cousin, as the poet Emily Dickinson warned, is not a package one can lay away."

But Sophronia was no pushover and could give as good as she got. She drew herself up. "Then I hope you have the courage for the unpacking." She cast one last glance at the garden. "You'll need a far larger patch of thyme for that."

CHAPTER 18

You can't depend upon your eyes when your imagination is out of focus.

—Mark Twain

The next morning, Marigold was still discomfited enough by her conversation with Sophronia to want the crowded, civilized comfort of the town.

"Wilbert," Marigold called before he could disappear from the kitchen. "I thought I might revisit the station at Pride's Crossing to inquire about my things that have not yet been sent on as I asked." And learn the schedule for trains back to Boston. "And with your escort, we could"—she lowered her voice, lest she be overheard—"visit the library to do some of that research we talked about. We might also check in at the Grange Hall," she suggested, "to inquire about the going price per head? Or the price of wool this year?"

If she had another reason for wanting Wilbert to accompany her, she would keep that to herself. *It takes some getting used to for some folks.* She hated that she was still one of the *some.*

"Pa don't like us leaving. Or taking the boat." Wilbert rubbed his shaved chin as if he missed the bristles. "And I'll admit I don't much like going to town. And they don't much like us. Never have." He squinted across the water. "It is a fearful long way to go."

"Less than two miles," Marigold reasoned. "And all the more reason to go and give them a good impression, looking as spiffy as you do." She was justifiably proud of the transformation of her cousin from the unkempt lurcher of their first meeting to the washed, combed, and cleanly dressed specimen who stood before her. "You may take confidence in your appearance."

Wilbert's cheeks turned so rosy a red that Marigold was momentarily alarmed that he might have gotten the wrong impression, but he agreed without any further sign of consternation. "I reckon I might could look into the Grange Hall."

Marigold was happy to find the row across Salem Sound was becoming more familiar and less daunting with every trip. But she still could not stop herself from searching the water for that remembered flash of red on the evening tide.

And thinking of drowning . . . "Do you like to swim, Wilbert?" She had thought herself a very proficient swimmer, especially once Isabella had designed her a swim costume without burdensome skirts. But she had never tried to swim in such cold water. "Perhaps when it's warmer or more placid in the summer?"

"Nah. I can't—none of us can," he admitted. "Pa always forbid us even wading into the water. Says it's not natural."

Perhaps that was why Cleon had been so edgy while she was clambering along the rocky foreshore? Had he assumed she wouldn't know how to swim either? It was another curiosity to add to the cabinet of curiosities that was life in the Hatchet house.

They crossed the sound without incident, stowed the dory on West Beach, and started the walk up the narrow lanes into Pride's Crossing, but while Marigold felt herself becoming more relaxed the closer they came to civilization, her cousin grew more agitated. "Would you like to accompany me into the library, Wilbert? Or would you prefer to head on towards the Grange Hall?"

"Sure, you go ahead and do that." Wilbert touched his hand to his hat before he slumped hastily off toward the plain clapboard Grange Hall down the street.

Marigold checked her own reflection in a window, making sure she could be seen as a stylish, impeccably mannered representative of her temporary clan before she passed through the doors of the library. "Miss Morgan," Marigold greeted the librarian. "How nice to see you again."

"Miss Manners! I am happy to see you looking so well and back at the library." The young woman hid her surprise by adjusting her spectacles. "What might I help you with this morning?"

"Some general reading materials on local agriculture, if you please."

"Arable or pasturage?"

Marigold had to smile at the preciseness of mind on display. "Both, I thank you, although I will admit to some greater interest in livestock."

"Any particular type or breed of livestock?

Until Wilbert had made up his mind, Marigold felt that risking her query about sheep might be trying poor Miss Morgan's local loyalties unfairly. "Just general information, although I am also interested in agricultural groups. I wondered if there were any publications from such any such local groups that would address best husbandry or stock management practices?"

"We carry the Farm Alliance's *National Economist*, as well as the *Rural and Family Farm Paper* out of Springfield."

"Those should do nicely. I appreciate your expertise, Miss Morgan."

"Thank you." Amelia Morgan's cheeks turned a charming rose. "I'll bring the latest issues to the reading room for you in just a moment."

"Thank you. I should also like to check out any primers you might have, both reading and writing, as well as mathematical."

That Miss Morgan was confounded by such a request was evident in the frown etched above her spectacles, but she did not demur—a very nice set of primers was delivered to Marigold's table.

"Thank you, Miss Morgan." Marigold turned her mind to the problem of making Hatchet Farm a going concern. She spent two hours working her way through the newspapers, seeking out pertinent information on forage and the like until she felt she had enough to advise Wilbert, whom she hoped would have finished his business at the Grange Hall and made his way to library.

He had not.

But no matter. It was only a short walk to the Grange Hall—Pride's Crossing was hardly Boston—but this time Marigold took her time, peering in the windows of the tiny nickelodeon reel house and dawdling to read the advertisements in the window of the druggist, where she bought a nickel's worth of penny candy at its marble soda fountain. Seeing and being seen.

While no one was what she might call friendly, people were civil, tipping their hats or nodding their heads to her. Marigold kept her smile warm—civility and respect were a good first step. Her plan to win over the townspeople was working, albeit slowly.

"Miss Manners?" The bell over the druggist's door jangled out its warning, and Marigold turned to find the silhouette of a tall man in a straw boater hat filling the door. "Marigold?"

Something within kicked free of her chest. "Cab?"

She said his name almost involuntarily, knowing it could not be true. Knowing her rebellious heart and even more ridiculously unhelpful brain had supplied some unmet, unnamed longing she would have to deal with at some later, less public moment. For now, all she could do was feel her cheeks flame and take solace in the fact that no one in Pride's Crossing could know who on earth Cab Cox was.

"It is you!" The silhouette doffed his hat and swept it under his arm so he could step near enough to be seen. And it really was Cab, stretching out his hand to her in greeting. "Marigold." He took hold of her nerveless fingers. "I can't tell you how glad I am to see you. I couldn't believe my luck when I saw your name on those broken-down crates at the train depot and realized what it meant—that you must be nearby."

"Cab," she said again, like the veriest peabrain, for her mouth could evidently produce no other word. "What are you doing here?"

"Now, that's a long story." He gave her that charming, self-deprecating smile that had so clearly imprinted itself upon her highly susceptible brain. "I suppose I wanted a change too—a bit of adventure."

There was no way that rural, plain Pride's Crossing, where the gossips had made a meal from Marigold's purchase of a carton of outhouse paper, could be construed as an adventure for a man of Cab's experience. "Really?"

"It was what you said about striking out on your own," he explained as he tucked her hand through the crook of his arm and led her, as docile as a lamb, away from the clerk's avid earshot. "You inspired me. My uncle Endicott—Mr. George C. Endicott, who is a landowner of some reputation in these parts—"

"Indeed, the name rings a bell." The Endicott family were well-known in Massachusetts for their fortune, built upon seafaring, as well as their political and military leadership. Although Marigold had never heard of any connection to the Coxes who lived on the North Shore, it would naturally follow that Cab would be related to one of the richest families in town, while she was related to the poorest.

"It's really his wife, my aunt, who's related through my mother's side," Cab was explaining. "You know how it is with family."

Marigold only knew how it was with her family—complicated and somewhat dangerous. "Naturally."

"Well, Uncle George had been asking for some help with a difficult lawsuit," he went on. "And as I'm only a junior partner at the firm, it was felt to be an advantageous use of my time. So here I am. But to see you here too—why, that's swell. You're looking well."

"Thank you," she said, because manners were manners and one had to have standards, even if one did want to reach up and tuck one's hair back under one's hat to make sure one did indeed look well and not as if one had rowed across Salem Sound in a stiff wind. "As do you."

And he did look well. Very well. His face was more handsome and square jawed than ever, and the boater hat, which he set back upon his head, balanced the architecture of his jaw quite nicely.

"I hope you don't mind." He was still holding her hand in a caring sort of way. "I don't want you to feel I'm horning in."

Thank goodness she was wearing good kidskin gloves to cover her washtub-reddened hands. "Not in the least," she said automatically. But her feelings were a tumult of conflicting emotions—elated and uneasy all at the same time. "I'm sure there's room enough in the state of Massachusetts for the two of us to pursue our own interests."

His delight gleamed down at her. "It's wonderful, isn't it—all this bright light and brisk sea air? Nothing like this in the city."

"Yes, it is *expansive*"—Marigold chose the word carefully—"isn't it?"

"That's right," he confirmed. "Just what we both wanted—wide open with all sorts of interesting possibilities."

CHAPTER 19

What are men to rocks and mountains?
—Jane Austen

The warmth of understanding lightened Marigold's chest. "Naturally." But as warm as her feelings were, her thoughts were decidedly scattered, especially when a bright-eyed young gentleman approached them.

"May I introduce you to my cousin, Mr. Thaddeus Endicott?" Cab asked as he gestured to the stylishly dressed young man. "My dear friend Miss Marigold Manners."

Marigold was delighted to find Cab had any relatives who weren't dyed-in-the-wool old puritans. "How do you do, Mr. Endicott."

The young man stuck out his hand, all enthusiastic equanimity. "Pleased to meet you, Miss Manners. Call me Tad."

The name sent a frisson of heady excitement—much like she imagined her father had felt when he gambled—running up Marigold's spine. If there had been only one Minnie, there ought to be only one Tad—or Taddy— Daisy's intended beau.

"I will, thank you, Tad. And you must call me Marigold." She took his hand with pleasure, for as well as being every bit as handsome as Daisy had claimed, the young man had a breezy kindness about him.

It seemed to run in the family.

But Marigold needed to dismiss her ridiculously complicated feelings about Cab Cox and concentrate on making the most of this introduction.

"I believe we may have a friend in common in my dear cousin Miss Daisy Hatchet."

"Oh, Daisy." Tad Endicott's eyes widened, and his cheeks gained encouraging warmth. "Why, she's just the swellest girl."

"Yes she is," Marigold agreed. "Just lovely. And very beautiful."

"Pretty as a daisy," the young man answered with some alacrity. "That's what I tell her."

"I'm sure you say that to all the girls," Marigold demurred, probing a new theory about Daisy's potential jealousy of Minnie. "A handsome young man like you must have any number of sweethearts along the North Shore."

"No, ma'am." Tad's face turned ruddier. "Only the one." He turned to his cousin and added, "But don't tell my father I said so."

"Not a word," was Cab's loyal answer.

"Your secret is safe with us," Marigold added with what she hoped was an encouraging smile, because her clever, determined, relieved brain was already making all sorts of interesting adjustments and addenda to her proposed plan for Daisy's education.

Tad smiled and ducked his head and swiped the back of his hand across his red-tinged cheekbones and tipped the brim of his hat up all at the same time—the very picture of the sweetly fumbling beau.

Oh, yes, if Daisy truly wanted him, Marigold could fashion her specifically for just such an open, engaging, well-connected, conveniently rich young man.

"Well, I best get on. Miss Manners, it's been a pleasure." Tad touched his hat politely and said to Cab, "Be seeing you."

"Be seeing you," Cab responded, before his handsome young cousin loped off, much like an exuberant but purebred puppy, all long, gangly legs and swinging arms.

"Now." Cab turned the bright beam of his gaze wholly upon Marigold. "How are you getting on out there on Great Misery, Marigold? I've heard some things . . ."

"What things?" Marigold was eager to hear exactly what the more prosperous people of the town thought of the Hatchets, so she might more effectively counteract such perceptions. A good cleanup could work wonders, but something more serious would require a different approach—or a hasty retreat. "I assure you, I am quite well. In fact, I've never been better."

"I can see that," Cab affirmed with a fond look.

Marigold deflected her blush. "Thank you. Are you also staying with your relatives, these Endicotts?"

"For the time being." A frown knotted up his perfect brow. "Got a nice little place along the water just south of here, George Endicott has."

Only a man of Cab's pedigree could call what was assuredly a summer estate a "nice little place." But she noted he said his uncle's name carefully, as if testing what she knew of the man.

"I take it he is the George Endicott of the Salem Endicotts? And the Massachusetts Supreme Court?"

Cab gave her that self-deprecating half smile. "Just so. He seems to fancy himself something of a local grandee."

Marigold could only smile back. "I expect he might, if he owns a large piece of the coastline."

"But not all of it." Cab doffed his hat and flipped it around in his hand. "That's why he brought me out here—to take a look at a lawsuit regarding some land that used to be his—or his family's."

"So, you're to litigate for your supper? I wish you luck." Marigold felt a bit sorry for whomever Cab had in his sights. His brand of well-bred intelligence seemed to come with a large share of well-camouflaged, steely determination—that trick he had for never letting on.

"Do you?" He looked at her askance. "You haven't heard anything about a dispute with Endicott?"

"No, but I am new to the area and not yet privy to much local gossip." A new thought came to her. "Is it to do with the Hatchets?"

"Well, on the face of it, it's an old dispute, started before either you or I were born." He looked serious again, as if there were more he wanted to say. "But when he wrote me with the particulars, I knew I had to come. I couldn't take the chance—"

"Is this stranger is bothering you?" It was Wilbert, looking far more dog in the manger than Marigold could ever have imagined.

"Wilbert, no, he is not bothering me. Please let me introduce you to an old . . . friend"—her tongue stumbled only slightly at the word—"of mine, Mr. Jonathan Cabot Cox. Cab, this is my cousin, Mr. Wilbert Hatchet."

Cab immediately put his hand out, disarming Wilbert with his natural, hail-fellow-well-met friendliness. "An honor to meet you, Mr. Hatchet.

And thank you for taking such good care of Marigold. It's a boon to her friends to know she's being so well looked after."

"Looking after us, mostly," Wilbert stammered. "But any friend of Cousin Marigold's is a friend of mine. She's a wonder, she is, helping out round the place. Don't know how we ever got along before her."

"Indeed?" Cab chuckled and shook Wilbert's hand in agreement. "That sounds just like her."

"There!" Marigold beamed at Wilbert as if to say, *See how easy it is to make friends in town?* But she thought it best to end the conversation before her cousin's store of social equanimity was exhausted. "Well." She extended her gloved hand for Cab to shake. "It's been lovely to see you, Cab."

He covered her hand with his own. "I hope to see you again, soon. Oh, I forgot—I have something of yours in my possession. I picked up some crates with your name when I arrived at the depot."

"My bicycle? How wonderful! Since it appears you are in possession of my prized possession, I do hope to see you sooner rather than later." Marigold's mind began to tick like a well-machined clock. "Might I trouble you to deliver it to me on Great Misery?"

"Sure, but . . ." Cab hesitated.

"How about tomorrow?" Marigold was anxious to get her machine—and her independence—back. And she could use Cab's visit to Daisy's advantage. "Bring your cousin, if you can."

Some of the eager warmth went out of Cab's face. "Tad?"

"Yes. I should very much like to introduce your young cousin to my two young cousins, Seviah and the aforementioned Daisy." She paused and attempted to give Cab a subtle sort of look that Wilbert might not understand. "It is so very hard for young people to meet one another, I'm sure you'll agree, when both live so far away from the town."

Cab's barely perceptible tension eased. "Up to your old tricks, are you, Marigold, arranging dates for everyone but yourself?"

Marigold refused to be baited. "Your cousin, being a local, will be able to direct you across the sound to the island."

"I suppose he will." Cab was too polite to contradict her. "Well then, I'll suppose we'll come tomorrow. But I need to tell you—"

"Excellent." Marigold stopped him from expressing any more personal thoughts. "Until tomorrow." She saw Cab off with a cheery wave, determined to dismiss the surprising tumult of emotions his appearance had engendered, but as soon as they were alone, Wilbert brought Cab up again.

"You know that fellow pretty well, then?" he asked.

"We were acquainted in Boston." Marigold gave him the simplest explanation. There was no reason to bring up the complicated hierarchy of Boston society and its relationship to collegiate social interactions.

"He courting you?"

"No," Marigold said firmly. Though she knew next to nothing of Cab's intentions—besides his ambiguous "interesting possibilities"—she knew her own convictions. "I am not, at present, interested in being courted with a view toward marriage. Now, let me relate some of the far more important information I learned at the library. The accepted ratio for keeping sheep is ten ewes and fifteen lambs per acre of good forage or pasture. How many acres is Great Misery?"

"Don't know really—ain't never seen the deed. But Pa's always said somewheres over a hundred acres."

"That big?" Marigold realized she had seen but very little of the property. "That's encouraging—there must be some suitable forage amongst so many acres?"

"Dunno. It's woods, salt grass, and rock. Not good for much."

"Well, the agricultural sources I consulted said that thirty acres, properly improved and fertilized, should sustain one hundred ewes and one hundred fifty lambs, but that the flock needs to be rotated, or moved within the property, to keep from overgrazing. And you need to have vegetation called *forbs*, which I had to look up, which is plant fodder with leaves."

"Huh." He made a thoughtful noise. "Leaves, not spears like grass? So, like the scrub or the understory of the woods?"

"There! You see, you have a vast deal of understanding, Wilbert, even if it wasn't learned in school or books."

"You reckon?"

"I do. But what's more interesting is that in the latest farm gazettes I consulted, many of the top agriculturalists are actually recommending restocking with sheep instead of cows or cattle after last year's bank panic forced so many farms out of business."

"Reckon that makes sense," he said slowly. "Things was never good, but a few years ago's when they turned particular bad—had to sell off the last of the bullocks. That's when the old man got stranger than ever. He was always a preachy sort, but the hellfire and brimstone came on him harder than ever."

"I am sorry. The past year has been hard on all of us. No one—not even my seemingly easy-living friend there, Cab Cox—escaped unscathed. The financial crisis cost him his father, dead from an attack of apoplexy at trying to prevent a particularly distressing loss."

"Wish my old man would drop dead of an apoplexy so's the rest of us might get on without any more distressing loss."

Marigold was not so much shocked by the sentiment as by Wilbert's honestly in expressing himself. "I'm sure you don't mean that, but I do understand your frustration," she consoled him. "The articles I read indicated that keeping sheep is being encouraged to improve range soil and vegetation by"—she consulted her notes—"*improving forage densities by reducing noxious plants and improving habitat conditions for beneficial wildlife.*"

Wilbert nodded along. "One of them fellas at the Grange was saying as he reckoned goats would even eat poison ivy for winter forage . . ." He trailed off as if still not convinced. "Don't know that might also be true of sheep. But wouldn't that make a change to get rid of some poison on Great Misery!"

Marigold could see that Wilbert was making a joke, so she stuck to the safer topic at hand. "I did read a news account about cattlemen setting themselves against sheep keepers." She felt it only right to admit to the bad as well as the good. "But most of those conflicts are over the rights to public grazing lands out west. And you own Great Misery, don't you?"

"Pa does, I reckon. And Little Misery too, though I can't remember the last time any one of us went there."

"Then it seems to me you've got enough acreage that actually belongs to you, so no one should have any objection."

"No one but Pa." But Wilbert looked as if he were beginning to actually consider it. "I reckon people don't much care what we do, so long as we keep to ourselves and it don't interfere with nothing onshore."

"There you have it." Marigold had formed her opinion, but she could see from the deep frown on Wilbert's face that he was not yet convinced. "I am happy to do more research, if you require it."

"At that library?" he asked.

"Indeed. You should come with me next time."

"Don't know as I could," he hedged. "Don't reckon I have enough learning."

Marigold saw her next opening. "Should you like to try to learn more? I can teach you," she offered. "I just happen to have the necessary books. We can start this evening."

"You won't tell no one?"

"Not a soul," Marigold swore. "You have my word. It will be our secret."

With so many secrets floating about Great Misery Island, what was one more?

CHAPTER 20

Always forgive your enemies—nothing annoys them so much.
—Oscar Wilde

Marigold began her morning with a walk in her garden, mentally preparing for Cab and Tad's visit. While she had spent the previous evening instructing Daisy on how to conduct herself, she had not yet done the same for herself. She needed to steel herself in advance against the tumult of uncomfortable and illogical emotions that had unfortunately already given her an uneasy night. Not that any night on Great Misery had been particularly easy with her mind awhirl with the strange circumstances of Minnie Mallory's—and *them other girls'*—drownings.

But Cab Cox's presence in Pride's Crossing seemed . . . too convenient. Too coincidental.

Marigold sensed Isabella's hand stirring the pot, but Isabella could not have invented a family for Cab to visit, nor a legal case that required a Harvard Law graduate's expertise. Yet despite Cab's sunny, well-bred assurances about change and adventure, Marigold couldn't shake the uncomfortable feeling of being pursued. Perhaps another woman might be flattered by such determined pursuit, but Marigold was . . . undecided. She would have to tread carefully with Cab Cox.

Right after she treaded carefully around the unreasonably angry man who suddenly appeared before her.

"What's all this?" Ellery Hatchet stomped into her budding kitchen garden. "I gave no permission for this."

"I beg your pardon, Cousin Ellery," Marigold began in a tone of voice that frankly did not beg at all. "This is a garden."

"I can see that," he all but spat as he crowded her back, trying to intimidate her much the same way his younger son had tried—and failed—that first afternoon. "I didn't give permission for this!"

"No?" There was something about his exaggerated posturing that stiffened Marigold's spine. She refused to be intimidated into politeness. "I did not know I needed to consult you before feeding myself, as you seemed particularly concerned with me taking foodstuffs meant for hardworking men. Accordingly, I made other arrangements for my board and also began this garden, although the bounty is meant to be shared with the whole family."

That he was confounded by her matter-of-fact, bordering-on-insubordinate tone was evident—he sputtered at her in outrage. "Why, you intrusive har—"

"Houseguest, yes, thank you." Marigold turned away to cut him off, just as she had successfully done her first morning, but she was surprised—and delighted—to find Sophronia standing nearby with a trug filled with mushrooms and some other forage her cousin must have been picking in the woods. "Good morning, Cousin. I should think some of that chervil looks like an excellent addition to an omelet this morning."

"Ayuh," Sophronia agreed in her cryptic New England fashion, but there was something else—a sort of slyness in the corner of her eye as she glanced at her husband. "With a mushroom or two. You used to like that flavor, Hatchet."

"I'll take nothing from your snake-fed hand," Ellery spat. "And well you know it."

Sophronia didn't so much as flinch, returning calmly, "What will be, will be, Ellery Hatchet. You know that sure as you know anything."

"Don't start at me, woman, with your witchy ways. This looks to be your doing." He tossed his chin at the garden. "For your witchy tonics and tarradiddles."

"Not a bit of it," Sophronia said, "though I like it well enough. Got a good patch of earth set. Deep enough to grow a good-sized rosemary." A small, nearly imperceptible smile creased the corners of her mouth. "Though I'd advise her to put in bird's-foot trefoil."

Ellery Hatchet's response seemed entirely out of proportion to the suggestion—he shook his fist at her. "You'll do no such thing," he cawed before he returned his displeasure to Marigold. "Where did all this come from?"

"The beds? Rest assured nothing was purchased," Marigold said to placate the unreasonably irate man. "Cleon and I cobbled it together from windfallen logs, chicken manure, leaf mulch from the woods, and seaweed from the tide line, though it was none too easy to haul it all the way here."

"From the woods?" He gasped, turning frantically back to the beds. "That stupid old man! Did he help you dig it up? Where? Where did you take it from, you cursed slommack?"

"Cousin Ellery!" No matter the man's clear perturbation, there was no account for such language.

He advanced upon her, looming over her, poking his dirty finger at her in hot accusation. "I was told to let you be to the Lord, but what ye hath sown, so shall the Lord reap!"

His rage spun itself into action—he went at the garden like a maniac, twisting up plants and kicking at the dirt to uproot what he couldn't pull. "Teach you to go against me," he ranted. "Who knows what you've taken! Who knows what you've ruined, you wretched girl. Coming here, digging things up. Ruined it all."

"Stop that!" Marigold cried, and would have tried to pull him away, but Sophronia was at her elbow with a clawlike grip, holding her back out of harm's way.

"Let him be. He'll only hurt you too."

"But . . . why?" Marigold struggled against both Sophronia and the hot, irrational mixture of anger and fear making a fist of her throat. "It's just a garden! How could a garden ruin anything?"

It was beyond Marigold's powers of logic to make any sense out of the man, who continued ranting and pulling, kicking and uprooting—ruining everything, even as he accused her of the same. He was utterly maniacal.

"What is wrong with him?" she asked no one and everyone who had come out of the house to gawk—from a safe distance—at the sight.

But only Sophronia answered. "Nothing you could ever hope to cure."

There was a weary fatality in her voice that finally pierced Marigold's armor of positivity. "Why does he hate everyone so much?" The words were more plea than question. "Why does he hate me?"

Sophronia answered by wrapping her arm around Marigold's shoulder, and Marigold didn't know what astonished her more—the affection from her cousin, or the naked hatred from her cousin's husband.

"Let him be for now," Sophronia advised. "Let him rant and rave and have his way. And when he's done, we'll put it to rights, just like we always do. We'll carry on. Just like we always do."

It was something so uncharacteristically lucid and kind and practical that Marigold was astonished into acceptance. "Thank you."

Perhaps something good might be salvaged from the destruction—perhaps this would be the impetus to finally convince Sophronia to talk lucidly and directly about the wrong done to Marigold's mother. And then Marigold could go back to Boston and escape this ridiculous abuse—although frankly, there was nothing she might be due that could make up for what had just happened, no promise of atonement that could be worth enduring another such experience.

Ellery seemed to have finally exhausted himself uprooting plants and turned what was left of his spite on her. "I'll trouble you to mind your own business and not be insinuating yourself with my family. I've seen you working your wiles on Wilbert."

"Insinuating?" Marigold's courage rose in proportion to the threat. "Why, you miserable old troll! It's a wonder someone in this house hasn't put you to bed with a shovel! I was invited here, not the other way around—your family are the ones who intruded upon me."

"You're no family of mine!" Ellery roared loud enough for all of Great Misery and half of Massachusetts to hear. "You keep away from what's mine," he screeched, spittle flying from his mouth, "or so help me, I'll get rid of you with my own two—"

"That's enough, Pa." Somehow, Wilbert was stepping between then, physically shielding her from his father's unreasonable aggression.

"Bah." Ellery flung himself away from his son before he pointed one bony finger at her in accusation. The look in his eyes was like nothing Marigold had ever seen—a roiling hatred that defied all logic and reason. "You keep her away from my woods."

With that ominous warning, the horrid man stomped off, and Marigold was left standing among the ruins. "Rest assured," she murmured more to herself than anyone, "I wouldn't go near you or your woods again, even with all the thyme in the world."

But Sophronia was looking at her with the same sort of pleased wonder Wilbert had evinced when Marigold had given him his money. "Well, look at you," Sophronia finally said. "Not a bit mothlike."

"Naturally," Marigold rejoined. But whatever stubborn determination or pride had carried her through the encounter ebbed away, leaving her feeling empty and shaken and remembering the hirsute clerk's prediction that *old man Hatchet was like to murder her.*

The hatred that had shone in Ellery Hatchet's eyes was a weapon far more dangerous than Wilbert's scythe or Seviah's matches or even Daisy's gun. Ellery Hatchet's hatred had no logic.

It was no longer hard to understand that he could have perpetrated a great and godless wrong against her mother. And instead of righting the wrong, he seemed determined to perpetuate his wrong a second time. On her. And Marigold didn't think she had anything left to combat such evil.

Nor did anyone else, it seemed—Daisy only approached once her father had retreated from sight. "Pa's just like that," she consoled, before she led Marigold away. "But we haven't got much time. I saw Tad's catboat cross Black Rock a while back."

Marigold took a deep breath. She could not crumble now. She was the incomparable Miss Manners, and she needed to act like a New Woman and not some shivering damsel in unreasoning distress. For Daisy's sake if not her own.

She had only a moment to calm her emotions, splash her face with cold water from the pump, and check her appearance as best she might in the reflection of the kitchen window before she joined Daisy on the path to North Cove. One problem at a time—she would deal with the garden later.

Daisy, she was pleased and relieved to notice, was dressed exactly as they had agreed, in a borrowed, freshly ironed, modern shirtwaist and sweeping skirt that hid her worn—but now well-polished—boots. She positioned herself precisely where they had rehearsed, within hailing distance in the deep shade of the woods, so she could act as if she had come upon the visitors unknowingly.

"Good morning," Marigold called with forced cheer as the graceful catboat slid onto the sand of North Cove.

"Good morning, Marigold." Cab vaulted from the bow across the surf line with athletically practiced ease. "I apologize for being so early."

"Not a'tall." She shook Cab's outstretched hand and had to belatedly steel herself against the warmth and intimacy of her palm and fingers fitted against his. To inure herself against the impulse to throw herself into his arms, lay her head against his starch-scented shirtfront, and beg him to solve all her problems.

Cab took advantage of their proximity to say in a quiet voice, "I had to come early. My uncle was none too pleased with the idea of me delivering your goods out here. Tad had to sneak off to join me, so we can't stay long before he'll be missed."

It restored some of Marigold's equanimity to find that even golden boys like Cab and Tad had their familial troubles—perhaps *some pumpkins* came at a comparable price to being *no-account*. "Thank you for taking such trouble to bring me my bicycle."

Tad was already unloading the smaller crate of books. Marigold would have assisted him, but Cab stayed her with that instinctive way he had of finding the soft spot of skin on the inside of her arm. "Marigold? What's wrong?"

"Nothing," she said automatically, before she could consider a better response. "I've just had a bit of a set-to with the overbearing paterfamilias, Ellery Hatchet. You know how families are," she quipped in an echo of his earlier words. "Nothing I can't handle."

But the truth hit her before she could finish the lie. The truth was that Ellery Hatchet's brand of distilled hatred was nothing she could handle, nothing she knew how to combat. Nothing she could change through her determined, practical tidying. Hatred of the kind that permeated the very earth of Hatchet Farm was well and truly beyond her scope.

It was going to take something far beyond cleaning and gardening.

Something she didn't know if she had in her to give.

CHAPTER 21

Get a bicycle. You will not regret it, if you live.
—Mark Twain

"Sure am sorry about your bicycle, Marigold." Tad's remark pulled her from her contemplation of her woes and directed her gaze toward the now-obvious fissure in the crate strapped athwart the sternsheets.

"Oh, no!" Dread leached back into her chest. "What happened?"

"Your machine is somewhat worse for wear, Marigold." Cab's concern was etched like a chasm between his brows. "I'm afraid it's been tampered with."

Tampered seemed such a tame word. "It looks as if someone took to it with a wrecking iron!"

"Or a claw hammer," Cab guessed. "I saw it off the end of the platform at the station when I arrived. Your name caught my eye." He passed his hand over the stenciled label to show where the raw wood had been gouged and cracked. "I intended to tell you yesterday, but . . ."

It was too much. Despite all her best intentions, everything was going wrong. One emotion piled atop the another until Marigold felt the heat of her unshed tears sting her eyes.

She tried to stave them off with righteous anger. "I shall have strict words with that confounded driver the next time I am in Pride's Crossing, see if I don't." But her throat felt so tight and raw, there was no hiding her misery.

"I already did." Cab laid a comforting hand to her shoulder.

"The nerve of the man!" Anger seemed a more productive emotion than this weeping distress. But in the midst of her outrage and upset, she could not forget her manners. "Thank you, Cab. You were very thoughtful to do so."

"Not at all." Cab began to untie the bindings that lashed the crate to the thwart. "I unscrewed the cover to take a look before I brought it along, and thankfully, other than the basket, which is unfortunately ruined, seems likely they were too damned lazy to do anything more than scuff the rest of the machine up. Your frame is nicked something fierce." He shook his head as if he could not fathom such malice.

And until five minutes ago, neither could she. But malice seemed to be all the rage in this part of the world.

The question she did not yet have an answer for was, what she was going to do about it? Was she going to give in to the inexplicably malevolent spirit of the place and tell Cab not to unload her machine, but to pack it up—the same way she was going to pack up her trunks and beg him to take her back to Boston?

Or was she the inimitable, accomplished Miss Marigold Manners, who had standards and a determined, logical character to uphold?

And Daisy was counting upon her—which recalled her to her object.

"I very much hope the tool kit I packed at the bottom of the excelsior is still there," she muttered, more to herself than anyone else. "If they haven't stolen that, I should be able to repair it." One would hardly call oneself a competent wheelwoman if one could not tend to one's own machine. "Let us open it up so we can find out."

Cab seemed to let out a breath. "You really are a wonder, Marigold."

"She is a wonder, isn't she?" Daisy appeared to wander down onto the beach to join the conversation as casually as a butterfly alighting upon an attractive flower. While Tad immediately doffed his hat in a bid for her attention, Daisy kept her warm smile focused on Cab, just as she had been instructed.

"Oh, Cab, may I introduce my dear cousin, Miss Daisy Hatchet?" Marigold took up her part. "Daisy, darling, this is my old friend Jonathan Cabot Cox."

"Mr. Cox." Daisy tucked her chin and looked up at Cab through soft eyes. "A vast pleasure to meet you."

And Cab, bless the poor man, was not immune—he unknowingly flattened his hat against his chest in wordless admiration. "My friends call me Cab, Miss Hatchet."

"And mine call me Daisy." The girl's smile somehow grew more luminous.

"Hey there, Daisy," Tad hastened to chime in. "Sure is good to see you." He rushed over to pump her hand while he beamed his admiration at her. "You're looking mighty fine."

Indeed, she was. Daisy looked every inch the epitome of Gibson Girl glamour, with her long blonde hair swept up into a loose chignon atop her head and a wistfully knowing expression on her lips.

"Aren't you kind." She blessed Tad with her soft smile. "Good morning, Mr. Endicott—Taddy." She lowered her voice to a breath of a whisper to pronounce his name before she retrieved her hand from his grip. "It's lovely to see you as well. Thank you so much for bringing my cousin's machine for her." Her voice was soft and sweet and just warm enough to encourage without being obvious. Perfectly calibrated to enchant. "I find myself quite curious to see it. Do you ride bicycles, Mr. Cox—Cab?"

"I do, Miss—" He fumbled briefly. "Miss Daisy. Not so well as Marigold here"—he seemed to recall her presence—"but I've enjoyed the exercise."

"And you, Mr. Endicott?" Marigold did her part to help the conversation along.

"Don't reckon I have," Tad was unhappy to answer. "Though I've seen them around Harvard Yard."

"Oh, Harvard!" Daisy sighed in wonder. "How marvelous. But don't feel too bad, Taddy. You can't do everything the best. You have to leave a little room for other people to do a thing or two nearly as well as you do."

The poor young man looked as if he couldn't figure out if he was being complimented or insulted—his smile filled his reddened face.

But Daisy, who was as clever a student as Marigold could ever have hoped, didn't leave him room to decide. "Oh, where are my manners. Wilbert, won't you come join us? And Seviah too." She gestured for her brothers—who had clearly followed the young women without Marigold being aware—to join them. "I understand you've already met Mr. Cox in town, Wilbert, but I don't believe you've been introduced to Mr. Endicott.

Mr. Thaddeus Endicott, these are my brothers, Mr. Wilbert Hatchet and Mr. Seviah Hatchet."

"Mr. Hatchet." Tad tipped his hat. "Seviah." He reached out a broad palm. "Been a while."

Seviah shook the hand Tad extended, nodding in response. "Tad. Reckon it has."

So Seviah already knew Tad? Marigold tucked that piece of information into the back of her brain for safekeeping.

"And Seviah, you must meet Mr. Cox," Daisy urged. "Mr. Cox is a friend of dear cousin Marigold's from Boston. Isn't that right, Mr. Cox?"

"Indeed." Cab extended his hand to both of her cousins in turn. "Mr. Hatchet, a pleasure to see you again. Seviah, very nice to meet you too. It's easy to see that you and Marigold are cousins."

"Is it?" Seviah answered with his usual brand of nonchalant defiance.

But Daisy was not going to let their carefully crafted agenda slip out of her control. "Marigold was just telling me last night that the last time she saw you, Mr. Cox, was at a lovely society dance back in Boston. Nothing is so lovely as a dance, is it? Marigold says you dance divinely."

"Well"—Cab had the grace to blush—"it's never a hardship to dance with a pretty girl."

"Oh, aren't you just the most gentlemanly fellow," Daisy attested. "I shall own it that you do dance as divinely as Marigold says you do everything—Oh, I shouldn't have said." Her cheeks obligingly stained themselves with a rosy blush that Marigold feared was mirrored on her own.

But any further revelation of feelings better left unexplored was interrupted by Tad, who broke in to declare, "Well, we're going to have a dance—a real one, for my twenty-first birthday. Mother's getting it all planned."

"Oh," Daisy breathed. "How lovely for you, Tad. I'm sure you'll dance superbly too."

Marigold didn't know when she had been prouder.

"Well, you ought to come, I reckon," Tad blustered, "and find out. Both of you." He pointed with his hat from Daisy to her. "All o' you." His gesture encompassed them all.

It was all faring better than Marigold could have hoped! She rewarded the young man with her warmest smile. "We would love to receive an invitation from your mother, if she would be so kind as to extend one. Wouldn't we, Daisy?"

"Oh, yes," her cousin agreed with a soft sigh. "Ever so kind."

"Well, that settles it, then," was Tad's satisfied answer. "I'll see to it that she does."

"Thank you, Mr. Endicott," Marigold was happy to add. "We'd—"

"What goes on here?" Ellery Hatchet made his untimely reappearance, bursting out of the woods like a rabid animal.

Marigold's heart began to pound in her ears as Ellery billy-goated his way into the middle of the group in what she feared was going to be a repeat of his earlier behavior. She was about to step in front of Daisy to shield her from her father's aggression when it was Daisy who stepped up to shield Marigold. "Now, Pa—"

"Who in the name of the Almighty are you?" Ellery peered hard at Cab before he switched his malignant glare to Tad. "I recognize you. You're Satan's spawn, you're an Endicott!" Ellery all but spat the name on the ground. "Get thee behind me, Satan!" Ellery bellowed and made as if he would take up his ever-present spade to strike the young man, but Wilbert and Seviah somehow hauled their father back before he could raise his backswing.

"Oh, Pa!" Daisy's voice shook from some too-familiar combination of embarrassment and anger. "Why do you have to spoil everything? Please accept my apology, Mr. Endicott. I reckon it's time for us to let you all get along home." She immediately began to push their catboat back into the water. "Mr. Cox, thank you so very much for your assistance to Cousin Marigold. We're indebted to your kindness."

"Yes, thank you, Cab." Marigold offered her own hasty goodbyes. "And Tad. As you fellows would say, I'm much obliged."

"Happy to help, Marigold." Cab shook her hand briefly before his gaze swung toward Ellery Hatchet. "Are you sure you're all right here?"

She heard the concern in his voice and thrilled to it—how wonderful it was to have someone care about her well-being. How tempting it was to share her worries and fears about Ellery's ugly threats. How lovely it might be to be sheltered from any potential harm.

But her pride was a dreadful, monstrous thing that found a sharp-enough sliver of pity in his voice to wound her. "Safe as houses," Marigold lied. Because she was the independent, accomplished, incomparable Miss Marigold Manners, and even if she had misgivings, she had a purpose.

If she let herself rely upon Cab to escape her present predicament, how was she going to look at herself in the mirror? And if she were gone from Great Misery, who was going to give two figs about her cousins? Who was going to help them discover what made them happy?

No one but her.

She was determined. For Daisy's and Wilbert's and Seviah's sake, if not for her own. See if she wasn't.

CHAPTER 22

I am suffocated and lost if I have not the bright feeling of progression.
—Margaret Fuller

Marigold returned to the garden after Cab and Tad's departure only to find the beds had already been salvaged. Herbs had been tamped back down and damaged plants pruned back and staked up with twine, and the soil was damp from watering with laboriously toted pails of water from the pump.

"Thank you, Cleon," she called to the old man. He had even left a gift of a new plant, a tall spike of beautifully speckled pink bells. "How kind."

"A pretty plant for a pretty lady," he said as he shuffled away with his fishing pole.

Marigold was cheered by this evidence of goodwill and was kept from any further contemplation of the evils of her predicament that afternoon when Daisy brought fresh intelligence about the party.

The celebration of Thaddeus Endicott's twenty-first birthday was to be held on the grounds of the Endicotts' expansive summer estate, Rock Ledge—the very estate Daisy had gazed at with such longing.

Marigold felt herself to be on firmly solid ground. If she could accomplish this one thing for Daisy, teach her that she had every right to make herself happy with Tad Endicott—or anyone else her beautiful cousin might fancy—Marigold could leave Hatchet Farm with her head held high.

Daisy was, as might be expected, in raptures. "Oh, I about swooned when he said he would invite us. Isn't he just the sweetest?" She sighed in wonder. "Isn't he just the handsomest boy you ever saw?"

"Very handsome," Marigold agreed, while making a mental note to include more of the precautionary arts in Daisy's schooling. "But we are not invited yet." And getting an invitation out of Mrs. George C. Endicott was not going to be easy—the party was a little over a week away, and Marigold was sure Mrs. Endicott had sent out all the invitations she had meant to send. "And I do want to warn you, as the host, Tad will be obliged to dance with a great number of other young ladies. It won't do if you're jealous."

"Jealous?" Daisy seemed genuinely astonished at the idea. "I don't reckon I ever thought of that. Ought I to be?"

"No." Marigold felt more than a twinge at having suspected such an artless girl of being in any way involved in any young woman's drowning. But Daisy's innocence also gave her a new goal—to increase her acquaintance with more young ladies in town. "You're an absolute lamb—but a lamb who needs to practice her response, should the invitation arrive. *Miss Daisy Hatchet accepts with pleasure,*" she dictated, "*on behalf of herself, her brothers, Mr. Wilbert Hatchet and Mr. Seviah Hatchet, the kind invitation of Mrs. Endicott, for the evening of May fifth, 1894.*"

"I've got to say all that just to say, yes, please?" Daisy said in wonder. "Fancy that!"

"Just the right kind of fancy—the correct kind," Marigold explained. "Because you want to serve notice to Tad's mother that you are every bit equal and indeed suitable to be Tad's bride, don't you?"

"Oh, I do," the girl swore.

"Then you must practice your penmanship." Marigold's feelings about penmanship remained quite strict. "A fine hand is seen as the indication of a fine mind and finer feelings, which you have in abundance and only need to refine."

"You think Will and Sev oughta to be our escorts and not the dee-vine Mr. Cab Cox?"

"Ought to," Marigold corrected. "Yes." She was enough in possession of herself to quash the ridiculous pang of illogical emotion attempting to rear its head at the mention of Cab's name and answered Daisy with equanimity. "Cab will surely have received his own invitation." And he might be kind enough to include Marigold. But Cab's decisions were not the point. "I think Wilbert and Seviah will greatly enjoy—and benefit from—the entertainment."

And Seviah especially would fill out an evening suit nicely, which would hopefully go a long way toward winning the favor of the town's daughters. Handsome young men prepared to dance with the wallflowers would be a boon to Mrs. Endicott's entertainment—if Marigold could finagle them suits.

"Oh! I know—" Daisy jumped up in excitement. "We can trade the invitation for borrowing Sev's gramophone, so you can teach me how to dance properly."

"Seviah has a gramophone?" Marigold had never heard any music in the house—though Seviah did seem to know all the popular vaudeville tunes.

"He's got it hidden up at the top of the barn. Thinks I don't know, but that's where he goes at night to listen to his songs after everyone else is abed."

For once, a useful secret. "Excellent. I will seek out Seviah and his hidden gramophone in the morning before I go to town."

"I can't believe your moxie in going across so often," Daisy exclaimed. "But can you get me a dress when you go there? Or let me borrow one of yours? I don't know how to sew anything so fine as what might impress Taddy's folks."

"No, I will not buy you a dress in Pride's Crossing nor let you borrow one, for everything I have is last season, which might be good enough most of the time. But this is not most of the time—this is special, in the grand ballroom of the grandest estate on the North Shore. But"—Marigold smiled to stave off Daisy's disappointment—"I have a plan. Let us get you into a decent, modern corset so I can take your measurements properly, which I will wire to my friend I told you about, Isabella Dana."

"The coo-tur-ee-yay?" Daisy sounded the word out carefully to get it right.

"The very one. She will know exactly what is called for on the occasion of a celebratory birthday supper dance given by Mrs. George C. Endicott." Isabella's encyclopedic knowledge of society could be counted on to establish the correct degree of deference in dress to please their hostess. And perhaps also find them a way in.

"But how are we going to pay for a dress from the House of Dana? I ain't got no actual."

"Haven't got any ready money," Marigold corrected her. "You let me worry about that. And it will not be a dress but a gown—an evening gown," she clarified. A stunning gown that would cement in partygoers' minds the image of the Hatchets as people of so much account that Daisy would appear to belong not only at the dance but also at Tad's side.

The truth of which Marigold was growing more confident. Daisy was proving an apt pupil of both elocution and vocabulary as well as in poise and self-assurance. While her young cousin was by no means fully a New Woman, she was affording herself more than enough self-respect to make Marigold proud.

Wilbert was also working studiously on self-improvement with his reading and writing. In fact, Marigold might soon need to combine her study sessions with her cousins into one, especially if Seviah and his gramophone were to be brought within their secret circles.

Marigold found her younger male cousin quite easily the next morning—all she had to do was set to repairing her damaged bicycle in one of the empty stalls in the barn and he appeared, drawn like a moth to the machine's modern, unconventional flame.

"That your bicycle, then?" Seviah slouched against the empty stall door.

"It is indeed. Isn't she a beauty?" Marigold had not quite felt her modern self without her own mode of independent transportation, and after yesterday morning, she was more anxious than ever to be able to be able to escape the oppressive atmosphere of the farm.

Luckily, her machine was not so badly damaged as either she or Cab had feared; although the creel basket was hopelessly crushed, the mainframe of the bicycle had suffered only minor scratches, which she would soon repair with a fresh application of black enamel paint. Which she would buy as soon as she got to town.

She finished mounting the handlebars onto the front tube as Seviah sauntered close enough to thumb the clapper of the bell. "Fancy."

"Yes, she is, my darling Victoria, queen of the safety bicycles."

"Safety bicycle? Doesn't look particularly safe, if you ask me."

"Oh, it's not," she agreed. "Riding it is still pleasurably dangerous. One can achieve speeds perilous enough to exhilarate." She smiled as she tested the brake levers and then moved on to lubricating the drive chain to keep the gear teeth meshing silently with the sprockets before she was satisfied enough to resecure the all-important chain guard—Marigold preferred more stylish split skirts to bloomers and took great care to mount the chain and wheel guards so her hems would not become fouled in the mechanism.

"Look at you," Seviah marveled, "all mechanical and all that."

"Look at me," she repeated with a smile as she secured the nuts. "And . . . look at me now!" She rolled the bicycle past her astonished cousin and mounted on the fly to pedal around the farmyard, testing out her adjustments.

"Look at you!" Seviah echoed before he broke into song. "*And you'll look sweet, upon the seat of a bicycle built*—for one!"

"What a marvelous voice you have, Seviah!" she encouraged, loving the joyous relief of pedaling her bicycle and wanting the moment to last. "Sing me the rest."

Seviah obliged with a laughing rendition of the popular tune. "*Daisy, Daisy*—but you're a *Marigold, Marigold*," he corrected himself before he continued. "*Give me your answer, do. I'm half-crazy over the love of you.*"

Lucy joined in from the water pump, and the harmonization of their two voices was sublime enough to make Marigold brake to a stop just to listen. "*It won't be a stylish marriage, I can't afford a carriage. But you'll look sweet upon the seat of a bicycle built for two.*"

"That was wonderful—as good as any music hall I've ever heard. Your talents are wasted here!" She said it to be kind and encouraging and honest all at the same time, but the moment the words passed her lips, she got the same sort of strange tingling quiet inside that she had felt when she first received Cousin Sophronia's letter—and when she realized Thaddeus Endicott was Daisy's Taddy. "Do you two sing together often?"

"Don't be ridiculous," Seviah scoffed. But there was something about the speed and vehemence of his response that made her think she might have struck a nerve.

"Have you ever thought of singing professionally, Seviah?"

He was less vehement but no less cagey. He threw up that defensive shrug. "Dunno."

"What about you, Lucy?" Marigold tried to keep Lucy from shying off. "Ever thought of it?"

"Don't suppose I have," Lucy answered carefully. "I do like singing with the choir at my momma's church when I can get over there. It's too far to go to town every Sunday, and anyways, Miz Alva likes her morning vittles special on Sundays." She exchanged an enigmatic look with Seviah before turning back toward her cabin. "But I got a job up here I'm meant to do, so I best get to it."

Meant to do was interesting language—it implied a hand not her own was pulling Lucy's strings. But who was the puppet master? Seviah had sauntered some small distance away to give the impression that it was certainly not he, but Marigold was not so sure.

But that was a thought for another day. Today, there was the freedom of the bicycle to be enjoyed and that time-sensitive wire to be sent to Isabella. And a gramophone to secure.

"Seviah! How should you like to escort Daisy to a dance in town?"

"What, now?" he laughed.

"No, in a week's time. At a summer estate. I'll vouchsafe you a dinner suit to wear."

"Could you?" He tried to couch his eagerness in a sort of jaded aloofness. "From that Harvard fellow, the one who sailed himself up here to impress you?"

"Actually, I asked him up here so his cousin, Tad Endicott, might impress Daisy, and she him."

"Them two's after 'impressing' each other—if that's what you can call it—for months now," Seviah scoffed.

"You know about Daisy and Tad?" Clearly, the Hatchets were better at ferreting out each other's secrets than she. "Then you'll agree to help her and go to the dance, and dance with her?"

"And dance with you?"

"Naturally, you shall also dance with me." Marigold saw her opening. "But I shall want something from you in return for the privilege."

For a moment he looked surprised, before he covered his expression with his usual wolfish leer. "And what do you fancy, Miss Frosty Boston Manners?"

"Your gramophone."

"Shh!" He clamped a hand over her mouth. "Who told you I've got a Berliner?"

Marigold tried to mumble around his palm. "Daisy."

"And how did she know?" He lowered his hand.

"Perhaps you're not so secretive as you—either of you—think," Marigold teased. But he looked so very nearly apoplectic that she quickly added, "But we're not about to tell anyone else, if that's your worry. We just want to play your gramophone so I can teach Daisy the latest dances in preparation for Tad's birthday party."

"You know all the latest dances, then?"

"I do. Or at least I did two weeks ago, but I don't think the fashion in dances has changed much since then."

"And you'll teach me and dance with me too?"

"Certainly." She ought to have anticipated that Seviah might know the music but not the steps. And that he was not as sophisticated or experienced with the world as he might want her to think—or as he clearly longed to be.

"And you'll really get me a fancy monkey suit, like those polished fellows in the traveling revues? Like that Barrymore swell?"

"Indeed." Marigold had seen Mr. Maurice Barrymore perform at Boston's Athenaeum Theater just last year but wondered how Seviah might have seen such a performer, who was not likely to have played on the sort of circuit that chanced through Pride's Crossing. "You're a handsome young man, Seviah. Indeed, you'll look quite the matinee idol. All the girls are sure to find you irresistible. But handsome is as handsome does, and you won't do a thing—or get the invitation to that dance—if you don't share your gramophone."

"It's yours!" he swore. "I got a little spot fixed up in the barn for the gramo, right and tight under the eaves, away from Pa and Granny. I don't get the Berliner cranked up unless I know the old man's asnore."

"Then we'll hope for an early bedtime, shall we, and meet you there later tonight?"

"You do that." He broke into a satisfied smile. "Look at you, making private arrangements and keeping secrets. We might make a Hatchet out of you after all."

CHAPTER 23

All the knowledge I possess everyone else can acquire,
but my heart is all my own.
—Johann Wolfgang von Goethe

Marigold's impromptu bicycle ride over the pockmarked paths criss-crossing the island began with a rush of pleasure so sharp she found herself laughing out loud at the simple joy of movement, but it ended the moment she spied Ellery Hatchet ahead with that long-handled spade over his shoulder.

She immediately dismounted, edging herself into the stand of birch trees so as to be as inconspicuous as possible. She might say it was easier to ask for forgiveness than permission, but it was easier still to avoid asking for anything at all.

And the awful, cold truth was, Ellery Hatchet terrified her.

He was pacing up and down along the low boggy spot where the woods met the shore—precisely where she and Cleon had shoveled up the sandy sediment for the garden. Hatchet was muttering to himself as he kicked the sandy earth to and fro, much as he had her garden, but she could not make out his ravings—whatever he said was lost to the wind.

Though she was rabidly curious, she kept herself resolutely still, afraid he would sense her presence or hear her heart pounding like a blacksmith's anvil. But when he was finally done venting his spleen, he tromped off, out of sight.

Relief left her drained. Marigold remounted in an unseemly rush, putting as much distance as possible between them as quickly as she could. But she could not escape the questions that revolved through her mind like a card catalog.

What could he have been looking for in such a spot? What had she overlooked? And what on earth was he always trying to dig up with that omnipresent spade?

But the feeling of needing distance—both emotional and geographical—pushed her across the beach to the dory, and without a second thought, she stowed her bicycle in the bow and put her back into the long pull. Fortunately, both wind and tide were in her favor, pushing her across the sound without too much exertion, so Marigold felt both rewarded for her choice and invigorated and reassuringly sporty as she pedaled through the placid streets of Pride's Crossing, very much enjoying the sight of the townspeople goggling at her beautiful bicycle.

By the time she had reached the library, a small pack of children were clamoring in her wake. "Yes, this is my bicycle, and no, you may not ride it. But I will pay you"—she picked out the tallest, most capably older-sisterish of the girls—"in penny candy to keep my machine safe and not let anyone else touch it."

The girl was delighted to be given license to boss. "You heard miss—no touching."

Marigold waved to Miss Morgan, who had come to the window along with a number of other patrons but was back behind the circulation desk by the time Marigold made her way inside.

"Good afternoon, Miss Manners." Amelia Morgan adjusted her spectacles. "What a beautiful machine."

"Thank you." Marigold made sure not to preen under such warm regard. "Do you cycle, Miss Morgan?"

"Alas, I have not yet had that pleasure."

"Then perhaps we can find a time of mutual convenience when I might show you the machine and teach you to ride?"

"Would you?" Amelia Morgan's face lit with astonished hope. "That would be marvelous."

"It would be my pleasure." There was more way than one way to make friends and bring townspeople—especially the young female townspeople—over to her way of thinking and prepare the way for Daisy. "Perhaps we might even form a Ladies' Cycling Club."

Miss Morgan's cheeks went pink with delight. "Oh my, what a stir that would make!"

"Miss Manners is well used to making a stir, aren't you, Marigold?"

Marigold turned to find long, tall Cab Cox filling the library's wide, arched doorway.

"Oh, Mr. Cox!" Miss Morgan's voice went breathless with suppressed excitement. "What can we do for you this afternoon, sir?"

"Miss Morgan, ma'am." Cab swept his hat from his head and tucked it beneath the arm of his somehow immaculate flannel spring suit, oblivious of his effect upon the poor woman. "I suppose I had to see what all the fuss was all about. I should have known it would be our Marigold."

"Our Marigold?" Poor Amelia Morgan sounded as if she might strangle on her disappointment.

Marigold decided to gift her with hope. "Mr. Cox and I are merely old collegiate friends, Miss Morgan. I do believe I've known Cab since he was in leading strings."

"Whereas no one has ever led Marigold about, not even when she was two years old."

"You flatter me, Cab."

And there was that charming, self-aware smile winching up one corner of his mouth. "I'll admit to trying. Might you have a spare minute to walk with me?"

"Yes, of course." She camouflaged her curiosity in politeness. "Let me just return my books." Marigold passed the small stack of primers she had copied into her own notebook over the counter. "Thank you, Miss Morgan. I'll be in touch about the cycling club."

"Yes, thank you, Miss Manners. I'd like nothing more."

"Making friends everywhere you go, Marigold?" Cab remarked as he held the door for her.

"Naturally." She fished the promised candy out of her pocket for the budding young extortionist in pigtails, who had likely been charging the congregated urchins a penny each to touch the bike—but who was Marigold to quash such an entrepreneurial spirit, especially in a young female?

"Let's head for the wire office, if you don't mind." She wheeled her bicycle along the sidewalk. "I've an urgent request for Isabella—an appropriate gown for Daisy for the Endicotts' dance. If she receives an invitation." Marigold stopped to focus what she hoped was the full force of her panache on Cab. "I'm hoping you can give me more information about your cousin.

He's told Daisy that he's a journeyman, but given his family name, I doubt that's true. Care to save me the indiscretion of asking Isabella?"

Cab smiled. "He likes to tell people he's a journeyman—a journeyman journalist, because he has been paying his dues and working his way up in the New York papers, where the Endicott name isn't so well-known as it would be in Boston. But truth be told, he's planning on taking the money that's about to come to him on his majority to start a magazine that I think is going to be a big success."

"You'd bet on him, would you?"

"I would," Cab answered without hesitation.

"Is he sincere and not just playing fast and loose with Daisy because she's poor?"

"Not Tad. I'd stake my life on it."

"Then that is good enough for me." Marigold's sense of responsibility was satisfied—for the moment. "I've a second request—might I prevail upon you to be Daisy's escort for the party?" She would work things out with Seviah later—after she was sure she had secured the invitation for Daisy.

Cab's expression was both surprised and unhappy. "I'll admit I was hoping to invite you, Marigold. After yesterday morning—"

"Why, thank you, Cab." If she had secretly been hoping the same, she ignored the ridiculous little frisson of pleasure that sighed across her skin in favor of a more careless sort of enthusiasm. "I would normally accept with alacrity—you do dance divinely." And she would quash the tiny shard of jealousy needling at her brain at the thought of him dancing with all the town's eligible young women—Amelia Morgan deserved not to be disappointed. "But I'm prepared to make the sacrifice of your exceptional company if you will instead escort Daisy. I should so hate to see her disappointed or shamed by not receiving an invitation. And if she's escorted by you, I know she won't be a wallflower without support."

"Oh, I doubt she'll be a wallflower," Cab said. "Tad seems quite taken with her."

"But your cousin will be the guest of honor and a host, and will have more pressing obligations than to dance with a beautiful but socially inconsequential girl. Which is why my plan is for you to make her the belle of the ball."

"Naturally, you have a plan." He turned that wry smile on her. "Happy to help as much as I'm able."

"Oh, thank you." Marigold reached for his sleeve in gratitude. "You're an absolute lamb."

"Not entirely a lamb," he objected, before he covered her hand with his own. "I shall want a favor of my own in recompense."

That little shiver of excitement slid deeper, under her skin. She made sure to answer in a self-possessed tone. "And what shall you want in return?"

His smile was so slow and subtly subversive, Marigold felt her breath still in anticipation.

"I'm not sure yet," he finally answered. "But I'm sure I'll think of something."

"Naturally." Marigold decided she didn't care if her voice had gone slightly stupid and breathy before she shook off the languid feeling in favor of more practical considerations. "In the meantime, I will make arrangements with Isabella for the perfect dress, so you can be assured that Daisy won't embarrass you."

"Under your tutelage, I could not conceive of such a thing." He smiled down at her in that way he had of making her feel like the best part of herself. Gracious, he was a wonderfully tall-boned man.

Marigold strove to return her thoughts to better-regulated order. "I suppose I must let you return to your lawyering. How goes your case—a dispute about your uncle's land, was it?"

"That's it," he confirmed. "Truth is, once I began to look into the particulars, I found out there really is no case to be made. The circuit and appellate courts had already rendered judgment that the deed was transferred fair and square some fifty years ago. My uncle wanted me to find some grounds for an appeal, but I could find none."

Trust Cab to do what was right instead of what was convenient for his uncle. "And that made him unhappy with you."

"Naturally." Cab's smile was somehow both so sweet and so subtly derisive that Marigold felt again all the force of her illogical attraction. He really was a formidably rational, attractively handsome man.

"As you predicted, he didn't care for my opinion," he admitted. "And he didn't mind letting me know, especially after our trip out to see you. Said what use was a Harvard law degree if I didn't know how to make the law do my bidding? And then he told me to get out of his house. So I have." He spread his arms in a gesture of chagrin. "So here I am, *not* doing what was expected of me this time." He shook his head at the strange wonder of it. "But I'm satisfied knowing I did the right thing."

Cab really was *such* a man. "As am I," she agreed. "But what does that mean for the party—are you still invited?"

"My Aunt Julia assured me my uncle's *cholers*, as she called his denouncement, were the product of the moment and would pass. So I've taken temporary rooms at a boardinghouse—though I'm told it's on the wrong side of the railroad tracks, I've also been assured it has the best kitchen."

"Dare I hope that means you are residing with Mrs. Bessie Dove, who is also a new friend of mine?"

"Trust you to have gotten there before me, Marigold. And yes, I am happily ensconced at Mrs. Dove's." He turned that formidable focus upon her. "And what about you? I'll admit to being worried about you, after meeting old man Hatchet. When do you think you'll return to Boston? Or your studies?"

"Oh," she said airily, as if she hadn't soothed herself to sleep last night with thoughts of resuming her archaeological studies. "I have no other plans at present. My cousins give me plenty of scope for occupation."

"Your cousins and not your mythology? Does that mean Isabella was right and you're tidying them up and making them over to your requirements?"

Marigold was going to have words with Isabella. "She would be doing the same, were she in my shoes—only Isabella would be making over their wardrobes instead of teaching them to read."

"Is that what you're doing? I thought you'd be teaching them to dance," Cab teased as he steered Marigold around two boys pasting up waybills for a religious revival on the brick wall of the druggist. "Far more practical."

"I assure you," Marigold rejoined, "I can do both at the same time."

"But not write your book?"

Damn him for being so insightful. "Practical considerations before the theoretical. And I only just recovered my books and notes from you yesterday morning."

"True." He stopped and looked down at her for a long moment before he tugged the brim of his hat. "You know, speaking of Isabella, I wonder if she might be the solution to both our problems."

There was something in his tone that prompted her to tease, "Do you need evening clothing as well?"

"No," he laughed. "I have dinner suits to spare. But let us both wire Isabella with our requests. But a word to the wise—I wouldn't get your hopes up."

"About Isabella, or about the party?"

"The party. I mean to warn you that there are other forces in play here—things that happened long before you or I came to the North Shore or were even born. So don't be surprised if all your plans come to naught, Marigold. There are some things—some minds—that won't be changed, no matter what you do."

Marigold took in the weight of this latest warning and made a decision. The time had come to ask for a different sort of help. "Then I should like your help acquiring a gun."

CHAPTER 24

We judge others by their actions, but ourselves by our intentions.
—Ralph Waldo Emerson

Her wire sent, Marigold tried to exercise her doubts and bolster her spirits by cutting a stylish picture as she pedaled back to the boat in time to catch the outgoing tide.

She had made progress on a number of fronts—though for others, not for herself. But progress was progress. Until it wasn't.

The moment Marigold remounted her bicycle on the twisting path through the island's woods, she was confronted by Ellery Hatchet himself. She debated keeping a safe distance, but he had already seen her—and Ellery Hatchet was a bully whose intimidation needed to be met head-on.

"Cousin Ellery." She greeted him coolly despite her hot palms.

"No cousin of yourn," he groused, looking askance at her bicycle. "What in thunderation is that infernal machine?"

"It is a bicycle," Marigold said, careful to keep both the machine and several yards of safe distance between them. She had no desire to goad him into another tirade, especially when no one else was there to keep him from physical violence.

He squinted his eyes in disapproval. "How in tarnation can that contraption stay upright if it can't balance on its own?"

Though Marigold was sure nothing she might say about the physics of propulsion would penetrate the wall of superstitious nonsense Ellery had built to keep out logic, her determined nature prompted her to try. "The chain drive exerts the force derived from the energy of my feet on the pedals to—"

"Serpentry, if you ask me. A menace, that thing is. As are you upon it. A heathen, no-account menace, showing your ankles."

As she had not asked him and was not showing any part of herself, clad in her well-polished bicycling boots, Marigold decided she might ignore his words the way he had ignored hers—though she would no longer ignore the fright she felt in his presence.

But gauging the distance between them gave her a narrow moment to observe that Ellery was dressed not in his usual grimy, soiled shirt and pants but in a rather cleaner, Sunday-go-to-meeting sort of suit. "You're all togged up, as Wilbert would say."

"I was to go preaching," he admitted. "Over to the Grange Hall, which lets the space every other Friday to meet and worship in the primitive faith, just as we ought."

Marigold did not want to enter into a discussion of faith—or lack thereof—but gauged it preferable to an investigation of where the boat that was to have taken him across to said Grange Hall might have been. "And how did your preaching go over?"

"Whatta you mean, go over?"

"I mean," Marigold explained, "how do your congregants like your sermons?"

"Didn't get to give it. The Lord saw fit to keep me from the water." He trudged unhappily up his side of the path. "But it doesn't matter what they like, they got to hear it. They got to understand they're sinners, every last lot of 'em, all iniquity and endless damnation. They're doomed to the fires of hell."

"So, in your belief, there is no room for redemption or forgiveness?"

"Only God can forgive. And only God will decide whether you're doomed or not. But we're camels before the eye of the needle, the Bible says. Doomed," he confirmed.

"I see." Marigold nodded politely, without any agreement. "And do you have a large congregation?"

His mouth turned down in sour admission. "I have a few."

"Less than ten?" she probed.

"Nyah." The word was a grumbled sound of neither admission nor defeat. "It's of no account. They're sinners whether they want to hear the word or not."

"I see," she said again, though at present she did not see—neither the point of Ellery's fruitless mission nor what she might do about it. "Perhaps your talents are wasted here," she added as a convenient sop to his pride, but the moment she said the words, the advertisement for the tent revival on the side wall of the druggist leapt into her mind's eye.

That same tingle of awareness she had felt that morning with Seviah resumed with a clamor—as if something within her had decided that Ellery needed her help as much as any other of the Hatchets—although she would be solving many of the others' problems too.

Can't ask you to clear out the place, can I?

"Have you ever thought of perhaps joining a tent revival to preach to a larger audience?" Marigold ventured. "I saw a waybill posted in Pride's Crossing about a religious revival taking place outside of Manchester—"

Hatchet made such a sound of derisive negation that she assumed he had no interest, but when they reached the barn, Ellery loomed close. "What was that tent whatsit you said?" he demanded. "What was it, now?"

Marigold instinctively stepped away to keep the threat that radiated off him like body odor at bay. "I believe the tent revival to be a traveling circuit of religious speakers," she said carefully, "who band together to take their message of faith to the people, wherever they might be, in this grand, expansive country of ours."

"And where did you say it was to be?"

"Manchester, Cousin Ellery."

"How many times I got to tell ye—you're no relation of mine!" But with that last piece of spite spent, Ellery Hatchet stomped away.

"Old man making friendly, was he?" Seviah teased from the ladder to the hayloft. "Wasting your breath with that one."

"Perhaps," Marigold agreed as the hectic pounding of her heart eased enough that she might be logical. "But I have better hopes for you."

★ ★ ★

The assignation with the "gramo"—and where had Seviah picked up slang like that?—did not commence until well after eleven o'clock at night, when the rest of the house had gone quiet and dark. Even Wilbert had finished off his writing exercises and taken himself off to his own room after refusing Marigold's whispered invitation to join them.

"That's not for me," he had said, shaking his head. "You already done me my good turn. You go on and do a turn for Daisy and Sev."

Accordingly, Marigold and Daisy tiptoed their silent way past Cleon, who was asleep, facedown upon the kitchen table. The thin moonlight was their only guide, but Daisy, who had clearly been sneaking out of the house for some time, knew her way and led Marigold unerringly through the darkened barn. "Sev?"

"Up here," Seviah's voice coaxed from high in the loft, but as Marigold clambered onto the bottom rung of the ladder, she could not shake the now-familiar, but nevertheless eerie, feeling that she was being watched.

She turned back to check the path behind, but there was no movement from the dark windows of the bleak house, no sound but the gentle lap of waves against the shore.

And yet the feeling persisted.

"Come on." Seviah broke the hold of Marigold's overactive imagination. "Up here."

When she emerged at the top of the ladder, Seviah's small safety lantern illuminated a makeshift room fashioned like a tent from canvas, burlap, and swags of circus-bright fabric—a surprisingly theatrical inner sanctum situated behind a wall made of thick bales of hay. Marigold's imaginings of her own excavation tent in Greece seemed decidedly drab in comparison.

"Boy howdy," was Daisy's exclamation of wonder.

Marigold settled for, "Seviah, I am all admiration." As well as all trepidation—it seemed an entirely flammable lair for a young man who liked to play with matches. The hay was old and so dry it crumbled to the touch.

"I fashioned it up pretty thick." Seviah patted a bale with more than a little pride. "With tarpaulins hung for walls and the door, so no light gets out and the sound gets muffled up." He lit a second shuttered safety lantern that illuminated the small square wooden box and large shellacked horn of the Berliner gramophone.

"I got rags and banjo music." He showed them his tidy collection of black rubberized recording disks. "And a turkey trot, a polka, a gavotte and a schottische, and two waltzes—the Belle of New York and the Aphrodite—for dancing. And songs, too, like they sing at the revues, like 'The Girls I Left Behind.' All the hits."

There was something in his phrasing—and a giddy sort of excitement in his voice. And Marigold noted that he had a second separate stack of disks.

far more faith in my own logic and determination than in the vagaries of inanimate objects which are only invested with *your* desires, not mine. So the question here is not whether I should believe you but why *you* clearly wish some terrible experience to befall me. Why, Sophronia, why? Why try to scare the wits out of me at two o'clock in the morning instead of talking to me like a reasonable, rational human being during the light of day? What is your intent?"

"I've said what I've said—"

"—and you'll say no more." Marigold stood back and crossed her arms over her chest. "So you've said, several times. And yet you persist in dropping these eerie little bon mots at all hours of the night and day. Why?"

Sophronia's answer was a thin whisper. "Because I don't know what else to do."

Marigold refused to be disarmed. "What to do about what?"

Sophronia's gaze went shiny and soft before a single tear slipped down her cheek. "About all the years gone. All the evil done before."

"My dear cousin." Despite herself, Marigold was filled with a weary sort of pity. "I know I said the past was not a package one could lay away, but neither must one tote it about endlessly like a heavy suitcase."

"No, no." Sophronia shook her head. "You don't understand."

"No, I don't," Marigold agreed. "And you are the only one who can help me to understand. So why won't you?"

"I—" Sophronia stopped and started and, in the end, only pushed a single card toward Marigold. "The Hanged Man."

The card in question looked hand drawn in pen and ink with watercolors, depicting a bound man hanging by his feet from a scaffold.

Despite the fright and revulsion that gripped her, Marigold made her tone cold. "And what do you suggest this upside-down fool means to me, Cousin?"

This time Sophronia laid her cold hand over Marigold's. "There is a painful sacrifice waiting here, Esmie's girl." She fingered the card. "Wisdom that comes at a cost."

"And what is that cost?"

Sophronia finally looked away. "Something I fear none of us can afford to pay."

Chapter 25

Let me tell you what I think of bicycling. I think it has done more to emancipate women than anything else in the world.

—Susan B. Anthony

Try as she might, Marigold could not dismiss the haunting image of the Hanged Man from her mind. Nor forget the strange sort of desperation Sophronia had conveyed—as if she were actually worried about Marigold's well-being. As if she really didn't want Marigold to end up like *them girls*.

And then there were the flowers—day after day, the little jam jar next to her bed was replenished with fresh rosemary and wildflowers. Their conversation in the garden—though it had yielded no useful information about the wrong done Marigold's mother—had revealed Sophronia's affinity for the language of flowers. Rosemary was for remembrance, her cousin had said— and she was quite purposefully leaving sprigs for Marigold in her room. But what—or who—was Marigold supposed to remember? And what were the other flora—today it was a delicate, heart-shaped fern—supposed to mean?

Was it more fortune-telling from Sophronia, reading her tarot and embers? *I saw it in the flames with my own ruined eyes. The curse will work its way.*

Superstitious nonsense! The sooner Marigold was done with Great Misery, the better. And she would be done as soon as she got the Hatchet siblings free from the repressive hold of their lunatic—

Outside the open window, her eye was caught by the astonishing sight of a neat little naptha launch sailing across her view, it's gay, striped awning dancing in the breeze as the eye-catching vessel came about some small distance off the point. And on that launch was a fashionably dressed woman, peering at the island though a telescopic glass—Isabella.

Naturally. First Cab and now Isabella—it was a wonderful thing to have friends one could rely upon.

Marigold waved elatedly and then gestured for the boat to proceed around the island to the west while she hastily retrieved her bicycle and made for North Cove, where the shallow vessel could safely put in on the sand.

"Isabella, you darling!" she called as she wheeled her bike down the beach. "What are you doing here?"

Isabella answered with a wave. "I've come to rescue you from the primitive. And not a moment too soon, from what I could see! Is the House of Usher open?"

Marigold laughed. "Absolutely not. You could have just written."

"You didn't think I was going to let a gown from the House of Dana be fitted by some two-bit country seamstress, did you? And for a party given by Julia Stuyvesant Endicott of the New York Stuyvesants and Salem Endicotts? I had to come myself, of course, and make sure about all the particulars you left out of your wire. Has she deigned to send you an invitation?"

"No." Marigold was both relieved and reassured that Isabella grasped the important particulars so readily. "But now that you are here, I'm sure we can overcome that hurdle. It is absolutely smashing to see you."

"And you as well, darling. Boston felt so dreadfully dull without your particular sort of panache. But you look a treat, despite"—she waved at their rural surroundings—"all the primitive. Dare I ask?"

Marigold gave her friend the gift of being right. "Primitive does, indeed, denote a lack of plumbing."

"Vindication," Isabella cried with a laugh. "The place looked ready to collapse down around your head. But no matter, you're safe now that I've come to take you away. Although why Cab didn't do that the moment he found you, I'll never understand."

"Because he knows I value my independence," Marigold answered. "And because I can't come away at present, although I will happily come aboard and let you serve me lunch so we can decide what's to be done about Mrs. Julia Stuyvesant Endicott."

Isabella's smile was delightfully conspiratorial. "But I've already arranged the answer. Emily Brinley Ryerson—you'll remember

Bunny—platinum-white hair, suffragette, piles of money for women's causes? Such a dear. Well, Bunny and I were finished together at Miss Porter's, and she and Bump Ryerson have got a lovely summer place just up the coastline from the George Endicotts, and she sent a note round to Julia that I was up to stay and we're all to be part of Bunny and Bump's party joining the festivities at Rock Ledge."

"All?"

"Anyone, and I quote, we feel inclined to include."

"Brilliant!" Marigold clapped her hands in relief. "Isabella, you are the most absolute lamb."

"Of course I am, darling," Isabella conceded, "but only for you. You mustn't tell anyone else."

"Never cross my lips," Marigold swore. "So does this launch of yours have a bar?"

"Fully stocked, darling. The champagne is on ice."

"Naturally!" It was a divine thing to have rich friends.

★ ★ ★

Once they had all the details settled amicably between them, Marigold left Isabella lounging comfortably on her deck after dropping Marigold off at the town dock, from whence she set off on her bicycle for her appointment with Amelia Morgan and the nascent Ladies' Cycling Club.

Amelia was waiting for Marigold in front of her rooming house on Grove Street with a small group of nervously hopeful young women. "I've invited a few select friends interested in the cycling," Amelia explained. "Everyone, this is Miss Marigold Manners."

"I am very happy to meet you all." Marigold felt completely in her element with a group of athletically inclined young women. "And please, call me Marigold. Why don't we use the lane behind Amelia's house, which will give us some privacy for our trials. What I recommend is that each of you begin by walking the machine, to get used to its weight and feel as it rolls along beside you."

They were a friendly, accommodating bunch, taking turns walking her bicycle up and down the narrow lane, calling out encouragement and individually introducing themselves to Marigold.

"I'm Sadie MacDonald and this is my sister Ellie, and we can't thank you enough."

"When Amelia told us at choir practice, why, we jumped at the chance to meet you."

"We saw you buying candy at the druggist the other day. So stylish," Ellie breathed.

"I'm Annie Farnsworth." The tallest of the four thrust out her hand. "I've been reading about bicycles in the *Ladies' Home Journal* at the library, and I've just been dying for a chance to ride one."

"Oh, don't say *dying*, Annie," Ellie whispered. "Remember Minnie."

Marigold jumped at her chance to investigate. "Was she a friend of yours, the late Miss Mallory? I read about her unfortunate death in the newspaper. I am so sorry for your loss."

"We weren't the best of friends," Sadie hedged. "But Pride's Crossing is a small place. We all went to school together. Everyone knows everyone."

"Naturally," Marigold agreed with all sympathy.

"So small we all have to make sure we're not using the same fabric to make our dresses for the Endicotts' big party next Saturday night," Annie joked to relieve the somber mood.

"Oh, yes!" Marigold let the conversation lead where it would. "I am lucky enough to have a friend from Boston who has promised me some fabric." No need to brag about Isabella's creations when all she meant to do was assure her new friends she wouldn't be copying their dresses.

"I'm so glad you've been invited too." Amelia Morgan's relief also admitted her surprise. "I mean, it's lovely that just about all the young people in town have been, even us year-rounders."

"How nice," Marigold agreed, curious as to when the invitations to non–society people had been sent. "We felt ourselves very fortunate to be invited—my young cousins, Daisy and Seviah Hatchet, and I," Marigold clarified, to the open delight of several of the young ladies.

"Seviah Hatchet's coming?"

"My cousin will be my escort." Marigold spoke carefully, curious as to their attitude about the young man. "How do you know him?"

"Well, the Hatchets didn't go to school," Annie explained. "Nobody'd heard of them much until that Ellery Hatchet started his preaching. But Minnie met Seviah and said that despite him being a Hatchet, he was a real gentleman when they walked out a time or two."

While Marigold was no longer sure her cousin's assignations with the departed Minnie had been more intimate than a mere "walking out," she was glad of the information—if only to confirm what Seviah himself had said of his relationship with Minnie. Not that Marigold had thought he had lied, just that he was withholding . . . something. "Despite him being a Hatchet?"

"Well, you see . . ." Annie looked at the others before continuing. "The Hatchets do have a certain . . . reputation as being—"

"Extremely private," was Amelia's tactful take.

"—different and standoffish," Annie finished.

"But Minnie said that was wrong," Sadie said. "She said Sev Hatchet was as sweet as pie and that he kept himself to himself. And that's certainly been true when we've seen him about town."

"Such a belvidere," Annie sighed, before clarifying, "So very handsome," in case Marigold didn't understand her slang. "Minnie met him at the nickelodeons, because she was the sort who didn't hold back introducing herself to people."

"To men?" Marigold asked.

"To them especially," answered Annie, a little wistfully. "She wasn't intimidated by anyone, leastwise by the type of fellows who think a girl owes them the world just for buying her a five-cent malt down at the soda fountain."

Marigold had had no idea the druggist was such a den of iniquity—she would have to visit more often. "I agree with the late Miss Mallory." She was surer than ever that she would have genuinely liked Minnie. "As I recently told my cousin, we women owe our suitors civility and respect only. We never owe anyone our very selves."

"No," Annie agreed solemnly, before returning directly to her point. "So you'll introduce us to Seviah Hatchet at the dance, won't you?"

"Naturally." After Marigold made sure Seviah would be on his best, non-Lothario-like behavior.

"And Mr. Jonathan Cox too?" Sadie asked in a rush. "We saw you talking to him outside the druggist, and Amelia mentioned something about your being old friends?"

"I do indeed know Cab Cox, and we are longtime friends," Marigold confirmed with a smile. "And I will also be sure to introduce him to you all that evening. He's a wonderfully accomplished dancer."

"Oh, yes, please," sighed Sadie. "I knew I was going to like you the moment I set eyes on you, riding down Main Street. I said, 'Now, that gal's got dash!' Didn't I, Ellie?"

"You did," her sister laughed, before she added, "I won't tell you what she said when she clapped eyes on Mr. Cox."

Marigold smiled despite the strange pang that arose within her. "He is indeed a man well worth admiring." Never let it be said that she wasn't fully prepared to sing Cab's praises.

"Have you set your cap for him?" was Annie's pointed question.

"I have not," Marigold told them with a clear conscience. "Though I warn you, I know many a young lady who *has* set her cap for Cab Cox, only to have those hopes dashed. Dance with him, by all means—but take care not to fall in love."

"As if you can help falling in love," Sadie laughed.

"I know it's all the fashion to fall 'helplessly in love,'" countered Marigold, "but I myself think it dangerous to cede one's ability to decide for oneself if a man is worthy of one's loyalty and fidelity—dangerous, not romantic. Look at poor Minnie, who, I've been told, threw herself into the sea because she was disappointed in love." She leveled her brows at them. "I don't think there's anything romantic about being dead."

"Certainly not," Amelia Morgan agreed.

But Annie crossed her arms over her chest and said, "Just because a cat has its kittens in the oven doesn't make them biscuits."

This was a New England aphorism Marigold had never heard. "What do you mean?"

"She means," Amelia answered carefully, "that we've learned not to believe everything printed in the newspapers, especially the local ones, run by gentlemen who are"—she lowered her voice, though they were quite alone in the lane—"more interested in keeping the status quo than in printing the truth."

"Oh!" Marigold couldn't help the gasp that slipped from her mouth. "I knew I was going to like you all—you've got gumption and you're logical. I didn't believe any of that romantic disappointment taradiddle myself. From what I've learned of Minnie's redoubtable character, it hardly seems likely." She could feel her archaeological need to solve the puzzle rise within. "So what do you think really happened?"

"Well," Annie answered in an urgent whisper, "we don't rightly know, but I'll never believe she pitched herself into the sea. More likely some bounder did her in. Minnie did walk out with a lot of different men."

Another round of glances were shared between the girls before Marigold probed, "And are there a fair number of bounders in Pride's Crossing?" At their silence, she prompted, "Ought I be worried about such cads at the dance?"

"Perhaps we should make you and your cousin a little list for your reticules," Amelia suggested. "So you can make a discreet check before you accept any invitations to dance."

"How brilliant of you," Marigold praised. "Thank you, Amelia. We would be very much obliged."

"Put down Jimmy Akers," Sadie offered. "And Billy Westbrow. And that awful old pill Wiley Jacobs. Even with all his money, he still can't find a decent woman between here and Boston willing to marry him!"

"Rest assured, I'll put them all down," Amelia agreed.

"Excellent," Marigold enthused.

Now this was progress indeed. Such a list of men would be the logical first place to search for the man who might or might not have put a bun in Minnie Mallory's oven but who very likely had done her in. And perhaps those *other girls* as well.

It was turning out to be truly frightening how often the sight of an independent young woman like Minnie Mallory brought out more than mere littleness in a man. Too often it brought out violence—hadn't she learned that herself out on Great Misery Island?

More than ever, Marigold was determined to find them all out. And stop them, no matter who they were.

See if she wasn't.

CHAPTER 26

I dwell in possibility.
—Emily Dickinson

After a week of surreptitious rehearsing and avoiding Ellery Hatchet at all costs, the day of the Endicotts' dance finally dawned—gray, raw, and uninspiring. But not even the prospect of dirty weather could discourage Marigold. Tonight the firstfruits of her labor would fall ripe, and she had every confidence in her plan. Daisy and Seviah were ready for this test. If they could keep it secret.

The trio slipped away from the island in the afternoon under a bank of darker-than-usual clouds threatening rain, but the storm held off, and they arrived at Bessie Dove's boardinghouse safe and dry. Despite Isabella's hostess's offer of rooms at Plum Cove, Marigold had decided to stick to their original plan of staying at the boardinghouse for Seviah's sake—the young man would need Cab's help and guidance in getting dressed.

If Marigold had another reason for wanting to spend the night nearer Cab, away from Isabella's all-seeing eyes, she kept that entirely to herself.

"I got your rooms all ready, child—two, for you and Miss Daisy, upstairs, and another for Mr. Seviah downstairs with the other gentlemen. And I got those dresses Mrs. Dana sent over all pressed out and hanging up ready for you. And Mr. Cox's suit for Mr. Seviah too."

"Thank you. You are a godsend, Bessie."

"Oh, you come on." Bessie led the way up the stairs. "Those dresses are just about the prettiest things I ever did see. You girls are going to look finer than anyone else in the whole of the town."

"Not everyone else, I hope." Upsetting the unspoken but ironclad social hierarchy of society would not endear Daisy to their hostess.

But Marigold need not have worried—Isabella had more than justified her faith. Daisy's dress was in a sweeping, unstructured style Marigold had not seen before. The puffed sleeves were fashioned entirely of extraordinary cream-colored lace that extended over the satin bodice and down the skirt, where pastel-colored chiné cutwork flowers were carefully sewn into the silk, making the dress into a pastel trellis of hand-painted blossoms. "Daisy will look as fresh and dewy as a rose in a garden."

"She sure will," Bessie agreed. "But I'm more partial to yours."

Marigold had given Isabella strict limits on her own gown, dictating that the dress be plain, as would befit her position of chaperone to her cousin. But Isabella clearly had her own ideas, because she had taken Marigold's stated preference for unadorned ice-blue satin and turned it into something altogether more whimsical. While the skirts were rigorously tailored, without the elaborate overlays and lace of Daisy's gown, Isabella had set the material on the bias in order to sew a line of embroidered butterflies into flight up the skirts. And while the sleeves were less elaborately puffed than Daisy's lace daydream, the sleek satin fabric was embellished by cutout butterflies set free upon a cunning net of tulle that swooped low across the bodice.

It was nothing Marigold had wanted and everything she secretly adored. "She is an infernal genius."

"You've got that right." Beside her, Bessie sighed. "Wish my Lucy could have occasion for a dress like this."

Bessie's wish pierced the haze of Marigold's euphoria. And left her ashamed. Ashamed, because it had never occurred to her before this moment that Lucy should attend. Because it had never occurred to the ladies of the cycling club, even as they had talked about "all" the young people in town being invited. Clearly not all. "Bessie, how ignorant of me. I'm sorry."

Bessie nodded even as she sighed. "Can't change but one thing at a time, they say, but Lord, I'm wearing out my patience watching progress for my people move along so slow." She took a deep breath. "But we've got to move fast now—we haven't got all night." Bessie was opening the connecting door to the adjacent bedroom. "You two are gonna look a treat. No way Mr. Cab is gonna take his eyes off you."

"Bessie, please." Marigold felt her face heat under the woman's watchful eyes. "That was certainly not my intention."

Bessie pursed her lips even as she smiled. "Well, that's gonna be your result."

Marigold kept that happy thought in the back of her mind as she called Daisy out of her bath—it truly was a marvelous thing to have friends with indoor plumbing—for her first look at her gown. Isabella had kept her in suspense by fitting her in a muslin blank. "Prepare yourself to be amazed and transformed."

Daisy gripped Marigold's hand, but all trepidation vanished the moment she saw the dress. "Oh!" Her hands flew up to her pinked cheeks. "Oh, my stars! It's prettier than I ever could have imagined. Oh, golly! Are you sure this is for me?"

"I am quite sure," Marigold was happy to assure her. "Only a girl as tall and willowy as you could do justice to these long, flowing skirts."

"Oh, Marigold." Her tall young cousin enveloped her in a bruising hug. "You are a wonder."

"Isabella gets all the credit so far, but just wait until I have worked my full wonder upon you. Now that you are thoroughly scrubbed, it's time to put up your hair."

"What about me?" queried Seviah from the doorway. "Do I get scrubbed too?"

"You shall have to scrub yourself, Cousin." Marigold was too used to Seviah playing the Lothario to mind his innuendo, but she'd have another word with him about this tendency before they left. "Downstairs."

Bessie chuckled and shook her head. "I'll show you to the gentlemen's bathing room, Mr. Seviah, but after that, you're on your own."

"What if I don't know how to get myself into the rig?"

Marigold heard the very real worry in Seviah's voice, but Bessie was briskly herding him away. "Oh, I reckon Mr. Cab can help you with that. He's already come home early to take his bath."

The thought of Cab Cox at his bath one floor below did strange—but entirely delightful—things to Marigold's sense of equanimity. Things she would think about later. After the party—or possibly during. "We're going to have a marvelous evening."

An hour later, she made good on the first of her promises. "There." Marigold placed the last hairpin in Daisy's softly upswept chignon and stepped back to survey her workmanship. "Yes, you'll do very nicely." She applied just the barest amount of rouge to augment Daisy's dewy-fresh look. "You're going to break his heart."

"Oh, golly, I hope not," the girl swore with a shy smile. "What use would it be to me if it's broken?"

"Quite so." Marigold smiled back at Daisy's reflection. "You're going to be a sensation."

"If I can be half the sensation you are, I'll be just fine." Daisy clasped Marigold's hand. "I'm ashamed I ever let myself think bad of you. Thank you for everything you've done, Marigold."

"You are very welcome. Remember, Seviah and I will be there to help you should you need it, but I have every confidence you won't."

"And I'll be there to assist you both," a quiet baritone added. "All you have to do is ask."

Marigold turned to find Cab standing in the doorway, perfection in a black dinner suit. There was something about the strictly tailored lines and the starched crispness of his evening attire that brought her attention to the architecture of his strong jaw and high cheekbones. Something that made her heart open without consulting her mind, which had more reasonable things to say. "Cab, you look wonderfully fine. But come, tell me what you think of Daisy."

Cab performed his duty without making it seem a duty at all. "Breathtakingly beautiful, Miss Hatchet. I predict you will be the belle of the ball." The smile he turned on Marigold was no less enthusiastic. "And you are a vision yourself, Marigold. The two of you will do your family proud."

"And what of me?" queried Seviah from behind him.

"Yes, let us have a look at you, Seviah." Marigold beckoned him into the room, anxious to have a look at her second charge. But she needn't have worried. Cab had clearly taken the young man under his wing—she recognized the studs shining from Seviah's shirtfront as well as the cuff links at his wrist. And the young man's unruly dark locks had been tamed into a neatly parted style.

"Look at you, Sev!" said Daisy. "You look like a thoroughbred."

"The very picture of a matinee idol, Seviah," Marigold confirmed.

He smoothed a hand through his hair. "Well, it looks like I'm painting the town red tonight."

"No malarkey, Seviah," Marigold warned sternly. "And no liquor. You're meant to be handsome and charming and a credit to your sister, so no spiking the punch. Behave, and you'll get your dance as a reward."

"I'm going to hold you to that, Miss City Manners." Seviah winked at her.

"And none of that. Endear yourself, charm certainly, but do not flirt. Are we all ready, then? Daisy, let's get you swathed in your wrap for the trip in case it rains. I've brought you one of my better shawls."

"Now, wait a minute now." Bessie was at the door. "I held a little something back—cuz your Mrs. Dana, that's what she asked me to do."

Bessie brought in two high-collared evening capes of velvet dyed to match their dresses, with a butterfly embellishment for Marigold's and a lace overlay for Daisy's. They were the perfect accompaniment. Isabella had indeed thought of everything.

Daisy sighed with happiness. "Only thing that would make it perfect is I wish we had matching shoes."

"Oh, no," Marigold contradicted. "What a disaster that would be, with new-made shoes stiff and pinching your feet. We will be far more comfortable in our own well-cleaned and polished, comfortable slippers, which no one will notice because of your dress. Your feet will thank me for it at the end of the night. Trust me," Marigold said, "to know how things ought to be. Cab, are you ready?"

The smile he gave her was bright with something just beyond anticipation. "Always."

CHAPTER 27

There is no charm equal to tenderness of heart.
—Jane Austen

*A*lways. Marigold's heart did unruly, very nearly unmannerly gyrations beneath the confines of her corset at his word. But this was Daisy's night, and Marigold needed to concentrate on her cousin and not on Cab Cox.

Yet Cab was persistent in his own way. "I hope you'll save a dance for me, Marigold," he said as he handed her into the hired carriage. "Though I should like to reserve them all, I know it's against the rules."

She touched his arm in gratitude but lowered her voice so they might not be overheard. "I would vouchsafe them all to you, Cab, so long as you remember your promise to dance the first dance with Daisy. You know you're the only one who can see her launched off in style."

"Not the only one—Tad may have plans of his own."

"He may, or he may not. You are the only man I can safely rely upon."

"I gave you my word." He held up his hand in pledge. "Just be careful who you dance with, all right?"

"Oh, you needn't fear, Cab. Seviah will perform the office of the first dance for me." *Perform* being the operative word—Seviah had an air of the stage about him this evening, as if the suit had invested him with a sort of presence. "And the ladies of the cycling club have furnished me with a list of all the bounders and mashers."

He seemed taken aback by the very idea. "Have they?"

"Of course. We young ladies try to look out for one another, so we know whom to avoid."

He seemed to want to say something serious—that frown had etched itself between his brows—but he said only, "Good to know," and settled himself into the carriage for the ride to the Endicotts' manse.

Rock Ledge was lit up like a wedding cake with gaslights twinkling in the twilight for the festivities. By the time they arrived, close to a hundred other people were already in the receiving line, but Marigold had timed their arrival so that they were perfectly placed just at the end.

"So many people," Daisy whispered. "Everyone looks so fine."

"They do. But after Mrs. Endicott, none look so fine as you." Marigold was glad to note that Isabella had been correct in her guess that Julia Stuyvesant Endicott would be trying to re-create the balls of her New York youth, when the Four Hundred were ruled by Mrs. Astor—a second cousin of Julia Endicott's, naturally.

Their hostess was receiving her guests at the door, just inside the house, a stately figure clad in a cream-colored satin dress fresh from New York with an asymmetrical overskirt of tawny sheer net, decorated in a swagged festoon of silk flowers and bows, all drawn back into a small bustle that was just at the last of its stylishness.

Marigold had never felt more beholden to Isabella's genius for setting, rather than following, the trends of the day. "And you also have the advantage of knowing how to conduct yourself just as we practiced."

"Yes." Daisy squeezed her gloved hand in gratitude, took a deep breath, and let her face relax into her naturally lovely smile. "Oh, there he is!"

And indeed, there was Thaddeus Crowninshield Endicott, standing next to his father, looking every inch the debonair man-about-town his parents clearly wanted him to be—with the exception of a small cowlick that had somehow managed to escape the strict confines of his hair tonic.

"Makes me feel all-overish, but in a good way," Daisy whispered. "I like that his hair is not quite perfect—makes him more real somehow."

"Exactly," Marigold murmured in encouragement.

But no encouragement was needed—Tad's mouth dropped open and his face lit like a beachside bonfire at the site of Daisy.

"Mr. Jonathon Cox and Miss Daisy Hatchet," the maître d'hotel intoned as Cab and then Isabella handed him her card with their names clearly written out. "Mrs. Charles Dana, Miss Marigold Manners, and Mr. Seviah Hatchet."

Daisy stepped forward as if on the impulse of the moment. "Oh, Mrs. Endicott, thank you so very much for your kind invitation."

"We're so glad you could attend, Miss . . . ?" Julia Endicott's patrician smile was firmly in place as she appeared to hesitate to understand who Daisy was.

But Marigold had prepared Daisy for such silly society games—the girl turned the benefice of her own dazzling smile upon Mrs. Endicott and simply carried on. "May I have the honor of presenting you to our party, ma'am?"

Julia Endicott made an equivocal sound of assent, but Daisy beamed at her as if she had been anointed for the task. "My dear cousin, Miss Marigold Manners of Boston and now of our island, we're happy to say."

"Thank you for your kind invitation, ma'am," was all Marigold allowed herself to echo before turning to Seviah.

"And my brother, Mr. Seviah Hatchet. And Miss Manners's dear friend from Boston, Mr. Jonathan Cabot Cox. Oh, but of course you'll already know dear Cab."

"Yes, yes, we do." Julia Endicott found herself smiling. "Good evening to you all."

"And Mrs. Endicott and I are old acquaintances." Isabella played her part to perfection. "How lovely to see you again, Julia. So kind of you to include me and my protégée, sweet Daisy."

"Yes, of course." Julia Endicott's brows rose in perfect arches of surprise. "A pleasure to have you here, Isabella."

"Thank you, Julia." Isabella was everything complimentary. "I am thoroughly enjoying my first glance at your beautiful Rock Ledge."

"That's swell." Tad beamed from the end of the line, effectively cutting out his father. "Glad to have you all here with us. Good to see you too, Cab. And Sev."

"A pleasure to celebrate with you, Tad." Cab had his own piece of social nicety at the ready.

"Oh, but there's the orchestra." Daisy turned her luminous smile on Tad as the band struck up a tune. "We won't keep you from your guests a moment longer, Mr. Endicott."

"Miss Hatchet," Cab asked, right on cue, "I believe this is my dance?"

"Oh, thank you, yes. You're too kind."

"Say, now." Tad stepped up. "I reckon the fellow whose birthday it is ought to have the honor of leading out the prettiest gal on the whole of the North Shore."

Daisy did the impossible—she looked at him with her heart shining in her eyes and said, "Oh, Mr. Endicott. I'd love to, but I've pledged the first dance to Mr. Cox." She looked mournfully at Cab, who took his second cue like the champion sportsman he was.

"I will cede the honor to my cousin, but only because it is his birthday. And only if you will do me the honor of your second dance, Miss Hatchet."

"You are kindness itself, Mr. Cox." Daisy was all gracious delight. "Of course, I'd be honored."

Marigold found herself drawing in a deep breath of relief as Tad drew Daisy to the place of pride in the center of the dance floor, though all around her the assembly seemed to draw its collective breath.

"Is that the Hatchet girl?" someone behind Marigold murmured.

"Couldn't be. Look at her! She looks divine. That dress!"

Marigold's satisfaction gave her enough ease to enjoy the sight of the two young people, so perfectly suited to each other, as they began a sedate waltz. Daisy moved beautifully and even laughed charmingly when Tad stepped on her foot. But oh, what a sublime couple they were, so clearly attuned to each other.

"Just as you'd plotted, no doubt," Cab said at her ear.

"Cab." She rewarded him for his part of the play with a smile. "That was perfect. Thank you."

"You're welcome. But I'm now free to collect on your promise that the rest of your dances are to be mine."

"You must recall I've pledged my first dance to Seviah, to help ease his way into society. I can't abandon him now."

"No, you dad-blamed cannot," Seviah retorted from her other side.

"And I will not," Marigold assured him. "Cab, the next dance is yours."

"All right, then, I'll sit this one out, secure in the belief that the best is yet to come."

"Oh, I beg you will not sit it out while there are so many young ladies without partners, Cab. Can't I persuade you to ask Miss Morgan—just to your left in a lovely aubergine-colored gown? As a favor to me?"

"Marigold." Cab almost sighed—almost. "Is it not enough that I'm letting you play fast and loose with Daisy and Tad? I won't have you playing fast and loose with me."

"Gracious, Cab. It's a dance, not a marriage proposal. If you mean not to dance with other young ladies, then you'll have to decline the honor of dancing with me."

"You're Machiavellian," he accused. "Though Machiavelli didn't look that good in blue satin." But he was smiling good-naturedly and straightening his cuffs before he went toward Amelia Morgan, so she took no offense.

Marigold let Seviah lead her out, secure in the hope that Cab would launch Amelia Morgan's prospects within society in the same manner she had planned for him to do for Daisy.

With that task accomplished, Marigold could turn her attention back to Daisy and Tad, who appeared to need no help—they were still blissfully twirling away, oblivious to Tad's mother trying to catch his attention to remind him of his duties to other young ladies.

"You're doing me no favors looking like you're bored to bits with me," Seviah complained.

"My apologies." She refocused her attention on her cousin. "You're right. I should be concentrating on whom your next partner should be. There appear to be slightly fewer ladies than gentlemen." She supposed a veritable *Who's Who* of the North Shore was in attendance, along with a number of townspeople—more than one fellow looked none too comfortable in his suit of evening clothes.

But not Seviah. He looked in his element—chin up, chest out, shoulders back. As if he were trained for the stage and the weight of an audience's gaze. "Do you like the theater, Seviah?"

"I reckon I do. Why do you ask?"

"Do traveling revues make it to the local playhouse?"

He somehow managed that careless Hatchet shrug even as he danced. "I've seen a few shows."

"And what did you like best about them?"

"Oh, the singers, standing up there, all fine. The duets with the fellow and a pretty lady were my favorites."

"Nothing better than a handsome man and a beautiful girl."

"Like us now," he offered with a sly wink.

"No winking. We're making over your reputation tonight too."

"My reputation? As a dangerous lover?"

"Is that really what you fancy yourself as?" she asked with all seriousness.

"Nah," he finally admitted. "That's all for show."

"Good. Because it's not me you want to impress with your gentlemanliness—it's them. Look at them—discreetly!" she hissed into his ear. Her glance took in more than one young lady gazing at Seviah with something more febrile than admiration shining in their eyes. "They're all hoping for a chance to dance with you, so as soon as this dance is done, I'll start introducing you to my friends."

"Imagine you, introducing me around my town."

"Imagine that!" Marigold laughed. Seviah would do just fine until she could figure out how best to help him off Great Misery as she had Daisy.

For now, she would turn her archaeological, puzzle-solving mind to the far more intriguing investigation of her list of Pride's Crossing's potential bounders.

And, very likely, murderers.

Chapter 28

The heart wants what it wants—or else it does not care.
—Emily Dickinson

As soon as the first dance was done, Cab appeared and put his hand to the soft, exposed skin at the inside of Marigold's elbow in that way he seemed to have of neither pawing at her like a masher nor startling her with an inappropriate touch—a delicate balance only he seemed able to achieve. "This is my dance, I hope."

"Naturally," she agreed. "But first, Seviah, would you be a lamb—and increase the suspense and anticipation of the other young ladies—by asking Miss Morgan to dance? I know you like the buttoned-up ones."

"Reckon I do," he agreed with a forbidden wink. But then he switched his dark focus to Amelia Morgan and set himself off. And if Amelia Morgan didn't find herself very much in demand as a partner by the end of the evening, Marigold would be very much mistaken.

"Arranging everyone to your satisfaction, are you, Marigold?" Cab asked as he led her into a slow, gliding two-step.

"Helping my friends make the most of their evening."

"It's just the evening, then, and not the rest of Tad and Daisy's lives you've got planned?"

"Tad and Daisy were secretly arranging their own lives long before either you or I came to the North Shore, Cab. I'm just helping them along by removing what obstacles I can."

"Removing. Arranging. Managing."

"Yes, arranging—arranging for a dress from Isabella. There is nothing sinister in that."

"No." He looked over to where Daisy was still dancing with Tad—a faux pas Marigold was doing nothing to oppose. "Isabella has done you proud. Though I don't suppose she actually sewed the thing. Such toil would never do for our Isabella." He turned Marigold's hand within his, finding that singular open spot at the buttoned wrist of her kidskin glove. "She's not like you, rolling up your sleeves and setting yourself to whatever work needs to be done."

"Are you saying my hands have grown so rough you can feel my calluses through my best gloves?"

"I'm saying I admire you for doing what needs to be done. All the work I hear you've done out on Great Misery at the Hatchet Farm—even if it is managing. From what I hear, it's for the best."

She could not deny that she was very proud of what she had accomplished for her cousins, but one didn't want to make too much of oneself. "I'm just doing my part."

"Your part seems to be dragging them into the nineteenth century."

"Just in time for the start of the twentieth," she joked. "And you? What are your plans now that I've exacted my promise from you?"

"I reckon I might extend my vacation a bit."

"You reckon," she echoed. "Just listen to yourself, Cab, talking like the veriest rural rube."

"When in Rome, Marigold."

"But this is not Rome, Cab."

"No. But I'm determined to make the most of it and think the best of its citizens without condescension."

Marigold was taken aback. "And is that what you think I'm doing—condescending?"

"With all this 'arranging,' it's obvious you think you know what's best for everyone—for Daisy and Tad, for example."

"No." For a man of such rare understanding, it was his attitude that was condescending—and infuriating. "They decided what was best for themselves," she repeated. "Again, I'm just helping remove the obstacles that might keep them from making it happen. That's what friends do for each other."

The smile he turned upon her was ironic—a full display of that steely way he had of never letting on. "Is that why you're so determined to keep me at arm's length, Marigold? Because you know, deep down, that I won't ever let you arrange or manage me?"

"Cab." Marigold was shocked into silence. "What—"

A spate of clapping brought their tête-à-tête to an abrupt end.

Tad had mounted the small dais where the orchestra sat and had raised his arms, calling for the assembly's attention. "Well, I reckon this is just about the swellest night of a fellow's life, to have such a grand party. I want to thank everyone for coming and my folks for giving me such an all-get-out party. But the best thing about tonight is that I'm the proudest man in all of Pride's Crossing and the happiest too, because I want to announce that Miss Daisy Hatchet has agreed to be my wife."

Around Marigold, gasps of delight and moans of despair were all melded into a roar of astonished clapping as Tad held his hand out to invite Daisy to join him. For her own part, Marigold could hardly breathe, so stunned was she.

"I'll ask you to raise your glasses in a toast." Tad drew Daisy to his side. "That's right—everybody get a glass of this swell champagne." He raised the coupe an obliging person pressed into this hand. "To my darling Daisy. What do you say, Daisy? Are you ready to become Mrs. Thaddeus Endicott?"

Daisy, bless her, looked genuinely shocked and happy and surprised all at the same time. She put her hand across her heart and looked at Tad with all the love in her eyes.

And behind Marigold, someone—was that Seviah's clear tenor?—broke into song.

"*Daisy, Daisy, give him your answer, do! He's half-crazy over the love of you!*" A little space cleared around him, and Seviah looked every inch the matinee idol as he crooned, "*It* will *be a stylish marriage, he* can *afford a carriage . . .*"

And then the rest of the crowd was swaying along as they joined in the popular song. "*But you'll look sweet upon the seat of a bicycle built for two.*"

Another round of applause broke out before the room quieted enough for Daisy to answer. "Oh, yes. Yes, please!" She threw her arms around Tad's neck in an adoring embrace.

Marigold let out her breath in stunned relief. She could not have hoped for a better result than a well-received engagement—it was well beyond her expectation, though not her imagination.

"You're to be congratulated," Cab murmured. "And only twenty minutes into the evening. That must be some kind of record."

"Cab." Marigold could only laugh at his ironic rebuke. "The secret is in the never letting on." When he smiled, she asked, in a repeat of her request at the boathouse, "Celebrate by taking a turn with me, for old times' sake, will you?"

"Love to," he answered, his voice full of amusement and regret all at the same time.

But before she could lose herself in the quiet steady companionship and fellow feeling of her partner's arms, George Endicott came bearing down upon them like a gunboat, all weapons showing.

"Brace yourself," was all Cab managed before Endicott launched his first salvo.

"Did you put him up to this?" the irate man growled. "If you—"

"Miss Manners, my uncle, Mr. George Endicott," Cab interjected evenly, trying to mitigate some of the man's apparent anger. "Uncle George, may I introduce Miss Marigold Manners, who knows nothing of your antipathy—"

"Antipathy? By God!" Endicott became so red in the face, Marigold began to grow alarmed for the health of his heart. "Did that demented Ellery Hatchet put you up to this? This is just his damn sort of goddamned gambit. I swear to—"

"No, sir." Cab purposefully steered the three of them off the dance floor. "You are ascribing to me powers I do not possess and schemes in which I would never participate."

"And what about her?" Endicott jabbed a finger at Marigold. "She looks every bit the schemer. Ellery Hatchet sent *her*, sure as day. He—"

"Knows nothing of this evening, nor this mooted engagement between your family and his." Marigold felt it was time to take up her part the conversation—if the low shouting match could even be called a conversation. "For if he did, I'm certain he would forbid it."

"Ha! As if we're not good enough for him and his lunatic kin?"

"Indeed, sir." Marigold's smile was all crocodile, but it served its purpose, alarming Endicott just enough that he stepped back to a more cautious, gentlemanly distance. "Clearly you feel the same."

"Perhaps, Uncle George, we may discuss this at another, less public time." Cab's voice was all low caution. "But I assure you, this was all Tad's idea. He never breathed a word of it to me."

Endicott nearly chewed his mustache in vexation. "Just remember who's side you're on, son. One word from me and those senior partners will jump to do my bidding."

If Cab was surprised by this indiscreet intimidation, he never let on. "I understand you, sir."

"See that you do." And with that, Endicott tugged aggressively at the waist of his evening vest and took his fulminating leave of them.

"Well," was all Marigold had to say in the moment. "That was . . . instructive."

"Indeed." Cab heaved out a sigh. "My apologies."

"You've nothing to apologize for," she assured him. "But perhaps you had best tell me what this antipathy—or is it really a full-on feud? I didn't lie that Daisy's father knows nothing of this, because Ellery Hatchet's adjectives for George Endicott are much the same as your uncle's about him. Well, you heard him that morning out on Great Misery—*spawn of the devil*, I think he said. Although he says much the same of his own progeny, so I didn't think it suspicious at the time." She considered. "But I sense there is more to the equation that mere antipathy."

"We're going to want a drink for this." Cab steered her off the dance floor, swiping a bottle of champagne and two glasses off a tray as they went by.

He let her out onto the wide, brick terrace overlooking the sound, where the dark shadow of Great Misery Island hulked against the wind off-shore. "You remember I told you about the legal case my uncle fetched me up here to try?"

Marigold made an encouraging, if not impatient, sound of assent to hurry him along—the party was proceeding apace, and she wanted to be able to support Daisy, should she need it. As well as get to her list.

Cab moved fractionally closer and lowered his voice to a confidential whisper, even though they were quite alone. "It seems some years ago, when the Endicotts were still clipper ship sailors and sea merchants in the tea and spice trade, my uncle's father, Captain Jacob Endicott, had a particularly unsuccessful voyage and gave a man who sailed for him a deed to some land in lieu of wages, with the unwritten—and perhaps unspoken—understanding that once Endicott had gathered enough money to pay the back wages, the fellow would return the deed." He paused and glanced around. "But by the time Endicott had the pay, this fellow had decided that he wanted to keep the land instead."

Marigold tried to understand what Can had *not* said. "Great Misery Island?"

"Naturally." Cab seemed relieved a little by the telling. "Elijah Hatchet was Jacob Endicott's first mate for many years and many voyages. But once Hatchet got the deed to Great Misery, he swallowed the anchor, as they say, took himself a bride, settled upon that rock. And then, strangely enough, promptly died."

"And the curse of Great Misery was born?"

"What curse?"

"No, never mind." Marigold didn't want to complicate the tale with extraneous superstition. "Why didn't you tell me this before?" This information seemed vitally important to helping her cousins, even if she didn't yet know why or how.

Cab looked unhappy. "I meant to, but the moment never seemed right."

"Well, it's certainly not right now!" Not when she ought to be paying all her attention to helping Daisy. "Perhaps you might tell your uncle that if he approves of the marriage, he might sooner get at least some portion of the island as her dowry?" She didn't imagine that Ellery had anything but some worthless, hardscrabble land to give his daughter. "And you might suggest to Tad that he hire you as his lawyer in drawing up the marriage contracts, so you could work to that end. I would trust you to see to Daisy's interests as well as Tad's." He had already demonstrated that he would do what was right instead of what was personally convenient.

"Perhaps I might." Cab cast his gaze through the open terrace doors to where Tad and Daisy stood arm in arm, their heads bent in an arc toward each other as they accepted kind congratulations. "They certainly do look happy."

They did—the complete opposite of how Mr. and Mrs. George Endicott looked on the other side of the room, heads nearly butting in heated conference. Watching them, one question, in particular, sprang into Marigold's mind—why should Mr. George Endicott, with a magnificent mansion on the North Shore and all the wealth of a revered old-money family, want a scrabbly, scrub-covered glacial island? And why should he try for so many years to get it back? And why should Ellery Hatchet, who hated to farm and was, to all accounts, out of money, not want to sell it to him?

A great mystery indeed. And one that Marigold most assuredly meant to solve as soon as she could set her mind to it. But now, as Cab had said, was not that time.

There was other work to be done this night.

CHAPTER 29

Success is a science: if you have the conditions, you get the result.
—Oscar Wilde

"I need to consult with Isabella," was Marigold's excuse for Cab to escort her back to the ballroom. If there were society secrets to be spilled about the Endicotts, Isabella would know.

She urged Cab on a circuitous promenade of the room, meeting and greeting the members of the Ladies' Cycling Club as well as other guests Cab knew while keeping a sort of maternal eye on her charges and also on George and Julia Endicott, the latter of whom bore an expression that Marigold recognized as akin to her own crocodile smile—she was all tight lips and anxious, lying eyes.

Daisy, on the other hand, seemed to be handling herself with perfect aplomb, being gracious and lovely and glowing with happiness by Tad's side—the very picture of elegant grace under pressure. "Why, Mrs. Endicott, I should love to come stay for a visit with you!" The smile Daisy bestowed upon Julia Endicott was calibrated to please, being open and guileless and grateful all at the same time.

Marigold was deeply relieved. And inordinately proud.

She brought her attention back to Seviah, who, she noted with some satisfaction—as well as trepidation—was surrounded by a group of young ladies of Pride's Crossing, who had somehow escaped their chaperones. Trepidation, because Sadie and Annie were among them. And because what Seviah required was quite different from what his sister needed—definitely not a marriage to a local beauty. And because Seviah was showing a side of himself Marigold hadn't fully recognized before—he was carrying himself with the innate confidence of the matinee idols he lionized. But Seviah was even more adept a student than his sister, because he had needed no tutor to learn how to show himself to best advantage.

They found Isabella deep in animated conversation with a distinguished older gentleman. "Marigold, darling, do let me introduce you to my dear friend Ben Keith."

And there it was—she saw her opening for Seviah as clearly as if it were a play upon a stage. Isabella might have addressed him familiarly, but Marigold was sure he must be Mr. Benjamin Franklin Keith of Boston and New York and the Keith-Albee circuit of vaudeville revues that toured up and down the New England coast.

"A pleasure to meet you, sir. But will you be so kind as to excuse me for a moment, Isabella? Cab?" Marigold made her hasty apologies before she made her way through the bevy of beauties surrounding her cousin and steered him and his coterie toward the elegant grand piano set up in the wide foyer just outside of the ballroom. "Why don't you favor your new friends with a song, Seviah?"

His assurance fled. "I've never sung in public."

"But we're not in public—we're at a private party, where you just made a lovely splash with your impromptu serenade of your sister, and as the orchestra seems to have taken a break so people might congratulate the happy couple, some small entertainment would be delightful. Also"—she slipped behind the keyboard—"I need someone to accompany my poor playing."

"Didn't know you played," he countered, as if she had hidden this from him.

"There is no instrument at Hatchet Farm," she demurred. "And I think of myself as merely good enough to accompany a far more gifted performer—in this instance, you. I do know the melodies of most of the popular tunes of the day, so why don't you pick a nice up-tempo piece, or perhaps a ballad, to delight the young ladies. You know 'After the Ball,' don't you?"

"Do I? By heart!"

Marigold quickly ran through an introductory arpeggio before she launched into the melody.

Seviah joined right on cue. *"After the ball is over, after the break of morn, after the dancers' leaving, after the stars are gone."* His rich tenor filled the room. *"Many a heart is aching, if you could read them all. Many the hopes that have vanished, after the ball."*

The young ladies were enthralled. As was Mr. Keith.

Marigold felt that telltale tingle all the way to her fingertips, and she had to concentrate on her playing lest she do less than her best for Seviah.

"Long years have passed, child, I've never wed." Seviah sang to his swooning damsels, raising his arm dramatically as he came to the coda. *"That's why I'm lonely, no home at all. I broke her heart, pet, after the ball."*

And there was Cab, behind the ring of clapping young women, looking at her with that wry, knowing, very nearly disapproving smile on his face. *Managing*, he was saying without words.

Accompanying, she mouthed back.

But why should she need Cab Cox's approval of her actions? Which progressed quickly when Isabella immediately brought Mr. Keith over to the piano to speak to her.

"I must congratulate you on your very accomplished playing, Miss Manners."

"Thank you, Mr. Keith." Marigold tried for an impromptu air. "Are you enjoying your evening?"

"Indeed, I am, I thank you. More so now." His eyes swiveled to Seviah, who was basking in the glow of Annie Farnsworth and the rest of the bright young things' adoration.

"Such a pleasure to get to show off my cousin's singing voice," Marigold enthused. "We live removed from the town some ways, and he doesn't often get such an opportunity."

"Do you think he'd like more opportunity?" Mr. Keith knuckled his mustache in contemplation. "I am a theater man, Miss Manners, always on the lookout for new talent. Your cousin seems to have what it takes to fill seats in spades."

Elation and satisfaction filled her being in equal parts—two triumphs in one night seemed even more success than she could have hoped for. "A strong voice that will reach the back of a theater?"

"A strong set of shoulders that fill out an evening jacket and appeal to the fairer sex," Mr. Keith corrected on a chuckle. "We men may think we make the world go round, but in my business, it pays to give equal attention to the needs of the ladies. The matinee seats must be filled, and handsome young men fill them quickly."

"Very astute, Ben," Isabella approved.

"And Miss Manners is an astute young woman to present her cousin's talents so well—don't think I don't see what you're doing." He chuckled. "I have half a mind to ask if you'd like to make the leap to the stage yourself, my dear, for you're uncommonly pretty and have a great deal of presence that could fill the evening's seats just as well as that young man will fill the matinees."

"You're very kind, sir, but my ambitions don't run in that direction."

"Marigold is sure to become a famous archaeologist," Isabella put in loyally.

"Alas. That will be my loss." Mr. Keith lifted Marigold's gloved hand to his lips for a courtly kiss. "But I'll remain hopeful that your cousin's ambitions do run in that direction?"

"I think, sir, that you should ask him."

There. That wasn't manipulating or managing. Seviah could say no to Mr. Keith if he chose—though she doubted he would. He was more likely to leave without a backward glance at Great Misery Island. *This cursed rock.*

Mr. Keith and Isabella moved on to speak to Seviah, but Marigold hung back, not wanting to influence her cousin one way or another. But Cab saw it another way.

"You're at it again," Cab said at her ear. "I saw that gleam in your eye the moment you recognized it was Ben Keith with Isabella."

"I shall have to work on my poker face."

"Your poker face is already spectacular, Marigold. I live in fear of it becoming any more formidable."

"Come, now." Marigold was done fencing. "Why this concern with what I'm doing? Why this double standard? When you were given the chance to help your family, you came all this way to do so. And you continue to—you aided Tad tonight, despite your uncle's opposition. Why should I not do the same?"

"Because I let the facts of the case guide me to the logical conclusion, even when it wasn't to my family's benefit."

"Do you think my plans illogical? Do you think that Daisy and Tad are not meant to be together?"

"I don't believe in 'meant to be,' Marigold," Cab countered. "I told you, I don't believe in predestiny any more than you do—we make our own fate by our choices."

"And that is how you might know this is *their* choice, not mine. I choose to be archaeological—the word *logical* is right there in the name of the profession. I would never have chosen *marriage*."

Cab absorbed her words like a blow—his head tipped back before he let out a breath. "So noted." He squared his shoulders within his evening suit and looked away for a long moment before he said, "Then let me congratulate you."

Marigold was not yet ready to make peace. "All I want is the chance for them to find out—to have time together, without any outside interference."

"Fair enough. But that means without any interference from you too."

"You have my word." But she also changed the topic to a more pleasant subject. "You know, we never did finish that dance I promised you."

"No," he mused. "We didn't." He took her hand and drew her from the salon out the terrace door and down onto the narrow walk along the shore that was clearing of partygoers now that the orchestra was striking up a tune. He took her into his arms and led her into a slow, lazy, close waltz, swaying gently side to side.

The press of his hand at the small of her back was just shy of seductive. "Cab?"

"Do you mind?" he asked quietly. "I fancy having you to myself."

"No." Perhaps he was finally ready to take a few well-warranted liberties. "I'd like that."

He answered by fanning his thumb along the line of her jaw, looking down at her in that way he had of scowling and searching and seeming to understand everything and nothing about her all at the same time. "I'd like to kiss you."

"Would you?" she managed to breathe.

"Would you?" he countered, his voice a slow whisper that managed to insinuate itself deep inside her.

"Yes. Yes, I would," she found herself answering, as any young woman of sense and panache would. "Rather desperately."

He smiled, that low melting smile that did delicious things to her insides. His hand around her waist tightened, and he picked her up and snugged her up against the seawall.

"Someone is coming out. Quiet," he instructed. "Not a sound."

Another secret. But this one she would gladly keep.

Against her back, the constraint of the wall was freeing. And encouraging.

"Kiss me," she whispered, raising her lips to his.

He lowered his head to hers slowly, glacially, incrementally, until at last they were nearly touching. She could feel the warm whisper of his breath, and she wet her lips that had gone suddenly dry.

But he did not come any closer. Did not kiss her. Did not explain why.

In another moment, he eased away from her and looked back toward the house. "They're gone." His thumb caressed along the edge of her jaw. "We ought to take better care. We can't have the inimitable Miss Manners looking all flushed, with swollen lips and hair mussed as if she's been kissing in the shrubbery, when she's meant to be chaperoning the belle of the ball."

"I suppose not," she answered, trying not to let her disappointment color her tone. "The secret *is* in never letting on. But I do have to say—I wish it were otherwise."

"Me too," he said. "I wish I could kiss you. And do other things that would put a glow in your cheeks without roughing them up."

"What other things?" she heard herself saying in a voice that all but pleaded to be shown.

"Let's just say that we'll have to take a rain check on the dancing and the kissing and the other things until we can find ourselves in a less public setting."

"Cab." She finally found her aplomb. "Are you by chance proposition-ing me?"

"What if I were, Marigold?" Cab's smile didn't falter, but his tone had gone serious. "What if I wanted a whole lot more than you seem prepared to give?"

"Cab." Marigold was astonished into silence. "You don't seem to understand—"

"I understand plenty." He smoothed an errant lock of hair behind her ear. "Think about it, Marigold, while you're arranging everybody else's life but your own." He stepped away. "Think about what you might have, if you'd only let yourself ask."

CHAPTER 30

There are only two tragedies in life: one is not getting what you want and the other is getting it.

—Oscar Wilde

The evening ended late. With Daisy and Tad so loath to be parted and Seviah completely engrossed in conversation with Mr. Keith, it was the wee small hours of the morning before they returned to Bessie Dove's, only to find an anxious-looking Wilbert sitting on Bessie's front porch in wait.

"It's Granny," he told his siblings without any further ado. "She's fit to be tied. Wanted an accounting of us all out of the blue."

"Oh, no," said Daisy at the same time that Marigold asked, "What's an accounting?" What had happened to the *each to fend for themselves* ethos?

Seviah whistled sharply. "Damn. How does she always know?"

"Don't matter how she knows, just that she does," Wilbert answered. "We got to fetch back to the island right quick."

Bessie already had their things bundled up and ready to go, so there was nothing to do but thank her and assure her they would all be all right. "I worry about you all," she fretted. "And my girl too, out there with Miz Alva fit to be tied."

"Don't worry, Momma." Lucy emerged from the dark boardwalk into the light of the porch. "I didn't like being out there either, so once I saw Wilbert going, I decided to pack up and get home while the getting was good."

"Did you bring everything?" Bessie's question was sharp with anxiousness.

"Not everything," Lucy admitted. "I'll get back when things . . . settle down. But I locked the place up good."

"All right then." Bessie's relief was only momentary. "If I were you all, I wouldn't go," she counseled the others. "Y'all can stay here—you already paid for the rooms," she argued. "I got a bad feeling about this."

Marigold was more than ready to bow to Bessie's wisdom—both her baser instincts for peace and preservation and her higher, more logical sense urged her to follow Lucy's lead. "Perhaps it would be best to return in the morning, when everyone has had some rest?"

But Wilbert was adamant. "We got to go. We got to get home now. No two ways about it."

And where Wilbert went, Daisy would loyally follow. "He's right—like you said to me before, Marigold, we can't turn tail now. But you'll come with me?" Daisy reached for her hand. "Won't you?"

"Naturally," Marigold said with far more assurance than she felt. "I'm sure everything will be fine," she said to bolster her own confidence as much as theirs. "We're in for a tongue-lashing, I suppose, but if that is the cost of an absolutely wonderful evening, then so be it. She can't take the experience away from us."

"She'll try," muttered Wilbert.

Cab took hold of her elbow in that gently insistent way of his. "Are you sure, Marigold? You don't have to go with them—I'm happy to have you stay with me." He seemed to realize what he had said. "I mean, as Bessie said, she would be happy to put you up here, where you'll be safe and I can"—he searched for the correct thing to say—"be of some assistance to you, should the need arise."

"Thank you, Cab. You're very kind to offer, but I need to stand by my cousins. We'll weather whatever storm might come for attending the party together. It's not as if we snuck ourselves out to a roadhouse, after all—we were at a perfectly acceptable, socially elevated ball," she said, to convince herself as much as him. "I'm sure there is nothing to worry about."

"Somehow, with you, Marigold, there's always something to worry about. Wait here," he admonished before he bolted into the boardinghouse. It was only a moment before he was back, pressing a small, unmistakably shaped object into her hand.

"Cab!" she gasped, half in jest, half in dawning terror as she palmed the gun.

"Do you know how to use it?"

"Yes, but—"

"Then take it. Like I said, there are larger forces at play here."

The seriousness of the situation pulled at her like a weight at her hems. "Then I will certainly look out for them—and defend my cousins if need be."

"Good." He nodded in grim satisfaction. "But promise me you will take care of yourself, Marigold."

"I promise." She gave his arm a squeeze before she kissed his cheek. "Thank you for the loveliest night."

"Remember that. Always."

★　★　★

Wilbert silently rowed the loaded dory across the darkened sound. Seviah sat in the bow, twisting forward to mark their way, while Marigold and Daisy sat together in the stern. Marigold kept up her purposefully cheerful, willfully positive demeanor despite the misgivings swirling around in her stomach like one of Cleon's fish stews until they finally fetched up in the slanted moonlight of North Cove.

"Gird your loins," was Seviah's advice as he handed them onto the beach. "Don't tell her nothing if you can help it."

"Seviah, there is no reason for anyone to conceal or lie," Marigold said as together the four of them dragged the dory high on the sand. "We did nothing wrong! I, for one, am exceptionally proud of you both."

"Thank you, Marigold." Daisy squeezed her hand. "That means the world to me."

"Why don't you let me take the blame?" Marigold suggested. "I'm sure I don't mind."

"No." Daisy was sure. "Like you said, we got into this together, and we'll get out of it by sticking together."

And stick together they did, until they reached the farmyard.

"Is that you, Daisy girl?" A querulous voice crept out of the ruined house like a fog. "Come here, child. I've been waiting forever for you."

"Coming, Granny," Daisy answered. "Stay with me, Marigold."

"Of course I will." But something about the eerie tension in the air had Marigold reaching into her pocket to check the small, steely, pearl-handled revolver—it was fully loaded.

Trust Cab to be thorough.

Marigold stuffed the uncocked gun back into the pocket of her evening cape before she took Daisy's cold hand and followed her into the dim kitchen. Except it wasn't dim at all but lit with oil lamps on the table and candles on the walls, illuminating a tiny old woman who sat like a queen in an ornate but tatty upholstered armchair of the last era.

Here at last was Great-Aunt Alva.

Marigold was decidedly underwhelmed. The woman who had loomed so large in her imagination was nothing more than a latter-day Miss Havisham, Charles Dickens's embittered character, fading away with the ages, down to her white hair and white gown, which upon closer inspection was not a wedding dress but a nightgown, buttoned up to its tattered lace neck.

This fragile old doily of a woman could not possibly be the malevolent presence Marigold had imagined her to be.

"Where have you been?" the old woman said to them in a soft, little-girlish voice. "Why were you not here when I called you to come to me?"

"We're all here now, Granny," said Wilbert as he took an empty chair.

And they all were. Marigold could see Ellery and Cleon seated around the table, while Sophronia hung back in the shadows near the stove.

"Indeed you are," the old woman said with sighing satisfaction. "Where you should be, for this is where Hatchets belong. This is our place, out here, away from the sinful turmoil of the world, close to God." Her little-girl voice gained some small strength as she continued. "But who is that?" She pointed to Marigold with arthritic, shaking fingers. "Who is she, who is not family?"

"I told you, Mother Hatch—" Sophronia began.

"I'm Marigold Manners, ma'am." Despite the late hour, Marigold was in full possession of her senses and preferred to speak for herself. "I'm Esmé Sedgwick Manners and Harry Minot Manners's daughter, as I think you know, for I told you so myself, at your door. I came two weeks ago at Mrs. Sophronia Hatchet's invitation." She extended her hand. "I'm pleased to finally meet you."

Great-Aunt Alva drew herself back. "I know who you are, Esmie's girl." She pinched up her mouth and face as if she'd discovered a particularly distressing smell—the very picture of offended sensibility.

But Marigold was unafraid to ruffle antiquated feathers. "Then why did you ask?"

Alva Hatchet's eyes flared at her audacity. "Because I expect to be answered," she quavered, all querulous hurt. "Mind your tongue, girl."

"I'll mind mine if you mind yours. My mother's name was Esmé." Marigold corrected her pronunciation. "As well you know, for you were, I understand from my mother, present at her christening to hear it spoken correctly."

"Well, don't you seem to know a lot of things that are none of your business?" The old woman retreated into pettishness. "Like encouraging your cousins into dangerous and foolish behavior, going across the water and cavorting in the town. Look at them, all dudded up in indecent glad rags."

"I think I look dashed fine, if I do say so myself," said Seviah, while Daisy made bold enough to say, "Not *cavorting*, Granny. Really."

"You may not say so yourself," Alva contradicted her grandson before she turned to her granddaughter. "And what do you think you *were* doing if it wasn't cavorting about in such indecent clothes? Why, I can see your *arms*," she said with outraged primness.

"We were at a dance—a lovely society party that we were invited to." Daisy's voice gained quiet confidence. "At Rock Ledge in Pride's Crossing, which is a lovely home, all beautiful and elegant and spacious. You were wrong about the town, Granny. Nobody was mean to us. We had a lovely, lovely time without a single moment of *cavorting*."

"Indeed." Marigold moved closer to support Daisy.

"You"—this time, Alva Hatchet shook her cane at Marigold—"will speak only when spoken to. And you two"—she returned her complaint to her grandchildren—"going over the water, letting yourselves go out amongst those people, disporting yourselves for their amusement and censure. Letting them make a mockery of you."

"There was no mockery," Daisy asserted. "We were most warmly received. In fact, the evening turned into a grand celebration of the fact that I am now engaged to be married to Mr. Thaddeus Endicott."

There was a lovely fraction of a second of silence before all hell broke loose.

"That will set the cat amongst the pigeons," said Sophronia, with what Marigold could have sworn was the beginnings of a smile, while Wilbert muttered, "Now we're in for it." Beside him, Seviah said, "Here we go," before he threw himself into a chair as if he were a character in a melodramatic play.

"No!" Alva's soft voice somehow cut through the din. She drew herself up like a displeased monarch. "I will not allow you to tell such an obvious falsehood, Daisy. How could this not be a lie? You were forbidden such contact with the town and the pernicious Endicotts. Forbidden to leave this island."

"*I* never promised," Daisy said with some spirit.

Alva gaped at her audacity. "Tell her again, Ellery." She turned to her son for support. "Tell her you won't allow it. Tell her you forbid it!"

Ellery Hatchet, who normally seemed ready to spit fire, was rather more subdued in his response. Though he said, "You'll marry that spawn of Satan over my dead body," his words lacked their usual bite.

"So be it," Daisy cried, and in the blink of an eye, she had pulled her own little gun from the pocket of her evening cloak and had it pointed at her father. "I *will* marry Tad Endicott, even if I have to do it over your dead body." And when Ellery Hatchet rose from his seat in astonishment, she raised her pistol with him, cool as any desperado. "Not a single step. Or I swear to heaven, I'll shoot your eye out."

Daisy rose to her moment. She spoke with absolute conviction. "I am my own woman, Granny, and I can decide for myself. And I chose love. I'm going to marry Tad Endicott if it's the last thing I do on this green earth, because I love him and he loves me and we're getting married and that's an end to it."

"But I forbid it," Alva insisted on a sob.

But the assembly was diverted from Alva's theatrics in favor of Seviah's—he shook off his indolent pose and stood as if he were in command of a stage. "I'm leaving too. If Daisy is leaving this godforsaken place for the life she was meant to have, so can I!"

"No!" Sophronia's objection was no more than a whisper, but she reached for her son. "Seviah! Not you."

"Yes, me!" he declared. "I'm tired of your doom and gloom and tea leaves and tarot. I'm tired of this rotten old place and of working for nothing. There's nothing for me here, so I've got nothing to lose. I've got a chance and I'm going to take it."

"A chance?" Sophronia cried. "But where will you go? What will you do?"

"What I was born to do." Seviah struck a dramatic pose that would doubtless soon be filling matinees and evenings alike. "I'm going upon the stage! The famous Mr. Benjamin Franklin Keith himself has asked me to join his traveling revue. And I'm going to do it. I'm going to be a vaudeville star, and there's nothing any of you can say that could stop me."

"If you go," Ellery threatened, "you'll get nothing from me."

"Ain't *never* got nothing from you worth having," Seviah scoffed. "Never paid me a wage. Never paid me so much as a kind word."

"You never deserved one!" his father bellowed. "And what's more, you sniveling ba—"

"Ellery! I won't have this. I won't." Alva had recovered herself enough to thump her cane to get their attention. "No one is to leave Great Misery Island."

"Not if they ain't in a casket," Cleon muttered sympathetically.

"I am leaving!" Seviah said with defiance. "I'm leaving on my own two feet right this minute, even if I have to swim across the sound. That Mr. Keith said as he would send his launch for me, but I didn't want him to see what a pitiful bag o' nails this place is. I didn't want him to pity or be ashamed of me, the way I am of you."

CHAPTER 31

A man who carries a cat by the tail learns something he can learn in no other way.

—Mark Twain

Inside her pocket, Marigold's hand clutched at her own gun, even as she was both astonished and thrilled to find she hadn't trained all the brash independence from Daisy's character. Across the room, even Wilbert gaped at Daisy.

"You wouldn't dare!" her father thundered.

"Try me," the girl answered with calm determination. "I've had about all I'm prepared to take. After all these years of your abuse," she swore, "don't think I wouldn't mind using you for target practice. Maybe I won't bother to shoot your eye out." She let her arm drop slightly. "I'll aim lower."

Ellery obligingly blanched, but Great-Aunt Alva clutched her chest as if she were suffering an apoplexy. "No, no! We'll go on like we did before. We'll return to the old ways."

"And what ways are those?" Marigold asked with all the unperturbed logic she could muster. "When an innocent girl could be forced into an arranged marriage?"

Great-Aunt Alva ignored Marigold's question, wilting into a tearful puddle of damp nightgown. "How could this happen?" she wailed piteously at her granddaughter. "How could you leave me? How could you abandon me?"

"Ashamed?" Ellery Hatchet's voice rose to a mean snarl. "I've never been anything but ashamed of *you*. You and your—"

"Seviah, I forbid you!" Alva gripped her cane so tightly her swollen knuckles shone white as bones against the handle. "You'll be cursed—"

"I'm cursed if I stay," Seviah returned. "Cursed by him"—he jabbed a finger at his father—"every blame day of my life no matter what I do. I've had enough. I'm leaving." He turned to his sister. "I'm going now—Daisy, if you want, I'll take you back with me."

"Yes!" she answered.

"Why, you ungrateful, unchristian succubi," Ellery fumed at his children. "I should have drowned you—drowned the whole lot of you! Ungrateful, unholy—"

"What will be will be, Ellery Hatchet." Sophronia stopped his rant with her quiet interjection. "You know that sure as you know anything."

"So you keep telling me, damn your witchy eyes." Ellery rose to his gaunt height. "Years and years of toil I've given, laboring under your curses—both of you!" He stabbed his fingers at both his mother and his wife. "The things I've done for this family. But no more. I'll not labor another minute for you ungrateful wretches. By God, I'm going too! I've made up my mind. I'm going to join the Revered Edison P. Cooper and his religious tent revival at Manchester. I'm dedicating my life to the good Lord from here on out, and I'll never think of you or this cursed island ever again."

And then, in the way of things, the evening really went downhill from there.

Alva screamed. Sophronia sank down into a chair in wonder. Daisy gripped Marigold's hand tighter than ever. Only Wilbert seemed to take the announcement in stride. "Well, I'll be doggoned. If that don't just seem like the fittest thing for you, Pa, I don't know what is."

"I forbid it, do you hear?" Alva cawed. "I forbid you!"

For a moment Ellery wavered under her piteous stare, but them he seemed to throw off her spell. "Mother, you have no hold on me now. I belong to no one but the Lord."

"You belong to me and this island," Alva insisted. "You promised," she cried. "You promised me."

"I'm done with the past," Ellery declared. "Done, I tell you. I'll go and take nothing but my Bible."

"You won't go. You dare not," the tiny old woman insisted. "You"—she turned on Sophronia—"you tell your husband he needs to stay. He belongs here. He belongs to us, here."

"Oh, nay," Sophronia disagreed with a wondrous sort of serenity. "He's none of mine. Hasn't belonged to me for years and years, nor I him. Best for him to follow his own way. What will be will be."

"I'll row you across myself, Pa," Wilbert declared. "If we go now, we can catch the tide."

"Have you all lost your senses?" Alva Hatchet asked everyone and no one in particular. "Don't you dare get in a boat." She seemed genuinely bereft, panting for air with her hand across her chest, as if she were having heart palpitations. "You know the danger of crossing—"

"I've broken the curse and the chains you've bound around me, Mother," Ellery said with an eye-rolling sort of wonder. "As sure as the dawn is rising upon us, I'll look to the new day and a new life. I'll go with God and pray that he has mercy upon your wretched souls."

He strode out of the room, deaf to his mother's wailing—which found a new target.

"This is all your doing," she cried. "You're the slommack who came to disrupt our ways." Alva stabbed the air in front of Marigold's chest with her cane as if she would lance Marigold like a boil. "You put all this nonsense in their heads, and you're to take it back out. They listened to me—they obeyed me before you came."

As Marigold had indeed quite purposefully helped both Wilbert and Daisy, encouraged Seviah, and told Ellery about the tent revival—and was frankly extraordinarily pleased at the result—she decided discretion was the better part of valor.

She kept her mouth shut. There would be time enough to savor her triumphs later. One never wanted to make too much of oneself.

But Sophronia found her voice. "I've told you again and again, Mother Hatchet, what will be will be. There's no way you can stop it, no matter who you blame."

"This is your doing too." Alva turned on her daughter-in-law. "You could have prevented this if you'd been any sort of decent wife."

"Would have needed a decent sort of husband," Sophronia returned reasonably, almost smiling at the sight of her tiny mother-in-law quivering with impotent rage.

In fact, the old woman looked so like a female Rumpelstiltskin that Marigold instinctively drew herself and Daisy back, lest the old lady go up in a flash of angry smoke.

But the movement brought Alva's attention back to her granddaughter. "How could you let yourself be led astray by one such as her?" she asked Daisy in a last-ditch plea choked with tears. "You were raised to be an unspoiled, natural, biddable creature, and you've turned into this . . . this . . ." She sputtered to find a word bad enough.

"This elegant, self-possessed young woman?" Marigold finished for her.

"Thank you, Marigold," Daisy said, before she addressed her grandmother again. "Marigold didn't lead me astray, Granny. She helped me find my way—the way I wanted for myself. The same way she did for Will and Sev, and even Pa, if I had to guess. She showed us that what we wanted for ourselves was possible." Daisy turned back to Marigold. "And I, for one, can never thank her enough."

"That's right," said Wilbert. "We each made our own decisions and followed our own conscience. Nobody can say we didn't."

Marigold found herself besieged by emotion. Darling wretches, defending her like that. She was uncommonly, unforgivably proud of all of them. "Thank you," she said when she found her voice. "And on that note, I should think the account is full and done, and I, for one, am for bed. It's been a very long but very fruitful day."

Marigold took Daisy's hand, and by silent consent, they went together up to Daisy's room.

But not before they heard Sophronia say with a sort of gleeful wonder, "Definitely not the same length as all the others."

Chapter 32

It has long been an axiom of mine that the little things are infinitely the most important.

—Arthur Conan Doyle

The next day was the most tranquil Marigold had ever spent at Hatchet Farm. Ellery was gone to Manchester and the Reverend Cooper at dawn, rowed away by a jubilant Wilbert.

Seviah had gone as well, sailing off in a canoe he had kept hidden on the southwestern end of the island—the means for secret trips to the theater and nickelodeon parlor revealed—anxious to make his appointment with Mr. Keith at Pride's Crossing's small opera house.

Daisy was packing her bags—which were, in actuality, Marigold's valises and trunks, as Daisy had never before had the opportunity for travel—for a visit to Rock Ledge, where she had been invited for a get-to-know-you stay by her future mother-in-law, who was very smartly trying to ease the antagonism between her husband and son that had arisen as a result of the latter's engagement.

Which left Great-Aunt Alva fuming in her room, audibly muttering on about the danger of boats, while Sophronia joined Wilbert and Marigold in quiet repose in the breezeway.

"It sure was a right good thing that you came, Cousin Marigold," Wilbert mused. "Because of you, everything's changed."

Marigold certainly felt her own share of contentment in knowing she had done well by her cousins. But while she might be forgiven some small private pride in her accomplishments, pride inevitably went before a fall. "Not because of me, Wilbert. You said so yourself last night—you all made your own decisions. All I did was help you find the information and means to make those decisions."

"I reckon you'll be gone soon too, same as Daisy." His tone was surprisingly wistful.

"I'm not going anywhere yet, Wilbert." Not until she saw them all settled in their new roles. With Ellery gone, she might stay as long as she wished now. The problem was in knowing what exactly she wished for—besides learning what great and godless wrong had been done to her late, beloved mother.

"I suppose that Harvard fellow's going to come calling?"

If Marigold had indeed expected Cab Cox to come calling that morning, she had been very much mistaken. She quashed her unreasonable disappointment with a stringent application of rationality. "You suppose wrong, Wilbert. Mr. Cox knows I have no interest in marriage."

"Way he looked at you last night . . ." Wilbert shook his head like a hound. "Like he's not the kind of fellow who's used to taking no for an answer."

"I assure you, Mr. Cox is a gentleman who is well able to take no for an answer."

"You'd really say no to a fellow like him?"

"I would." Despite her attraction to Cab, her feelings on the subject of marriage remained quite strict.

Wilbert's sigh was just heartfelt enough to be alarming. "Well, I guess now I won't feel so bad." He turned his attention to the problems at hand. "With Lucy gone, Granny will be fit to be tied over the food. Wonder if she left any foodstuffs behind?"

"Why don't I take a look in Lucy's root cellar," Marigold offered. She doubted Lucy would have had time to remove all of the canned and dried goods she had stored before she sailed to the mainland last night.

But the bulkhead latch was locked. Marigold would have gone to the door, or at the very least peered in the small windows—she had always been curious to see the inside of the place—when Bessie Dove emerged from it, walking purposefully toward the breezeway at the back of the house.

Bessie Dove, who had sworn to never set foot upon Great Misery again, was approaching Sophronia, who stood warily.

Marigold stepped back into the shade of Lucy's cabin to watch and listen.

"You know we got to talk," Bessie began.

"Ayuh," Sophronia was agreeing in her odd New England way. "After well on twenty years, I suppose we were due."

"Is he gone for good, do you think?" Bessie asked.

Sophronia almost smiled. "A body can only hope."

"And your boy Seviah?"

Sophronia's countenance seemed to cloud. "Gone with some theater fellow he talked about. Said he weren't coming back."

"He's got Lucy thinking the same," Bessie accused, "talking about striking out on her own. Which is all fine and good, but I can't like this closeness between my girl and your boy. He was at my house this morning, talking to her all secret-like, the two of them thick as thieves." Bessie put her hands on her hips. "Now, your man—"

"He's not my man," Sophronia broke in. "Never really was. Bound to follow no counsel or course but his own." She looked Bessie in the eye. "But you, of all people, knew long before me what he's like."

Bessie responded, almost too quietly for Marigold to hear, "I prayed he was done with that, for your sake."

"He was not." Sophronia's admission came on a sigh. "He always took what he wanted without so much as a by-your-leave from another soul." She drew in a long breath, as if she could draw strength or solace from the sweetening spring air. "He didn't ever belong to anybody except himself. And Mother Hatchet."

"That one," was Bessie's dismissal of the old beldam before she pressed her original point. "Now, I don't have nothing against your boy personally, but you know we can't let them think—"

"He is my boy," Sophronia confirmed quietly. "But he's not Hatchet's."

Marigold felt as if the blood had stopped in her veins—her skin went all hot and prickly and she had to put a hand across her mouth to keep from making another sound. But she must have made some noise, because the two women's heads swiveled toward where she hid. And then Bessie took Sophronia's elbow and urged her into the garden, on the other side of the runner bean frames—well out of earshot, damn it.

And although Marigold had strict feelings about eavesdropping, she had never been so tempted to break all her hard-and-fast standards of conduct as she was now. "Damnation." Marigold gave in to her vexation.

"That you, Marigold?" Lucy emerged from under the bulkhead door. "I thought I heard someone at the latch. What you doing here?"

"I was just coming to ask you about . . ." Marigold stuck as close to the truth as she dared. "About purchasing some of the canned and dried goods you might not want to transport back to the mainland."

"Oh, sure." Lucy frowned even as she agreed. "I'll set some things out for you." But she carefully reset the padlock on the outside of the cellar door.

Still so many locks. "Thank you."

"I was just about to clean out my stuff from the loft," Lucy said. "Care to help me?"

"Seviah's loft?" Marigold responded, more from curiosity than anything else.

"Our loft."

Marigold allowed herself the small pleasure of vindication before she followed Lucy up the ladder. Without the lamps, the loft at the top of the barn was dim and unlit and . . . empty. The colorful shawls and swaths of fabric that had decorated the walls were gone. The precious gramophone had been taken away, as had most of the rubber record disks—a scattered few were stacked in a cardboard tray, too numerous, she guessed, for Seviah to have packed in his hasty departure.

"I was just coming back for those." Lucy shrugged a leather satchel off her shoulder.

"These are yours, then?" Marigold started to collect the disks. "Are you going for good, then, too?"

"Everything has its season—that's what scripture says, anyway. And the season for my time on Great Misery has come to an end. But that's the way of it, isn't it?" Lucy laughed. "My momma used to say that when you find how you want to spend the rest of your life, you want that rest of your life to start right away."

"And is Seviah to be a part of that life?" Marigold asked cautiously.

"Sev?" Lucy's smile somehow widened. "You're just like my momma—she's got some worm eating at her brain that I'm all romantic about Seviah, but it's not like that between him and me. It was just being friendly, playing music, me teaching him about the blues and all. Him helping me with other things. Finding some small way to be happy."

Let that be a lesson to Marigold for jumping to unwarranted conclusions. "I had a hunch it was you two, together, singing and playing music late into the night, and not a haunted house at all."

"Oh, yeah!" Lucy's smile seemed to light the dim interior. "That was our secret, him and me. Treated me right," she averred with quiet conviction. "He helped me, so I helped him—helped us both to something better."

And here Marigold had thought she was the one who had put ideas of something better into her cousin's head.

Lucy put the disks into the satchel. "Sev couldn't afford much himself, what with old Ellery not paying them wages."

"But you got paid?" So strangely inconsistent, these quarrelsome, miserly Hatchets.

"Every week, in advance," Lucy confirmed. "Saturday morning, on the tray, in actual."

"Alva paid you herself?" What had Cleon, or was it Wilbert, said about the egg money? *Likes to know where every penny has gone.*

Lucy shrugged. "Don't know who else would have any money—no one else on this rock ever had more than a few cents to rub together before you came along. But I'm glad you did. Because things are different now, and that's a real good thing."

"Then I'm glad I came too." Marigold's smile felt bittersweet—to think she had made such friends only when she was losing them. "What will you do now?"

"Well . . ." Lucy hesitated a long moment before she made up her mind. "I've got this idea for a book on cookery. I've been working on my recipes, just getting them down exactly right, trying the tricky ones out on Seviah and then you, this last bit, before I served them to old Mrs. Hatchet—that's how he helped me before you came, tasting everything. So, if he liked it and then old Mrs. Hatchet liked it—because she hates everything—I knew my recipe was good."

"Excellent." Marigold heartily approved. "A book of recipes and instruction that could teach even me to cook?"

"Maybe not you," Lucy laughed. "It's meant to be for professional cooks, who cook for others." She fished a sheaf of papers out of her satchel and handed them to Marigold, who moved closer to the loft's hay door and the light.

"Why, Lucy!" Marigold's voice was full of admiration. "Your hand-writing is exquisite."

"So? I told you I went to a free school in Salem."

"A careful hand shows a careful mind. And this is meticulous, so I am quite sure without tasting this particular beef burgoo that it will be delicious."

"So, you think my idea could work?"

"Naturally! I will immediately make inquiries amongst my friends as to how to go about doing just that." Isabella would know somebody in publishing—she knew everybody. And young Thaddeus Endicott, who was about to launch a fashionable magazine, was likely to know whose door Lucy might knock upon. "We will make your plan a reality, Lucy. See if we don't."

"You'd help me?" Lucy's smile was all the thanks Marigold might need.

"Naturally! And as much as I hate to see you go, I know it will be for the best." Marigold was surprised by her own sentiment. "You must do what you're meant to do and let the world learn to catch up. Now, before I weep like a maiden auntie . . ." Marigold held out her hand to shake, but to her surprise—and delight—Lucy pulled her into a quick but heartfelt hug.

"I'm going to miss you, all improving like you are and everything," Lucy said as she stepped back. "And I'm going to remember you, too, when things need improving—how small things, like washing the clothes and picking up that junk, started to change everything."

"Thank you, Lucy. I'll remember you too. Especially when you're a famous chef and author. I'll be telling everyone, 'I knew her back when!' You and Seviah both."

"You do that, Miss Big City Manners," Lucy teased. "Well." She straightened her clothes. "You stay in touch."

"Naturally. Until then, goodbye and good luck!" Marigold called as she waved Lucy down the ladder. But Marigold didn't follow. Instead, she found a bale of hay near the open loft window and sat for a quiet moment to think.

Because what Sophronia had said to Bessie Dove to stop the worm of worry in her brain was that Seviah was not Ellery's son. Which meant that

Bessie had been worried that he was. Because when had she thought that Seviah was Ellery's son, he was unfit for Lucy's company?

Which meant either that whatever had happened between Ellery Hatchet and Bessie Dove in the past was so awful that she was carrying a grudge . . . or that the grudge she had carried might actually be Lucy.

Seviah Hatchet might not be Ellery Hatchet's child, but Marigold would bet all her accomplishments to date that Lucy Dove was.

CHAPTER 33

The possible's slow fuse is lit by the imagination.
—Emily Dickinson

Marigold had no idea what to do with her supposition—or her rage at what she assumed had been done to Bessie. There was no one with whom she might share such an awful, criminal conjecture until she had better proof.

"Marigold, are you up there?" Daisy called from below.

"I'm coming down." Marigold tried to shake off her consternation and keep her misgivings to herself.

"I was talking to some of the gals from town last night, at the party," Daisy began before Marigold reached the barn floor. "And they said that you had formed a Ladies' Cycling Club, and they invited me to be a part of it. I know I said I didn't want to learn to ride, because Taddy couldn't, but it would be nice to belong to a social group once I move into town, when Tad and I get married. So will you teach me?"

"Naturally."

Daisy threw her arms around Marigold's neck. "Oh, Marigold, thank you ever so much. You're the best friend a girl could have. I can't wait to see Tad's face when I ride by him, pretty as you please. It'll do him good to see other people do things he can't do—at least not yet."

"Indeed." Marigold could only agree. It would also do Daisy good to have accomplishments of her own going into her marriage.

Daisy whooped before she pressed a kiss of thanks to Marigold's cheek. "You really are the best, Marigold. Moments like this, you make me feel like I almost have a sister."

Marigold's heart, which she had been attempting to keep under strict, rational regulation, went soft and illogical. The heat of tears built behind her eyes, and it was everything she could do not to cry. She settled for a decorous sniffle. "I am deeply honored that you should think so. Now, let's get started."

They spent a companionable hour on the lesson—which Daisy really didn't need, because the girl was quite strong and physically adept—before Marigold turned her hand to helping Wilbert repair the henhouse.

"Sure was smart of you to get this new chicken wire. Must have cost you a pretty penny. Don't know as when I'll be able to pay you back for it. Don't know how in tarnation Pa did it," Wilbert admitted. "I mean, things were tight, you know? Weren't any sugar but once in a blue moon, or luxuries ever, till you came. There were always oats for porridge, and beans and bacon, and coffee, but I can't buy all that selling eggs!"

"Did your father not keep a bank account or some such?"

"Didn't trust banks. Kept his money to himself, Pa said. And he was such an awful cuss that he probably took whatever money he still had with him—kept it in an old talcum powder tin he kept hidden in an old boot."

"Lucy said she was paid every week," Marigold countered. "In cash money—left on her tray. So, does Great-Aunt Alva have her own money that ought to be put to Hatchet Farm's upkeep? And I will say, I will offer again to pay for my own room and board. I know," she said to forestall any objection, "your mother said you'd take nothing from me, but circumstances have changed. And we seem to be at an impasse that I could at least alleviate—at least until you get the legalities straight."

"What legalities?" asked Wilbert.

"Well, now that your father has left, are you legally entitled to run the farm?" Marigold spoke some of her musings out loud. "If Ellery has absconded from his responsibilities, can the deed to the island be transferred to your name—assuming there is a deed?"

"I don't know 'bout nothing legal," Wilbert admitted. "But I better find out, because now that old man is gone, I reckon I'm the one who's going to have to answer the letter old man Endicott gave to Daisy asking about her dowry."

"That was quick!" Marigold felt her brows rise.

"No grass that he can't sell grows under old man Endicott."

"May I see the letter? If you think that would help." She didn't want Wilbert to think she was horning in. Or doubting his reading ability.

"Sure." Wilbert dug the creased missive out of his vest pocket.

Marigold scanned the bold, typewritten letter wherein Mr. George Endicott, acting on behalf of his heir, Mr. Thaddeus C. Endicott, asked that a dowry be assigned to Miss Daisy Hatchet in advance of her "mooted" marriage to Thaddeus Endicott. "Well, it certainly is full of legalese. He even goes so far as to suggest that land would be an acceptable asset given in the 'dower proceedings.' Well, my, my." Exactly as she had so cavalierly suggested.

"Do you think that lawyer friend of yours, that Cox fellow, might mind taking a look to tell me what it says? It's all ten-dollar words," Wilbert fretted.

"Naturally, Wilbert," she assured him. "I will ask Mr. Cox to do so, if it isn't a conflict of interest." Especially if Cab had also taken her suggestion and was acting as Tad's attorney. "But first we have to ask ourselves something else." Something she had asked herself before and never answered. "If Endicott has long sought to get this land—Cab told me the man has brought any number of lawsuits over the years—but your father has long refused to sell, even though, as he stated the other night, he hated the place and needed the money . . ." Marigold tried to turn each fact logically. "Why would Cousin Ellery not sell?"

Wilbert threw up his shoulder in that world-weary Hatchet shrug. "The old man never said. Too contrary is my guess."

Marigold was not prepared to be so fatalistic. "Why on earth is Great Misery Island, a bald outcropping of rock that seems incapable of sustaining anything but sheep—and maybe not even them—so worth having that two men would fight over it for thirty-odd years?"

"Dunno."

"Well, if I were you, Wilbert, I'd try to find out."

★ ★ ★

Marigold could not sleep. The possibilities—about adultery and money and marriage and drowned girls—kept churning in her head, tossing and turning her in her bed, until sometime deep in the night, a loud noise brought her fully awake.

Her ears searched out the familiar rasping moans, but the usual melodic sounds of Seviah and Lucy singing blues songs in the wee small hours of the morning were absent. An eerie, ringing silence reigned.

Marigold was just about to turn over and plug her ears with her pillow when it came again—a loud, sharp concussion of a sound, like a door being thrown open or slammed shut. The vibration shuddered through the house.

She quickly threw back the blankets and fumbled in the darkness for suitable clothing in which to be abroad at night—one might alter one's standards but never let them down—all the while straining to hear what was going on.

Below, doors creaked open and shut, footsteps pattered along. A voice rose in muffled protest, but by the time she donned her long duster and cycling boots over her night clothes and went down to open her stout lock, she found the door at the bottom of her stair was wedged shut. From the outside.

Marigold rattled the panel in disbelief, before she put her shoulder into it and shoved, hard. The stout pine didn't budge.

She was locked in.

But by whom? And why? The undisciplined, fearful part of her brain readily supplied one obvious answer—to pen her up so they might do her a more specific harm.

An image of Seviah with his matches, crouching to light a fire at the other side of her door, leapt unbidden into her mind's eye before she could sternly ward it away with the clear, calm fact that Seviah was well away from Great Misery Island and Hatchet Farm and had no logical reason to return. He was going to go and never look back, he had said.

Likewise, Daisy and Lucy, with their guns and knives, were her boon companions now and could not wish her any harm. And the most obvious person who had so openly wished her to perdition—Ellery Hatchet—had gone off in the service of the Lord, with no mention of coming back.

That left Wilbert with his scythe, which seemed unlikely, given their obvious rapport. And, of course, Cleon with his clumsy shoves, which seemed too inept for door locking.

But then there was Sophronia, with her witchy ways and withholding of information—perhaps, after all her waiting, she meant to offer Marigold something other than atonement.

Marigold quickly retreated up the stairs to light her lamp to relieve the pitch-darkness—the full moon of the prior night must be obscured by clouds. But the lamplight illuminated the pearlescent gleam of the revolver that she had resolutely set aside in the belief that the moment of crisis had passed and she would not have need for it again.

Had the moment come again?

Better to be prepared and not need it than to be taken by surprise.

But she was still a thinking creature who would use logic before resorting to violence—just because she had a gun didn't mean she had to use it.

Her gaze fell on the little jam jar on the stool next to the bed. The water reflecting the dim light of the lantern held a fresh wildflower—a minty-looking leaf with tiny blue flowers—but tonight the jar could serve a different purpose.

Marigold dashed the flowers and water into the washstand and first put the glass to the door. What she heard could only be described as scuffling—chairs or heels scrapped against the floor or the creaks and groans of the old wooden planks. Words too indistinct to make sense. She could make out some more distinct sounds—low, short utterances from the front of the house, or possibly the kitchen—but could not distinguish voices or words. There was a heavy clatter, as if a chair—or a very large teacup—had been overturned.

And then there was nothing but silence.

So much silence, for so long, that she finally retreated to sit on the top step, still grimly gripping the pistol in her nerveless hand. Although she still strained to listen, the only sound she could distinguish was a sort of weathered sigh, as if the house had resettled itself. Or was that the kitchen door?

Marigold sat with her ears pricked for what felt like hours. But there was nothing more—nothing but the sound of wind and waves counting time through the night. Silence continued to reign.

No one called. No one came to explain what had happened.

Still, she sat, gun in hand, eyes on the door at the bottom of the stairs. Waiting.

For whoever it was to come and try to kill her.

CHAPTER 34

The best way to cheer yourself up is to cheer somebody else up.

—Mark Twain

Marigold awoke with a start some hours after dawn, stiff and uncomfortable after falling asleep on the floor, disoriented by fitful dreams in which Minnie Mallory's red skirts had swirled around Marigold's feet, dragging her down into the icy water.

How strange to dream of someone she had never met.

But the first thing she did—carefully, with her pistol firmly in her grip—was try her door, which inched open freely at her tentative push.

Cleon was in the hallway, retrieving Aunt Alva's sparse breakfast tray. "Morning, Miss Girl." He was his usual shuffling self. "Yer down late." He took a second look at her. "You all to rights?"

"Yes, I thank you, Cleon." She hid the gun behind her back and smoothed her tangled braid to repair something of her appearance. "But I had a most uncomfortable night. What went on here?"

"Went on?" The old man was the very picture of wide-eyed bewilderment.

"You didn't hear all the commotion?"

"Didn't hear nothing," he swore. "Though the house, she makes odd moans and groans in the night, cursin' us in the darkness, you know."

"So I've heard." Marigold expressed her skepticism through sarcasm but did not waste any more time debating Cleon, who seemed to have the intellectual capacity of a pet goldfish—all gulping vacancy. He must be as deaf as a goldfish as well to have heard nothing.

"Marigold?" Daisy came down the hallway in a rush. "Why are you not dressed? You promised to help me with the valises. Aren't you coming to see me off?"

"Yes, of course. I'll only be a minute."

Marigold took, in fact, about five minutes to dress herself suitably in a well-tailored ensemble of chocolaty linen that made her feel jaunty and smart and not as if she had spent the night fighting her worst imaginings. And the jacket had a sufficiently deep pocket within which to stow her revolver without ruining the line of the suit. There was no excuse for looking less than one's best, even while one was armed.

She retrieved her bicycle from the barn, which already had Daisy's valises strapped to the back. "Well, you've been busy. Could you not get back to sleep either?"

Daisy shot her a quick look as she strode toward the path. "Well, I'm less all-overish now that the moment is finally here. I want to get away before the air turns—it's a weather breeder today, for sure."

It was, in fact, a clear, cloudless day with no wind—but in New England perfect conditions were mistrusted as the harbinger of a particularly mean storm. Daisy was understandably on edge.

"Did all that commotion last night keep you up too?"

"What commotion? I didn't hear nothing," Daisy vowed.

"Anything," Marigold corrected automatically. "Are you sure?"

"Why are you eyeing me all slantandicular?" Daisy reverted to her vernacular, something Marigold felt she did when she was uncomfortable. "What do you think you heard?"

There was something . . . probing about her question. Or was there? "I heard a commotion," was all Marigold could say. "Some sort of disturbance."

"Did you go see what it was?" Daisy asked.

"No," Marigold admitted.

"Then it can't have been particular interesting if you didn't."

"Particularly," Marigold corrected again. "I couldn't investigate the sound—my door was locked."

"Oh, sure," Daisy said nonsensically. "Mine, too, on the regular. Come on, I'm allafire with the need to get away." She darted ahead, past the path to North Cove. "I can't wait to get away for good."

"Where are you going?"

"I've got a little pinnace hidden up near the rocks—that ledge across from Taddy's place? Sev hid his sailing canoe on the southwest side, but Tad and I decided to put mine nearer the ledge so's I have some independence and be able to come see him."

Such a lot of hidden watercraft scattered about the island. Every day, it seemed, new secrets were revealed—the exception being the one secret that had brought Marigold to Great Misery in the first place.

"Daisy, do you think there's room for my bicycle in your pinnace?" Marigold felt the need to escape as keenly as her cousin, albeit for different reasons. Too many questions—as well as unspoken threats—remained unasked and unanswered. She wanted the calming exertion of a bicycle ride to get fresh air into her lungs and calm her racing thoughts. She might ride to the Ryersons' estate to talk with Isabella—although Isabella was likely to be deeply engrossed in planning Daisy's wedding ensemble, a topic that could interest Marigold only as an aesthetic exercise. Instead, she might visit the library, where she might research the potential messages of Sophronia's wildflowers. Or perhaps she might visit Cab instead, at Bessie's, to try to make sense of the strange events of the night.

"Surely." Daisy was all agreement. "We'll have to snug up, but we can make room for your machine."

"Thank you."

The lovely sweep of the short sail was exactly what Marigold wanted— the physical sensation of wind and wave helped quiet and focus her thoughts. With her Hatchet relatives finally sorted out, she could turn to the still-disturbing problem of what had really happened to Minnie. And those as-yet-unnamed *other girls*.

The bracing bicycle ride that followed bolstered her nerve. It seemed as if it were no time before Marigold was coasting comfortably through the town, plying her bell with a mixture of purpose and delight—she was going to ask the questions that needed answering—especially when she pedaled up to the library to see another women's bicycle leaning neatly against the lamppost in front of the library.

"Dare I hope that new machine is yours?" she asked Amelia Morgan, who came to the door to greet her.

"Isn't it marvelous?" The quiet librarian was bouncing up and down on her toes with suppressed excitement. "First the dance, and now this!"

Amelia could hardly contain all her delight. "I borrowed tools and I read the assembly instructions twice, but I would appreciate it greatly if you could take a look before I take it for any ride longer than a few blocks."

"It would be my pleasure." Marigold stripped off her gloves to test the tautness of the various nuts, especially the top head lug and the steering lock. "May I ask how long have you lived in Pride's Crossing? I only ask because I recall the other girls talking about their families and going to school here, while you live with a landlady."

"Almost two years now. I came east directly after finishing my degree at Mount Holyoke, near where I come from. Why do you ask?"

"Oh, nothing of import." Marigold waved her hand to signify that she was just trying to sort through her thoughts. "Did you come because you were offered a job at the library, or did you find the job after you came?"

"Oh, I was hired right out of college by Mr. Coolidge, our head librarian, who was hired by Mr. George Endicott, who had read of Mr. Andrew Carnegie's library patronage in Pennsylvania and fancied that Pride's Crossing needed a library to become a place of import, where summer folks from Boston would entertain themselves and the locals could educate themselves and their families. With the library and the theater, Pride's Crossing is becoming quite the sought-after destination."

Hardly, Marigold thought, but then she chided herself for being so uncharitable—good logic had no room for snobbery. What would Cab say if he were to hear her speaking so?

Marigold focused her logical mind away from Cab. "Would you have come, do you think, if you had visited in advance and known what Pride's Crossing was really like?"

"Of course," Amelia answered immediately. "Professional librarian positions are not so thick on the ground that I could afford to pass the offer up, even when it meant moving away from my family."

"I understand the professional implications, but what about all the things we talked about at the Ladies' Cycling Club—all the dangers to young, unmarried women? Like Minnie?"

Amelia took a long moment before she spoke carefully. "I suppose it's just as you said—human nature is much the same no matter where you are. You know, there was a river at home in South Hadley too—the Connecticut River—where young women every so often drowned. I just keep sure to stay well away from the water."

The water being a metaphor for any number of things dangerous to young women. "Well, your machine appears to be in very fine shape. Perhaps we can take a short ride together after the library closes for the evening?"

"That would be wonderful. Are you staying that long today?"

"Yes. I have a number of things I should like to research, starting with information on the folktale language of flowers."

Amelia nodded. "I believe we have at least one title on the topic."

Marigold followed her inside, and in no time at all, she was ensconced in the reading room, making a quick sketch of the delicate frond that had lately graced her jam jar.

"That looks like a maidenhair fern," Amelia commented as she brought Marigold two well-illustrated titles. "They grow wild in the low woodlands around town."

"That must be it." Marigold flipped open the first book, scanning the *f*'s. "Here! And they mean . . . secret bond of love? And if you are fascinated by a woman, it is a good gift to present her with?"

"Did someone give you a fern? Mr. Cox?"

Marigold was determined to keep all thoughts—and questions—about Cab under strict regulation. "No, my cousin Sophronia, who is conversant in the language of flowers, left the frond in a little vase in my room, along with a sprig of rosemary."

"Now, rosemary is for remembrance—even I know that. But . . ." Amelia sat next to Marigold to scan through the entry. "This reference says in folklore, the maidenhair fern is seen as a symbol of protection."

"So, the protection of a secret bond of love? Along with remembrance?" Was Marigold the one who was supposed to remember? Or was the message not about Marigold, as Sophronia had warned, but about someone else's secret love?

The baffling question of Seviah's parentage loomed large.

"What about bird's-foot trefoil?" That was the plant that Sophronia had mentioned when goading Ellery Hatchet the day he had tried to ruin the garden. Which reminded her of the tall pink flower Cleon had planted for her—but which she couldn't remember seeing since then. How curious.

Amelia had scanned through the index to find the entry. "*Lotus corniculatus* is the taxonomic name of bird's-foot trefoil. And the symbolic meanings is—" She looked up, startled. "Retribution. And revenge."

"Revenge?" Marigold pulled the book over to look at the illustration of the innocuously pretty little yellow flowers and tried to remember Sophronia's exact words. Had she advised Marigold to enact revenge, or to prevent Ellery from doing so?

"Why would someone want revenge on you?" Amelia was even more dumbfounded than Marigold, not having been witness to the antagonism between the inhabitants of Hatchet Farm.

But whatever revenge was to be exacted was a moot point now that Ellery was gone. And Marigold planned to be long gone too, back to Boston, before the old rattletrap ever made his way back to Great Misery. If only she could get through Sophronia's bizarre reluctance to tell her about the past—

"I hope you don't mind my asking," Amelia asked tentatively. "But I heard—perhaps it's just a rumor, but I did wonder—that the senior Mr. Hatchet has left Great Misery Island and taken up with an itinerant preacher."

News certainly traveled fast—too fast for Pride's Crossing to qualify as a place where "folks kept to themselves."

"It is true that my cousin's husband has joined a religious tent revival circuit," Marigold said, mostly to gauge Amelia's reaction—which was very clear relief. "Would Ellery Hatchet have made it upon your list of men to avoid?"

"Well, I've never met him," Amelia hedged, because she was trying to be polite. "But he does have a reputation as quite a strange and unforgiving man, always carrying on about hellfire and damnation."

"Yes. Quite so." But it seemed unlikely that Ellery's fiery preaching had anything to do with the "great and godless wrong" done to Marigold's mother, though it might have many things to do with other, present-day antagonisms.

"If I may, I should like to learn more about the history of Great Misery Island. And other islands like it along the coast," Marigold added to deflect her particular interest in why George Endicott might feel so proprietary about the island.

"I'll bring a few local histories, shall I?" Amelia suggested.

Marigold spent the rest of the afternoon searching and sorting through the local annals, all of which repeatedly featured the Endicotts as well as their Peabody and Crowninshield relations, looking for some reference to the ownership of Great Misery Island. But apart from a tale about the name of the island—a shipbuilding Peabody ancestor, who had gone out to the island to cut timber, was shipwrecked by a winter storm for three days of the greatest misery—there was no hint of *why* George Endicott should spend so many years and what had to be a small fortune in legal fees for a mostly barren piece of rock set an inconvenient distance out to sea. A rock that seemed to impose both misery and poverty upon its inhabitants in equal measure.

What was it about Great Misery that drew such contention?

"You 'bout ready to be done?"

It was Wilbert, standing at the end of the reading room table, wringing his hat between his hands. "I come to fetch you back," he said. "Saw you'd gone over with Daisy this morning and thought you'd need to get home."

"How thoughtful, Wilbert," was all she could think to say, even as some strange, unspecified instinct tried to find a reason to stay.

Wilbert nodded and shuffled a step or two backward. "I'll wait outside." And before she could introduce him to Amelia, he did just that.

And there was nothing else for Marigold to logically do but make her goodbyes. "Good afternoon, Amelia. I'll see you next time." And hope against the strange uneasiness that settled upon her, like a raw mist off the Atlantic, that there would *be* a next time.

CHAPTER 35

When the gods wish to punish us, they answer our prayers.
—Oscar Wilde

The long pull back to Great Misery was accomplished in silence but with speed—the rumbling clouds of a thunderstorm were building from the mainland and the rising wind rushed them toward the island. Only when the bow of the dory slid onto the sand of North Cove did Marigold relax enough to help Wilbert beach the boat and overturn it in preparation for the rain.

"Do you think we'll actually get any?" she asked with a glance at the dry stubble of the sparse grass. The spring rain that greened the coastline never seemed to reach across Salem Sound to relieve the persistent dryness of Great Misery.

"Dunno, but I don't like the look of it," her cousin declared. "Best get home either way."

But Hatchet Farm wasn't Marigold's home. And despite the improvements she had made and the friendships she had formed on Great Misery, the urge to be done with the place was growing ever stronger.

Accordingly, she went straight to her room, passing up Cleon's latest addition to the glutenous, never-ending chowder pot—"Raked up some quahogs today, Miss Girl"—set her own lock on the door, and fell into a fitful sleep.

She was awakened deep in the night by what she might have assumed was thunder, as lightning flashed through her curtains. But the sound had been too soft, more of a low, creaking sort of sound, as if someone were sitting heavily in a leather armchair. But that was nonsensical—there were no leather armchairs anywhere at Hatchet Farm that she knew of—although the rooms behind the still-locked doors might hold any number of unknown items.

After her regrettable overreaction to last night's strange sounds, Marigold was determined not to let her imagination get carried away, though she couldn't stop herself from retrieving her pistol from the stool next to the bed.

She was just about to give herself a stern reproof when she heard another loud noise—something that sounded very much like a hard slap—from the farmyard below.

Marigold bolted for the window, scanning the yard as her eyes adjusted to the light of the two-day-old moon. She fancied she saw some furtive movement at the far side of the yard, near the refurbished chicken coop, and wondered if some wolf or fox had swum across to try to steal away the skinny hens.

She had thrown up the window sash to listen for any panicked squawks of alarm when something else hit her senses—the smell of smoke, strong and pungent and coming from someplace near.

Who could be cooking at this hour—

A hot spark of orange flared out of the night and slowly grew, inch by inch, into the shape of a rectangle—the barn's loft door.

The loft, where Seviah had stacked all that old, dry hay.

"Fire!" she bawled at the top of her lungs as she lunged for her boots and linen duster and bolted down the stairs, her fingers fumbling clumsily on the wretched lock. "Godda—" She bit off her curse to save her breath and focused on inserting the key. "Wilbert! Cleon, wake up! Wake up! The barn is on fire!"

But it was Sophronia who pulled her door open and reached for her hand. "Come out of here."

Marigold went. As fast as her feet could carry her.

They came out into the yard in time to see Wilbert flinging the swinging barn doors wide.

"The mules?" was her first thought.

"Already loose," he rasped as he turned back to haul out the dilapidated, smoldering wagon. "I'll get the cart, you get your bicycle."

"Yes!" Marigold was thankful for such incisive direction. She covered her mouth with her sleeve and followed him into the smoke-filled barn.

The interior was shrouded in murky darkness, but her machine was just where she had left it, next to the now-empty stalls. She ran her bicycle through the door and out into the yard, gasping and hacking at the acrid smoke.

"Cleon, find those mules!" Wilbert called as the old man wandered into the yard. "They can't have got far."

Marigold ran to help Wilbert haul the heavy cart to a safer distance, but he redirected her. "Get as many shovels as you can find out of the shed."

"What about buckets or pails to form a bucket brigade from the pump?" she asked.

Wilbert shook his head. "Fool's errand—just get the danged spades!"

Marigold fumbled her way back into doing as asked and came out with two shovels and a hoe.

"That'll do. Thank God you're out," he rasped. "The floor's about to collapse down. We'll each take a side." He gestured about the barn. "Use the shovel to stamp out any sparks so's to keep the fire from spreading. The barn can't be helped," he said with another resigned shake of his head, "nor Lucy's place, I fear, but I'll be damned if I let him burn down the whole of this farm."

Him?

"You take the windward side." Wilbert gave her no time to think but pushed her toward the safer side of the barn while he ran downwind, where the sparks were beginning to fly fast and furious.

Sophronia took the flank with Cleon, while Marigold defended the chicken coop and henhouse with as much vigor as she possibly could, working like a dervish in the hellish light of the growing, glowing fire to stamp out any wayward embers carried by the onshore wind.

Marigold had no idea how long she toiled until Sophronia appeared at her side in dawning daylight. "Drink." She took the shovel from Marigold's hands and thrust a cool tin cup of water into her raw palms.

"Thank you." Marigold drank, wondering idly if she herself looked as bedraggled, soot stained, and worn as her cousin did.

Sophronia eyed her over too. "I'll say one thing for you—you don't spare yourself."

"No," Marigold agreed on a smile. "We have that in common."

Sophronia almost smiled too. "Happen we do."

The companionable moment might have stretched had not Wilbert waved them over to the pump, where he was drinking his fill. "Why don't you two rest a spell, and then we'll see what else ought to be done?"

"Ought to eat," Sophronia advised, "to keep our strength up. If those hens haven't been put off laying in all this to-do . . ." She plodded off toward the henhouse to find out.

"I'll make tea," seemed the most sensible thing for Marigold to say. Strong, hot tea to revive and slake their smoke-seared throats. But first she took the opportunity to douse herself beneath the pump and wash her hands and face before she headed for the kitchen. One might alter one's standards . . .

As she passed onto the porch, her eye was caught by the motion of Great-Aunt Alva letting her tattered curtains fall. So she had been watching, had she, as others toiled on her behalf? Marigold would make sure Great-Aunt Alva was served her tea last—hopefully when it had gone cold.

She put the water in the kettle to boil before heading for the outhouse past the A-frame rack of scarlet runner beans. The scarecrow had been moved to a new position and was fully dressed in a new suit of clothing.

"Oh, Cleon, thank you," she called over her shoulder. "I hadn't noticed you'd finally found a hat. It looks—" Well, frankly, it looked . . . odd.

"Miss Girl?" the old codger called from where he had subsided at the pump. "'Tweren't me, Miss Girl. Don't got no hat."

"No, not you—on the scarecrow." Marigold pointed at the figure at the far end of the garden, where Cleon must have relocated it. After his initial objections, he had proved surprisingly faithful in moving the straw man every few days to keep the rapacious crows from getting too used to the careworn figure, who was folded over his crosstree, kicking up the rosemary. Hanging—

She tried to scream, but the sound that tore out of her mouth was more like a gasp. It was as if something within her understood before her normally acute mind could articulate what she was seeing.

Because what she saw was Ellery Hatchet lurched on top of the scarecrow's crosstree. Still dressed in his Sunday-best going-preaching shirtsleeves, as if he had prayed himself out and fallen asleep there. Except that his feet were high off the ground, dangling in the rosemary, stirring up the scent. And his eyes were open wide, staring in glassy oblivion.

Because he was dead. Quite dead.

"Lawd, keep us from being murdered," whispered Cleon as he came up behind her. "He came back," he marveled. "Said as he were bound for Jordan, but he come back."

Wilbert, who had followed Cleon, stopped in his tracks at the sight. "Is he dead?"

"I fear so." Marigold found her voice.

Sophronia came to stand just behind them. "Saw there'd be a Hanged Man, didn't I? Just didn't know who it'd be. But there he is."

There he was, in a manner too calculated to be either a coincidence or an accident of the fire.

"What should we do now?" Wilbert's decisiveness seemed spent.

"Get him down, surely," was Marigold's most rational thought. "Unless we ought to notify the authorities first?"

"Why do that?" Sophronia asked at the same time Wilbert said, "We can't leave him up there—it ain't decent." And indeed, Ellery Hatchet's body was a horrible sight—the man looked as venomous in death as he ever had in life.

"What goes on here?" came a querulous demand from the kitchen door, where Great-Aunt Alva appeared in one of the newly bleached nightgowns Marigold had recently laundered—a slightly brighter, more boraxed Miss Havisham but still trailing her moth-eaten shawls and gray braids. Great-Aunt Alva, who had never come out of her room until three nights ago.

"It's Hatchet," Sophronia said in her flatly factual way, gesturing toward the body. "He's dead."

"He can't be," Alva swore, not a second before she accused, "You must have poisoned him."

"Not I. Hasn't taken a sip or a scrap from my hands these twenty years past," Sophronia said in the same even tone. "You know that."

"Bring him to me," Alva ordered. "Bring him to me so I can see what's wrong with him."

"Granny." Wilbert shook his head. "He's dead."

"At long last," Sophronia said with a touch of wonder, as if she were convincing herself. "Years and years he put it off. But what will be will be, just as I always told him."

"No!" Great-Aunt Alva tottered across the rutted yard in her carpet slippers and nightgown like a wizened fairy, swinging her cane as if she could shoo death away like an errant crow. "Cleon, tell him to get up. Tell him I insist!"

"Now, sister," Cleon said sorrowfully. "Ain't nobody left to tell."

"Nobody but the undertaker," Wilbert added.

"And the police," Marigold put in.

"What for?" Wilbert asked.

Marigold thought the reason was obvious. "He couldn't have placed himself on the crosstree. You can't imagine that he just happened to have an attack of apoplexy last night and then hoisted himself on top of the scarecrow to ease his pain?" Marigold looked from Wilbert to Sophronia, willing them to see what she saw. Willing them to understand—the devil did indeed have long arms. "Someone had to have put him up there, so high that his feet are off the ground."

"Who would do that?" Wilbert's face was tight with disgust.

"You!" Aunt Alva found the easiest target for her agitated accusations in Marigold. "You, who seem to know exactly what happened. You're the serpent with the apple, with your garden and your interference and your bad influence."

"That'll do, Granny," Wilbert instructed in a weary rasp. "We'll take him into the house and lay him out, decent like, but won't do anything else without your say-so, Cousin Marigold."

"Her say-so?" Alva cried. "Who gave her leave? Not I! *I* say what goes here."

"No, Granny," Wilbert contradicted. "You've got to see how it is. You got to understand."

"I'll do no such thing," Alva countered. "I want . . . I need . . ." She turned around in a full circle, as if looking for a new angle of accusation or a fresh source of agitation. "Tell him. Cleon! Tell Ellery I want him to get up and come to me."

"He can't and he won't, Mother Hatchet," Sophronia told her bluntly. "Justice has finally prevailed. Because he is well and truly dead this time."

"And," Marigold clarified, "very likely murdered."

CHAPTER 36

What is right to be done cannot be done too soon.
—Jane Austen

A steady rain began to fall. Finally. Too late to do anything more useful than douse the last smoldering embers of the fire.

Marigold breathed only a temporary sigh of relief. The situation demanded explanation—which she couldn't yet imagine.

"Marigold!" a low voice called over the rising patter of the rain.

"Cab!" It was just the man she needed—a man who knew the law. He had come at a run, clearly—he was in his shirtsleeves. Behind him, Bessie and Lucy came into view farther down the path.

"We saw the fire from the mainland. What happened?" Cab demanded, reaching her hand. "Are you hurt? Was anybody else hurt?"

"No. I am quite well," she assured him. Apart from being clothed in only sooty, smeared nightwear and dirty cycling boots and surely reeking of smoke. "The barn burned down last night." Best to start at the beginning with the bare facts with no suppositions about the cause of the blaze. "And Lucy's cabin too, I'm sorry to say."

But Cab's gaze had gone over her head, to the scene in the garden behind, where Wilbert and Cleon were just managing to take the stiff body off the crosstree.

"But obviously that's not all," Marigold added. "It's Ellery Hatchet. I just found his body this minute. He's dead."

"Good Lord." Cab doffed his hat in respect as he stepped into the garden. "I'm so sorry, Marigold. Then how did he get up there—?"

"Had an apoplexy during the fire, maybe?" Wilbert suggested, though the hope in his voice was thin.

"No." Marigold kept her voice as kind as she could. "At least, I never saw him during the fire. We hadn't seen him for two days now and assumed he was well away in Manchester or Gloucester or points beyond, with his traveling tent revival." It was astonishing how strangely their lives had kept changing in the past few days. "He was stiff, hanging up there"—she pointed to the crosstree—"on top of the scarecrow, with his feet a good foot and a half above the ground."

"No chance he could have got up there himself?" Cab asked.

"I guess I don't reckon so," Wilbert relented. "The back side there's got nails sticking out"—he gestured toward the post—"that nobody in their right mind would want to mess with."

"But was he in his right mind?" Cab asked.

Trust Cab to ask the pertinent questions.

"They's for holding the straw man, the nails," Cleon put in. "Powerful full of bad luck, just like I said. Didn't I say?"

"Yes, Cleon, you did say," Marigold agreed before she returned them to a more logical line of thought. "The point being that even in the dark, if Ellery Hatchet were having an apoplexy or heart attack, I should think he would have tried to get our attention by coming out into the yard instead of climbing onto the scarecrow."

"Cousin Ellery never did like that thing," Cleon insisted. "Graven idol."

Marigold has some insistence of her own. "So he would hardly replace it with himself, don't you think?"

"So someone put him there," Cab agreed. "We'll need to speak to the police—you'll need to go, Marigold, since you're the one that found him. But"—he looked at each of them in turn—"it might be best to take statements from each of you about your whereabouts last night."

"Ever the lawyer?"

"Marigold," he answered quietly. "From what I can see, you're going to need one. If this really is a murder—"

"You think so too!"

"I didn't say that," Cab was quick to counter. "But from where I stand, looking at the possibilities, you need to understand that you, just as much as anyone else in the house—or the town—are very much suspect, at least until we can get further information." Cab leveled them all with his steely gaze, all take-charge directness. "We can't proceed any further until we can get the authorities out here. All right?"

"All right," Wilbert agreed. "Does that mean we got to leave the old man out here in the rain? Doesn't seem decent."

"We'll disturb him as little as possible," Cab decided as he looked around the garden. "Marigold, did your bicycle make it through the fire?"

"Yes?"

"Then I'm going to ask you to get dressed and go to the authorities." He walked her toward the house away from the others. "But first, I have to ask . . ." He lowered his voice so only she might hear. "Did you kill him?"

"Cab!" She was truly shocked—it was as if he didn't know her after all. "Of course not. Why would you ask such a thing?"

"Because a lawyer can best defend his client when he knows the truth."

"Why should I need defending? He was the one threatening me, not the other way around."

"What about the others?"

"We were all fighting the fire—all four of us together, Wilbert, Sophronia, Cleon, and I, in plain sight of each other. There was no one else here—except Great-Aunt Alva Hatchet, who was in her room, like she always is. The others were all gone."

"That accounts for a vast deal of last night, but the truth is, we don't know when he died or was killed," Cab said, holding up his hand to forestall her tirade of questions. "Everyone on Great Misery Island will quite naturally be suspect."

"We can eliminate some, surely? Daisy was with the Endicotts and Seviah off with Mr. Keith. And Lucy, as you know, was with her mother in town."

"Perhaps," Cab agreed slowly. "Again, that would account for last night, and—"

"—we don't know when he died," Marigold finished. "Or was killed."

"You understand me." Cab nodded grimly. "So I'll ask Bessie and Lucy to take you to town to fetch Officer Parker from the town hall, and also Doc Oliphant, I think."

"Naturally," she answered, unsurprised that he had gotten to know the town so well. "I'm happy to be of use. After I do that, I'll let Seviah and Daisy know."

"I'm going to ask you not to, Marigold"—Cab looked at her soberly—
"but to come back here directly. I'll help your cousin in your absence."

There was that steely determination—he would not eliminate anyone
as a suspect until proven otherwise. And she would be just as wise to do the
same.

Seviah's defiant words echoed in her head. He'd sell Hatchet Farm, he
had said. *Or burn it to the ground.* Was this his revenge? But why would he
come back just when he had escaped? And why would he kill his purported
father when he finally had everything he wanted?

Or could it have been Wilbert, left behind and resentful at the others
for leaving? Might he have killed his father to prevent his coming back to
interfere with Wilbert's new plans for the farm?

And Daisy, with her gun and her secret boat and her dead aim? She had
been in an awful rush to leave the island yesterday. And how strange that she
had denied hearing any of the commotion of the night before. How uncharacteristically unforthcoming.

And Lucy had been cagey locking up the root cellar. Making sure that
neither Marigold nor any of the Hatchets could get into her place before it
burned to cinders?

Two weeks ago, Marigold might have happily suspected them all, but
now the thought brought her nothing but misery. Surely she knew each of
them well enough to be able to believe them innocent—they were her
friends now, not merely distant relations. She had helped each of them find
their path in life in the past few days—how could they turn back and turn to
murder now?

Marigold had no answer for her own questions but to get dressed. She
hardly wanted to arrive at the sheriff's office looking like she'd been dragged
through an ash pile—Ellery Hatchet wouldn't be made any more or less
dead by a slight delay to make herself presentable.

One had one's standards, even with a corpse in the garden.

She washed and dressed hurriedly in a clean, soot-free shirtwaist and
warm jacket along with a water-defying canvas mackintosh—though she
took the time to secure her pistol in her pocket. If there were murderers
abroad, she wanted to be prepared.

Across the empty farmyard, Lucy's former abode had been reduced to
two upright, charred corner beams and a few smoldering planks that pro-
truded up from the debris-filled root cellar—a historical wreck, but a

complete wreck nonetheless. There was little left for Lucy to salvage, but Marigold could see that she and Bessie had tried—a trail of ashen footprints led up from what remained of the charred cellar steps. So much for replenishing the larder with leftover canned goods.

Marigold pushed aside all questions of larders and empty stomachs and whether the fire had been an unfortunate accident or maliciously set, retrieved her bicycle, and set off for North Cove with alacrity. She had just rounded the great protruding glacial rock at the wooded part of the path, where she could see Lucy and Bessie on the beach ahead, when the bicycle seemed to skid out from beneath her for no reason.

There was something fouling the spokes—a piece of fabric that resolved itself into Ellery Hatchet's suit jacket. His "preaching" suit, for want of a better term.

Marigold reached to pick it up before she stopped herself—anything that was associated with Ellery Hatchet was now likely to be accounted evidence. Especially since his jacket was there, on the path, well apart from his body.

But she couldn't leave it fouling her spokes. Marigold pried the material away from the fender, and in the process, an empty bottle of tonic, similar to the bottles Marigold had seen on the shelves at the druggist in Pride's Crossing, fell out.

Had Ellery been secretly drinking? Such tonics typically contained a large dose of alcohol. Or had he been ill? The jacket certainly stank with a particular odor that wasn't just sweat and lack of washing. Perhaps he had simply died from whatever ailed him.

No—the remembrance of his feet hanging over the rosemary gave lie to that theory.

Another image caught her attention—the fluttering of the white sail swinging on the boom, signaling that Lucy and Bessie were ready to set off.

"Wait!" Marigold called, making the decision to leave the suit jacket for later, when she could show it to the authorities. "Wait for me!"

"You all to rights, child?" Bessie queried when Marigold joined them at the skiff. "You've had an awful shock."

"Yes," Marigold admitted, "but I suppose we all have." Bessie especially could be expected to have complicated feelings about the death of her child's father. "How are you two?"

"We're keeping just fine. Now we best get on, then, and let you get to your business in the town." Bessie directed Marigold around to the port side so she could stow her bicycle in the prow. "You get that in and then push us off."

Marigold noticed that Bessie's hands were smeared with ash and soot. "Were you able to retrieve your belongings?" She looked to the small collection of things at Lucy's feet in the stern.

"Just this and that," Bessie answered, rearranging her skirts as she sat, more interested in catching the tide. "Let's get on and get out of this rain."

Marigold shoved the laden skiff off the sand, just managing to belly flop into the prow, almost on top of her machine, as Lucy put the helm into the wind.

"You hold on to that bicycle of yours, there," Bessie advised. "It looks like it might get choppy."

But the water looked as flat as a cast-iron skillet under the dull pounding of the spring rain. Still, Bessie could be expected to know better than she. And it was just as well—Marigold had too much to think about. Like the realization that Ellery Hatchet might have died just yards away from her while they were fighting the fire. How had she not seen him? Or heard him? Had he called out?

Nobody, not even hateful old Ellery Hatchet, deserved to die like that.

But how had he gotten there?

Marigold instantly looked behind to the beach, but the angle of their steerage, combined with the curtain of the sail and the rain, kept her from being able to see if there had been any evidence of another boat or other footsteps in the sand. She would have to hope Cab had noted such evidence when they had arrived at the island that morning—and be more observant herself in the future.

What else had she missed? What had happened the night before last— the disturbance that no one else had claimed to hear?

Marigold was sure of what she heard—as sure as she had been about Minnie's body in the water that first evening. Why would no one on Great Misery acknowledge what had happened?

But did she really want to get to the bottom of the mystery? Especially if it was going to prove that one of her Hatchet relatives—one of the people she had come to care for and champion—was a murderer. Not that they all didn't have good reason to want Ellery Hatchet dead.

"We'll put you in at the town dock." Bessie called Marigold's attention back to the logistics of reporting the death. "You can go ahead with your bicycle and don't wait on us."

"Yes, ma'am." Marigold jumped nimbly onto the wooden dock as Lucy neatly brought the skiff alongside.

"You let us know how it goes," Bessie called as they pulled sharply away.

Almost as if she wanted Marigold gone. As if all her work bettering the reputation of the Hatchets had already come to naught and she had fewer friends than she thought. Murder, she supposed, had a way of driving people out.

She was entirely on her own.

CHAPTER 37

It is a capital mistake to theorize before one has data. Insensibly, one begins to twist facts to suit theories, instead of theories to suit facts.
—Arthur Conan Doyle

Marigold pedaled swiftly to the town hall, where she entered at the side door marked POLICE. The Office of Public Safety was a wholly masculine preserve—a single rectangular room with a large, grubby desk in sore need of a good scrubbing situated in front of two iron-barred cells along the back wall.

Though it was not the first jailhouse Marigold had ever entered—agitation for universal suffrage was often looked at askance by the powers that be—it was the first time she had done so as a material witness to murder. Even though it was likely the second murdered body she had seen.

"Officer Parker?" She addressed the blue-uniformed man with his feet up on the desk. "I'm Marigold Manners, cousin to the Hatchets of Great Misery Island. I've come to report Ellery Hatchet has been murdered."

Her pronouncement was met with all the éclat of a dud.

"Well, what do you know. Heard about you." The laconic officer let his feet slide to the floor but did not rise. "Oughtn't be surprised someone finally settled old Ellery Hatchet's hash. But I heard he'd left town," he mused. "Run off and joined the preaching circus?"

"He had joined the Reverend Cooper's tent revival, yes. Or at least we thought he did. But we found his body this morning, in the garden at Hatchet Farm."

"This morning? I heard another rumor there was a fire out there last night."

The news had certainly traveled as fast as stink, as these New Englanders might say. And yet the officer had not stirred himself to investigate. "The barn and one of the outbuildings were consumed in the flames."

"Consumed"—he mimicked Marigold's pronunciation—"was it? Burnt down," he amended. "Well then, I reckon he went and had hisself an apoplexy at the sight," the officer reasoned, settling back into his chair like an exemplar of Occam's dullest razor, judging from the thick, unworn shoe leather on the bottom of his soles. "Old man Hatchet was well-known for getting himself hot under the collar. It figures that he'd finally blow his gasket for good."

"While that assessment of Mr. Hatchet's character may be true," Marigold reasoned, "the circumstances in which the body was found are suspicious."

"Says who?"

Marigold wanted to answer, *Says me*, but she amended her response to, "Says his son, Mr. Wilbert Hatchet, and Mr. Hatchet's attorney, Mr. Cox."

"That so?" Parker had his own theory. "Reckon he changed his mind about wanting to go off with the tent revival. Wanted the comforts of home."

"Hatchet Farm hardly offers comfort, sir," Marigold countered.

"If that's so, why're you out there?" Officer Parker demanded. "Fancy Boston girl like you? You know, there's not a person in this town doesn't wonder what you're up to out on Great Misery."

"Cleaning," she said succinctly with a feeling of rising hauteur. "As any of my Hatchet relatives can attest."

"That so?" He met her nearly insolent tone with sarcasm of his own. "You don't look much like a skivvy. Look like one of those damn *sportswomen*. Getting up clubs to wheel around on your bicycles instead of minding your own business."

Marigold very briefly debated giving the condescending fellow more than a piece of her mind, but she was a woman of reason and instead did what any frustrated, thinking woman who wanted to get her way as quickly and easily as possible had to do—she spoke more softly in order to force him to listen, while wielding the cudgel of influence.

"I am very much minding my own business, sir, when I report to you that my cousin's husband has been found dead in suspicious circumstances. Mr. Jonathan Cabot Cox, their lawyer, who is nephew to Mr. George Endicott, sent me here to inform you and Dr. Oliphant, and to tell you he is awaiting your investigation out on Great Misery."

"He said that, did he, this Cox? Endicott's nephew?"

Marigold took what satisfaction she could in discommoding the man. "I am merely his messenger."

Officer Parker rather predictably changed his tune. "I suppose it wouldn't hurt to take Doc Oliphant out there to Great Misery to take a look. And we'll figure it all out, nice and easy, and that'll be an end to it. Then you all can bury the old bastard in peace."

"Excellent." Marigold produced an audible sigh of thanks. "I know my cousin, Mrs. Hatchet, would appreciate that."

"Would she? From what I hear, if anyone murdered him, it's likely to have been her that put poison down his gullet."

All playacting was immediately forgotten. Marigold was sure she blanched—her face went hot and cold all at the same time.

Parker smiled coolly. "Or maybe it was you. There's been a betting line round town, wondering which one of you would get to the other one first."

Marigold swallowed the bitter bile of her indignation and gathered her aplomb. "Well, if you'd be so good as to do your job, then I'm sure you'll be able to figure out who got to whom. I have my bicycle." She tugged at the hem of her glove in a gesture of impatience. "I will meet you at Dr. Oliphant's." It would be better to speak to the doctor without the officer's clearly prejudicial attitude standing in the way of the facts.

"Well, I got a bicycle too." Parker came up and around his desk with alacrity, suddenly all afire to get to his job. "So, unless you want to be trounced in a race, I suggest you wait a doggone minute."

Marigold waited. Not because she was afraid of competition—far from it—but because she was a New Woman who didn't need to prove herself to any man. Especially not to a thin-necked know-nothing like Officer Parker. It again remained damnable how easily the sight of an independent young woman brought out the littleness in any man.

She pedaled sedately in the officer's hasty wake to the white federal farmhouse that housed the doctor's practice.

"Doc?" Parker bawled as he stomped through the side porch door to Dr. Oliphant's office. "We got ourselves a poser."

"Parker." Dr. Oliphant nodded in greeting. "I take it this isn't a social call?" The physician was nearly exactly as she had pictured him—a gray-haired, spectacled owl of a man with a large, well-brushed mustache and a perpetually perturbed demeanor.

"This girl's from Great Misery," Officer Parker announced, "where she says Ellery Hatchet's been murdered."

"I'm Marigold Manners, sir." Marigold spoke for herself. "And I have come over from Great Misery Island, where, just a little over two hours ago"—she consulted the clock on the wall—"Ellery Hatchet was found dead in suspicious circumstances."

"I get to say what's suspicious," Parker interjected.

But the doctor's face registered neither censure nor doubt. "That's quite an accusation, Miss Manners. Care to tell me what's got you suspicious?"

"The position of his body," Marigold began. "He was draped"—she chose the most decorous word she might—"over a scarecrow, and his feet were several feet off the ground. Too far to jump. His body was also quite stiff when the family tried to take him down. So aside from the curiosity of his position, there is some doubt as to when exactly he died."

"I'll get my bag." The doctor rose. "I'll admit to having some curiosity myself about the Hatchets out on Great Misery all these years."

"You've never had occasion to visit the island before?" Marigold asked. "Not even for a birth?"

"Not once. They keep to themselves, those Hatchets." The doctor was mater-of-fact. "That or they've enjoyed exceptionally good health."

Which was exceptionally unlikely, what with all the drowning and scythes and matches and guns and shovels. Marigold could only think it something of a wonder that they hadn't been steadily burying each other through the years.

Or perhaps they had been and nobody like her had been around to insist upon consulting the authorities? If past experience was any indication, the future would hold even more secrets Hatchet Farm might be dying to keep.

★ ★ ★

Officer Parker commandeered a large sailing dory at the town dock and proceeded to steer them toward Great Misery.

Marigold sat as quietly as possible until they came to the spot where she had seen the woman in the water that first day. "On the evening of my first arrival in Pride's Crossing, I believe I saw the body of Minnie Mallory just about here, beneath the surface of the water. She was wearing a mulberry-red skirt. But perhaps the color appeared darker because of the water."

"All the way out here?" the doctor queried at the same time Officer Parker asked, "Why didn't you tell anyone?"

"I did," she informed him shortly. "But no one believed me."

"Not that it makes any difference," Parker finally said, but Marigold noticed the doctor looked pensive, or at least slightly more pensive than before. It was hard to tell with the mustache.

So when they debarked at North Cove—where all evidence of any boats had been washed away with the high tide—and began the walk across the island, it was Dr. Oliphant's gaze that she directed to Ellery's jacket. "Look at that!" she exclaimed as they neared the spot. "That looks like Ellery Hatchet's suit jacket."

"Don't you have an eye for dead people's garments," Oliphant commented wryly.

"So?" Officer Parker said, looking down at the jacket with little comprehension. "So he lost it."

Marigold went ahead and picked the coat up, hoping the empty tonic bottle would fall to the ground, which it obligingly did. "What's that?"

"Let me see that." Dr. Oliphant took a moment to read the label before he took a decorous sniff. "Patent medicine," he decided before passing the bottle to the policeman. "Cider tonic."

"Seen the like at the druggist's," Office Parker said. "Taken the like myself a time or two."

"Indeed," Oliphant agreed. "Common enough."

Marigold was underwhelmed by their lack of enthusiasm for these clues. But as she all but rolled her eyes in frustration, something at the edge of the bracken on the other side of the rock caught her eye. "But what's . . . why, it's a Bible," she said as she retrieved the battered, soft leather–covered book. "*His* Bible, do you think?"

She handed it to Dr. Oliphant, who took a quick look inside the cover. "Ellery Hatchet," he confirmed.

"I should think he dropped his Bible first." Marigold tried to envision the fall of objects along the path. "And then his coat and . . . what else?"

MISERY HATES COMPANY 237

It was Parker who saw the man's tie, dangling from a shrub by the side of the path some twenty feet ahead. She must have missed it when zooming past on her way to catch Bessie and Lucy.

"Also Ellery's," she attested. "He was wearing this ensemble the morning he left Great Misery. So he must have lost or discarded them the night he came back?"

"I reckon," was all Officer Parker would agree to.

But Dr. Oliphant was sharper. "Do you mean last night?"

"I don't know," Marigold answered honestly. "There was some disturbance two nights past that I wasn't privy to. But what would bring Ellery Hatchet back to a place he had been so determined to leave? It's all so curious and strange."

But as the answer was not to be found in any more objects upon the path, they pushed on to Hatchet Farm, where they found Cab, Wilbert, Cleon, and Sophronia in the kitchen, standing around the table, where Ellery's body was now laid out, still in his preacher's shirtsleeves.

Which was also curious and strange—Ellery Hatchet looked far cleaner in death than he ever had in life. Perhaps they had plumbing on the tent revival circuit? Everyplace was more modern, it seemed, than Hatchet Farm.

The doctor immediately put his ear to Ellery's chest. "He's dead, all right. And damp from the rain?"

"Washed clean of the stain of his sins," Cleon said solemnly.

"You washed him?" Dr. Oliphant examined one of Ellery's hands.

"No. We thought to," Wilbert began with a glance at his mother. "We brought him in just as it started to rain. But then Mr. Cox here bid us wait. So we just laid him out, decent like, until . . . well, you'll see."

"What will we see?" the doctor asked, before he began opening up the clothing that had already been unbuttoned, exposing Ellery's chest and two pale, gaping purple holes for all to see.

"Well, there you have it," Doc Oliphant muttered. "This man's been shot. He's most definitely been murdered."

CHAPTER 38

Apparently there is nothing that cannot happen today.
—Mark Twain

Marigold's natural impulse to say, *I told you so,* was completely overridden by her astonishment—and terror. The image of Daisy brandishing her pistol in the blink of an eye was stark in her brain. And if Ellery had somehow taken a detour from preaching to try to interfere with Daisy's newfound chance at happiness . . .

"When?" she asked, hoping to put paid to such ghastly suppositions. "And why wasn't he covered in blood?" Marigold pointed at the fabric of his shirt, which was remarkably unstained.

The doctor shot a hard look at her over the top of his spectacles. "Hard to say. But from the size of the wounds, I'd say he was shot with a thirty-eight caliber or so."

Cab's gaze immediately shifted to Marigold, because he knew the caliber of her gun quite exactly—but with any luck, he might not know Daisy's. "Did any of you hear gunplay?"

"Nope." Wilbert was quick to answer.

"No, no. No guns here," Cleon agreed.

"I didn't hear a gun," Marigold added in her own defense, as well as that of her absent cousin, while cleaving closer to the truth than addlepated old Cleon. "But I did hear a scuffle the night before last."

"What sort of scuffle?" Officer Parker asked.

"Noises, doors slamming, that sort of thing. Loud enough to wake me from sleep. But when I went to investigate, I found I was locked into my room—from the outside. I never left my room, though I could hear people abroad in the house." Marigold noted that Wilbert kept a careful watch on his boots while she spoke and neither added nor contradicted her version of events, while Cleon gazed at her in stupefaction.

"And what about last night?" Cab asked. "We saw the fire from the mainland. How did that happen?"

"No idea how it started—except that a noise woke me," she said. "And when I looked outside, the barn was on fire."

"I was woke the same way," Wilbert said. "Ma and I came down together and went out straightway."

All the while they had been talking, Dr. Oliphant had been making acute observations of the body, sniffing and poking and prodding, peering under Ellery's eyelids and examining his fingernails. "Let me see that bottle from his pocket."

"Why, that looks like the ones Crestfield sells of mine," Sophronia said. "Apple cider vinegar tonic for digestion and chronic complaints."

"You make these yourself, here?" The doctor's question was quiet but sharp. "Where?"

"Stillroom." Sophronia cocked her head toward the back of the kitchen, past where the larder and the broom closet were located. She drew a key strung on a worn ribbon around her neck out of her bodice. "Kept locked, you see. Fermented spirits," she explained as she led the way.

Her key opened the door to an immaculately clean and neat workroom, with dried herbs hanging from a rack—there were the chives hung to repel evil spirits—and shelves filled with neatly labeled bottles. Clearly, this tidy stillroom—an astonishing contrast to the rest of the previously unhygienic house—was the source of all those unexplained, astringent smells.

"Those, there, are the elderberry tonic." Sophronia gestured at the well-organized shelves. "Elderberry, honey, ginger, cinnamon, and clove. That's a strengthener if you find yourself under the weather or such. And the digestive, there. And that dark one is rose hips and coneflower with honey for a cough."

Dr. Oliphant put on his spectacles to take a closer look. "These aren't labeled."

"I trade them with Crestfield over at the druggist. Puts his own labels on. Doesn't want people to know he doesn't make them himself." Sophronia's mouth twisted into a sardonic smile. "Or mayhap he doesn't want people to know they came from a Hatchet."

Sophronia, busy with her own business, just as Cleon had said that first morning. "Is that how you made money, Cousin Sophronia?"

"Ayuh. Traded for credit with Crestfield, but he'd get what I needed elsewhere so's I'd only have to deal with him. Ingredients for the tonics. Beans and bacon, flour and rice. Sugar every now and again. Whatever I needed. Kept on credit. Never too much at one time. Never wanted it to be so much it'd excite Hatchet's attention."

This explanation went a fair way to answering Marigold's earlier questions about how the house had sustained itself. So like Hatchets to keep beans and bacon secret. "How did you get to town if your husband didn't like anyone leaving the island?"

"Got a little peapod sailer hidden away from his notice," Sophronia admitted.

Naturally. Each to fend for themselves. It seemed that Marigold was the only one without her own hidden boat.

"Did you pack the tonic for your husband when he left?" the doctor asked.

"He never got that tonic from me," Sophronia said with a mirthless laugh. "He'd never have touched it had he known it came from my hand."

"And why was that?" was Dr. Oliphant's next question.

"He'd taken a bad turn once before and accounted it was my hand that poisoned him. It weren't," she avowed, with that sly half smile, "but it kept me from having to do any cooking for nigh on twenty years."

"You keep this room locked?"

"Alcohol," was Sophronia's explanation. "There's them that don't hold with spirits and them that the spirits get hold of too tight."

Cab sent a questioning look Marigold's way.

"Ellery for the first," she answered quietly. "Teetotaler. And Cleon for the second. Hopeless drunk, according to him, though I've seen him muzzy headed only once, the day I arrived." The others in the household, she could not vouch for.

"I'll take the key, if I may," the doctor said.

Sophronia handed over the black ribbon without any objection.

"Well?" Officer Parker demanded. "What gives?"

Dr. Oliphant answered obliquely. "Let's get the body decently wrapped up to take back to my surgery."

"What for?" Wilbert asked. "Ain't no surgery going to revive him."

The doctor looked at him over the top of his spectacles. "For what we call an autopsy."

"No," came that frailly authoritarian voice. "I forbid it." Alva Hatchet stood in the doorway to the kitchen, looking far older and more like Death than Miss Havisham with each passing appearance, which Marigold noted was her second of the day. For an old woman who never left her room, she seemed surprisingly mobile.

"Mrs. Hatchet, I presume." Dr. Oliphant nodded his head in greeting. "I know the idea is upsetting—"

"A desecration!" Alva's voice choked with tears. "And on whose authority?"

"Generally," the doctor began reasonably, "it's for the coroner to decide. But I am the coroner in Essex County. And I've decided." The doctor gestured to Cab and Wilbert. "If someone would help me get the deceased wrapped up in a clean sheet or blanket—"

It was Marigold who overcame her horror of both the body itself and its frankly fetid smell to help. "There's clean linen here, in the cupboard." She retrieved the sheet and brought it to the table. "Should you like me to remove his wet shirt beforehand?" The shirt fabric was coolly damp, chilling in a way that had nothing to do with temperature.

"No. Don't let her touch him." Alva's voice was thin and frail, but she strengthened as she spoke. "You leave him and take her. *She* did this. She wanted him dead—she said so!" she accused. "I heard her with my own ears threaten to put him to bed with a shovel. Her exact words! And tell them what else you told me," she commanded Cleon.

"Oh, it's true what Alva says." Cleon shook his jowly hound's head. "Told Cousin Ellery right to his face, right out there in that garden, Miss Girl did. And she did swear to Wilbert she'd get rid of Cousin Ellery for him. But that was in the kitchen, next to the fire, not the garden."

Well! That eavesdropping old son of a . . . How rude, to appear to be such an addlepated old codger when all that time he was practically memorizing their conversations. At least he couldn't have heard Wilbert saying he wished his father would drop dead.

But she had some information of her own. "Why don't you tell them that Ellery Hatchet was an awful man who threatened to strangle his children and to strangle me with his own two hands and throw me in Salem Sound just for making a garden?"

"Marigold," Cab said in a warning undertone. "You're not doing yourself any favors. That's what's known as a motive."

"Then there were a great many people before me who had both the motive and the means to murder Ellery Hatchet. There is no shortage of people who hated him with every emotion from fear to vengeance—your uncle, Mr. Endicott, included! I myself felt mostly fear. And revulsion. I'm quite particular about people who don't bathe."

"Marigold," Cab repeated. "You're *not* helping yourself."

"She'll have poisoned him." Alva took up her accusation again. "Ellery knew she had it in for him—that's why he left us, because he was afraid of her! She stole rat poison from Cleon."

"Afraid of me?" Marigold all but guffawed. "I've never heard anything so preposterous. I've stolen nothing."

"Tell them, Cleon," Alva insisted.

"Took the store of poison I was keeping safe, she did," Cleon confirmed. "First thing she got here—took that straightaway."

Marigold very nearly gaped at the wretched old man in incomprehension before she recalled herself. "Do you mean the dirty sugar I cleaned out? The little sugar pot, you called it, from over the stove that was full of rust and dust? I certainly did throw it away and replace it with real sugar."

"Stole it away," Cleon reasserted.

"Well, if it was poison, you had no business keeping it in a sugar pot over the stove." Marigold tried to inject some reason—and hygienic standards—into the proceedings. "No wonder you Hatchets all feared poisoning."

"Marigold." Cab was at her ear again. "Again, I don't think this is helping."

"What am I to do, then? Stand quietly by while Mr. Bumble and Miss Havisham here tarnish my good name?"

"You might try a different tactic," Cab advised with quiet exasperation. "You might not have the right to vote, but you do have the right to remain silent."

"And that's what women are always meant to do—stay silent and let someone else defend them? Do the laundry and clean the cupboards and let mean-spirited people make farfetched accusations?"

"Let someone else help defend them," Cab insisted. "We're on the same side here, Marigold."

"Well, I'm on the other. I've heard enough." Officer Parker hitched up his britches. "You fellows take the body," he directed Cab and Wilbert. "And I'll take the girl. I'm arresting you, Miss Marigold Manners, on suspicion of murder."

While Marigold was neither surprised nor overly concerned by Parker's ploy—her assessment of him as the type of man who would only reach for the low-hanging fruit was merely confirmed—she was surprised by Cab's vehement reaction.

"I'd advise you against using hearsay to base an arrest, sir." His voice had lost any semblance of "not letting on"—it was cold and chiseled and as hard as granite.

"Well, I reckon if both Miz Hatchet here and Cleon can say—" Parker hedged.

"I don't know as what their part is in this . . ." It was Sophronia, strangely calm as ever, interrupting Parker. "You don't need to take the girl—she's no part of this. I can vouch for her whereabouts and her character. She might not know this"—her dark eyes darted to Marigold's—"but every night, I lock her into her room."

Marigold felt the blood leave her face before it rushed back up her neck from the realization that all the while she had thought she was locking the Hatchets out, they had been locking her in. "Whyever would you do that?"

"Wanted to make sure you were safe," Sophronia answered.

"From what?" Marigold heard her voice crack.

"From Hatchet, for starters." Sophronia's expression—that stoic acceptance—never varied. "He could always do more harm."

More harm? For the first time, Marigold understood that the locked doors at Hatchet Farm might have had another purpose than solely keeping her out—they were meant to keep others out as well. She felt rather warmer toward Sophronia's actions. "Thank you."

"What will be will be," was all the older woman said before she sat down at the table, patient as Job, as if she were confident that what would be would have nothing to do with her. "It'll all come out now, the litany of Hatchet's sins." Sophronia shook her head even as the corners of her mouth twitched up in a rueful smile. "Because of you. Determined, that's what you are, aren't you? Esmie's girl. You'll uncover his sins against us all."

"Will I?" Was this another of Sophronia's prophecies, like the Hanged Man, or was she actually encouraging Marigold to carry on asking questions and prying into dark, undusted metaphorical corners?

"What will be will be." Sophronia repeated her bywords. "No sense in trying to put it off. Told Hatchet that, time and again. But he had his mind set a long time ago—set and closed as the grave."

"And so have I," said Officer Parker with finality. "It sure does seem suspicious to me that she's the one with poison and she's the only one hearing sounds and she's the first one to see the fire." He ticked off the accusations on his fingers. "And the one to find the body, and the coat, and the Bible too. Too convenient, if you ask me." He jammed his hat back on his head. "So, like I said, I'm taking her in. And I don't want to hear another word against it."

CHAPTER 39

Nine-tenths of the world is entertained by scandalous rumors, which are never dissected until they are dead and, when pricked, collapse like an empty bladder.

—Horace Greeley

"You'll have to hear more than a word against it, sir." Cab's tone was just shy of adamant. "As I said, you'll need more than the hearsay accusations that have already been refuted by another witness. And frankly, those accusations are suspicious—Dr. Oliphant said that Hatchet was shot. He said nothing of poisons. It won't hold up, sir, and you know it."

Parker looked as if he did not, in fact, know it, but Cab wisely gave him ground to cede. "But I do understand your need to get to the bottom of this," Cab went on, "so I will give you my word as both a gentleman and as an officer of the court of the State of Massachusetts, and more personally as the nephew of retired Justice Endicott, that I will keep Miss Manners in my custody with the promise to deliver her to you if any further evidence of her alleged guilt should come to light. I'll sign an affidavit, if you like."

Officer Parker conceded as gracefully as such an awkward man could. "I don't reckon that'll be necessary."

If she were a romantic, she might interpret Cab's oath as heroic. But she was a New Woman who didn't like the idea of anyone else giving their word for her, though she was also a realist, who would be sure to put Cab's protective instincts to good use.

So, the moment after Officer Parker and Dr. Oliphant finally departed with the body in the singed mule cart driven by Wilbert, Marigold pressed her advantage into insistence. "Did you take a greater look around the island while I was gone? I was wondering if you noticed any indications of other boats landing at the cove. The tide's come up now, but the question of how Ellery Hatchet—or his body—got over here from the mainland is vexing me."

"There were no other marks in the sand." He walked beside her as they followed along in the cart's wake. "The beach at North Cove was quite unmarked when we arrived."

Marigold was momentarily stymied. "It seems unlikely that anyone would have attempted to put in anywhere else—especially on a cloudy night with no moon. Although the others all had boats hidden all over the island, so clearly there are other landing spots to be found."

"Yes, but also, the tide must have turned after he arrived," Cab acknowledged, before he tried a question of his own. "Does your cousin, Mrs. Hatchet, always sound as if she's fresh from reading some tea leaves?"

"Tea leaves, tarot, and embers," Marigold confirmed. "*What will be will be* seems to be one of her favorites. She said those exact words to Ellery Hatchet about some mushrooms in the garden that morning before you first came with my bicycle. But he said, 'I'll take nothing from your snake-fed hands.' Those were his exact words, but I thought he was just making a sort of biblically allegorical reference to her being female and therefore a descendant of Eve and therefore responsible for all of humanity's sin. All that is to say, I really do think her husband would refuse any tonic from her."

"She also said you were going to uncover all of Ellery Hatchet's sins," Cab added.

"I'm not sure I want to, even if that's the real reason I originally came out here. I'm sure Isabella told you"—judging from Isabella's past behavior, Marigold was sure her friend had given Cab every detail she could—"but I came out here at my cousin Sophronia Hatchet's invitation, when she wrote me that Ellery Hatchet had done my mother—my sweet mother, who never hurt anyone but herself—a great and godless wrong. But now it seems as if Ellery is the one who has been done a great wrong."

Except this wrong wasn't that godless—Ellery Hatchet seemed to have earned his deservedly messy fate. *What ye sow, so shall the Lord reap.*

He certainly had been reaped. But how? And when?

"Do you think they're going to be able to establish a time of death as precisely as the cause?"

Cab nodded. "It will depend upon the doctor's skill, but with the state of forensic science today, it is possible to establish."

"And once we know *when*," Marigold mused, "it will be reasonably easier to estimate *where* he might have been when he was shot. I'm sure it wasn't at Hatchet Farm, because I was listening two nights ago—I had a glass pressed to the door—and I'm sure I would have heard a gun go off. But I didn't hear any. So he must have been shot elsewhere, and if we can determine—"

"*We* are not going to determine that, Marigold," Cab said with some feeling. "*I* will. Or rather, Officer Parker and Doc Oliphant and I will."

"Don't be absurd, Cab. I do understand your desire to protect me, but as I was present the whole time at Hatchet Farm, where clearly something was afoot the last two nights, though no one admitted, and you didn't ask, what went on—" Her archaeologically trained mind ticked off the outstanding evidence. "And furthermore, I have questions about why, if he was shot, there was no blood on his body or clothes, or about the house, which I clean, so I would have noticed. And then there's the empty bottle of tonic—Ellery Hatchet must have purchased it at Crestfield's in town before he came, or was brought back, to the island. So, if we can place him in the town, we can establish a timeline of the events leading up to his murder."

"Agreed," Cab said. "But *we* will not establish a timeline of events— they will. You will—" He stopped himself—his head went back, as if he had pulled his metaphorical reins. "I would ask you to please give me leave to sort some things out on your behalf. You've been accused of a crime by two people." He reached out, as if he would take her hands in his. "I don't think you realize—"

She brushed his hands aside to get a better look at something near his feet. "Cab, look!"

"Damn it, Marigold—"

"No." She was too impatient to explain. "Look!" She picked a dusty talcum powder tin out of the overgrowth. "It must be Ellery's money tin that Wilbert assumed he took with him when he left. Ellery definitely must have dropped this unknowingly, or lost it in a fight, just like his suit and tie and Bible—for why would a miserly man like Ellery Hatchet knowingly throw away money?"

Cab pried open the tin and shook out the change. "A dollar ninety-six," he counted out. "That leaves out robbery for a motive."

Marigold looked back up the path, gauging the distance to the spot where she had found the Bible, bottle, and jacket. "Can't you just see him, trudging along here?" Much as Ellery had been doing the day she had impetuously suggested he join the tent revival, she imagined—harried and a little unkempt, even in his suit. "He dropped or threw away his Bible? But he's a preacher man—more likely he just set it down and lost it in the dark. But why set it down?" She let her thoughts spool out logically. "Because he needed his hands to reach into his pocket—for what? Money? What would he buy on Great Misery? Or he was after something else and was so impatient and distracted he either didn't notice the money falling aside, or he tossed it aside? It's the tonic he wanted, then—a tonic for stomach complaints, Sophronia said. So perhaps he's feeling poorly— so poorly he's come all the way back from Manchester, when only a day or so before he couldn't wait to shake the dust of this place from his shoes . . ."

Cab nodded even as he frowned. "Go on."

Marigold was beginning to envision the sequence of events more clearly now. "So he's plodding on, rifling through his pockets, but he stops and guzzles down the tonic—he empties the bottle. But he's still feeling so poorly he shucks off his jacket and flings away his tie? Because he's in distress and hot and sweating?" Maybe that was why his clothes smelt so oddly. "Maybe he really was poisoned!"

"Seems reasonable," Cab said. "But that's an awfully plausible scenario from someone who claims not to be involved."

"You mean me?" Marigold felt herself bristle like a cat—she very much wanted to hiss and spit at the insufferably perceptive man. "I didn't say I wasn't involved, only that I didn't kill him. I merely put forth what I think is the most logical, likely scenario. That is what archaeologists do, Cab. We take a few items of material culture, be it two days, two years, or two thousand years old, and we try to envision the most rational way people might have used them, to piece together a complete picture of what occurred. Do you have a better suggestion?"

"No," Cab answered. "I don't make suggestions or scenarios—I'll let the facts speak for themselves. So best let me go ahead and find those facts out. Marigold." He reached again for her hands. "Please."

Something within, something vain and hopefully foolish, prompted her to push a stray bit of hair out of her eyes, the better to see Cab's face. But her fingers were permeated by the faintly rank, damp scent of woodsmoke and . . . something else. Was it rosemary?

The smell must have transferred to her hands from Ellery's shirt. How strange. The rosemary could be explained on his pants, she supposed, but nothing else. "Maybe I was wrong," she said. "All of his clothes smelled of smoke. So perhaps he was on the crosstree the whole time the fire burned. And we never saw."

"Maybe someone didn't want you to see him. Maybe whoever put him up there on the scarecrow's crosstree lit the fire as a diversion." Cab looked especially grave at the realization. "I'll speak to Officer Parker about that."

Marigold wished she hadn't said anything. If her suspicions about Seviah proved correct—

She tried to divert Cab's line of thought. "I know we must wait for the doctor's report to establish the time of death, but how did Ellery get all the way from the mainland back out to Great Misery, do you think? Where would he get a boat? And if he did get a boat, where is it now?" She started off down the path with greater urgency.

"That is something else I will be investigating as soon as—" He broke off, catching up with her to take her arm in a rather implacable grip. "Damn it all, Marigold—a man has been murdered and you're as cool as a cucumber, spinning out likely scenarios—"

"Would you rather I was in hysterics?" She rounded her elbow out of his possession. "If you're implying that I haven't any proper feelings, I assure you, I was as horrified as you could wish. You didn't see me at six o'clock this morning."

"I saw you at six thirty," he acknowledged. "And I will grant that you looked terrible enough then."

"Thank you," she answered with only a modicum of sarcasm. "I am as frustrated and baffled as you, Cab. And frankly afraid too—it's never a pleasant thing to find oneself accused, even by an interfering old eavesdropper and a superannuated harridan, or to be threatened with a jail cell even when

one is confident one didn't do it! But what I can't figure out is, if I didn't
shoot him—and I didn't! By the way, I suppose now is as good a time as any
to show you my gun. It's quite the same as you gave it to me—it has not
been fired." She fished the pistol out of her pocket.

He quickly took the gun, checked the mechanism, and put it into his
own pocket. "With five bullets," he agreed with some relief. "Thank you.
And you sure you didn't hear any other shots?"

"Quite sure," she swore. "Not last night nor the night before. Which I
think means that he was shot someplace else before he was brought to
Hatchet Farm and put up on top of that scarecrow."

"Agreed," Cab said grimly. "I can at least easily acquit you of that—as
athletic as you are, you're too petite to have slung such a tall man up there."

"Thank you." It was less work to keep the sarcasm from her tone this
time.

"But Marigold, Ellery Hatchet was murdered, and I've learned from my
readings in the new science of forensics that, once a person has killed somebody,
they're not likely to hesitate to kill again. And you, with your reasonable suppositions and keen observations, may present a threat to them. Do you see?" He
gripped her shoulders, not unlike the way he had gripped her in the dark of the
Endicott's terrace. "I'm goddamn worried *for* you, not *about* you."

"Then, thank you." She meant to be cool and perhaps even a bit sarcas-
tic, but he had that same look on his face as when he had almost kissed her
in the dark of the Endicotts' terrace.

But he didn't kiss her this time either—he took her hand and started all
but towing her down the path. "I'm not leaving you out here in this godforsaken place one more night. You're coming with me, and I don't want to
hear another word about it."

"You'll have to hear another word about it, Cab. One word in
particular."

"And what would that word be?"

"Please." She drew a long breath to try to settle her feelings into some sort
of more reasonable order. "As in, *please* come with me to Bessie's, or my cousin's, or wherever it is you mean to stash me. I will surely come, Cab, for what
you said makes remarkable sense. But I should very much like to be asked."

He kept himself from sighing. "Then ask I shall. Marigold, would you
please, please for the love of God, come with me?"

"Naturally," she replied with a smile. "I'd love to."

CHAPTER 40

The truth is rarely pure and never simple.
—Oscar Wilde

Cab rowed the dory not west toward Pride's Crossing but north across the sound, toward Manchester, where the coastline curved east into the Atlantic and he hailed the first lobsterman they came upon pulling up pots in the channel.

"Are you getting us dinner?"

"Better." Cab finally cracked a smile. "Information. Sorry to bother you," he called as the dory bobbed alongside. "I'm looking for information on whether anyone from the harbor might have picked up a preacher from the traveling revival out at the fairgrounds and taken him out to Great Misery in the past few days?"

"You'll want Roger Brown and his boy, Harv." The lobsterman thumbed a glove over his shoulder, toward the harbor, where numerous dories were being oared to and fro. "Said something about taking a crazed-up preacher man over. Had to be crazy—who else'd want to go to Great Misery, eh?"

"Do you know when that was?" Cab pressed.

"Day before last, was it?" The fellow checked with his dory mate.

The day of the commotion. Marigold was beginning to get the timeline straight in her head. "Did they say if he was hurt or injured in any way?"

"Davie"—the lobsterman put the question to his mate—"you talked to Harv?"

"Sweating like a sow, Harv said, and just as sour," Davie related. "Complaining of stomach pains, raving like a lunatic that he'd been poisoned. Guzzling down a bottle of patent medicine, Harv said."

"Much obliged." Cab tossed the men a silver dollar.

Marigold was already taking stock. "It really might be poison—but how did Alva know that? And if he came back two nights ago, that was the commotion in the house, although no one else admitted to hearing it, not even Daisy."

"Is that so?" That serious scowl was carving a trench across Cab's otherwise perfect brow. "Doc said a thirty-eight. That's a lady's gun."

Marigold wished she had held her tongue. "Well, you've got my gun and you know it's never even been fired—it's as pristine as if it came out of a box."

"So noted," Cab agreed grimly. "Let us get back to Bessie's and get a decent meal into you. I doubt you've had anything to eat today."

"Are you saying I look starved?"

"I'm saying you've looked better, but you still look so good I'm tempted to ship my oars and show you just how good."

"Cab." She gave him her most encouraging smile. "I wish you would."

"I wish . . . you're in the middle of a murder here, Marigold, and such things will have to wait."

"Spoilsport," she teased. "I know ladies are meant not to seem too eager"—she paraphrased dear Miss Austen—"but you are very much increasing my anticipation by suspense, according to the practice of elegant gentlemen."

"I try," he answered with that deliciously self-deprecating laugh. "I surely try."

The rest of the row across the sound was accomplished in silence but with a great deal of attention paid to the marvelously rippling sinews of Cab's forearms, which were nicely exposed by his rolled-up shirtsleeves. Gracious, but he was a well-put-together man.

Marigold ogled him until they arrived at Bessie Dove's dock and the aroma from the house captured all of her attention. A few gulps of cold pump water only went so far in sustaining a person.

"Oh, child. You look like you got one foot on a banana peel and the other in the grave." Bessie turned on Cab. "What took you so long to get her out of that place?"

The woman's obvious worry was such that Marigold could only chide herself for earlier fretting that Bessie might not be her friend.

"My apologies," Cab demurred. "But I've brought her here now."

Bessie harrumphed but immediately brought a pungently spiced, burlap-wrapped ham to the table and proceeded to carve off slices. Marigold's mouth all but watered as she took a deep inhalation. And came to a stunning realization.

"Marigold?" Cab was watching her. "What is it?"

She shook her head, as if she could dispel the notion—the reason Ellery Hatchet's shirt smelled like woodsmoke—but her thoughts had finally become clear. "Cab, would you give me a moment alone with Bessie? I have a question of a . . . feminine nature to ask her."

"You ailing?" Bessie's smile was tight with worry. "I've got just the tonic for female complaints. Make them up myself."

"Yes," Marigold agreed automatically, because while Bessie's concern was all for her, Marigold was now more concerned for Bessie than before—her expertise with tonics opened up new and dangerous possibilities. "How did you know just what I wanted?"

"A body knows," Bessie answered, satisfied to be proved right. "You get that food in you." She watched as Marigold took a few sustaining bites. "That's better. Now, what you need is my black cohosh tonic—mixed with plum cherries and clover mint." Bessie rose and opened the door to her larder.

Marigold could see shelves full of canned and pickled foodstuffs along with an array of bottles much like those in Sophronia's stillroom. "I've seen tonic bottles just like these somewhere else."

Bessie's laugh surprised her. "You likely seen them down to the druggist. Mr. Crestfield buys them from me and puts his own labels on them. Like he doesn't want folks thinking they're buying their medicine from a Black woman's hands."

Crestfield clearly had a great deal of outsourcing—as well as a great deal of pride—to answer for. But so did Bessie.

"What I need from you is not tonic but answers. To questions like"—she lowered her voice to a whisper—"exactly when was Ellery Hatchet at your place two days ago, and why? Did he come to you before he went out to Great Misery?"

Bessie pressed her lips together. And stared.

"I mean to help you, Bessie," Marigold promised. "But you have to tell me the truth."

Bessie was silent for another very long moment until she finally answered, "Lucy warned me you're a sharp one. How did you know?"

"The smell of your smokehouse was on his shirtsleeves, though nearly masked by the smoke from the fire. And I'm sorry to trouble you about this, but," Marigold began, trying to steer carefully between her own need to know and her instinct to keep what she supposed private, "he was Lucy's father, wasn't he?"

"Jesus Lord." Bessie let out a long, low sigh, as if she had been holding that particular breath for years. "Nothing gets by you. And how'd you suss *that* out?"

"A number of inferences, including the difference of age and appearance between Lucy and Samuel. But mostly by your reaction to Seviah and Lucy's presumed romance and your hushed conference with my cousin Sophronia that next morning."

Bessie shook her head. "Now I wish I'd held my peace, the way things are working out so nice. Seviah brought that Mr. Keith here to my place, and now he's thinking of turning my boardinghouse into the headquarters of the new all-Black revue he's proposed to build. My boardinghouse on permanent lease, always paid up. That's security."

"And very well deserved, I'm sure. Congratulations." Marigold was delighted at such an extraordinary outcome. But she couldn't let Bessie divert her. "But if you hadn't made a fuss out at Hatchet Farm, I daresay you wouldn't know about Seviah's parentage either."

"Lord, there's no keeping things from you." Bessie sighed. "But that's right."

"Lucy is Ellery Hatchet's child, while Seviah Hatchet is not." Marigold felt some small satisfaction in discovering herself correct. But more questions remained. "Did Ellery Hatchet know? About Lucy?"

"He knew."

"And is that why he came to you?"

"Oh, no, he didn't come to me. Least not in the way you think. But it were yesterday morning, early, before the sun was full up." She let out each piece of information carefully, as if she were weighing Marigold's trustworthiness.

"Bessie, as long as you didn't kill him—though I am quite sure you have more than reason enough if you did—"

"Oh, no. He was already dead."

The enormous sense of relief Marigold felt was second only to her astonishment. "How could that be?"

Bessie lowered her voice to the barest whisper. "He was in the cove. I'd gone out to my smokehouse to check on some hams I got curing on order for the grocers. And there he was, tangled in the reeds, washed up in the shallows."

"Washed in from Salem Sound?" Clearly the preferred mode of getting rid of a body. "That's why there was no blood." But Marigold's next question was the same horrible one she had had about Minnie. "Was he tossed in after he died, do you think, or was he thrown in so he would drown?"

"All I know is what I seen," Bessie said. "And that was that he *was* drowned. The gracious Lord seen fit to take him at last."

"You're sure he was dead?"

"Put my ear to his chest and my hand to his wrist," Bessie confirmed. "He was already as cold and dank as a tombstone."

"All right." Marigold accepted Bessie's admission as truth until proven otherwise. "Then what happened?"

Bessie's face closed up a little, as if she were having second thoughts about confessing to Marigold. "Well, then I'm not so sure."

Marigold leaned closer to assure her. "Bessie, I swear to you, whatever you tell me, I promise you I will not tell a soul, not even Cab."

"Too late," that unmistakable deep voice behind them answered. "You already have."

CHAPTER 41

How often have I said to you that when you have eliminated the
impossible, whatever remains, however improbable, must be the truth?
—Arthur Conan Doyle

"Really, Cab!" Marigold remonstrated. "Eavesdropping. You're as bad as old Cleon and Alva. And awfully darn soft-footed for a city boy."

He was unapologetic. "A man has been murdered, Marigold—it's my job as your attorney to listen to everything and everyone I can." He turned a chair backward and sat down across from Bessie. "Now, suppose you tell me from the beginning how you fished Ellery Hatchet out of the cove."

Bessie was adamant. "Didn't fish—he fetched up in the reeds, facedown in the shallows. It was at the end of the dirt path, just where the boardwalk rises off the shore. I was standing right there when I saw him. And I swear to you, he'd already breathed his last."

Cab narrowed his eyes. "So how did Ellery Hatchet, who gets a lobster-man to drop him off on Great Misery, sick as a dog, find himself fetched himself up at your dock the next morning?"

Marigold's mind's eye supplied the red swirl of the only body she had actually seen in the water. "Floated across-sound, much like Minnie Mallory?"

"Interesting connection," he posited, unaware of her witnessing the prior crime. "But where did he go into the water and how?"

"I don't know about that," Bessie averred.

"But what I think you do know, Bessie Dove"—Cab turned all that steely intelligence upon his landlady—"was how his body got from your dock all the way back out to Great Misery and the garden at Hatchet Farm, with no one the wiser, to be planted in the rosemary."

The rosemary—for remembrance.

For the first time, Marigold thought Bessie looked scared. "Now, he was already dead, you understand? And I didn't want no more trouble with that man than I already had."

Cab shook his head. "Then why didn't you wake me?"

"For all your kindness and honesty, you're one of them," Bessie replied defensively. "You don't understand what it's like to be a Black woman in a white town."

The truth of this Cab acknowledged with a nod. "So tell me."

"It's danged precarious is what it is."

Cab again nodded his understanding. "So what did you do?"

"Only Christian thing I could do—I hauled him out. I put him in the smokehouse so he wasn't laying there in the open, all indecent like. Then, once I'd had a minute to think, I put him in the skiff to take him back where he belonged," Bessie finished. "Where he couldn't trouble me no more."

"All by yourself?" Cab scratched at his chin, where the barest beginnings of whiskers were starting to make their appearance. "Why? Why did you not take the body to the police, or better yet, since I was here, come get me to take care of things and call them here for you?"

"Well, I thought of that, but I've lived in this world long enough to know that sometimes, oftentimes, a Black person is made to take the blame when they ain't done nothing wrong. I knew that if that policeman heard I found that body, he wouldn't look no further to make up his mind, and not even you might could change it."

Cab heaved out a sigh of acknowledgment regarding the character of Officer Parker. "How tall are you, Bessie?"

"Oh, it weren't no bother. Skinny old man like him—bones like a bird, nothing but air and resentment. Didn't weigh much."

"It took two grown men to move him this morning," Cab observed. "You dragged him out of the water to the smokehouse, then the length of the dock to your skiff, sailed him across to Great Misery, dragged his body more than a mile across the island, through the woods, and propped him up in the garden? Alone?" Cab repeated his question. "You sailed Ellery

Hatchet up to Hatchet Farm by yourself in the dark and got back in time, against the tide, to be home at dawn to give me the news that Hatchet Farm was on fire? Or did you set that fire while you were out there?"

"No, now don't you go looking for trouble where there is none," Bessie complained.

"Bessie." Cab's voice was quiet, but all the more steely for its softness. "Please don't lie to me. It wasn't you, because I saw you in your kitchen late last night. I was awakened by voices and came down to see you pacing up and down as if something heavy were weighing on your mind. And that's when Seviah came in."

Marigold heard her own gasp.

Cab's gaze pinned Marigold just as sharply as it had Bessie, telling her not to interfere.

"Seviah came in before dawn, along with your Samuel—through that porch door. Which is when I smelled the ash on the wind and noticed the glow of the fire out on Great Misery all those miles away. But I wrongly thought that whatever mischief Samuel and Seviah had been up to could wait until we'd sorted out whatever was wrong at Hatchet Farm. Only what they'd been up to was part of what was wrong at Hatchet Farm, wasn't it?"

"Could be." Bessie put a gentle hand to Cab's arm. "But we don't need to bring Samuel, or Seviah for that matter, into this, do we? You know what the police are like—always ready to let a Black man take the blame. You mix my Samuel up in this and Parker will put a noose around his neck, sure as wonder. And Ellery Hatchet was dead already. I swear to it. And I'll swear to it in court."

"If you want to keep safe from prosecution, Bessie, both of those men will have to corroborate that fact—swear to it in a court of law."

Marigold was not sure how much swearing Seviah might do under oath, but she recalled vividly his swearing that night they had talked about Minnie in the breezeway. *Sell Hatchet Farm*, he had said. *Or burn it to the ground*.

"Marigold? What is it? What are you not telling me?" Cab insisted. "What does it have to do with Lucy being Ellery Hatchet's child but Seviah Hatchet not? Tell me the truth!"

Her poker face was clearly slipping under duress. "Eavesdropper," Marigold accused again. The truth was as mutable a thing as justice in this circumstance—there was no one absolute. And these truths were not hers to tell.

But Bessie was more than equal to the moment. "Ellery Hatchet was Lucy's sire. By force—do you understand?" She leveled Cab with the fierceness of her gaze. "And Samuel was twelve years old back then, just a boy. But Lord, he seen it, what Ellery Hatchet done . . ." Bessie shook her head, too overcome by the memory to speak it. "That man had the devil in him, and no mistake," she finally said. "It's the Lord's work that he's finally gone."

"Yes," Marigold agreed, taking Bessie's hand, though she knew it was small comfort for the violent crime done to her, and years too late. "It most assuredly is."

"He was a mean old rip, as savage as a meat ax." Once Bessie admitted the truth, the words came tumbling out of her. "Ask anyone—mean and hard, they'll tell you. So mean and so hard I packed myself and my boy up from that place without a penny I was owed. After what he done to me, I had rather take my chances in the world than stay there a minute longer."

"So how did you get the money from him?" Marigold prompted, trying to get the information Cab needed to understand the history that had indeed gone on long before the two of them ever came to Pride's Crossing or Great Misery. "The money that paid for this boardinghouse, as recompense?"

"Ain't nothing could be true recompense for what he did to me," Bessie swore. "But I had to think of my children."

"So you took the money he offered?"

"Never offered so much as one thin dime. But I was determined to take what I could, so I packed up everything I had canned or put up—everything, down to the last potato in that root cellar. And the Lord provided the rest."

"Just like you did when Lucy left, and again this morning." Marigold didn't mean it as a question—she was thinking of how careful Lucy had been with the contents of that root cellar—but Bessie took it like one.

"Lord, there's no getting anything past you." She sighed. "I thought no one would ever know—or notice. I said those Hatchets didn't know about it all those years and weren't likely to do anything to put things to rights anyway. But Lucy said you'd set to cleaning things up and that you'd surely find it."

"Find what?" Cab persisted.

"The money." Bessie took a deep breath. "I'd took all I could carry with me that first time I left Great Misery behind, before Lucy was born, but it still wasn't all I was owed or had earned. But we got the rest of what I was owed out eventually, a little at a time over the past few years, every time Lucy came back over."

"What money?" Cab probed.

"Or should we ask, *whose* money?" Marigold clarified, because there was something tickling at the back of her brain about money and the lack thereof on Great Misery Island.

"I was my money—what I was owed," Bessie swore. "There, in an old sea chest covered in dust and bushel baskets down in the root cellar—a strongbox filed with what was called specie."

"Coins of different metals?"

"That's right. Mostly Mexico silver dollars—what they told me was *reales*."

"Who told you that?"

"Friends in Boston who know about money. Friends who didn't ask questions about how a Black woman got ahold of Mexico silver coins but understood that money was provided to me by the Lord. I didn't take anything that I hadn't already earned by my work and by my labor, you understand." She looked Cab in the eye, daring him to contradict her. "Years of back wages I was owed. Years. And other costs as well."

"Quite right," Marigold agreed. "So you took the chest? Is that what you had in the stern of the boat this morning?"

"Lord, but you are a sharp one. But it wasn't the chest itself—that old chest was banded with iron bars. But there was a smaller strongbox inside that we took with the last of what I figured I was owed—Lucy and I both. Because it was rightfully mine by then—I worked out the terms of Lucy's employment in a contract that said the contents of that little house and root cellar was ours. Got it right there in writing."

"Very smart thinking, but I'll have a look at that contract, if you please," Cab asked.

"Sure. I got nothing to hide. Because I left the rest of it for them, that chest, just as was right. The rest is out there for that Wilbert to find. Poor boy deserves something for all his years of labor, just like the rest of us."

But Marigold's reasoning had turned in a different direction. "After what had happened to you, whyever did Lucy come to live and work out there?"

"Now that was the hand of the Lord again. Miz Sophronia sent a letter, asking if Lucy was available to cook for old Alva. I reckoned the old biddy had a scare about poisoning or something. Or had to eat too much of poor old Cleon's cooking, which is about the same thing. But Miz Sophronia, she worked out the terms with me so I could feel all right about Lucy going out there. I didn't think she knew, that Sophronia, but after talking to her, I reckon now that she did know all along—about Lucy, not the money—and was trying to put things right."

Sophronia, with her letters, trying to put right what Ellery Hatchet had long ago put wrong.

Cab cleared his throat. "So, Samuel had good reason to hate Ellery Hatchet—"

"I told you," Bessie insisted, "Hatchet was already—"

"—dead." Cab held up his hands to forestall her. "I'll need to corroborate that fact with Samuel and Seviah."

Bessie folded her hands in her lap. "Well, I reckon it's too late for that now—they're already gone. All of them. I advised them all to clear out until all this blows over and it's safe to come home again. And I don't know where they've gone, so don't ask me."

"Seviah? Samuel? Lucy too?" Cab pushed to his feet and raked his hands through his hair. "Blast it, Bessie. As an officer of the court, I'm sworn to do everything in my power to serve justice, and justice is finding whoever shot Ellery Hatchet—"

"But he weren't shot!" Bessie insisted. "He were white as a dead cod's belly, not a bit of blood on him. He drowned—water come all up and out of his mouth when we moved him. You mark my words, that man drowned."

"Agreed." A new voice intruded on their conversation. "Ellery Hatchet was drowned."

CHAPTER 42

It is considered good sportsmanship not to pick up golf balls while they are still rolling.

—Mark Twain

D r. Oliphant stood at the porch door with Officer Parker trailing behind coming up the porch steps. "Although something did put a hole in him—two holes, deep enough to puncture his lung and perforate his liver, right between the fifth and sixth ribs." He made a thrusting gesture with two fingers. "But it wasn't bullets—the holes were clean. Whatever went in went back out."

Marigold felt a relief so profound she nearly gasped—she had not realized quite how anxious she had been for Daisy until that moment.

"And whatever did that probably would have killed him eventually," the doctor continued. "But he drowned first—his lungs were full of water."

"I told you," Bessie muttered.

Cab spoke over her to divert the officials' attention. "Along with the evidence of Mr. Hatchet's things you collected on the path on Great Misery, we've taken some testimony from lobstermen Roger and Harvey Brown that they rowed a preacher presumed to be Ellery Hatchet out to Great Misery Island two days ago. Harv Brown related that Hatchet was in a bad way—sweating and doubled over with stomach pains, guzzling down that bottle of patent medicine you've got."

"Which I tested for poison—that accusation having been made, however recklessly or without evidence." Dr. Oliphant nodded toward Marigold in a rather nice form of apology. "I found no trace of strychnine or arsenic, the most common domestic poisons," the doctor informed them.

"He wasn't poisoned!" Marigold felt a second wave of relief—this time for both Bessie and Sophronia and their larders full of tonics.

"I didn't say that." Dr. Oliphant looked over the top of his glasses. "I said I have yet to identify the poison. But I still suspect it."

"Was he poisoned, stabbed, or drowned?" Officer Parker was still confused.

"All, maybe," the doctor declared.

"So let me get this straight." Parker hitched up his pants, as if that helped him think more clearly. "Hatchet left to preach with that tent revival over in Manchester—"

"But then he left the revival and came down to the fishing docks"—Cab added their new information to the narrative—"wanting passage to Great Misery. It seems pretty clear from the lobstermen that Hatchet thought he'd been poisoned, although it might have simply been something he ate. But he was sick enough to leave the tent revival and go home to Great Misery. He must have made it home before he was stabbed, since there was no sign of blood on the path or in the house."

Marigold tried to picture the sequence of events—given that Ellery was already dead when Samuel and Seviah hung him up on the scarecrow, something must have happened at Hatchet Farm two nights ago—something no one else in the house wanted to acknowledge. *Washed clean of his sins*, Cleon had said. Which made Marigold wonder what else gawney, gulping, eavesdropping old Cleon knew.

Cab had his own line of reasoning. "Perhaps it might make more sense," he offered, "if we don't assume only one person was responsible for all that happened to Ellery Hatchet."

"More than one?" Officer Parker was baffled. "What in tarnation? How many god-blamed people did it take to murder Ellery Hatchet?"

Cab looked at Marigold. "I think we'll have to return to Hatchet Farm to find out."

"Aww." Officer Parker rubbed the back of his neck. "It's nigh onto supper time. By the time we get all the way out there, it'd be full dark. And . . ." He groped around for an excuse.

"And I'd like to take another considered look at Hatchet's liver first," the doctor offered. "I'd like to see how the cat jumps before we proceed."

"All righty then." The policeman seemed relieved to have that settled. "We'll maybe get some of Miz Dove's good ham, then reconvene in the morning and head out to Great Misery once the tide turns." He cast a narrow-eyed glance Marigold's way. "Tho' I can't say I like leaving her at loose ends. Or anyone—I want to get ahold of the rest of these Hatchets, the other son and daughter. And it seems like"—he scratched his head, as if it would stimulate his brain—"there's something else . . ."

Cab stepped forward into Parker's line of sight. "Then I'll reiterate my earlier pledge as an officer of the court. Miss Manners will abide here for the night, if that's all right with Mrs. Dove?" But he seemed conscious of turning Parker's attention from Bessie. "Miss Manners will be here under my supervision, just as I attested to you before, sir. And we'll get out to Great Misery first thing in the morning, just as you said, and get the answers to your questions."

"Fair enough," Parker conceded.

"Fair enough." Dr. Oliphant took his leave. "I'll see you all in the morning."

Once both officials had left, Bessie sat heavily. "Thank you, Cab. I appreciate your keeping my Samuel out of it."

"I've done what I can—for now." Cab swept his hair off his forehead in a gesture of frustration. "But I doubt I can shield him, or Seviah—or anyone else, for that matter—forever."

"Like a dog who can only smell the first rabbit, that Parker," Bessie muttered. "Lazy, no account—"

"I've often noted how the mere sight of an independent woman brings out the littleness in some men," Marigold agreed. "But I had not understood how the sight of an independent Black woman would bring out more than littleness. I am sorry you have had to endure that meanness, Bessie. Deeply sorry you should have to endure any of what has befallen you."

"Thank you for that kindness, child. I don't dwell in pain—I've made a good life for me and mine. And I tell myself I'm not alone—that men like old Hatchet been taking their selfish pleasures down through the ages—though I do worry about what might happen should word get out. You know how folks like to talk."

"I do," Marigold acknowledged. "Which, by the way, is why I need to send a message to Mrs. Isabella Dana at the Ryersons' home. I'm sure rumors have been circulating, and I'd like to let her know that I'm fine. And that I'm here with Mr. Cox." That would suit Isabella's sensibilities.

"One of my other boarders can do for a messenger. Consider it done, child." Bessie squeezed Marigold's hand before she wagged her finger at Cab. "But I'll be back in no time, you hear me?"

"You mistake me, Bessie," Cab swore with his hand over his heart.

"I doubt that!" Bessie sighed as she made her way out of the kitchen. "I've got eyes!"

Once Bessie had taken her leave, Cab held out a chair for Marigold. "I doubt you've had anything to eat today."

"Nor you." But Marigold sat. "Another one of those excellent biscuits wouldn't go amiss."

"I'm sorry you have to endure this, Marigold."

"I've endured nothing compared to Bessie." She gave him a confident smile. "I'm quite sure we will prevail upon Officer Parker to see sense."

He reached out to hold her hand, but of course he found a soft spot just beneath the cuff of her shirtwaist—which she noted was smudged with dirt from the rigors of their day. "I'll have to wash this out. I didn't think to pack a change of clothes when I decided to come with you."

"No." He shook his head. "But I have to admit, I'm glad you're staying here tonight—I'll be able to sleep." He took a deep breath and let it out. "In fact, I'd like to ask you to stay here until we can get this business sorted out at Hatchet Farm. With your sharp mind and eye for the telling details, you'll be needed tomorrow. But"—he looked her in the eye—"it's not going to be easy, Marigold. One or more of your relatives is more than likely to prove themselves to be a killer."

Trust Cab to get right to the heart of the matter. "I know. And I know I don't want it to be any of them."

How strange—when she first came to Hatchet Farm, she had been rather convinced that more than one of them might be trying to kill *her*. But not anymore. "Ellery Hatchet was clearly alive when he set foot upon the island, but . . ." She shook her head, as if she might bring her thoughts into better order. "Something happened at the house, but it didn't sound like murder."

"It need not have happened at the house," he reminded her. "There's also the fire. So, Seviah is Sophronia Hatchet's bastard?"

"Cab." Marigold's tone was chiding. "Illegitimate will do, please. And I for one don't fault her for looking elsewhere. Ellery Hatchet raped Bessie, Cab." She hated saying the ugly word, but it was an ugly truth and an even uglier crime that had long gone unpunished. "He was a terrible husband and a worse sort of person."

"I don't dispute that." He put his hands up to placate her not-unreasonable anger. "But however much I might agree, that gives them all motives, Seviah and Sophronia as well as Bessie, Lucy, and Samuel."

Marigold hated to agree with him. "But Ellery knew about Seviah—he must have for years—just as Sophronia knew about Bessie and Lucy."

"Do you know who Seviah's father is?"

"I haven't figured that out yet." Not that it mattered, as far as Marigold could see—Seviah had wanted to leave Great Misery and not look back, and he was sure to stay away now.

Cab exhaled on a little huff of laughter. "You will figure it out. And likely before the rest of us do. So where does that leave us?"

"Can we eliminate Daisy as a suspect?" Marigold knew this was wishful thinking, because instinct told her Daisy had lied to her about the commotion the night before she left.

"I was relieved Doc found that Hatchet hadn't been shot—I was worried about Daisy's thirty-eight." He ran his hand through his hair before he tipped his head back to look at the ceiling. "You weren't going to tell me about that, were you?"

"Not until I had to," Marigold admitted. "How did you know?"

"Tad—he told me all about getting a gun for Daisy when I inquired about getting one for you."

So Tad had armed Daisy—there was a certain poetic justice in that. "One has to admit, as a romantic gesture, it cuts a certain dash."

Cab laughed. "So . . . any thoughts about your part of all this?"

"My part? I told you, I had no part in this!"

"Don't be disingenuous, Marigold. You're a part of it, because I have no doubt you *did* say, 'Leave him to me,' and make one of your Machiavellian plans—"

"All I did was to suggest—*suggest*," she emphasized, "that Ellery's ambitions as a preacher were wasted on Great Misery and that he might think to try the traveling tent revival circuit. He was the one who decided to go, not I—I did nothing to coerce the man. He went of his own accord."

"You certainly did manage a heck of a lot in a few short weeks."

"Don't flatter me."

"I don't mean to. You did put the idea in his head. Same as you did with the others."

Marigold threw up her hands. "You call me managing just because I can articulate a goal and recognize the steps needed to achieve it? Were I a man, the world would be acclaiming my skills and acuity and offering to make me a junior partner in a law firm or the head of the archaeology department. But since I'm a woman, the world just calls me bossy and interfering."

"I did not call you bossy."

"You called me Machiavellian, which is a ten-dollar way of saying bossy. And also a way to flatter the college girl in me."

She finally managed to break the strange tension between them—Cab smiled. "So where does that leave us?" he repeated.

"Alone," Marigold said, determined to get some small victory from the day. "And wondering if, by any chance, you'll engage in some of those liberties you alluded to earlier?"

"Marigold." His voice was full of something that wasn't quite a warning.

"I wish—" She wished they were on his narrow bed there at the boardinghouse, or even on the lumpy mattress in her attic at Hatchet Farm, alone and free with nothing between them but their attraction.

She felt his hands rub up and down her arms as if he wanted that, too, before he set her away. "Marigold, I wouldn't do you the dishonor."

"Cab, I'm not some medieval maiden—my honor is mine to share as I choose."

He nodded and leaned in to kiss her forehead. "So is mine, Marigold. So is mine." He stood and stepped away. "I'll see you in the morning."

She took her defeat like the sportswoman she was—bested but vowing to try another day. "You most assuredly will."

CHAPTER 43

I distrust those people who know so well what God wants them to do, because I notice it always coincides with their own desires.

—Susan B. Anthony

"Rise and shine." Bessie was at the door of her room. "I brushed out your clothes and drew a bath for you in the washroom."

"Thank you, Bessie." It was a glorious thing to have friends with plumbing. "You are a lamb."

Marigold allowed herself the luxury of a good long soak before she was obliged to face the wolves at the door—this time in the form of Mr. George Endicott, who seemed to have hauled himself to Bessie Dove's boarding-house at a clip, pillows of dust rising behind his elegant piano-box carriage. He barely took the time to secure the horse to the hitching post before he accosted Cab and Marigold on the porch, clutching a letter of some sort in his fist.

"Did you know about this?" He thrust a crumpled paper at them.

"Is this about the murder?" Cab asked.

Everything within Endicott stilled and shifted and recalibrated within an instant. "So, it was murder? By God, if that isn't the fittest thing."

Cab tried to curb his uncle's unseemly enthusiasm. "We're currently waiting upon the coroner's report for confirmation—"

But Endicott was only temporarily diverted—his frustrations found a new target in Marigold. "Did you know? Did *she* write you?"

Marigold decided she didn't like his tone—and frankly, she never had. "Did *who* write me about *what*?" she asked for precision's sake.

"The Hatchet girl." He all but spat the words. "Was this her idea?"

"Then, no, my dear cousin Miss Daisy Hatchet did not write me. Although I wrote to her at your address condoling her for her father's death, I've yet to receive a reply."

"Then you knew nothing of their plans?"

Marigold had had enough vagueness. "Who are *they*, and what, specifically, were *their plans*?"

"To elope!" Endicott thundered in the violently threatening way that powerful men who are thwarted too often employ. "My boy left a note that they were bound for New York early this morning and that they'd be married by the time I found them."

Marigold was of two minds simultaneously—she was both delighted that Daisy had gone ahead and done what she wanted to do without waiting for the world to catch up to her and terrified that her cousin's departure might be seen as fleeing the scene of her crime. But it was the accompanying swell of emotion within her that took her entirely by surprise—Marigold could not have been any prouder. "Brilliant, headstrong, independent girl."

"Brilliant?" Endicott echoed in disbelief. "First there was a fire, then Ellery Hatchet was shot, and then the girl conveniently leaves town to elope with my son, maybe so he can't testify against her? I've seen that little gun she tries to hide in her skirts, and I don't like it. I don't like how any of this looks for that girl."

"Your gossip has served you ill, Uncle George." Cab's tone indicated he had taken more than enough of his uncle's guff. "Ellery Hatchet wasn't shot. He drowned, after being poisoned."

Marigold's emotions took another leap from relieved—for Daisy—back to concerned—for Sophronia and Bessie. "Cab, what do you know?"

"Dr. Oliphant arrived earlier, while you were . . ." He diverted himself from blushing over Marigold's bath by gesturing mutely toward Bessie's stillroom. "He's inside, taking samples."

"I've got nothing to hide in my larder," Bessie said from the doorway, as if she hadn't a care in the world. "Most I make goes to Crestfield, the druggist, and the rest is for my own people, who come to buy it from me here. I don't have any complaints. My room is clean as clean can be."

Judging from the generally immaculate state of the house, Marigold didn't doubt it. But one could be hygienic and still be a poisoner, she supposed.

It didn't help that Dr. Oliphant came out of the larder a short while later with no expression on his face. "I have what I need."

Marigold was going to have to trust that the doctor would be of the same mind as Cab and let the facts lead him to his conclusion and not the other way around.

Those same facts also led them back to Great Misery after taking their curt leave of Cab's uncle. The sail out to the island—in a blessedly comfortable catboat that Marigold suspected Cab had borrowed from his Endicott cousin—was both a timely diversion from the reckoning to come and an unexpected pleasure. Cab commanded the helm as elegantly and efficiently as he did everything else, and Marigold could only wonder at the extraordinary circumstances that had thrown them together so much—she never would have gotten to know him so well had she gone to her archaeological field season in Greece.

But it was an unproductive thought. Despite her current circumstance, despite the murder, Marigold remained determined that her future was going to include going to Greece to study and excavate and no amount of attraction ought to sway her from her plan. She was more than glad of the brisk wind that blew them along and cooled her heated cheeks lest her poker face give way.

"Now, where is everybody else?" Officer Parker asked when they arrived at the farm. "Ought to be a passel of Hatchets out here."

"My cousins Daisy and Seviah Hatchet have lately moved into Pride's Crossing, as has Lucy Dove," Marigold interjected before Cab might be inclined to offer more than was necessary. "Seviah to join the theater companies of Mr. Keith of the Orpheum and Daisy to a visit with her betrothed's family, the Endicotts."

"And didn't that engagement surprise us all," Parker said under his breath as he headed around the house. "Let's have another look at where you found the body."

The body. How strange that Ellery Hatchet, a man who was such a force in life, had been reduced so completely in death.

Sophronia hung back in the doorway but was looking at Marigold in that strange, mutely searching way that unnerved her so—watchful and probing. "You cipher out what happened to him yet?"

"We know some," Marigold admitted out of earshot of Officer Parker. "Like how he ended up in the garden—propped up on the scarecrow by Seviah and Samuel Dove."

For all her vagueness, Cousin Sophronia instantly understood the implications of her son's involvement. "And then set the fire in barn," she sighed with that fatalistic shrug. "What will be will be."

"I see you have a number of medicinal plants in your garden, Mrs. Hatchet." Dr. Oliphant addressed Sophronia.

"Not my garden," she answered with a glance at Marigold. "Grown for the table, not the stillroom. I forage for my tonics."

Marigold spoke up for herself, though she did so tentatively. "I'm the one who started the garden shortly after I arrived, to improve the culinary variety."

"If it's a kitchen garden, why do you cultivate foxglove?"

Behind Marigold, Sophronia made a sound of frustrated derision. "Fust! That weren't there afore," she stated. "That weren't there when we took Hatchet down. It's been planted in since."

"That tall, spire-shaped pink one?" Marigold asked. "There was one before—another plant just a pretty as this one, planted the day Ellery tried to uproot—" But perhaps it were better to exclude all references to her prior conflict with Ellery. "But the flower disappeared. I thought it died or was eaten by some scavenger."

"You'd know if it were eaten. Dangerous stuff, that," the doctor returned.

"Ayuh," Sophronia agreed tersely. "That's why I pulled it out—before. Don't use it in my tonics."

"We'll see about that." Doctor Oliphant led the way inside before he disappeared into the stillroom with his bag, presumably to test the veracity of that statement, much as he must have done with Bessie's stock.

"All right then." Officer Parker addressed the rest of them in the kitchen. "I'm going to need some answers to my questions. We've established that Ellery Hatchet made his way here, to Hatchet Farm, two nights ago. Who saw and who talked to Ellery Hatchet that night?"

"Not me," Wilbert said. "But my room's up at the top of the house."

"I locked him in too, along with Marigold." Sophronia didn't blink. "And Daisy. Have for years. To keep Hatchet getting to them in one of his rages. Seviah was already gone."

"So you did see old man Hatchet?" Parker probed.

"Ayuh," Sophronia admitted freely. "I seen him. But I kept my distance, same as always. I let him be."

Cab tried to be patient with Sophronia's melodramatic vagueness. "Where, specifically, did you see him, ma'am?"

"Here, in the kitchen." She gestured to the hearth end of the room.

"And where were you, ma'am?"

Sophronia tossed her head toward the stillroom. "End of the hallway, next to my room. Retreated there behind my lock once I'd secured the others, same as I normally did when Hatchet was in one of his takings."

Which left . . . "Cleon?" Marigold ventured. "This seems to be where you sleep most nights, here at the table. Did you see Cousin Ellery when he came in?"

"Oh, I surely did," Cleon admitted, as if he had only just thought of it. "He come home all boogered up, he was."

"Boogered?" Marigold had not heard this particularly expressive description before.

"Bent over, like he was crippled, maybe," Wilbert clarified. "Or boozy." Wilbert's shrug was a mirror of his mother's. "Figure he fell back on the booze—the old man claimed to be a teetotaler, but that was on account he used to be a bottle hound once."

"That's not true." Great-Aunt Alva appeared among them again as if she'd been conjured, thumping her cane, an insistent hodgepodge of shawls, nightgown, and defiance. Her voice was small but furious in her grief. "He was a good man, my Ellery was."

"Ellery Hatchet was a son of a bitch," Officer Parker declared baldly. "Begging yer pardon, ma'am, but I don't think there was a body in Pride's Crossing he hadn't argued against, especially Mr. Endicott."

"Which is why we keep out here, to ourselves on our island, away from the Endicotts' pernicious influence." Alva shook her cane at Parker.

"This island was deeded to Mr. Elijah Hatchet, Ellery's father, by Captain Jacob Endicott." Cab put forth the history between the two families as it was known to him. "As payment for a debt of wages."

"It was all as it should be, legal and binding," Alva quavered. "You can't take it away from us now."

"No, ma'am," Cab confirmed. "Just as you say."

"Hatchet gave up drink back in the year eighteen and seventy-five," Sophronia put in. "He swore on a Bible he'd give up the drink if the Lord would spare his life. Traded liquor for milk."

"But the milk of human kindness still never flowed in the old man's veins," Wilbert claimed. "He *was* a right mean old cuss. Thought all fathers were like him—all people. But now I know better." He looked at Marigold.

"No. She made him that way," Alva insisted, pointing her arthritic white finger at Sophronia. "With her sour looks and heedless—"

"Mother Hatchet." Sophronia cut Alva's tirade short with a withering look. "He was a grave sinner, like us all, no more, no less. You know that."

"But he were washed clean of his sin," Cleon claimed. "Just like he asked. Wanted to be washed clean." He nodded as if agreeing with himself. "He said so to me."

Marigold felt the hairs on her skin tingle in that strange way. "Exactly when did he say that, Cleon?"

"What sin?" asked Cab.

"Don't rightly know which of them all." Cleon looked puzzled. "But it were spilling out of him. Like Jesus and the centurion's lance, he said, 'cept it weren't water and wine coming out from his side."

A realization came over her. "Was he bleeding, Cleon?"

"Like a red gum stump," the old fellow admitted. "Looking to die with the pains. Going on and on about the sin and how he needed to be washed clean of it, he was. Begged me take him down to the water."

How horrifyingly biblical. "So did you take him down to the water's edge? To Salem Sound?"

"I surely did," Cleon assured them. "I do as I'm told. Same as always."

"He was alive when you took him there?" Cab asked.

"Ayuh. Took him to his praying place, where he'd go so's the Lord could speak to him direct like."

"God spoke directly to Ellery down on the shore?" Marigold had assumed that Ellery Hatchet's conversations with his maker were strictly one-sided.

The old man just bobbed his head in agreement. "I laid him down there just like he asked. And Cousin Ellery patted my face when he look up at me. Said I looked all yellowed with the moon behind my head like a saint."

"There wasn't a moon that night." Marigold recalled the inky blackness perfectly. "It was cloudy."

"Xanthopsia," the doctor muttered. "From digitalis, the plant of the foxglove or nightshade," he explained. "Digoxin is the poison extracted from the leaves of the foxglove." Oliphant's gaze landed squarely on Marigold. "When given in large enough doses, it can occasion sickness, purging, giddiness, confused vision, objects appearing haloed in yellow or green, increased secretion of urin . . . beg your pardon." The doctor left off his list. "All leading to death. In short, all the symptoms that have been reported for Ellery Hatchet."

CHAPTER 44

Not knowing when the dawn will come, I open every door.
— Emily Dickinson

"Didn't get it from me," Sophronia reiterated. "You'll have found none of in my room or in my tonics." She held out her hand for the key to her stillroom.

"True," the doctor agreed without returning the key. "I have not found evidence in your stillroom, though I tested every bottle I could find."

"Hope you cleaned up after yourself," was Sophronia's only complaint. "The girl works hard enough to keep the place as neat as a pin and shining like a copper penny. Don't want you giving her any extra work."

It was as close to a compliment as Marigold was like to get. "Thank you."

"I'll want to retest for digoxin in the bottle we collected from Ellery Hatchet's pocket," Oliphant confirmed.

"More tests?" Officer Parker was getting frustrated again. "Are you looking for more evidence of poison? Or of stabbing?"

"Perhaps we should look for evidence in the place where Ellery Hatchet was last seen alive?" Marigold redirected their attention to Cleon. "Ellery was bleeding and you helped him down to the water's edge, Cleon?"

"Ayuh. Sat him down against the rocks." The old fellow pointed out the window toward the shoal of glacial moraine that formed the southernmost point of the island. "So's the water could flow over him and wash him clean."

"Was he still bleeding?"

"Red as a tide," was Cleon's answer. "That's why I brung him. But I left him be there, cuz that was his private place for praying, see, where I wasn't allowed. Got to thinking I might shouldn'ta put him down into the water like he asked, cuz he didn't go down to Moses on the River Jordan like he said. Next morn he was back up in the garden, and I knew it were the curse that put him there."

"The curse? Oh, Cleon." Marigold was nearly overwhelmed with pity for the old man, but she wasn't about to tell them that Samuel and Seviah had actually put him there. "There is no curse."

"There surely is. I were here the day he cursed the place," Cleon swore. "Rained that hex down on sister and Cousin Ellery's head. Made her hair turn to white, it did that day. Cursed us all."

"Who did?" Parker asked.

"He doesn't know what he's talking about," Alva insisted. "Never has. He's gawney—always has been. She did this," Alva accused in that pleading quaver, pointing first to Sophronia before she switched to Marigold, as if she couldn't make up her mind. "She's the one that made him go away, for her revenge. She put the idea into his head. She's the one that did all of this."

The policeman was rightly confused. "Now, was it you," he asked Marigold, "who cursed him?"

"Not I," Marigold swore. "I assure you, I've cursed no one." Deserving boarding school girls and recalcitrant clerks excepted.

"I heard her with my own ears," Alva countered. "She said, 'You leave him to me.' Right there in that yard, bold as day, she swore that to Wilbert." She turned on her grandson. "Tell me she didn't, boy. Tell them what she said to you."

"No, no," Wilbert stammered. "I mean, she did say that, like, but that's not . . . I didn't think she meant anything."

Marigold spoke for herself. "I didn't mean anything more than that I would help Wilbert with his plan—"

"Aha!" Alva crowed. "There you have it. It was her. She was planning her revenge all along!" She had their attention now. "From the moment she came here, all insinuating and curious, nosing and pushing her way into our business. All for what she could get from us. Well, I won't let her take this place."

Marigold's normally banked temper finally began to flare. "I do not want this place—who in their right mind would? Sorry, Wilbert." She apologized to her cousin but would not be put off having her say. "But I did not come out here to pry. I came at my cousin Sophronia's invitation—but for her letter, I would never have known the Hatchets even existed."

"Admit you wanted him gone," Alva insisted.

"*He* wanted gone!" Marigold abandoned grammar for the sake of expediency. "Ellery Hatchet hated Hatchet Farm. He talked openly and incessantly about how cursed the place was and how nothing would grow—until I made a garden and showed how wrong he was. But he resented the garden as much as he resented his sons." But perhaps it would be better if she did not supply those sons with motives in front of the police. "What he wanted was to preach. All I did was encourage him to do just that—to join the Reverend Cooper's tent revival that I had seen advertised in waybills about town."

"I saw the waybills too." Cab quietly added his support. "I reckon we all did."

"Well, that's beside the point." Officer Parker wasn't letting go of the low-hanging fruit. "And maybe he didn't want to go, so you—"

"But he *did* want to go!" Marigold swore. "He said so in front of the whole family the night of the Endicotts' party. He told them all, including his mother, that he was leaving to go on the revival circuit and that there was nothing she could say to stay him. And he left that very next morning."

"That's exactly what happened," Wilbert averred. "I rowed him over myself. Happiest I'd ever seen him. Talking the whole time about the plans the Lord had for him."

"Said the Lord would provide," Cleon confirmed. "The Lord would give it to him if he were good and holy."

Marigold had learned to take Cleon literally. "Give what exactly, Cleon?"

"What he were looking for! Years he spent looking. Years he spent praying, asking the Lord." Cleon gazed out the breezeway toward the point. "Though he never did find it."

Had Ellery been talking to God that day she had seen him kicking up the bank? He had been swearing in a manner more fit for Lucifer than the Lord, but . . .

Another thought occurred. "Cleon, is that why Cousin Ellery was always digging holes wherever he went on the island? What was he trying to find?"

"The chest."

"What chest?" Wilbert asked.

Marigold let Cleon answer, though she was sure she already knew. "Old Elijah's chest," Cleon said, "that he brought out here and hid, even from sister."

"Sister?" And for the first time, Marigold understood that singular word—*sister*. And it all began to make sense—the old man sleeping on the kitchen table all night and most times of the day, waiting to do his sister's bidding, after the rest of the house had gone to sleep or was up in the barn playing juke music or locked into their rooms by Sophronia to keep them safe not only from Ellery Hatchet's volcanic tempers but also from the one person who was entirely unaccounted for at Hatchet Farm—Alva Hatchet. Alva, who never came out of her room but somehow knew word for word what conversations Cleon had been listening to on his sister's behalf.

"What was in the chest, Cleon?"

"Don't rightly know, since he never could find it. But it were supposed to be treasure."

"A child's tale, foolishness." Alva contradicted her brother. "He's gawney. Always has been. Doesn't know what he's talking about."

But Marigold felt the old man knew perfectly well. "Like an iron-banded tea chest, Cleon? One the clipper ships would have brought back around the horn from China?" China, where Elijah Hatchet had sailed as first mate to Jacob Endicott in the tea trade.

"Ayuh," Cleon agreed. "The very like. Elijah told sister he'd hidden it on the island."

Marigold looked over Cleon's head at Cab.

Who looked back at her with the same sharp understanding—that the chest Bessie had discovered in the root cellar, the chest that was full of silver specie of the sort used by American clipper ship captains to buy their cargoes, and this treasure were one and the same. "Wilbert, remind me that I have an important—but welcome—chore for you later."

"Don't be making Wilbert into your cat's paw to do as you like—like you did to my Ellery." Alva reinserted herself in the conversation. "She's a she-devil, come here to have her revenge."

Marigold held her temper in favor of logic. "That's the second or third time"—frankly, with so much to keep track of, she had lost count—"you've said that, Great-Aunt Alva. But I should like to ask, quite particularly, revenge for *what*? What on earth would I want revenge for?"

The silence that met her question was deafening.

"You know," Alva finally insisted.

"I do not know," Marigold responded. "Though I came here at my cousin Sophronia's invitation to find out." She pulled the smooth folds of Sophronia's letter from her pocket and held it out to her. "Without her letter, I would not have known the Hatchets existed. Don't you think it's time you told me why I was invited to stay?"

Alva retreated into pettishness. "I never wanted you to come. I forbade it."

"Naturally." Marigold gained some respect for Sophronia. "Look at you," she teased gently. "Going against her wishes. Not a bit mothlike."

The faintest beginnings of a wry smile warmed Sophronia's face. "Ayuh. For all the good it's done me."

"What are you talking about, Ma?" Wilbert broke in. "Cousin Marigold's done us a world of good. Just look around this kitchen, this farm. Even with the old barn gone, this place has never looked so good."

"It used to look fine, until she came," Alva accused with a glare at Sophronia.

"So it might have," Sophronia agreed in her laconic way. "But nothing any of us did—not Bessie, and certainly not me—were ever enough to please you. So I stopped trying. Until she came." She looked at Marigold. "You changed everything, just as I feared and hoped you would."

"Yeah, yeah." Office Parker was like a dog with a dry bone. "But what I want to know is what in tarnation this has to do with Ellery Hatchet's murder."

"Nothing and everything," Sophronia said in her cryptic way.

"This would sure go a whole lot easier if one of you would go ahead and confess," the policeman groused.

"We cannot confess to that which we did not do," Marigold returned tartly. "And Cousin Sophronia attested that it could not be either Wilbert or Daisy or I, since she had locked us into our rooms on the night in question. Just as she was locked in her stillroom."

"That's right," Sophronia affirmed.

"All I have is your say-so," Officer Parker returned, "with no way to tell whether or not it's a dad-blamed lie. But I ain't leaving here until I find out."

"Oh, you'll find it out," Sophronia murmured, returning her gaze to Marigold. "It's time you found out. You'll need this." She fished another long key on a string out of her bodice and handed it to Marigold.

"What are you doing?" Alva cawed in protest. "I forbid—"

"Which door?" Marigold asked, cutting her off.

"Mine."

Marigold rushed to the central stairwell, above which Sophronia's and Wilbert's rooms lay. Wilbert's she had seen before—so spare as to be Spartan—to deliver clean laundry, but Sophronia's had always been locked. Though her dread increased with every step, Marigold stepped through the doorway into Sophronia's chamber. And was immediately taken aback by the cozy simplicity and order.

The bed was covered by a worn but well-made quilt—similar to the one on her own bed. Checked curtains, though sun-bleached, hung neatly over the clean single dormer window. A chest of drawers and dressing table held not a speck of dust.

The contrast with the rest of the disordered house was so great as to be bizarre.

But what was most bizarre was the dressing table, decorated with an array of small, framed tintype and sepia-tinged photographs—most of which were of Seviah, all "togged up," as he had said, in his dinner suit from the evening of the party. "But how did he have his photograph taken—"

The answer came to her on a gasp when she picked up the frame. It could not be Seviah—the style of evening clothes was thirty years old if it was a day. The handsome young man who gazed so calmly from the portrait could be none other than the charming rogue who had been Harry Minot Manners. "It's my father."

"I thought I recognized him." Cab had followed her up and put a warming hand to her elbow in unspoken support. "I suppose I can guess who that is too." He pointed to another frame, which Marigold had, upon first glance, assumed to be Daisy but upon closer inspection proved to be her own darling mother, Esmé Sedgwick Manners. This, then, was the photograph both Cleon and Bessie had remarked upon.

The resemblance was indeed uncanny.

More photos, of small children, clad in the long, androgynous dresses of an earlier time, whom Marigold could not immediately identify—the pronounced likeness between Daisy and Esmé and between Seviah and Harry had her utterly confused—were tucked into the sides of the frame of the folded mirror.

"Look." Cab pointed into the shallow open drawer on the left side of the dressing table, which contained more photos—warped and curling with age—alongside newspaper clippings of Marigold's preparatory school graduation and a photogravure of her winning the collegiate championship in golf.

"Why are there so many pictures of Seviah and so few of Wilbert?" She pulled open the other drawers, only to find more of the younger son, including a photograph of him as a solemn-faced, dark-eyed child staring forthrightly into the camera.

And felt a strange stillness overcome her.

"That's—" Her voice sounded quiet, subdued, even to her own ears. "That's Seviah, isn't it? But it looks just like me." Her parents had kept a similar photograph of her on top of the piano in the Beacon Hill house.

"Yes," Cab murmured. "The resemblance is pronounced."

The wonder and strangeness of it all crashed into stupefaction. But she could see the truth in the faces staring out at her from the photographs. It was obvious. And inevitable. "Are Daisy and Seviah Esmé and Harry's children? Are they my brother and sister?"

"Perhaps," Cab cautioned quietly.

"I don't understand." Officer Parker—whom Marigold had entirely forgotten in her wonder—stood in the doorway. "This Harry and Esmé are, or were, your parents? And how are they connected?"

Her mouth spoke the words even as she struggled to make sense of them. "My mother is Sophronia Hatchet's first cousin. But that does not explain how their children got here, to this godforsaken place." Her mind was whirling ahead. "Unless this is the 'great and godless wrong' that Ellery Hatchet did to my mother? Oh, dear heavens!"

The truth hit her like a golf club to the back of her head. "That horrible, hateful old man! He stole my beautiful mother's beautiful children."

Chapter 45

A father may turn his back on his child, brothers and sisters may become inveterate enemies, husbands may desert their wives, wives their husbands. But a mother's love endures through all.

—Washington Irving

"My God." Marigold invoked a deity she would have sworn she didn't believe in.

The enormity of the sin—the crime!—was overwhelming.

She found herself sitting on the edge of Sophronia's bed, steered there by Cab, who must have feared for her normally impervious constitution.

How could she have no memory of them? How could she not know? "Do you think they know?" she asked him.

"Seviah and Daisy?" He shook his head but said, "You would be a better judge than I."

"Would I?" For once, Marigold could not agree with him. Her powers of discernment had failed her so utterly. "Even Cleon could see! He told me I would see how Daisy looked like Esmé. And I did, but I didn't understand. And Seviah! I discovered he was not Ellery Hatchet's son, but I never suspected he was my brother—though you saw it, the resemblance, it never occurred to me."

How blind she had been in thinking she was the only one who knew how things ought to be at Hatchet Farm. She had never questioned her own assumptions of rightness. She had never asked why things might have gotten so out of hand in the first place. "What a fool I've been."

To her chagrin, neither man in the room disagreed. "Well, this is certainly a whole lot of jiggery-pokery," the officer surmised. "But it still doesn't tell me who killed Ellery Hatchet."

Except it added an entirely new set of stunningly compelling motives—the knowledge that Ellery Hatchet had stolen children gave those children an even greater motive to exact their retribution. To *burn it all to the ground*. Or *shoot his eye out*. Or *clear the place out*.

To put it all right—just as she had been invited to, by Sophronia, in her letter.

Marigold could see the awareness of that exact truth reflected in Cab's eyes—he was more deeply worried for her than ever.

"I didn't do it," she assured him. "However much he clearly deserved it, the thieving bastard. I had no idea until now."

"No," he agreed. "I think we can both see that." He looked to the policeman for confirmation.

Who gave it reluctantly. "Nevertheless—"

Nevertheless, one of them—someone at or involved with Hatchet Farm—had killed him.

But Marigold no longer cared who. She could only think of her poor mother, deprived of the daughter and son she must have so desperately missed. No wonder she had spent her life in a whirl of dissipation—she had spent her life trying to forget. While Sophronia had clearly spent her life trying to remember, keeping the collection of photographs like talismans of the sin. Signposts to the past. "Sophronia knew all of this, all along."

"Yes," Cab agreed. "I think we had best go talk to her."

Marigold descended to the kitchen on legs that felt numb. She laid the photographs of Esmé and Harry on the table like a pair of Sophronia's tarot cards and asked only, "Why?"

"Jealousy," was Sophronia's whispered but honest answer.

Marigold wanted far more explanation, but she settled for asking, "Whose?"

Sophronia settled back into her chair. "Mine. His. Both."

"Please." Marigold could feel her composure crack. The depths of her well-cultivated aplomb had run dry. "For once, will you please, please, kindly, simply explain."

Sophronia pulled the photograph of Esmé, sublime and ethereal on her wedding day, toward her. "She was a beauty, wasn't she?"

"She was." Marigold could only agree. "And Daisy is the picture of her, isn't she?"

"She is," Sophronia sighed. "Though on a grander scale." She smiled a little wistfully, making a gesture to acknowledge Daisy's towering stature before she went back to fingering the worn edge of the photograph, as if she had beheld it thus many times over the years. "She was like a tiny fairy queen that day."

Marigold felt a strange twinge of uncomfortable empathy. But the time for uncomfortable truths had come. "Were you jealous of her beauty?" She gave Sophronia's hand a little squeeze. "I was too, growing up. Always wondering why I wasn't as beautiful as she."

Sophronia squeezed Marigold's hand back, but she said, "You don't need beauty—you've got something more. But I was once as beautiful myself. Beautiful enough to rival even Esmé." She pulled her hand away and sat back in her chair to remember. "So I set myself after her suitor—to prove I was still . . . someone. To show I was still . . . I don't know. It was all for naught. Still ended up here. Still had to endure Hatchet's displeasure."

"You set your cap for Harry, my father? I don't understand."

"Jealousy," Sophronia repeated. "That was my sin in all of this. But it started it all."

Marigold tried to understand what her cousin had not said. "You married Hatchet after Harry chose Esmé over you?"

"Before," Sophronia corrected. "I married the miserable man before. That was what drove me back. Drove me toward Black Harry."

"But why did you marry Hatchet in the first place if he was so disagreeable?"

"Oh, he weren't always such a . . . He was charming and handsome once too. Courted me with posies and the language of flowers—he's the one taught me that. But that was afore." She paused and looked out over the kitchen table as if she could see back across time. "Afore his mind started getting all twisted up with anger and greed and . . . and that evil unholy holiness. All that preaching—ranting, it was." She sighed. "But that came on gradually, though it came on strongest after."

"After he stole my mother's children?"

Sophronia shook her head—whether in negation or rejection of the deed, Marigold could not tell—before she returned to her story. "Had this place already when I met him. Made out like we were going to live the life of Reilly in this big house. Said the place was a treasure." She shook her head again. "But he soured and the land soured around him when he couldn't find his treasure, though he couldn't bear to leave. Nor would Mother Hatchet let him leave. Nor leave herself. She squatted in there, like a dragon in her lair." Sophronia flicked a dismissive finger toward Alva Hatchet's room. "Hoarding what she considered hers, giving nothing in return—no love or affection. Not even a bit of work after I came here as a bride. Expected us to do for her."

"Why didn't you leave?"

Sophronia tossed up that unaccountable shrug. "I loved him once, you know. Or thought I did. But then we came out here to this lonely living with Mother Hatchet—" She closed her eyes, as if it might help her see back across the years. "And then, when I had my first baby, my blessed Wilbert, Hatchet's attention wandered, and I wanted to get back at him for catting about the town like a tom."

"Ellery was unfaithful?"

"More than unfaithful." Sophronia pursed her lips, as if the taste of the words themselves was sour. "He was criminal."

"Bessie Dove?" Marigold whispered.

"And others." Sophronia took another deep breath, as if it were hard to draw the air into her lungs. "They lured him, he said, with their wicked ways. Said Satan sent them. But I didn't care who sent them, did I? It was his fault and none other. But it made me powerful angry, and so I run away home. Back to Boston. But Mother Hatchet, she came after me. Told me I had to come back for Wilbert's sake. But I'd got my revenge, I thought. I'd got myself with child by my cousin's man."

There was so much pain in Sophronia's voice that it took another moment for Marigold to begin to understand. Everything within her went still with dread—like an animal that, too late, sees the hunter. "By Esmé's husband? My father?"

Sophronia's expression was bleak. "He weren't her husband then—just her suitor. But ayuh, he was your father."

It was as if her body had its own logic apart from her mind—Marigold felt a pain in her chest, as if her heart had stopped working or, more likely, that the overstrained organ had split itself in two and was pouring molten blood within her chest.

She could not make herself believe such an impossible thing. "But he was devoted to her—to my mother—as she was to him. They loved each other. They could not stand to be apart."

"True," Sophronia agreed grudgingly. "She was the making of him. Or would have been, but for Hatchet."

The enormity of the implications—

Marigold tried to reassert her powers of logic. "Did he know, my—" She was too confused to sort out the ties. "Did you tell Harry you were pregnant?"

"Never told him. Would have taken it to my grave." This time Sophronia's characteristic shrug was weighted with regret and longing for something that could almost have been. "I don't rightly know—I never spoke to them again. I was here, kept here under lock and key by Mother Hatchet."

"And the baby? Seviah?" Marigold picked up the portrait of her father, photographed as a young man, in his finest. The familial resemblance to Seviah was so strong, it was a wonder she had not remarked upon it before. Seviah was her half brother!

But Sophronia was still lost in the maze of the past. "I'd had my babies, but they locked them away from me. Because Hatchet and his mother took one look at them and knew they weren't his."

This time Marigold's head kept working, even as her heart seemed to stutter to a painful stop within her chest. "They? Babies, plural?"

"Ayuh." Sophronia looked into Marigold's eyes for a long time before she finally told all. "You and your brother. The spit of him, you both were—of Black Harry."

"My brother." Marigold repeated the word carefully, as if it were a shard of broken glass balanced on her tongue. "Seviah is my brother?"

"Ayuh." The word was nothing but a sigh. "My sweet babies. Twins."

CHAPTER 46

Until you have loved, you cannot become yourself.
—Emily Dickinson

Marigold felt a strange sort of painful numbness—she didn't actually feel her knees give way, but she was sinking and Cab was there, steering her into one of the kitchen chairs.

She latched on to the only solid fact. "You're my mother."

Ma is always going on about you.

"Ayuh." Sophronia's admission came on the merest whisper, as if she too were holding herself in dread.

But Marigold was too numb to account for anything more than plain fact. She took refuge in logical deduction. "And Daisy is Esmé's and Harry's daughter, isn't she?"

"Ayuh." Finally, a tear rolled down Sophronia's cheek. "When she was born, Hatchet stole her away." Her voice broke. "And gave you to them instead. Took one and left the other as punishment and reminder of my sin."

My darling changeling. It was all so painful and unfathomable all at the same time. The heat in Marigold's throat was unbearable. Her chest felt hot and tight.

But if Sophronia had suffered even half of Marigold's current pain, it was no wonder she was so brittle and broken. "That must have been . . . devastating." The word could not possibly be adequate. "I am so sorry."

"Wasn't your doing." Sophronia sniffed and wiped her eyes on her shawl. "You were but a babe. But to never look upon you until you came—"

She drew in a sharp breath. "It has been an awful penance to pay. Knowing when I finally saw you that Esmie never got to do the same—that she died not knowing her daughter's face."

The ache within Marigold grew. "I am so sorry," she said again, even though she knew the sympathy was inadequate.

"So am I. So am I." But Sophronia seemed a little relieved, finally, at the telling. "It is the curse and the blessing of motherhood that you're only as happy as your saddest child. But I never knew if you were sad or not—I only knew I was." She reached for Marigold's face with a shaking hand, exactly as she had that first night—as if she were afraid to touch her. "I couldn't allow myself to imagine what you looked like for the longest time. Wouldn't let myself wonder if you looked like your brother."

Oh, but she had wondered, hadn't she, with her strange collection of photographs of Seviah as a child, dressed in the old-fashioned genderless dresses of the time.

"Do they know, Seviah and Daisy?"

Sophronia shook her head. "There's only three people alive who know. And we're two of them."

"Great-Aunt Alva?" And where had the old besom disappeared to? The chair she had languished into was now empty.

"Ayuh. Knows it all, she does. About my babies and Esmie's. About Lucy. And about other things, too, I reckon. Who knows what else that evil old woman is keeping to herself with her blackmail and her curses and her forbiddings? She said I had to forget. But I never forgot you. Never." There was a sort of pleading desperation in Sophronia's voice. "Wasn't a day that went by that I didn't think of you. Look for you in Seviah's face. And hope that she was loving you the way I would have wanted to."

What had Marigold said to Isabella all those weeks ago? *They loved me in their own way.*

But Sophronia needed forgiveness, not just reassurance. "She was very loving, Esmé—if, I see now, a little baffled. Much the same way you seem to feel about Daisy?"

"That's another punishment, you see," Sophronia acknowledged. "Trying to love another's child. I did try, for your sake. God knows, I tried. But all I could see in her face was my betrayal of poor Esmie. I never was as good as her. So I thought the best thing would be to leave the poor child to herself, not to burden her with my sorrow and regret, and just make sure that

Hatchet couldn't plague her. Let her free to be herself without his interference."

"And she is an admirably independent spirit—seizing her change to take her happiness and letting no one stand in her way. I hope you'll be happy to learn she's eloped with her Mr. Thaddeus Endicott. She's run off to be married."

At that news, Sophronia's stoic veneer cracked. She turned away, blinking and swiping at her eyes with the cuff of her sleeve. "She's safe, then, from Hatchet's plans. That's what I wanted—why I wrote you. I've done my duty."

"Why, what do you know?" Wilbert let out a relieved chuckle. "Little Daisy went and got herself married."

"You did that," Sophronia said to Marigold. "You gave her the confidence I couldn't give."

"If I did, then I'm glad. And proud. But I hope you are proud too—she is the woman you let her be."

But pride went before the fall. The truth was, if Marigold hadn't come and meddled in their lives, Ellery Hatchet would likely still be alive. "Why did you not simply tell me when I arrived? Or sooner? You could have written all this in your letter."

"Didn't know how. Didn't think you'd believe me."

"Of course I would!"

"Maybe. Maybe not. I feared you'd be like me, maybe, beaten down by the sorrows in life. But you're so like him, that Harry. You've got his way of making obstacles disappear. Of seeing the best in people." She shook her head in wonderment. "You've got such force of life." Sophronia drew something from her pocket—the painted tarot card of the woman seated on a throne with a scale in one hand and a sword in the other—the same card Sophronia had shown Marigold late that night. "Justice," she said. "Always the same card for you. Even in the very beginning. Justine, I named you, before Esmie called you Marigold. I should have trusted you'd bring justice."

Had she brought justice—or only retribution? All Marigold felt she had proven was that even good actions, taken for the best of intentions, could have awful, unforeseen consequences—consequences that could have been avoided. "Why didn't you come get me? Why didn't you take Daisy back to them? Why didn't they come get Daisy?"

"I prayed they would come, but they didn't. Mayhap they didn't know where to look. Mayhap Black Harry didn't know whose child you were. Mayhap there were others besides me—he was no saint. Or maybe he didn't want to break poor Esmie's heart a second time and never let on. I'll never know. As for me, I didn't have the courage," Sophronia admitted. "Couldn't leave my boys. Had to hope Esmie was doing better for you than I could do for Daisy. She did—just look at you. But Daisy seems to have found her own way—or did with your help."

"We'll need to tell them, Daisy and Seviah, eventually."

For the first time in her telling, Sophronia turned squeamish. "They're already gone on to better things. Why tell them now?"

"Because it is the truth."

"Be it on your head," Sophronia warned. "I've said what—"

"—you've said and you'll say no more." Marigold had to laugh. "Hardly. But I don't mind telling them," she declared. "Frankly, I think they'll both be relieved to find they aren't related to Ellery Hatchet." Which also made her sadder for Wilbert, who had no such reprieve.

But Wilbert, who looked just as astonished as she at the revelations of the day, had other compensations—there was the remaining share of some Mexican-minted silver dollars to be collected from the cellar and counted. But first, there was still a murder to be solved. And Minnie's probable murder as well. Something Sophronia had said was tickling at the back of Marigold's brain.

But Ellery had been poisoned before he drowned. Poison, the popular wisdom said, was a women's weapon—so that ruled out Wilbert, Seviah, and Old Cleon, she supposed. Marigold, for her part, also ruled out Sophronia as well as Bessie—who, if they had really wanted to see Ellery Hatchet dead, might have done so years ago, with no one the wiser. Instead, Bessie had taken her small revenge in the return of Ellery's body—though Seviah and Samuel had actually done the deed with the scarecrow.

So why had he been killed now, when so many years had passed? What had changed that made killing Ellery Hatchet necessary? Was it true that nothing would have changed had she not come to Hatchet Farm?

Officer Parker, whom Marigold had frankly forgotten about in the midst of all the familial revelations, was thinking along the same lines. "This is all very heart stringing, but what I still don't know is which one of you confounded people actually killed Ellery Hatchet. Which one of you poisoned him? And stabbed him? And drowned him? Well, I guess we know he sorta drowned himself, with Cleon there's help."

"I only do what I'm told," Cleon objected. "Only speak when I'm spoken to. And Ellery, he told me to put him in the water, just like Alva told me to—"

He cut himself off before he said anything more, but Marigold heard something different in his recitation this time. "Cleon," she pressed. "What else did Alva tell you to do?"

Cleon was hesitant to answer, looking at the ground and away so as not to meet Marigold's eyes. "I'm not supposed to say," he finally whispered.

"Cleon?" she asked again in her kindest, softest tones, because the old fellow was a lot of things—gawney, superstitious, buffle-headed, very dirty, and very likely deaf—but he was not a liar. At least not a good one. "Did she tell you not to say?"

He nodded obediently. "Ayuh."

For such a tiny woman, Alva Coffin Hatchet had certainly cast a very long shadow over Great Misery Island. But Marigold was determined to shed light on every single shade. "Are you not supposed to say anything about the foxglove?"

"Pretty plant for a pretty lady, I always said."

"And did she ask you to plant it in my garden while I was away from the island?"

"Ayuh." He turned his rheumy eyes to her in appeal.

"So how did Ellery take the foxglove, Cleon? He left immediately after he declared his intention to go. Wilbert, you rowed him over—I thought he took nothing but his Bible?"

"He took a satchel with his things," Wilbert said. "Cleon brought it out—"

They all turned back to the old man, who looked at them with wild eyes, like a dog that knows it's about to be whipped. "I only do as I'm told."

"Yes, you're very good in that way." Marigold made her voice gentle, just as if she were talking to that frightened dog. "But what did Alva tell you to do? Did sister give you something to put in the bag?"

"Ayuh. Said it were a tonic that would make him want to stay home."

Officer Parker stepped forward as if he might arrest Cleon, but Cab intervened. "Cleon?" Cab asked slowly, as if he were reasoning it out. "Was Mrs. Alva Hatchet present when Ellery Hatchet came here and spoke to you the night you took him down to the shore?"

Cleon was misery itself. "Ayuh."

"And where is Alva now?" Marigold asked.

"Gone back into her room, I reckon," was Wilbert's answer. "And good luck getting her out. She won't come willingly now."

Cab looked back at Sophronia. "I take it your mother-in-law's door is locked? And who has that particular key?"

"Not I." Sophronia was succinct. "Mother Hatchet's the only one with all the keys, except for my little padlocks and my stillroom. I've kept those from her, no matter her threats."

"Or her curses?" Marigold was beginning to realize that Great-Aunt Alva's malevolent presence had loomed as large as she had imagined.

"Sister only said we'd be cursed if we tried to leave Great Misery," Cleon said. "Old 'Lijah cursed her first, but she said it was like the water, surrounding us all. Keeping us here so's we wouldn't drown like old Elijah."

Another person drowned? The newspaper had stated that Captain Elijah Hatchet had passed away at home. And who would have told them that? "But you came across the water to fetch me," Marigold reminded him. "And you didn't drown."

Cleon shook his shaggy head. "Sister said I wouldn't, because I was supposed to drown you."

Marigold felt the same sort of chill she had experienced that first cold spring evening crossing Salem Sound. She saw the scene before her with new eyes—Cleon fumbling when he had tried to strike her overboard.

Horror rose like gorge in her throat. "To think I almost joined Minnie."

"What does Minnie Mallory have to do with this?" Cab asked.

"I'm not sure," Marigold answered. "But it feels as if it must."

"One dang thing at a time, if you please." Officer Parker hitched up his pants before he gestured to Wilbert. "I want to talk to Alva Hatchet, even if I have to break down the door. The rest of you"—he especially fixed Marigold with his eye—"stay here."

They did. But only until the sounds of Wilbert knocking at the door had been followed by thuds and ended in a splintering of wood.

"By jeezum," Parker exclaimed.

"Would you look at that," was Wilbert's contribution.

Marigold—and Cab and Dr. Oliphant and Sophronia—immediately dashed down the hallway to see what lay behind the formerly locked door, into the chaos that was Great-Aunt Alva's room.

The lair was a veritable rabbit's warren of old, tattered furniture of a previous era, piled high with stacks of paper, old clothing, and assorted ancient and unidentifiable items the old woman had somehow accumulated over the years—the physical manifestation of her darkly twisted mind. The comparison to Miss Havisham had been apt indeed.

Someone threw back the tattered drapes to let in more light, making dust motes dance across the room but revealing Alva herself in the middle of a massive old four-poster bed piled high with dingy linens.

The old woman smiled at them, her thin grimace shiny with the drink she clutched in her hand. "I always said the only time I'd let someone into my room was over my dead body."

CHAPTER 47

It is my belief . . . that the lowest and vilest alleys in London do not present a more dreadful record of sin than does the smiling and beautiful countryside.

—Arthur Conan Doyle

"Poison." Marigold was horrified by such an act of self-malice.

With her long white hair in a frizzy braid and her oversized, overlong nightgown tattered at the sleeves, Alva Hatchet looked more like a hopeless, rather lost old lady than an evil goblin, but Marigold suspected the malevolent spirit that haunted Hatchet Farm was merely hiding, lying in wait.

Dr. Oliphant went close enough to the bedside to examine the glass she clutched. "A solution of crushed foxglove leaves," he surmised.

Alva chuckled, and all the layers of falsity and old-lady befuddlement were stripped away. "It's too late now. I'll never leave Hatchet Farm." Some of the old woman's resolve seemed to waver—tears gathered in her eyes and her voice caught. "He never should have left. None of this would have happened if he'd just stayed like I told him. He should have stayed." She all but bared her teeth at Marigold. "This is all your fault." Alva's spite held. "I hope you're happy—having your way and ruining everything."

But Marigold was a Manners—still—and had her own crocodile smile, along with as much persistence as the old woman had ill will. "I am happy for them," Marigold said more reasonably than she felt. "Because I didn't have my way—they had *their* way. My way would never be to marry like

Daisy nor go on the stage like Seviah. Nor preach like Ellery, nor even to stay here and run the farm like Wilbert. But to each their own."

"They were *all* meant to stay here," Alva insisted. "None of it would have happened if you hadn't come—if they had listened to me and driven you away or done you in, like I asked. But you turned their heads—made them over to you. Just like she knew you would." Alva transferred her odium to its timeworn target. "Sophronia ruined everything by writing you. I told her she'd rue the day, and now I'll tell you. Esmie's girl, they call you," she taunted. "Trying to convince you. Trying to convince themselves! But she knows the truth." She pointed her bony finger at Sophronia. "That you're not Esmie's girl at all."

Marigold broadened her crocodile smile. "Indeed, my mother told me. I know that it is Daisy who is dear Esmé's daughter. And by the by, she got married today, our sweet Daisy, to young Mr. Thaddeus Endicott. She is free from your pernicious influence."

"No!" Alva's eyes darted back and forth between Marigold and Sophronia, trying to gauge the truth of Marigold's statement. "You told them of your adulterous sin?"

"Are you sorry she spoiled your surprise?" Marigold probed. "But you seem to like trying to spoil people's days—just like you spoiled your son, Ellery Hatchet's chance to get away from here, by poisoning him, didn't you?"

Alva narrowed her eyes. "Who told you that? Cleon?"

"You did," Marigold answered. "Right now."

"You think you know everything, don't you?" Alva's smile was full of spite. "Well, you don't know everything. None of you do."

The malice in the old woman nearly took Marigold's breath. "Why did you poison him? Because he left and wouldn't be bound by your curse?" Marigold persisted. *I've broken the chains you've bound around me, Mother.*

"To make him come back and stay as he ought! Just like before. Just like he promised."

It wasn't much of a confession, but it was enough for the law. Still, there was the question of the stabbing. Alva didn't look as if she could have stabbed a piece of cake with a fork—she looked so old and fragile, her oversized nightgown enveloping her, like the ghost of her former self. She put her hand to her chest, as if it pained her, and Marigold was momentarily diverted by pity.

But Alva had nothing of pity in her. "I should have killed her too." Her spiteful gaze found Sophronia. "And those Black women too—both of them."

"One of those women is your granddaughter," Marigold reminded her.

"Never," the old woman fumed. "You're none of you mine but Wilbert."

Poor Wilbert looked horrified by the distinction. "You killed Pa!"

"All he had to do was stay." Alva melted a little more into the little puddle of nightgown and shawls. "Same as my Elijah. Stay put and stay with me. I couldn't let him leave too."

This time it was Sophronia who asked, "Did you poison your husband too?"

"I had to." Alva's breath began to come in pants. "He was going to leave—leave me here alone." She closed her eyes and gripped the crumpled linen. "I showed him. He wanted to go to sea, so I put him in the sea. Just like I did with all the others."

"What others?"

Alva turned her mouth down as if she would say nothing more, but she was ready to unravel the web of lies she had so carefully spun over the years. "All of them, those women and girls he brought here. Drowned them all to keep him safe. To keep him home. Any of them that tempted my boys, my Ellery, or eyed my grandsons. Luring them away from where they belonged."

Marigold remembered how Minnie had talked to Seviah of leaving their one-horse town. It was Alva and not some bounder who had done her in.

"Hatchet always did have a careless, roaming eye," Sophronia observed.

"He wouldn't have if you'd have done your duty and been a better wife to him," Alva rasped.

"I tried that, didn't I? You made sure I did." Sophronia shook her head at the old harridan. "I did love him once. Enough to marry and leave my family and come over the water out to this place. Had my son here and put down roots. But Hatchet wasn't satisfied. Didn't know how to be happy with what he had—didn't know how to be happy at all. So he looked elsewhere."

"Who wouldn't?" was Alva's response.

"You," was Sophronia's mirthless rejoinder. "You did everything you could to tie him to the place—tie us all down here like tethered stock.

Cursed us all, calling down misfortune like the rain that never came. Keeping him so no matter what he'd done or how many sins he committed, you'd find some way to bring him back. You'd keep this place and keep your secrets."

"You're happy he's dead," Alva accused instead of answering. "You wanted him gone."

"Made me no bother that he'd run off to join his circus," Sophronia observed frankly. "I didn't need him dead."

"No one did," added Wilbert.

"I needed him to find the treasure," Alva hissed.

"What treasure, Granny?" Wilbert asked. "Why have I never heard of this before?"

"Because it was mine—what he promised I'd have if I married him and came out here to this godforsaken rock. But he hid it from me—told me he'd buried it away where I'd never find it."

"Pa?"

"No, no. Elijah. My Elijah."

"I know where the treasure is, Alva," Marigold told her. "All these years, and it was never more than a few feet away."

Alva's black eyes widened. "You!"

But it was too late now. Alva Hatchet took her last rasping breath and was dead by her own hand.

Dr. Oliphant retrieved the glass she still clutched. "I'll have to test this, to be sure—"

"It'll be the foxglove," Sophronia remarked, "not arsenic. Took that on the regular, she did. Has for years."

Dr. Oliphant frowned. "Poisoning herself?"

"Building up her immunity. Slow like, bit by bit, for years. Reckon you'll find that in there too"—she nodded at the various piles of detritus—"if you keep looking." Sophronia let out a long sigh, as if she'd been waiting years to have her say. "Keep a bit of rat poison, like all farmhouses," she explained. "Had a scare, if you like, some time ago. It wasn't enough to do him in, Hatchet—just enough to make him know it was done. Keep him obedient, was my guess. Hatchet accused me of poisoning him. But it weren't me. So I locked the larder up and gave Hatchet the key."

I'll not take anything from your snake-fed hands.

"That's why Cleon cooks?"

"Ayuh." Sophronia nodded. "But Mother Alva had keys to all the rooms, she did, all but mine—reckon you'll find those, too, in here if you look." She waved her hand at the piled refuse. "That's why I got my own locks—traded for them with the druggist. To make sure I wasn't gone crazy."

"You're not crazy," Marigold swore. "You may be the only sane one left amongst us."

Sophronia's eyes grew surprisingly glassy. "She tried it on you, her poison, just as I suspicioned she would—first dinner you took at this table. Had Cleon put it in your bowl."

The wedding china that ended up crashed to the floor. "You broke it on purpose."

"Looking out for you," Sophronia said tersely. "So's you could do what you were meant to do."

To find out all of Hatchet Farm's secrets.

It had been Sophronia who had been watching—and watching out—for her. All those uncomfortable moments when Marigold had felt a presence—it had been her mother trying to take care of her, keeping her from harm.

Marigold reached for Sophronia's hand.

Sophronia raised it to her lips, to kiss her daughter at last. "Ayuh," she said through tears. "You've got some powerful magic in you."

CHAPTER 48

A faithful friend is a strong defense;
he that hath found him hath found a treasure.
—Louisa May Alcott

Officer Parker was more concerned with the harm that hadn't been prevented. "Alva Hatchet poisoned her husband and son and then poisoned herself?" he asked. "We know that, and we know how Ellery got into the water . . ." He scratched his chin in contemplation. "What about the stabbing?"

There was only one person left who had been present for the commotion that fateful night. Marigold turned to Cleon.

"They argued, didn't they, Cleon? Sister and Cousin Ellery. Did he know she'd poisoned him?" All this time Marigold had thought the Hatchets' worry about poison excessive—perhaps it hadn't been enough?

"Ayuh." Old Cleon crumpled to his knees next to his sister's bed—the sister he had blindly obeyed, eavesdropping on conversations, planting poisonous plants, and putting bodies into the silent waters of Salem Sound. "Never did like to be crossed, sister." Cleon began to cry, streams of tears creasing his face.

"He wanted revenge against sister—even though it were my fault, for giving him bad tonic. He come at her hard, Cousin Ellery did," Cleon told them. "He knew he were dying, and he were full of God's righteous anger. Said he'd drown *her* and be done with her. Do to her what she'd done to his pa. What he had always been afeared she'd do to him if he didn't mind her ways. I had to stop him."

Marigold made herself ask, "How did you stop him?"

"He pushed me away, back against the stove," Cleon admitted. "And I flung my arm out for a handhold."

Marigold looked back toward the hulk of the cast-iron stove. "The toasting fork! The perforations—the two holes in Ellery Hatchet's side."

"By God," the doctor said.

"You stabbed Pa, Cleon?" It was Wilbert who voiced the unspeakable.

"He come at me." The piteous creature gulped through his tears. "I just wanted to be let be."

Marigold could see the scene in her mind's eye—Cleon in a crumple on the floor, holding the fork, and Ellery Hatchet impaling himself in his blind rage.

"By jeezum." Wilbert sighed and drew the crying old man to his feet. "It's all right, Cleon."

"It's not all right," Officer Parker insisted. "He stabbed him and then left him to drown? And when he'd done his worst, then he hauled Hatchet up on the crosstree to dry out like a scarecrow?" He scratched his head under his hat. "Suppose the old fool lit the fire too?"

Cab looked at Marigold. Marigold looked to Sophronia. Who closed her eyes.

It was Wilbert who put an end to it. "Reckon it was just an unlucky lightning strike that night. Bound to happen someday with all that old, dry hay."

Marigold all but held her breath, but Parker was quick to choose the path of least resistance. "Well, I reckon," he agreed.

And with that, what would be, was.

Justice, though hard-fought, seemed to have been won. The bad had been punished and the good—or at least the good *enough*—were left in peace to contemplate their sins, exhume their secrets, and bury their dead.

Officer Parker and Dr. Oliphant left soon thereafter, presumably to make their reports and sign whatever official papers were necessary for the town of Pride's Crossing and the inhabitants of Hatchet Farm to resume their otherwise quaintly eerie lives.

"Well, it's a good thing we saved the shovels," Wilbert said wearily. "I've got two graves to dig."

"I'll help you, Wilbert." Cab, always ready to do the right thing.

As was she. Marigold decided that the best thing she could do for her family was what she did best—clean. Starting with the age-old mess that was Great-Aunt Alva's room.

She gathered her necessary buckets and hygienic supplies and set herself to making order from chaos. The cluttered interior so reminded her of the littered yard when she had first arrived that Marigold felt she was starting all over again.

"Surprised she didn't go up in flames years ago," Sophronia commented from the doorway, gesturing to the melted wax and sagging candles perched atop some piles. "And all of us with her. No idea it'd got this bad. Don't think anyone but Hatchet or Cleon had been inside in years."

But her comment gave Marigold her solution. "Perhaps a good bonfire in the remains of the barn might be the best solution—if there are some embers still smoldering? But wait—Wilbert!" Marigold chased her half brother—her *brother*—across the yard. "The graves can wait. First, we need to sift through the ashes of the root cellar."

"What for?"

"Your treasure."

She led him behind the charred remains of the barn, and there it was, just as Bessie Dove said she had left it, in the soot-filled cellar. Wilbert swept aside the ash and cinders to reveal the charred remains of an iron-banded, wooden chest.

"Well, I'll be." He traced the initials engraved in the metal. "*J.E.*" he read. "Wonder what the *J* stands for? Didn't know Pa's father had another name besides Elijah."

"That's the Crowninshield family cipher," Cab said quietly into Marigold's ear. "With likely Jacob Endicott's initials."

Another thought struck her. "Your uncle Endicott must have known. Why else would he keep trying to buy, or recover through litigation, a bald, bankrupt, rocky island?"

"Indeed," was all Cab would allow.

"So, what do we do?" she asked. "Will the contents change the Endicotts' fortunes? Or will it be a more suitable reward for this young man who has nothing else of value to his name?"

"Nothing but his excellent remaining family." Cab smiled at her in that way he had of making a person feel like the best of themselves. "Wilbert, why don't you have a look and tell us what's in there?"

If there had once been a lock guarding the chest, there was not now—a benefit, Marigold suspected, of Bessie's raising her son to be a blacksmith. But the less said about them the better—Wilbert didn't need to know that someone else had already taken their own suitable reward.

"Holy smoke—" Wilbert's oath transferred into a long whistle. "Will you look at that."

Inside were large, blackened disks, tarnished by age, filling the bottom half of the chest.

"Must be—more'n a hundred!" Wilbert was beyond astonished. "All these years, this was what Pa was digging for? And it was here all the time?"

"Yes," was the simplest answer Marigold could give. "And now it is yours."

"Mine?" He blinked at her, all disbelief. But then he seemed to grasp all the ramifications of the day. "By jeezum. You really aren't here to take anything from us, are you?"

"All I have ever wanted was information about my mother."

Wilbert drew in a breath that seemed to expand his chest and shoulders before her eyes. "You're plumb crazy if you think I'm not going to share this! With Ma and Cleon and Sev and Daisy, and you. We wouldn't never have found it if it hadn't been for you. And we're family still. Reckon a half sister's as good as a full one. Makes no difference to me."

"Thank you, Wilbert," Marigold returned. "That means the world to me."

Marigold felt a strange, numb sort of peace settle upon her—she had done what she was meant to do, and the world had finally caught up. Wilbert, Seviah, Daisy, Lucy, Bessie, and even Sophronia were all poised to embark upon new and hopefully better phases of their lives. The wrong Marigold had come to Hatchet Farm to discover was known, and although it could never be righted—as Sophronia had so wisely said—Marigold could go on with her life.

She had not drowned in the well of her family's troubles, though she felt as if she might have gone under a time or two. Order had been restored to, or rather imposed upon, Hatchet Farm.

Whichever it was, Marigold could be proud of all she had accomplished for her cousins—her *siblings*—and might leave in good conscience. "What do you think you'll do now?"

"Sell up," Wilbert said immediately. "Sell it back to old man Endicott, if he still wants it. Sell it on to anyone who'll take it. Take what we want and burn down the house behind us and move on to someplace better, someplace without any bad memories or secrets. Move on."

"That sounds like a very sound plan for such prime coastal real estate," Marigold agreed.

"S'pose you'll be moving on too? I hope you know you're always welcome with us, Ma and me," Wilbert offered.

"Wilbert, you are a lamb." But *always* had always seemed longer than she wanted to think about at present. Always meant permanence, which made her desperately uncomfortable.

Always made her think of Cab.

Who was watching her carefully.

"Care to take a walk with me, Cab?" Though where they were to go seemed problematic—the garden felt too filled with ghosts.

"Naturally," he said as he fell into step beside her. "Glad to have a moment alone." He swiped his hat from his head. "I see your poker face is well in place. Happily, I've bought the necessary medicine to cure a bad case of poker face." He held up a flask of delightfully demon liquor.

"You have no idea how welcome that is! Let's try the breezeway." She was suddenly wearier than she'd ever been. "It's not the salon at the Copley Square Hotel, but I hope it will do. What have you brought me?"

"Port. Fortified and strong. It's been a hell of a day."

"It has indeed, but as I told you, I'm no damsel in distress."

"No," he agreed. "But perhaps I am."

Marigold laughed and raised the flask. "I'll drink to that. I would drink to a willing foe again, but how horribly prescient was that toast?" She took a deep drink. "Thank you. This is exactly what I needed—forgetfulness in a flask."

"That's where we started, back in Boston, isn't it?" Cab sighed in easy agreement. "Maybe I should have said my piece then, and maybe then none of this might have happened."

"What piece?"

"Marigold." There was something in his tone. Something bare and plain. And unsure. "Surely you know?"

"That this was all my fault? I do—"

"No. Surely you understand." He reached for her hand. "I'm utterly mad about you."

Heat and something more fragile kindled in her chest. "If you must know, I'm desperately fond of you too . . ."

"But?"

"But I've just had my life upended," she finished.

"I understand that," he said. "I want to give you some surety—someone you know you can count upon."

She had to smile. "Yes, I think I have learned that I can always count on you—to do the right thing even when it is inconvenient. Thank you—you have been an astonishingly good friend." Letting Seviah, Samuel, and Bessie off the hook was only the beginning of friendship. "You are the rare man who can be counted upon to know the different between punishment and justice."

"Thank you. But why should my friendship astonish you?"

"Because, at the moment, it seems I have nothing to offer you in return."

"Nothing?"

"I'm not who I thought I was, Cab. It was bad enough being a pauper, but now I'm a bastard—to use your plainspoken word—as well. It's a bit much, even for me."

"Marigold." His tone was gently chiding. "You always said people make their own decisions, regardless of their blood or family name."

"That was before my name was in question—although I suppose I am still a Manners."

"Marigold, you must understand that no matter your name, or your parents, or your execrable habit of managing others, I love you? That I always have? And I always will."

For once in her life, Marigold was nearly overcome with raw, painful emotion, as if her heart had gone weak and wavering within her chest.

And that was the problem—the way she felt about Cab was unsettling. Whenever she was near him, all her well-honed reason seemed to desert her. Emotions were not nearly so reliable as logic. "*Always* seems untenable," she returned cautiously.

"Please believe me," he began slowly, as if he were feeling his way as carefully as she. "I know I love you. I have from the first moment I met you. And I fear, no matter the outcome of this conversation—because I see that alarmed look in your eye—I always will. I'm afraid you've ruined me for all other woman, Marigold. You and you alone will do for me."

"Cab, I—"

"Don't say it. If the answer is no, don't say it, please. Let me hope. Let me hope for just a small while."

"Then I won't say no." She reached out her hand. "I'll say, kiss me instead."

He was astonished. "Is that a yes?"

"It is a please. Right now, after everything that has happened, I would like to be kissed. By you and no other."

"Then, yes." He pressed a kiss to her hand.

Marigold felt clarification was in order. "On the lips, Cab. On my lips."

CHAPTER 49

As to marriage, I think the intercourse of heart and mind may be
fully enjoyed without entering into his partnership of daily life.
　　　　　　　　　　　　　　　　　　　—Margaret Fuller

Cab finally kissed her. Oh, sweet heaven, so deeply, completely, thoroughly, she wondered if she had ever known how to breathe.

She leaned into the solid, sure strength of him, into the scent of starch and virtue. "Cab."

"Marigold." He spoke her name against her lips, teasing her with each breath and syllable. His kiss was gentle and bold, exactly as she might have wished. Perfect, in fact.

Until he spoke. "Marigold, I must ask. Will you marry me?"

Marigold's eyes filled with unexpected tears—heat and love and despair all piled up behind her lids until they spilled down her cheeks.

His arms around her gentled. "I didn't mean to make you cry."

"Naturally." She managed a smile. "I'm crying because I love you."

And she loved him because he was smart enough and perfect enough to understand what she hadn't said. "But"—he let out a breath even as he kissed her hand again—"not enough to marry me."

"More," she corrected. "Too much to marry you."

"That makes no sense to me," he objected. "I love you. I want you here with me, like this, every day. Knowing that you'll be by my side wherever we go. Together." He let out a breath. "But that's not what you want, is it?"

"Not exactly. Because the world doesn't work in the reciprocal way, does it? I'm not allowed to expect that *you'll* be by my side wherever *I* go."

"What is the difference?"

"The difference is in our world."

"Then damn the world." He gripped her hand and then, more carefully, her face. "I won't change my mind. I'll just keep asking."

"Do you think you'll change my mind?" she asked, before she added quietly, "Or find I just can't do without you? But the problem is, I can, you see. I already know that. And that's what makes me unsuitable."

"You're not unsuitable."

"Let me ask you this—when you were a boy and read the stories in fairy tales, did you imagine yourself the dragon or the knight?"

"The knight," he said immediately.

"Naturally." She reached out to touch his forearm—that strong, steady sword arm. "Because that's who you are. But not me. If you asked me if I would rather be the witch or the princess, I would have chosen the witch, not just because she had power, but because she was the only person who never had to please anyone else."

Cab tried to hide his disappointment. "And is that so bad, pleasing someone else?"

"No," Marigold admitted. "It is sublimely pleasurable when I can choose to please you. But it's pleasurable because I can *choose* to do it, or not."

"And marrying me stops you from choosing?"

"You're the lawyer—you know it does. You know under the law, I—or any woman—would be nothing more than an extension of you. Your name becomes mine. Your word, that of mine. Your will, superior to mine." She shook her head. "I couldn't abide that."

"Does the fact that I love you count for nothing?"

"It counts a great deal. It nearly counts for everything, because I love you too. With my heart and soul and body. But not with my very person. Do you see the difference?"

He was enough of a lawyer to understand. "I do. And once again, I lament that such is our world." He drew in a deep, reconciled breath. "So, no is for always?"

"No." She couldn't let him think that, even as she couldn't let him think it was yes. "It's no, not now. Not when things . . . when I am so unsettled. I feel much the same way I felt when my parents died." The remembrance brought a fresh wave of understanding. And sorrow. "Only they weren't my parents, were they? Only Harry Manners was."

"Who your parents were doesn't change anything about you."

"Doesn't it? I heard how you referred to Seviah, Cab, when you thought him a bastard. And that's what I am as well. I *have* always said that people make their own choices, regardless of their family's blood, but now that tie has been taken away from me, I understand that it was the bedrock upon which I constructed my life. Without it, I feel . . . adrift."

"I thought you were a New Woman, who didn't care what the world thought of you."

"I've always cared. Always cared that the world knew I was accomplished—" she began.

"You are accomplished—just look at how much you accomplished at Hatchet Farm. I fear for your becoming any more accomplished," he laughed softly.

"And therein lies the rub, dear Cab. Because I do plan on becoming the very thing you fear—more accomplished. I don't think I'll ever stop wanting and trying to be . . . more. More educated, more experienced, more admired, and more accomplished."

"Marigold, I was only joking. I don't fear you."

"Don't you? You're a man formed for hearth and home, Cab. You want a wife to be by your side."

"And you don't want that? You, who never had a permanent home? I thought you—"

"—would feel hemmed in," she finished. "I still aspire to becoming an archaeologist. To travel and study and research and dig."

"Can you not do that by my side?"

"Can *you* still conduct your life the way you want and be by *my side*? Living in a tent in Greece, or wherever else my studies might take me? Would you leave Pride's Crossing and Boston and the law to come with me, if I chose to go?"

"Go where?"

She rose, the possibility pushing her to her feet. "Wherever life might take us."

He came to his feet with her. "Life needs to be paid for, Marigold. With a job."

"Then that's a no."

He sighed. "That would be a not now."

"But not a not ever?" She wanted to hope, but she had to make sure she understood.

"Yes." He reached for her hand and kissed it one last time. "And please know that no matter what, no matter where you go or what you do, I'll always love you."

"And I love you, in my own way." Marigold came into his arms, to the comfort of his broad, safe chest, where she could give in to the impulse of the moment and bask in the warmth and surety of his embrace. Just this once.

Because she didn't know when she would ever get to do so again.

And that would have to be fine.

Epilogue

Independence is happiness.
—Susan B. Anthony

There wasn't much else for Marigold to do—she had done all she had set out to accomplish at Hatchet Farm. And there was nothing left in her pocketbook for her to do anything else.

Isabella heard her sigh. "You know what you need?" she began as she supervised the loading of Marigold's trunks onto the launch.

"Money," Marigold answered.

"Some occupation," Isabella corrected. "And before you say it, I mean an occupation that will bring you the money you need to resume the life you want to lead."

"Naturally," Marigold agreed. "I seem to recall having this conversation some weeks ago."

"Well, you hadn't solved a murder some weeks ago."

"Two murders, actually?" Plus those poor, as-yet-unaccounted "other girls" done in by Alva. "Do you mean I ought to set myself up as a sort of a consulting detectivist?"

"Too dangerous," Isabella advised. "Why don't you just write about it? All the gory, grisly, gothic details that the public loves?"

"Isabella," Marigold chided. "One doesn't want to appear ghoulish."

"Nonsense," Isabella countered. "Take up a pen name like that savage man you mentioned. Because if anyone can tell such a tale with style and panache, it's you, my dear."

"I am all for the idea of writing, but I am meant to be working on my mythology."

"Think of the money." Isabella tried again. "The paying press is always hungry for the sensation and scandal of an interesting murder. It's bound to be more lucrative than your worthy, but frankly boring, academic tome."

"The classical myths are far from boring—not the way I'll retell them."

"Darling, please. You need *money*."

"True." Isabella's idea began to have some appeal. "Perhaps I might try," Marigold reasoned. "I did enjoy Wilkie Collins' mysterious novels—perhaps I could write my own."

"Perhaps?" Isabella repeated theatrically. "The inimitable Miss Marigold Manners says *perhaps*? My dear friend, I truly begin to worry."

"*Begin*?" Marigold had to smile. "I will admit to being rather shaken by all that has happened. It was one thing to find myself a pauper, but now to be a pauper and a bastard—" She shook her head. "It's all just too sordid, even for me."

"Darling," Isabella said with feeling, "if you can give bastardy as much style and verve as you've given paupery, you'll be a smash. Write your murdery story. It will do you good."

It might. Even if the experience did nothing more than sort out her still-conflicted thoughts and feelings—it would never do to exist as a slave to her emotions.

"Perhaps I will." It would certainly be something different.

Marigold picked up her pen.

The first thing she noticed was the scarecrow's hat, battered and torn but still somehow familiar, tilted at a rakish angle, as if the wearer had some style or panache—but panache was what gave one style, if you asked her . . .

AUTHOR'S NOTE

MISERY HATES COMPANY began it's journey from my head to the page chiefly as an homage to one of my favorite books that I read as a young woman, Stella Gibbon's *Cold Comfort Farm*. While I loved the improbable plot of that story, I never really believed the benign outcome—I just knew there were dead bodies hidden somewhere in the hayloft or along the edge of the marsh. I wanted the Gothic overtones to come with real shadows, filled with cobwebs, more than a little malice and murder.

And I wanted to make my heroine, Marigold Manners, a very particular American sort of heroine, who while she owes much to the practicality of *Cold Comfort*'s Flora Poste, owes more to the illustrated cover of "Wellesley College, by Miss Goodloe" for Scribner's Magazine for May, c.1897 by Charles Allan Gilbert. In Gilbert's illustration, young women walk and gather on the women's college campus with their bicycles and field hockey sticks, while wearing crisp, fashionable shirt waists. These girls, my imagination insisted, could solve crimes in between classes, all while suffering no fools. These girls needed murdery stories of their own.

I hope you have as much fun with Marigold as I had creating her.

Acknowledgments

Very few books—and none of mine—are conceived of, researched, written, or published in a vacuum. My books are always the result of a generosity of spirit from myriad other people, among whom Tracy Brogan and Sherry Thomas feature most prominently. Our daily Tortoise Conclave of encouragement, brainstorming, goal setting, and experience-sharing texts has helped me beyond measure.

Similarly, sensitivity reader and dear friend Cheryl Morgan Kennedy read an early draft and made astute suggestions for the betterment of the novel, as did my agent, Danielle Egan-Miller, and her team at Browne & Miller Literary Associates, who have seen me safely through the arcana of the publishing process.

And my greatest thanks must include the entire team at Crooked Lane Books: Dulce Botello, Megan Matti, Mikaela Bender, Thaisheemarie Fantauzzi Pérez, Rebecca Nelson, Marisa Ware, designer, and Rachel Keith, copyeditor, who, under the leadership of Matt Martz, publisher, and Holly Ingraham, editor, have made the process of bringing this book into the world a delight. A tip of Marigold's chapeau to you all!